A SUMMER
OF MURDER

Also by Oliver Bottini in English translation

Zen and the Art of Murder (2018)

OLIVER BOTTINI

A SUMMER
OF MURDER

A Black Forest Investigation: II

Translated from the German by
Jamie Bulloch

MACLEHOSE PRESS
QUERCUS · LONDON

First published in the German language as *Im Sommer der Mörder*
by Fischer Verlag in 2006, and reissued by DuMont Buchverlag, Cologne, in 2016

First published in Great Britain in 2018 by

MacLehose Press
An imprint of Quercus Publishing Ltd
Carmelite House
50 Victoria Embankment
London EC4Y 0DZ

An Hachette UK company

A CIP catalogue record for this book is available
from the British Library.

ISBN (HB) 978 0 85705 767 9
ISBN (TPB) 978 0 85705 739 6
ISBN (Ebook) 978 0 85705 738 9

10 9 8 7 6 5 4 3 2 1

Designed and typeset in Minion by Libanus Press, Marlborough
Printed and bound in Great Britain by Clays Ltd, Elcograf S.p.A

For Chiara

There can be no long-term politics without an ethical principle.
ANDRÉ GLUCKSMANN

There are a few more stories, let me tell you . . .
SEYMOUR HERSH IN AN INTERVIEW
WITH *SÜDDEUTSCHE ZEITUNG*

Prologue

Adam Baudy didn't see the fire until they had reached the outskirts of Kirchzarten. A glow, a narrow streak of light on the pasture between the road and the forest, flames flickering sluggishly at the break of day. The fire was dying out; they had come too late.

The command vehicle ahead of him slowed and turned onto the farm track. Baudy followed. Where the fire raged, the last corner upright toppled to the ground, sending a cloud of sparks flying into the air, a swarm of frenzied red insects extinguished moments later in the dark grey of the morning. Nothing remained of Riedinger's wooden shed but embers and ashes.

"You can open your eyes, sweetheart," Baudy said, taking his phone from its cradle. As he dialled Martin Andersen's number, it struck him that already he'd forgotten what the shed looked like. He'd been passing this way every day for decades and he hadn't consciously looked at it once. He wondered how hard you had to look to see everything that existed. The important things and the unimportant ones.

It went straight to voicemail. "Call me back," Baudy said.

"It's already out, the fire," Lina said.

"Yes, thank goodness."

The headlights of the first fire engine loomed in his rear-view mirror. On either side the blue light picked out a few metres of field from the dawn gloom. Baudy suppressed a yawn. He felt tired for the first time that morning. Whenever he had Lina he didn't sleep much. He would lie awake for ages, thinking how she'd soon be gone again.

"Papa, was there someone inside?" Lina whispered.

Baudy turned to look at her. Lina had leaned forwards in her booster seat to catch a glimpse of the fire. He gave her a reassuring smile. "No."

"What about any animals?"

"No animals either."

"Maybe two or three mice."

"They move so quickly, they don't hang around when there's a fire. They scuttle away, sweetie."

Lina looked at him. "So what was in there?"

"Just a bit of hay."

Baudy checked the time: a quarter past five. Riedinger had rung the emergency services fifteen minutes ago. Thirteen minutes ago Freiburg had notified the Kirchzarten volunteer brigade via the radio alarm. Ten minutes ago, with Lina in his arms, he'd left the apartment, "without brushing our teeth?" Three minutes ago they'd set off from the fire station. The blaze must have started at about a quarter to five. It took half an hour to die out and the little old wooden shed, which he'd never consciously looked at, no longer existed.

"Are we going back to your home now?" Lina said.

"Soon. Have another little sleep."

His mobile rang. "No fuel, no gas bottles, no fertiliser," Martin Andersen said. He'd been on the phone to Riedinger. Baudy peered at the command vehicle. Andersen had stuck his hand out of the window and was giving the thumbs up.

"O.K.," Baudy said.

They pulled over onto the verge soon afterwards. Baudy turned around again, pulled the blanket over Lina and stroked her cheek. "Papa's got to do some work now, sweetheart."

"It's a shame hay can't run away," Lina said quietly.

Baudy waited beside the command vehicle until the two fire engines had come to a stop, and then gave the order to get out. His voice was deep and hoarse with tiredness. While the sixteen men took up positions between the vehicles, he went to within ten metres of where the fire had burned. He wasn't wearing a respiratory mask; they didn't have to worry about carbon dioxide as the fire had been too small and they were in the open air. Baudy checked for odours as he breathed in through his nose. No petrol. In the centre of the scorched area a slim flame darted upwards, unable to find sustenance, and was then extinguished. Ten square metres of embers and a few fire pockets. "Two B hoses," he said, without turning around.

Lew Gubnik and the leader of the second squad relayed the order.

Baudy could now make out the contour of the belt of trees fifty metres away, behind which ran the B31. A slender band of darkness and silence. Above the trees flashed the warning lights of the Rosskopf wind turbines, like four synchronised stars. In the north-east he saw a flickering blue light. A third fire engine: their colleagues from Zarten.

Slowly he walked forwards. No people, no animals, Riediger had told the control room, and Martin Andersen too. Only a few old tools and some hay. The unused wooden shed had stood in the middle of a pasture, and nobody lived within two hundred metres of it. But you could never tell. If you couldn't see what you passed every day for forty years, then anything was possible.

Baudy stopped when he could feel the heat of the embers. No casualties, no fatalities, that was the important thing. He let his eyes wander across the burnt area. Again he checked for the smell of petrol, or of any other accelerant. Then he stepped aside and gave the signal to start operating the hoses.

Smoke rose into the air, the embers hissed.

Once they'd dealt with the fire pockets they could all go home. He would take Lina to kindergarten in Freiburg, sit with a cup of coffee in the carpentry workshop and finish Gubnik's strange casket. This had been a short, safe operation. But he wasn't feeling the usual satisfaction of having won the battle. Maybe because he was so tired, or because there had been no battle.

"Fire under control!" Gubnik called out. A few of the men laughed and Baudy joined in.

*

Then the squad from Zarten arrived. Baudy raised a hand and waved at the driver's cab. All that was missing were the police. He wondered what might have caused the fire. A cigarette butt? The hay spontaneously combusting? Or was it arson? But who would set light to a hay shed? He thought about the asylum seekers in Keltenbuck, all those Dutch at the campsite, the American students camping in the Grosse Tal. About Riedinger, who was capable of anything.

The first rays of sun flared on the horizon. From one moment to the next the light in the east became friendlier. It occurred to Baudy that this was the least worst time for a fire. A new day was breaking. A seed of hope, even in the face of the devastation wrought by fire.

He took a few steps into the heat beyond Gubnik and young Paul Feul on the first hose. Baudy heard Gubnik curse. They needn't have come, not with three engines and two dozen men. The fire was out and there was no other building far and wide that needed protecting. A few buckets of water would have sufficed. Baudy smiled. Lew Gubnik, the Russian-German, had put on a fair bit of weight in Breisgau and regretted every movement that wasn't strictly necessary.

Karl, head of the Zarten squad, appeared beside him. "Was anyone in there?"

"No."

"Horses? Cattle?"

"No."

Karl nodded. "Do you need us?"

"No," Baudy said for the third time, holding out his hand. "But thanks for coming." Karl nodded. The two men didn't like each other. Too many fights as children, and later often running after the same girl. When neither invited the other to their wedding or Christenings, it was too late to change anything. But none of this had any bearing on joint operations; then it was as if the fights and the girls had never existed.

"There's somebody over there," Gubnik said.

Baudy now saw a man in the grey morning light. He was standing about thirty metres away, staring at the ashes.

Hannes Riedinger.

Baudy approached him. He wanted to tell Riedinger about the seed of hope, even if it was only a shed that had burned down. Everybody needed some hope, didn't they?

Riedinger's wrinkled, unwelcoming face glistened with sweat. "A little bit of hay doesn't go up in flames that easily," he said.

Baudy nodded. "Not at night."

The charred planks crackled, the hissing of the embers was not so loud now. A few metres away Gubnik was muttering.

"It looked like someone had opened the gates to hell," Riedinger said, as if talking to himself.

Baudy looked at him. "Are you sure it was just hay in there?"

Riedinger nodded curtly.

"No fertiliser? Gas bottles, fuel, quicklime?"

"How often do I have to say it?"

Baudy remembered that Riedinger lived alone. His wife had done a runner, the children had moved abroad and the neighbours avoided him. He'd driven them all away. "Well?"

"No."

In spite of the darkness he could see the severity, the ruthlessness in Riedinger's eyes. Baudy jerked his head towards Gubnik and Paul Feul to signal that he had to get back to work.

"A little bit of hay doesn't go up in flames that easily," he heard Riedinger say behind him.

Shortly afterwards Baudy gave the order to reel in the second B hose. Only Gubnik and Feul remained at the site of the fire, the others were gathered around the manifold or by the fire engine, chatting about the Tour de France as they watched Gubnik and Feul. Baudy could see the blue lights of a patrol car in the distance. Officers from Freiburg South. The Kirchzarten police were still asleep; their shift began at half past seven.

Baudy got into the command vehicle and switched on the blue

lights to help the police locate them. Then he went back to his Passat and gently opened the rear door. Lina's eyes were closed. He waited for a moment to see whether she really was asleep or just playing her old Am-I-Asleep? game, from when there wasn't a "his home" and a "her home". By now Lina would have grinned if she were still awake.

Only the kindergarten run left, and after that he'd have to be without her for another fortnight.

"Water off," he heard Gubnik shout.

He shut the door. "Water off," he ordered. The hose slackened. Baudy glanced at Riedinger, who was staring at the scorched ground, hands in pockets. His home, her home. The idea that they had some things in common made him uneasy.

"Josef, the infrared camera."

"Is there any point looking for more fire pockets?" said Josef, the longest-serving Kirchzarten volunteer. Most people became more cautious as they grew older and more experienced, but Josef had become more reckless.

"The camera," Baudy repeated. Josef nodded and went to the fire engine. The men at the manifold were discussing Jan Ullrich's unsuccessful challenge on the Col du Tourmalet a week earlier. Their voices had got louder.

"Quiet!" Gubnik grunted, but nobody apart from Baudy seemed to hear him. Gubnik had raised one hand and turned his head to the side, as if listening for something. "*Quiet*, you arseholes!" he yelled and dropped his hand.

The voices fell silent.

Baudy took a few steps towards Gubnik. Now he could hear it too. A sound like water on stone. But the shed wasn't made of stone and the hoses were off. "Does the shed have a cellar?" he called out to Riedinger.

"No."

"Josef?" Baudy said.

Josef, who was a few metres away from Gubnik, already had the camera to his eye. "Nothing."

Gubnik let go of the hose, took off his helmet and stepped onto the ashes. Seized by a sudden fear, Baudy called out, "Stop, Gubby!"

Gubnik stopped mid-stride.

"Put your helmet back on, for God's sake!"

Gubnik grimaced, saluted him and put on his helmet at an angle. Baudy heard Paul Feul giggle.

No fire pockets, but water on stone, he thought. As he went over to Josef he gave the order to get the second B hose ready again.

"It's all out,' Josef said. "Not a straw smouldering."

"Underneath, perhaps?"

"What do you mean underneath, if there's no cellar?"

Baudy took the camera and twice scanned the area of the fire, but found nothing. Plenty of grey, no white. There really wasn't a single straw smouldering.

"Listen," Gubnik muttered.

Now other sounds mingled – earth, stones, sand, all falling. "The ground's giving way."

Then they saw it too. Roughly in the middle of where the fire had burned, the damp ashes began to move, and all of a sudden a metre-square hole appeared. "Get away from there!" Baudy said, yanking Gubnik back onto the grass. Their eyes met. Gubnik nodded in satisfaction, as if to say: Maybe there *is* more to be done here. He plodded back to Feul by the first hose.

"I see something," Josef said, the camera at his eye. "Diagonally beneath the hole."

"Engine one, first and second hose at the ready!" Baudy instructed. "Josef?"

"It's spreading. Something's burning down there."

Gubnik and Feul aimed the first B hose. A few metres away the second squad got into position. Baudy gave the order to engage. Water shot from the hoses.

"There's no cellar there," said Riedinger, who'd gone closer.

"Stay where you are!" Baudy barked. By the time he turned back more holes had appeared. He couldn't hear a thing; the rushing of water drowned out all other sounds.

"Shit, something's burning underneath," Josef said again. Seconds later a few sparks flew out of one of the holes.

"Everyone back!" Baudy ordered. Those manning the hoses as well as Josef, Riedinger and Baudy all retreated a few steps. He turned and instructed Martin Andersen to recall the Zarten team, just in case. Dark shapes emerged from the Freiburg South patrol car, which had just arrived. The strip of light on the horizon was now orange and had spread across the sky.

Baudy looked back at the site of the fire.

"Something's really brewing down there," Josef said.

Baudy put the whistle to his mouth to give the danger signal. At that moment came an ear-splitting detonation and a fountain of flames, rocks and earth erupted from the ashes. Paul Feul let out a shrill scream, Gubnik began to curse wildly and Baudy held his breath. Stones and earth peppered the ground, particles of ash danced in the air.

Then there was silence.

Nobody moved a muscle; everybody appeared to be waiting.

"Martin, take Lina away!" Baudy yelled without turning around. Barely five seconds later the engine of the Passat sprung to life.

"What is that arsehole storing down there?" Gubnik growled.

Baudy was gripped by a sudden panic. He blew his whistle and shouted, "Retreat! Get back!"

The entire ground on which the shed had stood caved in, flames shot metres into the air. The blast from another explosion threw Baudy backwards. He got to his feet again, all but deaf. With Paul Feul screaming on one side and Josef on the other he staggered to the fire engines. In the light of the flames he could see that the men from the second hose were running back to the engines, with Riedinger and the police officers somewhere in the chaos too. There was frenzied shouting up ahead, a number of voices yelling all at once. He couldn't make out what they were saying. Baudy opened and closed his mouth but it got no better.

A few metres away the red manifold lay on the ground, the two hoses dancing about freestyle. "Water off!" he cried. Nobody appeared to react, but the water stopped a second afterwards. He changed direction and sprinted over to one of the hoses. Then he noticed that Gubnik wasn't amongst the men. Baudy stopped and called out, "Gubby?" Two more explosions, and someone pulled him to the ground. Riedinger's words shot through his mind: the gates to hell.

Then he heard a sound that was far too quiet to be coming from outside his head: a high-pitched, desperate whimper.

"Adam," Josef said beside him.

Baudy tried to stop the whimpering. But it wasn't coming from him.

"Adam," Josef said again. His eyes were fixed on the burnt-out hole from which bright flames were jetting upwards. Baudy spun around. Beside the fire Gubnik was on all fours, as if trying to peer into the cellar that didn't exist. Individual flames seemed to be making a grab for him, wrapping around his torso. He was no longer wearing his helmet; his hair was on fire. Feebly he moved a leg to the side and raised his backside. But he couldn't get up. His body swayed back and forth as if on a listing ship. His arms gave way.

Again Baudy called his name. A whimper in response. Baudy leaped forwards, but Josef was quicker, planting himself in front. Four or five hands grabbed Baudy and held him fast.

At that moment Gubnik toppled forwards and vanished into the sea of flames.

Barely an hour later everything was over. The cellar was half under water. The remnants of wooden crates, bent pieces of metal, splintered wood and charred planks floated on the black surface. Gubnik's body in a red protective suit, only the helmet missing.

Baudy turned away.

He went to his men sitting by the fire engines. The sun was now above the horizon. The seed of hope that had brought death.

Officers from Kripo – the criminal police – the constabulary and the fire service kept arriving. On the farm track one of Freiburg's fire chiefs was in conversation with Almenbroich, the head of Kripo, and Martin Andersen, Baudy's deputy. A local politician whose name he could never remember, the mayor of Kirchzarten, a public prosecutor and Heinrich Täschle, the chief of the local police station, were with them too. The first reporters, photographers and camera teams had by now appeared on the scene. A Special Support unit kept them behind the cordons. The spokeswoman from police H.Q. was with them, wearing a high-visibility jacket with PRESSE POLIZEI on the back. Officers from Freiburg's professional fire service and a handful of men in white disposable suits were standing or kneeling around the site of the fire. He couldn't see Hannes Riedinger. Maybe Kripo had taken him away.

Baudy thought of Lew Gubnik's last words. *What is that arsehole storing down there?* The black water concealed the answer.

He stopped in front of his men. They all looked at him, even Paul Feul, who lay on his side curled up like a foetus. "Have you got his helmet?"

"No," Josef replied. He was wearing a bandage over his right temple. Dried blood stuck to his cheek below it. He explained what had happened: Gubnik had stumbled and lost his helmet. On his knees he'd turned around and obviously hadn't been able to see for a few moments. Then he had crawled in the wrong direction. A few men yelled out warnings, but Gubnik hadn't heard them.

"What are they doing here?" Josef said, gesturing with his head.

Baudy looked up. The fire chief, the head of Kripo, the local politician, the mayor. Professional fire service, crime scene investigation department and an army of uniformed police and Kripo officers.

There it was again, Gubnik's question.

He shrugged. He didn't have the energy to think about it.

"Let's fetch him," he said.

The undertakers put Gubnik's corpse into a metal coffin. One of his friends said, "Don't forget, Gubby, we're going bowling on Wednesday," which elicited a smattering of laughter. Banter and laughter would help drive his grisly image from their minds. His face had been burned to a cinder.

Baudy followed the undertakers to the hearse. He thought of Gubnik's casket sitting half-finished in the workshop. What was he going to do with it now? He couldn't throw the thing away.

The undertakers lifted the coffin into the hearse and closed the door. Gubnik's body had been impounded. His last operation was to end in forensics.

Baudy stepped back. He had wanted to say a few words of farewell. But he could only think of the clichés he churned out during operations: "Everything's going to be alright", "Heads up, it's not that bad" and "Courage, men, tomorrow is another day".

So he said nothing.

Later Baudy was approached by Berthold Meiering, the mayor of Zarten and a Swabian Allgäuer by birth. Beads of sweat stood on his bald head and his eyes strayed in every direction. After Baudy had filled him in on the situation, Meiering said that, as far as he was concerned, Baudy was in no way to blame for the death of his "comrade", a view shared by Baudy's "colleagues", if the mayor had understood them correctly. His round, fleshy face was ashen. There was empathy in Meiering's voice.

Baudy shuddered as he considered the mayor's words. He began to suspect that the key criteria of his twenty years in the volunteer fire service – analysis, facts and loyalty – no longer counted. Now it was about interpretation, interests, recriminations. Despite this, Baudy felt that Meiering's empathy had been genuine.

He nodded.

"And please, Adam, not a word to the media. They have to talk to the police spokeswoman."

They looked each other in the eye. Once more Gubnik's question hung in the air, and once more Baudy had no wish to contemplate an answer. But now he felt the question taking root in his head. Not because he was especially interested in the answer, but because as time went on this question would be all that remained of Gubnik. A question and a half-finished casket.

Meiering put his hand to his head. "Your eyebrows."

"Yes?"

"They're singed."

Baudy nodded. At least his hearing had returned to normal.

Martin Andersen, who seemed to be everywhere at the moment, came to whisper in his ear that his wife had taken Lina back to their place. Lina was O.K., he said, she hadn't registered much. "Come past when you're finished here." Baudy nodded and Andersen left.

"Kripo want a word," Meiering said.

"Yes."

"And headquarters wants a report."

"They'll get one."

"This one's too big for Kirchzarten, Adam. Freiburg's going to deal with it."

Baudy nodded, then shuddered again. "It's *Kirch*zarten, not Kirch*zarten*," he said.

"What?"

"You said Kirch*zarten*."

Meiering didn't respond.

"Here we say *Kirch*zarten," Baudy said again, softly.

"O.K. Thanks."

The two men watched the professional fire fighters begin to pump the water away from the site. The level sank rapidly. For a moment

Baudy thought he could see Gubnik's yellow helmet bobbing on the surface, but he wasn't sure.

"What's that smell?" Meiering said in sudden exasperation.

Baudy breathed in deeply. It smelled as it usually did after a fire. Then he detected some other, very faint odours. Vinegar. Honey. Something else he couldn't identify.

This one's too big for Kirchzarten. Freiburg's going to deal with it.

"What was that arsehole storing down there?" he said.

"Weapons," Meiering whispered, as if hoping no-one else would hear.

I

The Hellish Legions

1

A time of firsts, Louise Bonì thought as she took a bottle from her shoulder bag and lay down on the grass. The first overtime, the first visit to Kirchzarten, the first dead bodies. Last night the first serious crisis, a few days ago the first sex with Anatol, a week ago her first row with Rolf Bermann. The first nightmares, the first doubts about whether she'd make it. Her return to normal life was accompanied by premières.

She undid the screwcap and gulped down half the bottle. Almost forty-three and life – *this* life was starting afresh.

Not an altogether pleasant thought.

She looked over at Schneider, who'd been standing motionless at the edge of the scorched area for some minutes, his gaze fixed on the forest or the hills beyond. Handsome, dull Schneider, lost without Bermann as ever. Like five months ago, in the snow near Münzenried, on the day Natchaya and Areewan died.

Since her return, she thought, everything was happening for the first time and yet all of it led straight back to the life before her time at the Kanzan-an. She put the bottle to her lips, finished it, opened a second and drank half of that. She could drink as much water as she liked, but she was still thirsty.

Thirsty and sleepless.

At three o'clock that morning she had been at the till of a Freiburg petrol station, packing four bottles of high-percentage alcohol into a bag. Back home she'd set the bottles on the coffee table in front of her. Right, she said, if you really want to drink, then go ahead! Do you want vodka? Bourbon? Have what you fancy! Vodka? Yes? Go on, then, drink! Drink what you want!

Yes, yes, yes, the demons in her head called out.

No, Louise cried. Not tonight!

Instead she'd left her apartment and driven to a deserted police headquarters. She was still without an office, a desk or a telephone. So she sat in Almenbroich's office, because he had the most comfortable chair, was the head of Kripo and supported his officers through their battles with their demons.

But that morning Almenbroich hadn't come into the office. The control centre had notified him at home and he'd driven straight to Kirchzarten.

Her gaze wandered across the site of the fire. At this stage she knew very little; Bermann hadn't let her come until late afternoon. Weapons in a cellar nobody had known about, beneath a wooden shed nobody had used, in the field of a farmer nobody liked.

And a dead fireman.

She hadn't yet read any eyewitness statements, nor had she taken part in the first meeting of the "Weapons" investigation team earlier that evening. Cautious Bermann. He wanted to integrate her back into normal life slowly. We mustn't expect too much of her, he'd said last week in front of the assembled team. She's been away for quite a while. She was ill. But now she's better again. That's right, isn't it, Luis? You're better again?

To begin with he'd toyed with the idea of seconding her to a different section. How about vice, Luis, wouldn't the vice squad be right for you? Wouldn't that be good? Or youth crime? Rubbish, she'd said.

They'd agreed that she would remain in Bermann's D11 squad, but at first only "helping out", as he'd put it. He hadn't said what he meant by "helping out".

She emptied the second bottle and put it in her bag. She would have liked to stay away a while longer. Far away from the world and life, from outside influences and feeling like an outsider. On the other hand, returning a changed woman was exciting. Detecting curiosity in every glance, in every voice, and sometimes surprise. And occasionally, in Bermann and other men, even a peculiar intensity that she hadn't sparked for centuries.

It was impossible to ignore the six kilos she'd lost, or the four months in the fresh air.

Schneider came alive again. He turned to her and pointed towards Freiburg. Shall we go? His face was lit up by the last rays of the sun. A friendly, empty, clothing-catalogue face you couldn't take your eyes off until you realised that it might be forever devoid of any spirit.

She shook her head. We're staying. Waiting for the ghost to reappear.

Half an hour went by. The sun disappeared behind the hills. Schneider was in the car; she could hear him talking on his mobile. One of the Kirchzarten patrol cars drove past slowly. Heinrich Täschle, chief at the local station, was also doing overtime. She'd seen him that afternoon, but hadn't had the opportunity to meet him. A tall, somewhat gauche police inspector in his fifties, he'd been born in Kirchzarten, gone to school in Kirchzarten and got married in Kirchzarten. Täschle had hurried along beside Bermann warily, holding his cap. Later, from his car, he'd watched Kripo comb *his* field centimetre by centimetre. The old rivalry between the constabulary and the criminal police. He'd left around seven o'clock, since when he'd driven past three or four times.

Eric Satie rang out on her mobile. It took Boni a while to find it amongst the empty plastic bottles in her bag. It was a new phone, so far she'd only saved a few numbers. This was not one of them. Wilhelm Brenner, a firearms expert at the forensics laboratory. "I heard you were back. How was life with the Buddhists?"

"Like life with Buddhists."

"What, do you meditate every day?" Boni laughed politely. "You'll have to tell me about it sometime."

"Yes." For a moment she imagined that such an opportunity would actually arise, and she smiled to herself. Had she become naïve at the

Kanzan-an? Or was she simply not in the habit of hearing everyday platitudes?

Schneider came and squatted beside her. If she could judge its reddish hue in the evening sunset, his face bore a shimmer of embarrassment or nervousness. She mouthed the word "forensics". Schneider held out his hand for her mobile, but the gesture lacked conviction.

He was right, officially she was only "helping out".

Louise flashed him a menacing smile and Schneider withdrew his hand.

Brenner had examined the first of the destroyed weapons and identified some manufacturers' markings as well as model numbers: model 57 pistols, the Yugoslav licensed version of the Russian 7.62-millimetre Tokarev; small model 61 submachine guns, the Yugoslav licensed version of the Czechoslovak Škorpion; Kalashnikovs without model numbers, but the manufacturing style suggested that these were also Yugoslav licensed versions of the Russian original.

"Yugoslav," Louise told Schneider.

"Yes," Brenner said.

"The weapons?" Schneider asked.

She nodded.

"Rottweil," Brenner and Schneider said simultaneously.

Brenner added "early nineties" and Schneider "last year". The weapons find in a garage in Rottweil the previous year could be disregarded. Gun freaks apparently preparing themselves for World War Three had stockpiled submachine guns, machine guns, pistols and other munitions. But more interesting was Rottweil in the early 1990s, when the Baden-Württemberg Criminal Investigation Bureau came across a ring of Croatian arms dealers. If she remembered correctly, some of those weapons had come from Yugoslavia.

Brenner promised to find out the types and models of those weapons back then.

"Have you counted the stuff yet?" she said.

"Yes. Twenty-four boxes."

"And?" Schneider whispered.

"They haven't counted yet."

"Who are you talking to?" Brenner asked.

"Schneider."

"Schneider, Schneider . . . Which one's he again?"

"The good-looking one. When will we get the official report?"

Schneider frowned, Brenner sighed. "In a fortnight."

"You lot haven't got any quicker during my time with the Buddhists."

"Oh yes, we have. It's just that we've slowed down again since you came back."

She smiled and said goodbye.

Schneider's knees creaked as he got up, and it struck her that, against expectation, the ugliness of ageing was beginning to rage beneath his handsome exterior. He was in his late forties, not a problem from the outside, just from within.

Just then she glimpsed the ghost standing absolutely still, barely twenty metres behind Schneider in the twilight, and staring at her.

The day of motionless men.

She'd been expecting to see Baudy, the commander of the Kirchzarten volunteer fire brigade, but it was Riedinger, the farmer. That's O.K. too, she thought.

When they arrived at the scene of the fire that afternoon, Riedinger was standing at the edge of the belt of woodland, surveying the activity. Bermann said he'd been questioned all day long, by Kripo, C.S.I., the fire brigade, the mayor, the public prosecutor, the press and "wassisname, Däschle". Riedinger had worked himself up into such a fury that no-one dared approach him anymore. He'd threatened one of the reporters and insulted a uniformed officer. She was about to go and talk to him when Bermann held her back. "You're only helping out here, Luis," he said, staring at her with this new intensity. The male gaze. Ludicrous as it was, Boni took it as further proof that she had changed. That she'd ridden out the storm and that she would be able to survive every future minute, hour and day.

Looking now at Hannes Riedinger, she decided against approaching him straightaway; she would wait a while longer, show him she was relaxed. She gave him a polite smile.

"So what's Brenner saying?" Schneider asked.

"Tell me first what Riedinger's saying."

"Why Riedinger?"

"When did he notice the fire?"

Schneider snorted indignantly.

Riedinger explained that he'd got up at around half past four, seen to the cows and put the dog on the tether. As he was heading back to the farmhouse he caught sight of the first flames in the darkness. He climbed onto his tractor, but when he had gone fifty or sixty metres he realised that he wouldn't be able to put out the fire alone, and certainly not without water. So he turned back and rang the fire brigade. He then returned to the shed with a few buckets of water, but by now the flames were already several metres high. As if someone had opened the gates to hell.

"He said that?"

Schneider nodded. "Now tell me about Brenner."

As she summarised her telephone conversation she realised she'd forgotten to ask Brenner about munitions and explosives. Whether the fire could have triggered the explosion. Louise looked at Schneider.

"How did the stuff go up then?"

She sighed and gave a shrug.

Schneider went to the Kripo car to pass on Brenner's information to Rolf Bermann. Louise noticed that Riedinger was still staring at her. A small and insignificant shed burning down – the gates of hell? She knew almost nothing about Riedinger, apart from the fact that nobody liked him and he lived alone. That he could see the gates of hell in the blaze of a wooden shed. Not much in the way of information. But if you considered that Kirchzarten was inhabited by the affluent, educated, wholesome middle class, then perhaps it was enough.

"Rolf says it's time to return to H.Q., so let's go," Schneider said on his way back.

"What else did he say?"

"That Löbinger and D23 are on board too."

"I mean about the fire and the weapons."

Schneider hesitated.

"Come on, Heinz."

Schneider crouched beside her. Although he'd been on duty for fourteen hours, the knot of his tie was still impeccable and there wasn't a speck of dust or a blade of grass to be seen on his light-brown corduroy suit. Insects landed on other people, but not on Heinz Schneider. Not even the high summer temperatures seemed to bother him. Louise thought of Hollerer – unshaven, stained police coat, crumbs down his front.

The round, white face beside the shadowy, bloody snow at night.

There were firsts still to come – paying Hollerer a visit, going to Niksch's grave.

Louise tried to focus on Schneider. Twice today, he said, Bermann had pointed out that a disproportionate number of arsonists came from the ranks of the professional or volunteer fire brigades. It was possible that one of the Kirchzarten volunteers had set the shed on fire. She nodded pensively. The ideal target for a pyromaniac. The fire couldn't have spread or injured anyone.

Schneider stood up and his joints creaked again. "Can we go now?" He froze. "There's someone standing . . ."

"Riedinger." Louise got up and slung the bag over her shoulder.

"How long's he been there?"

"A few minutes. Come on, let's have a little chat!"

Schneider held her back. Riedinger was dangerous. A man the neighbours avoided, who'd unleashed his dogs on asylum seekers and Dutch campers because they'd set foot on his land. Who'd beaten his wife and children, driven away his employees and sold the lion's share of his land for financial reasons. Who was facing ruin.

Stories told to him by Berthold Meiering, the mayor of Kirchzarten.

"Just be careful, Luis."

"Is he an alcoholic?"

Shocked, Schneider looked away.

She grinned. "Come on," she said.

Riedinger was barely taller than she was, but twice as broad. His expression was cagey, his eyes clear, the irises bright. No, not an alcoholic. This thought comforted her, but she couldn't have said why.

Schneider introduced Bonì as a "colleague" and said they had a few more questions. Riedinger told them he didn't want to answer any more questions, he'd been answering questions all day. "I've got some different questions," Louise said.

Schneider looked at her in surprise; Riedinger spat to the side.

"Where are your children?"

Riedinger laughed angrily.

"Your wife, your employees? Why's there nobody here anymore?"

"Luis," Schneider warned.

"These sorts of questions, Herr Riedinger."

Riedinger had stopped laughing. His round cheeks had turned red, his eyes were smaller. Something about him or inside him seemed to be vibrating. Schneider's hand grabbed Louise's arm and pulled her back. She realised that both men thought she was trying to provoke Riedinger, and that he was on the verge of hitting her. She held up a hand and made a dismissive gesture. Sometimes when she was speaking she found it hard to coordinate the old, gruff Louise and the new, more relaxed one. Then the old Louise formulated thoughts that passed through the head of the new one.

"These sorts of questions," she repeated, feeling exhausted all of a sudden. But Riedinger had already turned his back on her and was heading into the darkness.

*

Schneider said nothing until they were in the tunnel on the B31. Then he muttered, "What kind of questions ... Are we psychiatrists? Come on, we're police officers . . ." Louise had no desire to enter into this conversation. She thought of Riedinger back there in the darkness, furious, but with nobody left to hit. Louise was convinced that somewhere in his head was the information they needed, to make some initial progress. It was his shed, his pasture, and it was not as if these had only recently come into his possession. Even if he really *had* known nothing about the weapons store, he was the link between the cellar and those who'd used it.

She wished she could speak to Reiner Lederle about this. Engage in some brainstorming without running the risk of being declared mad. But Lederle was in a cancer rehab centre somewhere in Franconia. Five months ago he'd told her he was going to win the battle. But he hadn't. The cancer had come back in another place. A few days before her return he'd had a tumour removed from his gall bladder, along with his gall bladder itself.

She was still thinking of Lederle as she climbed the stairs behind Schneider to the third floor of police headquarters. In the corridor the sound of their footsteps was swallowed by the low ceiling. Schneider seemed careful to be always one metre ahead of her. Outside Bermann's office he straightened his tie and collar, as if the few hours in her company had sullied his appearance.

Almenbroich was perched on the edge of Bermann's desk. He looked overtired. From the breakfast table straight to Kirchzarten, back to Freiburg for the mid-morning weekly management meeting, then out to Kirchzarten again, and all this in 36-degree heat. But he gave Louise a fleeting smile as she came in. The severity with which he'd packed her off on sick leave almost six months earlier had given way to a discreet leniency. Almenbroich also seemed to be reacting to the changes to and within her. But she couldn't tell whether this was in his capacity as a man, or as a caring boss.

Bermann was sitting on his chair, swivelling from side to side. Anselm Löbinger, head of the organised crime section, stood at the washbasin. He grinned at Louise in the mirror.

"Is that sorted out then?" Almenbroich said, standing up.

Bermann nodded and Löbinger said, "Yes." Anger was written across Bermann's face, but not Löbinger's. Ever since it had become known that the head of Division One was retiring at the end of the year, they'd become rivals – both had applied for the post. Being the boss of Division One meant serving as deputy head of Kripo; running five sections, including two key ones, the serious crime squad and national security; and promotion to detective chief super-intendent in salary bracket A13. It was worth the fight. The position was advertised throughout the entire administrative district, but Almenbroich had of course tailored the job profile to Bermann and Löbinger – experience in running a section, heading up task forces and cooperation with the French police, and someone under the age of fifty. He wanted one of those two, but he hadn't indicated which. It was making communication difficult.

Almenbroich went to the door. "See you then," he said, and left the room.

Löbinger, a compact man in his early forties, with narrow glasses, dried his hands and turned to Bermann. "Neither of us got what we wanted. Let's make the best of it."

Bermann gave an apathetic nod. "Tomorrow," he said.

For Bermann, "tomorrow" began the moment Anselm Löbinger had gone. "Rottweil 1992," he said. "Look at everything the Criminal Investigation Bureau collected. Get in touch with Pilbrich, he was head of the investigation team at the time. Check the names of every-one that was involved in any way." He was squinting with concentra-tion and there was power and assertiveness in his movements. We'll nail them, promised his expression, gestures and poise. Schneider hung on his every word, as did Louise. "Defendants, lawyers, witnesses, suspects, relatives, the whole lot of them. Do you understand?"

They nodded.

Bermann propped himself on his desk. "Is something wrong? Have I missed anything? Heinz?"

Schneider fiddled with the knot of his tie.

"What do you mean?"

"He doesn't want me to help him," Louise said.

Schneider looked at Bermann, opened his mouth, then shut it again. Bermann leaned back and crossed his arms. "What happened?"

Schneider told him about the questions Bonì had fired at Riedinger. He raised his hands, shook his head. "What sort of questions are those?"

"Buddhist questions," Bermann explained.

"You two haven't changed," Louise said.

Bermann yawned pointedly. "Well, we haven't been on a withdrawal treatment programme, have we?"

Bermann solved the problem rapidly and with astonishing composure. Schneider would investigate Rottweil in 1992 with a different colleague, Louise the fire in Riedinger's shed with another officer. Were there suspects amongst the fire brigade? Had there been any unexplained fires in Kirchzarten over the past few years? "You know what I mean."

She nodded. "Two large fires in the past two years. The Dold sawmill in Buchenbach, one year ago. An old farmhouse with a pottery in Falkenstieg, two years ago. The Dold fire was down to a technical fault, the one in Falkenstieg because of a problem with the insulation."

Bermann raised his eyebrows. "She hasn't forgotten," he said, without taking his eyes off her.

"That's enough, Rolf."

"Of what?"

"You know very well what."

Bermann looked at Schneider. "Would you go and get us something to drink, Heinz?" As Schneider left the room, the two of them listened to his footsteps recede into the distance. Then Bermann swivelled his chair in Boni's direction and looked her up and down. After a while he said, "O.K." She waited, but he said nothing more. From the calm expression in his eyes she thought she could infer that he meant it seriously.

Bermann's O.K.s.

Just as at the Opfinger See a few months ago, to Louise it sounded as if this O.K. concealed a whole string of other words too. Words such as, We're delighted you're back. You were at rock bottom and now you're back. Respect. You'll get your chance. All the best for the time *afterwards*.

Words like that.

She nodded. "O.K."

Schneider brought Coke and crackers from the vending machine outside the cafeteria. As they ate and drank, Bermann gave a resumé of the investigation team's preliminary meeting that evening, which had been more of a quarrel over who was in charge. Operations had notified the serious crime squad in the morning, then Bermann assembled and dispatched his team. Afterwards, Löbinger called Almenbroich in Kirchzarten. This amount of weapons, he argued, pointed to organised crime and therefore *his* section was responsible. On Almenbroich's instructions, the investigation team was to be jointly led by Bermann and Löbinger, and would consist of an equal number of officers from each section, plus a firearms expert and someone from C.S.I.

"And Täschle?" Louise said.

"Who?" Bermann said.

"The chief of Kirchzarten station."

"Oh, come on. It's too big for them."

"He knows the place and the people."

"Luis, they clock off at five in the afternoon. How's that going to work?"

After Schneider had called him earlier with an update, Bermann had rung Wilhelm Brenner at the forensics laboratory himself. From now on, he said amicably, Brenner would report in to him alone. If he was taking a piss, Brenner would notify Löbinger, and if Löbinger happened to be taking a piss too, Schneider. Louise smiled. "What if all three of you need to take a piss at the same time?"

Bermann grinned.

Brenner didn't have an answer as to the cause of the fire either. No accelerants such as petrol had been used. One possibility was that the hay had combusted spontaneously, the cause of many fires on farms. In this case it was unlikely as the fire had broken out in the early morning, when it was cooler.

"How did the weapons go up in smoke?"

"That's the big question."

"Were there explosives down there too?"

"That's what we're assuming."

Crime scene officers identified yellow residues on several stones which they assumed had been catapulted from the cellar into the field. And for a while after the blaze a number of detectives as well as fire officers said they could detect the faint odours of vinegar, honey and wax. Both the yellow residue and the smells suggested Semtex.

Another question yet to be answered was whether thermal updrafts produced during the fire could have caused the detonators and thus the explosives to blow up. Brenner thought that Semtex reacted to thermals as well as pressure surges, but he wasn't totally sure. He would check with an expert at Stuttgart police H.Q. the next day. It was also theoretically possible that a stone or plank might have fallen directly on top of a detonator and triggered the explosion.

"And there's one other possibility, of course," Bermann said hesitantly. Louise nodded. Not very likely, not very plausible, but a possibility all the same. Maybe the fire and the explosions were linked.

Maybe someone had set fire to Riedinger's shed in order to blow up the weapons.

With that, the decimated investigation team's unofficial conversation was at an end. They took the lift to the ground floor. "Rottweil 1992 was Croats," Bermann said, more to himself. "Rottweil 2002, arms obsessives." And Kirchzarten 2003? Louise thought. Former Yugoslavs, gun freaks, neo-Nazis, Islamic fundamentalists? None of whom were pleasant prospects.

They came out of the lift and headed for the main entrance. Louise held her card to the reader, Schneider opened the security gate. They waved to Gregori, the porter. "Where's your car, Luis?" Bermann said as they stepped outside.

"I walked."

"I'll give you a lift home."

"Thanks, but I'd rather walk."

"Fine." Bermann touched her bare arm. "See you at *seven* tomorrow morning, but beforehand, read . . ."

"Seven?"

Bermann nodded. Because of the heat the daily meetings were scheduled for seven in the morning and seven in the evening. "Oh yes, and after the meeting I'm going to need you for an hour or two."

"Why?"

"We're going on a drive . . . somewhere."

"Somewhere?" she said.

Bermann nodded and looked at her arm where he'd touched it, then at the writing on her T-shirt: PLEASE MARRY ME OR AT LEAST TAKE ME OUT TO LUNCH. He looked up. "Hard facts, Luis, it's all part of the job."

"And what's that supposed to mean?"

"Tomorrow, Luis."

*

She got home at eleven. No post, no messages on her answerphone. The bottles were still on the table by the sofa, as if they'd been waiting for her.

From the work surface in the kitchen she picked up the activity schedule she'd drawn up the week before and scanned it. Maybe she would find something you could do at eleven at night, which would help combat not just the craving for a drink, but also the fear of Bermann's menacing "Tomorrow, Luis". She could eliminate cinema, the theatre, museums, church, Italian videos or a trip over to Schauinsland, and taking a walk hadn't helped. Going to Enni's for some sushi, calling Richard Landen, visiting Hollerer in Konstanz, going to Niksch's grave and reviving old friendships were out of the question too. Sex was a more viable option, as were the gym, jogging or a nightclub. Visiting Mama in Provence or Papa in Kehl – only in an emergency. Reading, listening to music or meditation would be no use. Tidying the apartment, cleaning the apartment, rearranging the apartment? Not again. Looking for a new apartment, looking for a second-hand car . . .

She put on her coat. You could look for second-hand cars at night too.

2

Once again she drove in the darkness to police H.Q. Once again she sat in Almenbroich's chair and hoped he would come, at the same time hoping he wouldn't. She set his alarm clock for half past six. Seconds later she was fast asleep.

When she was woken by Almenbroich's cold hand on her shoulder it was a quarter past six. "If I'd known," he said, "I'd have brought croissants." There were little yellow balls in the corners of his eyes. His face was pale and streaked with red blood vessels. He looked depressingly tired and feeble. But what she really needed at the moment was a strong boss.

"Not hungry," she said, getting up. "Sorry."

As he slumped into the chair Almenbroich waved away her apology. He wasn't sleeping much, he said, because it was hardly cooling down at night, and when the air finally did become fresher he couldn't sleep because he was too cold. He tried a feeble smile.

She felt the urge to lay her hand on his cheek. Kripo bosses needed a bit of comfort now and then too.

His face was as cold as his hand.

Almenbroich looked at her in surprise, but not unhappily – an exhausted old man who'd aged years in a few weeks of intense heat, receiving a little unexpected comfort.

"Is it really hard?" he said after a while.

"Sometimes."

"Very admirable. How do you manage it?"

Louise took away her hand and sat on the armrest. "I tell myself:

Not today. I'm not going to drink today, under no circumstances. I've no idea what tomorrow will be like, but today I'm not going to drink."

"Like a mantra?"

"Sort of."

"And you say it every day?"

She nodded.

"Well, it seems to help," he said.

"Along with a few other techniques."

"Really admirable."

They looked at each other for a while in silence. Louise wondered if Almenbroich knew where Bermann was taking her later. Did she want to ask him, and perhaps find out now? She stood up. "The worst thing is the self-pity."

"From you that's hard to believe."

She smiled, even though she couldn't be sure exactly what he meant by the comment.

"Have you seen your Buddhist expert again?"

"My . . ." She could feel herself blush. "No."

"Maybe you ought to."

"Maybe." She was about to leave but Almenbroich pointed to the visitor's chair on the other side of his desk. Louise sat down. He rested his elbows on the armrests and the fingertips of either hand formed a triangle. The last time she'd seen this gesture he'd sent her on sick leave.

Another first that took her back to the time before the Kanzan-an. Although she'd led a completely different life for four months, every day since seemed to be connected to her life before, as if it had merely continued.

But this was about the case rather than her illness. "Pay careful attention . . ." Almenbroich said almost guardedly, and then he paused. "Pay careful attention to who gets involved with the investigation. Keep an eye on the investigation team and anyone else hovering around the case, or trying to. Don't get me wrong, it's . . ."

"I'm not getting you at all."

"O.K., let me put it another way. My impression is that too many people are interested in our work."

"What sort of people?"

"Well, for example, the Baden-Württemberg Criminal Investigation Bureau showed a keen interest rather too early for my liking." He looked her in the eye and waited.

She didn't think it particularly unusual for the Bureau to have stepped in at this stage. Had the weapons cache been larger they would have taken over the case by now anyway. She raised her eyebrows.

"Yesterday evening a permanent secretary called me to ask how the investigation was going."

Louise didn't find that especially strange either. Permanent secretaries loved making calls, often to people who didn't want to talk to them.

"And then there was a call from F.I.S. asking that we provide them with the official forensics report and the results of the inquiry into how the weapons came to Germany."

Bonì nodded. This was surprising. Kripo and the Foreign Intelligence Service rarely had anything to do with each other. The Service sat in its fortress in Pullach and looked after Afghanistan, Chechnya, Iraq, Al-Qaida . . . not Freiburg or Kirchzarten. Cooperation between the authorities, especially the Criminal Investigation Bureau and the Foreign Intelligence Service, had gradually improved since August Hanning had been made boss of the latter a few years earlier. He aimed for openness and more cooperation, and hoped to improve the image of F.I.S. But he was in a minority, especially since the Service's move to Berlin had been made definite.

"That was one thing," Almenbroich continued. "The other is that they're passing *us* information. The Bureau is suggesting that neo-Nazis from Munich are stockpiling large quantities of weapons – possibly in Baden. The permanent secretary says that although the threat from the extreme right has been significantly checked, it hasn't yet been defeated. He has information that Baden-Württemberg neo-Nazis may be planning an attack. And according to F.I.S., U.S. intelligence has intimated that neo-Nazis in southern Germany have been buying weapons with American money."

"All very possible."

Almenbroich nodded. "Nonetheless—" At that moment the clock started beeping and he flinched. "What's that?"

"Your alarm clock."

He grabbed it. "How do you turn the damn thing off?"

"Hit the top."

Almenbroich did as instructed and put the clock down with a grin. "Nonetheless," he said again.

But he couldn't give concrete reasons for his unease. Somewhere between the external heat and the internal cold, a strange feeling was lurking inside his body which said. How nice that they're showing an interest in our work and giving us tips. But it's very odd. Everyone wants something and to get what they want they're all sending us in the same direction. But, said the feeling, are they just trying to prevent us from going in a different direction? He smiled grimly. "Am I being paranoid?"

"A little."

"Perhaps you're right. Ten years with national security have left their mark."

It hadn't occurred to Louise that Almenbroich had himself once been a national security officer. All national security officers were paranoid, and that was a good thing. Almenbroich had run the section for five years before it was liquidated in April 2000. After 9/11 it had been revived as D13, but by that time Almenbroich was already head of Kripo.

He got up and walked around the desk. "Nonetheless," Louise said, "I'll keep my eyes open." Now she too was struck by a peculiar feeling: Almenbroich was hiding something from her. He knew more than he'd let on.

But that was inconceivable. All the others, yes, but upright, dour Almenbroich? Never.

He grasped the door handle. "If you think it was neo-Nazis, then focus on neo-Nazis. If you don't think it was them then go down the other route, no matter what Rolf or Anselm say. Only one thing counts: the truth." He smiled. "The good old truth. The older you get the better you understand that it's all we've got. It's at the heart of everything, the most important asset for any enlightened society. Unfortunately it's the most uncomfortable one too, which is why we like to avoid it. But ultimately, Louise, everything's about the truth. From the truth of birth to the truth of death. Our lives in-between are more meaningful, more fulfilled and more Christian if they're lived in accordance with the truth."

She frowned. "I suppose."

Almenbroich laughed and put his other hand on her back. She winced; the hand was even colder than before. "But why me and not Rolf? I've got less influence, and no-one who speaks up for me."

There it was, the self-pity. She knew she would keep talking. Another little helping of self-pity. Voicing her grievances to Almenbroich for seconds, minutes, hours. Lock the door then talk about the days, weeks, months and years past, when everything, everything just went wrong. Did Almenbroich know that her ex-husband had cheated on her with half of Baden-Württemberg? That her brother Germain had died in a car crash in 1983? That her parents had waged real war against each other between their marriage and divorce? No? She'd tell him everything. All this and everything else.

Four months in the tranquillity of a Zen monastery had been good for self-discipline, but they hadn't done anything for the self-pity.

She cleared her throat but said nothing.

"Rolf respects authority. You don't." Almenbroich smiled. "That can be a good thing sometimes."

He opened the door, but Louise didn't move. Seeing as she was in her self-pitying mode . . . "One more thing," she said, and she put the question that had been bothering her since the evening before: Where was Rolf Bermann driving her?

Almenbroich closed the door. He knew the answer.

They had found the monk.

She stayed with Almenbroich until just before seven. Sitting on the window sill with a cup of tea, she watched the light and traffic flood into the city below her. The old town and minster, the Schlossberg, the thousand different reflections of sunlight, a picture of peace and relentless indifference. Truth and lies in one. The life before, the life after – no matter what came between, life always leapfrogged it.

Taro hadn't been murdered, he had frozen to death. Walkers had found him at the beginning of March halfway up the Flaunser, far from any path or hiking route. Propped up against a tree, he'd been overlooking Liebau, Freiburg and the Dreisamtal when he died.

Almenbroich and Bermann had decided to keep this information from Bonì until she was back. And when she did come back Bermann had said, "We mustn't overburden her. What does it matter if Luis knows or not? The important thing now is to look after her." Almenbroich said, "Talk to her. Drive her over there."

The good old truth.

It occurred to her that Taro may have been searching for the truth too. For some reason she was convinced that for him the truth boiled down to one question: Who am I, in the middle of everything that's going on?

But who could say what had been going through his head? Louise had come round to Richard Landen's way of thinking: you could never completely understand another person, especially if they were from a different culture.

"Are you alright, Louise?" Almenbroich sounded concerned.

He had turned his seat to face the window. She nodded. As absurd as it sounded, the fact that Taro had frozen to death instead of being murdered made it more bearable.

All the same, she was in no hurry to see the pictures of his body.

The life before, the life after – no matter what came between, life always leapfrogged it. As she rinsed out her cup in the small washbasin she realised how closely she'd adhered to the laws of an indifferent life. But Taro's death gave her a reason to contact Richard Landen.

Five officers each from the serious crime and organised crime squads attended the second meeting of the "Weapons" investigation team in the task force room, plus Bermann and Löbinger, the section leaders. Also present were a crime scene officer, a weapons expert and two secretaries. They sat around a U-shaped table, the D11 officers down the side nearest the door and the D23 officers on the other side, their backs to the windows. Sixteen people in a room for eighty; three taciturn groups eyeing each other warily.

The hot, sticky air inside the room didn't make it any easier.

There was only one of Löbinger's people Louise didn't know, a nervous young, blond chap who must have started during her absence. She kept feeling his eyes on her, and whenever she returned his gaze he looked away. This was no confident, laid-back Anatol, more like a younger, shier brother who didn't allow himself to dream of older women. It seemed she hadn't lost the power of attraction over men who were half her age. Louise could only hope that after four barren months in the Alsatian forest, men of her own age would show an interest in her too.

"Let's begin," Bermann said.

"Let's begin," Löbinger agreed.

"Open the windows," the D11 team demanded.

"Too loud," the D23 lot objected.

After they'd agreed on breaks for fresh air, Bermann reported on the findings Wilhelm Brenner and the forensics laboratory had delivered so far, as well as the outcome of yesterday's questioning. Then Löbinger gave a preliminary resumé: ex-Yugoslavs, weapons obsessives, neo-

Nazis, Islamic fundamentalists – all areas that would have to be investigated even though there were indications that here they were dealing with neo-Nazis. They discussed probabilities, improbabilities, the extent to which the fire was significant for the weapons investigation. Each time they came to the sobering realisation that they had hardly anything to go on. Then the discussion became more heated. Bermann's interjection that it was theoretically possible somebody had set fire to the barn in order to blow up the weapons divided opinion and both squads down the middle. Löbinger calmed the heated discussion. Seeing as they still had next to no information, he said amiably, they simply couldn't gauge this possibility.

Louise did her best to follow the conversation, but her mind kept drifting to Taro. Whenever she'd thought about him over the past few months, she had pictured him wandering through the snow, away from Liebau, away from her. Now in her imagination he was sitting up on the Flaunser with his eyes closed. He'd come back.

The background voices suddenly fell silent. All eyes were on Alfons Hoffmann, one of the chief case officers in Bermann's section.

"Lew Gubnik, please," Hoffmann said. "Not 'the dead Ruski'." He'd crossed his arms in front of his chest. His face was a deep red and he was breathing fast. Drops of sweat ran down his neck and his shirt was sticking to his voluminous stomach.

"Yes, yes," Bermann said, rubbing his face with impatience.

"His nickname was Gubby, if you really want to know."

"We don't have *time* for that, Alfons."

"I think you always have to have time for that."

"Did you know him?" asked Tomas Ilic, a colleague from Bermann's D11.

Hoffmann wiped the sweat from his face. "From bowling. The Kirchzarten volunteers have a bowling club, sometimes we play them."

"Nice," Bermann said. "So let's think of Lew 'Gubby' Gubnik now and then. We'll throw flowers on his grave and pray that there's a bowling alley in heaven. But in the meantime let's try to find out who's been stockpiling weapons and munitions under our noses, and more importantly," he added, slamming the palm of his hand on the table, "*why*."

The door opened and in came Almenbroich followed by four men. Two of them were with D13 – national security – but Louise had never set eyes on the other two. Almenbroich apologised for interrupting, gave their names and then, staring into space, said, "Criminal Investigation Bureau."

"Perfect," Bermann said, standing up. "We were about to take a break anyway."

The break lasted a quarter of an hour. Louise made use of it to skim the reports, protocols and statements. Bermann and Löbinger had vanished along with Almenbroich, then they all came back. Bermann couldn't hide his tension; Löbinger seemed calm.

Bermann rapped on the table. "O.K. Let's move on."

The two D13 men were added to the investigation team, which everyone thought a sensible move. If the weapons hadn't belonged to an obsessive or a collector, then national security had to be on board. The Criminal Investigation Bureau officers, on the other hand, were only being brought in as "external support", and to ensure a smooth flow of information between Kripo and the Bureau. They were quiet, reserved and friendly and Louise felt she could trust them. One of them reiterated the vague suspicions about southern German neo-Nazis that Almenbroich had voiced in his office and Löbinger had mentioned earlier. One of the men from national security said he had similar information from a reliable source in his section. "Yes, thank you, we talked about that earlier," Bermann said. "Let's work out the teams so we can finally get going."

As coincidence or fate would have it, Louise was allocated as a partner the least popular officer from Löbinger's section, if not the entire Kripo. She knew him only by his first name, rank and shoddy reputation: Günter, detective chief inspector, uncommunicative loner, grumpy colleague who came when he liked and left when he liked. Right now he was in the toilets.

Bermann and Löbinger had conferred earlier, so the pairs were quickly formed, comprising in each case one from Bermann's D11 and one from Löbinger's D23. Nobody was pleased, but nobody grumbled. The chief case officers, those responsible for the investigation file, were Alfons Hoffmann from D11 and Elly, the only female officer from Löbinger's section, a small, focused redhead. The D13 men made up a pair of their own. National security officers were secretive and preferred to keep to themselves.

Louise paid little attention to how the officers were divided up. An indefinable feeling had taken possession of her, and she was struggling to give it a name. She had the impression that the investigation team wasn't at the heart of the investigation. That the really important things were happening outside it.

Almenbroich's touch of paranoia had rubbed off.

Soon afterwards they left the task force room and hurried to their respective floors, corridors, offices. Bermann made sure that Schneider, Anne Wallmer, Alfons Hoffmann and Thomas Ilic followed him. "You too," he said casually to Louise.

She went down the stairs beside him. "Have I got you to thank for Günter?"

Bermann gave her a bleak smile as they went into his office.

"Right," Bermann said. "If any of you want to moan, do it now and then shut up."

"I mean, *Günter*," Louise said.

"Point taken. Anyone else?"

Nobody said a word.

Bermann sat behind his desk. "Let's move on to the next point, then. Illi, what if we're talking about Croats here?"

Thomas Ilic returned his gaze. "And?"

"Not a problem for you?"

"No, not at all."

"I'm counting on it."

Thomas Ilic nodded. His dark, distanced eyes met Louise's. The half-Croatian man, the half-French woman. Mothers German, fathers not, both born in Germany. Was he thinking the same?

She didn't know much about his family. Once in the cafeteria he'd told her that his father had become more Croatian as the years went on. She'd replied that her father had always tried to be more German than the Germans.

A moment of familiarity thanks to their fathers' aspirations.

"I've got a fucking awful feeling about this case," Bermann said, "and I bet you lot feel the same." He was interrupted by the telephone on his desk. He picked up, growled "yes" a few times, then hung up. "We're going to have to postpone our brainstorming session. Our excursion too, Luis. Almenbroich's got Andrele in his office."

"Andrele?" Louise mumbled, and thought: A trip up the Flaunser.

"Marianne Andrele, a new prosecutor from Munich," Wallmer said. "She started while you were away." Wallmer looked at her sheepishly. The eyes of the others were on her too. She nodded. "Away", their synonym for "alcoholic".

But now she was back.

A short while later she went over to organised crime to pick up Günter, but couldn't find him. His office was empty, his colleagues in the other rooms just shrugged. She opened Löbinger's door and the team members from D23 stared at her. Only Günter was missing. "Yes?" Löbinger said cheerfully.

"Where's my Günter?"

"Waiting for you outside the cafeteria."

"Thanks." She went into the room, closed the door and leaned against it, waiting. Nobody said anything, nobody moved. Löbinger and the shy boy read the writing across her T-shirt – DO YOU WANT

TO STAY FOR BREAKFAST? The boy blushed, Löbinger gazed at the words a while longer. Power games from the gender toy box.

"Was there anything else?" Löbinger asked her breasts.

"My dear friends, how awkward things are between us," Louise said.

Löbinger looked up. "We were just planning our bowling evening."

"So were we."

He nodded and pursed his lips, but said nothing.

"Maybe we ought to go bowling together."

"Now, that's an inclusive idea."

"The only question is whether we actually want to go bowling together."

"The question won't arise, Luis. But I could think of other questions that most definitely will."

"Are you talking about me?"

"I'm talking about Rolf. Arms dealing is D23's business, not D11's. Rolf can't go running around claiming jurisdiction over cases he's not responsible for."

"We don't even know yet if this is about arms dealing."

Löbinger waved a hand dismissively. "Do you know why he's doing it?"

"I know why he's doing it and I also know why you're getting your knickers in a twist."

"Oh, really?" Löbinger's eyes sank to the level of her breasts, then looked up again.

For a moment she let him sit there, unsure as to whether she would actually spell it out. Here, in the presence of his officers, at a time when D11 and D23 needed to save their energies for the joint investigation rather than squandering it on the battle for leadership of Division One.

She opened the door and said, "See you at the bowling alley some-time."

*

As she was on her way to the ground floor Wilhelm Brenner called. He had news – and had "misplaced" Bermann's number. He cleared his throat.

"And Löbinger's and Schneider's too, I suppose," Louise said.

"We're getting older."

They laughed.

"I don't want you getting the wrong idea," Brenner said.

"You just like my voice."

"I'll say it again: I don't want you getting the wrong idea."

Louise smiled. She stopped on the last landing. Günter was sitting on the radiator in the corridor to the cafeteria, a can of Coke in his hand. His legs were crossed and he was leaning against the window. He gave her a curt nod, she nodded back. Black jeans, black T-shirt, black denim jacket, black hair. A pale messenger from the darkness. This is what writers looked like, film directors, people in advertising. Police officers looked different.

"I wanted to ask you something," Brenner said.

"Go on."

"Let's get the business out of the way first."

The suspicion that Semtex may have been stored or ignited in Riedinger's cellar had become more concrete. It could not be proven 100 per cent, but the yellow residues and the Semtex-like smell after the explosions pointed in that direction. Semtex itself was not susceptible to impact or flames, which means it must have been detonated. Brenner saw three possibilities: first, a time fuse connected by wire to an electric detonator; second, a non-electric detonator set off by impact or perhaps by a fuse that had caught fire when the shed was burning; and third, a radio-controlled detonator.

Her gaze returned to Günter, who'd stood up, tossed his can into the bin and was heading for the gents. "We have a few possibilities then, but nothing is certain."

"Exactly."

"So which is the most likely?"

"Hmm."

She waited patiently. Her colleagues in forensics didn't like to speculate, even though sometimes their intuitive guesses hit the bullseye. They saw themselves as analysts, empiricists, scientists. They wanted to provide proof, not intuitive guesses, and for that they used their knowledge of chemistry and physics alongside computers and microscopes. And they were right to; their assessments had to be defended in court.

"The second," Brenner said. A detonator, a little bit of fuse, a little bit of luck and patience. And, of course, a few matches to set the barn alight. But Brenner wouldn't be pinned down. They hadn't yet found any trace of a fuse. In fact so far they'd found as good as nothing. It was a tricky search. There had been the explosions, the fire, then hundreds of litres of water had gushed into the cellar. The concrete walls of the cellar had been partially destroyed and the whole cavity was full of earth and rocks. "But one thing's for certain: the Semtex didn't go up by accident."

She nodded. Günter was back. He glanced up at her as he sat down. He appeared to be out of breath, as if he'd been running.

She went down the last few steps. "So no accident."

"Absolutely not."

In the meantime Brenner had got up to speed on the 1992 Rottweil case. Some of the weapons in Riedinger's cellar did indeed come from the same manufacturer. Zavodi Crvena Zastava, a state arms manufacturer in "old Yugoslavia", as he put it. He and his colleagues had also made an inventory of the twenty-four crates. The depot had stored at least one hundred pistols, fifty sub-machine guns and fifty machine pistols. "Someone's up for a war. The question is: here or abroad?"

"Shit," Boni said. "Call Bermann."

"If I can find his number."

"You will."

"I think I will too. One more thing, Luis. There were no munitions in the cellar. Not a single round."

Two hundred weapons, but no bullets.

Günter was on his feet again. She could hear him coughing, clearing his throat. He took a few steps in her direction then turned and went back into the gents. A man with a bladder problem *and* a breathing problem, not to mention the problems with his team.

Two hundred weapons, but no bullets. Who needed weapons without munitions? Who bought or sold weapons without munitions? Sure, she thought, many things are possible. But in all likelihood there was another depot somewhere with thousands of rounds for pistols and submachine guns manufactured in former Yugoslavia.

"Good luck with your search," Brenner said.

3

Half past nine in the morning, twenty-eight degrees, the air outside was perfectly still. They drove with the windows open because Günter didn't like air conditioning. It dries out the mucous membranes in your nose, he said, you can't breathe properly. Not even down by the feet? No, not there either. The air rises from the feet to the nose, all it does is take a little longer till you can't breathe properly.

Irritated, Louise kicked off her trainers and called Brenner. "You wanted to ask me something."

"Oh, let's do it another time," Brenner said.

They ended the call.

Günter drove hectically, jerkily, too fast. His fingers clenched the steering wheel like iron talons, his breathing was shallow. In his pale, uptight way he wasn't unattractive, she thought; maybe his face was a bit too bloated, and a bit too standoffish. He was a few years older than her, but one rank lower. One of those officers hauled up by the state of Baden-Württemberg from the middle ranks into the higher levels of service via the W-8 course. Eight weeks of instruction without examination, replacing the three years of study at Villingen-Schwenningen College including state examination and thesis. No wonder some colleagues turned their noses up.

But Günter's bad reputation had nothing to do with the W-8 course.

"Tell me something about yourself," she said.

"I'd rather not," Günter said.

They drove into the tunnel and had to brake after the first bend when they ran into heavy traffic. In front of them was a sea of brake lights, moving at walking pace. At the end of the tunnel Günter accelerated and said in an almost jolly tone, "I'm not a fan of friendships between colleagues."

"Christ, I'm not trying to be your friend."

"I mean, what can you really say in four or five minutes?"

"The essentials."

"Fine, then tell me the essentials about you and then I'll tell you the essentials about me."

"Not worth it," she said. "We're almost there."

They parked the car by the side of the road and followed the track to the site of the fire. The track and the field were scored by the tyres of numerous emergency vehicles. Where there were no ruts the subsoil had been dried out by the heat, and in some places it was breaking up. The grass was yellow and parched. They ducked beneath the police tape. The smell of ash still hung in the air, but the cocktail typical of Semtex – honey, vinegar, wax – had dissipated. As they approached, Louise kept her eyes lowered. She didn't know if you could see the Flaunser from here, and she didn't want to know either.

"Can you smell that?" Günter said.

"What?"

"It smells of burnt human flesh."

"Rubbish."

"Try again."

"I don't smell any human flesh."

"No?" Günter sniffed. "I do."

She resolved to be as patient as possible. At least as patient as Reiner Lederle had been with her at the beginning of the year.

But then she would send him packing.

Within fifteen metres from where the shed had burned down the dry earth was darker, and covered in deep prints from shoes and boots. Adam Baudy's report, which had arrived at police H.Q. by fax at three in the morning, contained sketches and detailed descriptions. They knew where the fire engines had stood, where the manifolds were positioned, for how long the hoses had been left unmanned, how many litres of water had been pumped out.

Bonì tried to picture the shed. Years ago she and Mick had driven out to Kirchzarten a couple of times to visit friends, but she hadn't been back since. She did, however, remember the crooked, dilapidated wooden building. Maybe because she hadn't been able to work out what purpose it served. If it was no longer used, why it hadn't been torn down.

They stepped up to the jagged edge of the pit, where the cellar began.

Günter sniffled.

The cellar hadn't been very deep, around two and a half metres. The explosions had partially destroyed the concrete walls and ripped out the earth. In silence they looked at the concrete floor, which had been completely cleared by forensics and C.S.I. The cellar had not had its own entrance, it was only accessible from inside Riedinger's shed. C.S.I. had found the remains of hinges, as well as long rusty nails that may have been part of a ladder. Wooden planks had lain over beams. Riedinger had said that he knew nothing about any beams beneath the wooden floor. He'd never noticed that some of the planks could be removed, which was hardly surprising as over decades a layer of earth, straw and dust several centimetres thick had built up on the floor.

Louise gathered her hair and tied it up with a hairband. "Right," she said and relayed the latest information from Brenner.

Günter listened in silence, nodding occasionally. "Two hundred weapons but no munitions," he repeated when she had finished.

"Almenbroich is going to put together a task force," Louise said. If there was a second depot with munitions it suggested that the people behind this were very well organised. And it may also mean that there were other depots elsewhere. Anybody who could get hold of two hundred firearms from former Yugoslavia could easily procure four hundred or a thousand.

It was not especially reassuring.

They walked around the pit in opposite directions and glanced at each other when they met again.

There was something else that connected Louise to the Kirchzarten valley and Mick. A few kilometres beyond Kirchzarten lay Buchenbach, where Mick had wanted to spend their wedding night in Hotel Himmelreich – for where could be better suited to such an occasion than the "Kingdom of Heaven"? Himmelreich, she'd said, was at the beginning of the Höllental – "Hell's Valley". Was that really the place to start a marriage? But Mick remained obstinate. As he came from Titisee-Neustadt, for him the Himmelreich was at the *end* of the Höllental. Just look at it that way, honey. Louise did look at it that way and gave in.

Two different perspectives that culminated in humiliation, a catastrophe, and the demolition of a life plan. From that moment everything, absolutely everything, had gone wrong. But in fact it had started earlier, much earlier.

Would Günter listen patiently if she let her self-pity off the leash? Hardly. No friendships amongst colleagues. On the other hand, friendship was not mandatory for this.

"We don't need a task force," Günter muttered. "Small teams work much better."

"Did you know that there's a hotel in Buchenbach called the Himmelreich?"

"I'm asking you, why do we need a task force? Himmelreich? No, I didn't know that. Is it significant?"

She sighed. "Let's try to reconstruct this."

They circled the cellar again. Günter began with the reconstruction. "Someone gets hold of pistols and submachine guns manufactured in old Yugoslavia, and probably the munitions for these too."

"Someone with contacts to old Yugoslavia or to arms dealers with contacts to old Yugoslavia."

"Why are we calling it 'old Yugoslavia'?"

"That's what Brenner in forensics calls it."

"Is there a 'new Yugoslavia'?"

"More likely 'rump Yugoslavia'."

"So what's 'former Yugoslavia'?"

"Our 'old Yugoslavia'?"

Boni gave a quiet moan. "Thank God no-one can hear us."

"Let's move on."

But they didn't progress much further. Someone obtained weapons manufactured in former Yugoslavia, brought them to Riedinger's shed and stashed them in the cellar. Someone else – *presumably* someone else – knew about this, or found out about it, installed an explosive device and set fire to the shed. The weapons were destroyed. Two unknown parties – *presumably* two unknown parties – linked in some way.

Günter stopped. "Look, our colleagues."

On the edge of the belt of woodland between the pasture and the B31 stood Anne Wallmer and her partner from Löbinger's section. Louise suggested they go over and swap notes. Günter said she should go alone as the stench of burnt flesh was making him queasy. "I'd rather wait in the car and breathe some fresh air. You go."

Louise asked if he wanted some water.

No, he didn't want anything.

She watched as he walked away. Deep inside her stirred an inkling of what he might have told her had he not rejected the idea of friendships amongst colleagues.

Anne Wallmer and Peter Burg, a veteran detective chief superintendent who'd turned prematurely grey, brought information from C.S.I. The weapons had probably been in Riedinger's cellar for weeks, if not a few months. Since March or April was their guess. They also believed that two large blocks of Semtex had been detonated in different places.

The craters in the ground and the effect of the blast on the walls allowed them to roughly identify the positions: one in the northern third of the cellar, the other at the southern end. In addition, it looked as though two smaller blocks had been fitted with detonators. All four detonators had evidently been connected by fuses – and one or more fuses had led up into the shed. The rest of the floorboards were being examined right now. So far one thing was clear: they were ancient and must have burned like tinder.

"Where's Günter off to?" Wallmer said.

Louise whipped around and was surprised to see Günter turn out of the farm track and speed off down the road to Kirchzarten. She shrugged. "No idea. We're not quite coordinated yet."

"If it were up to me I'd boot him out," Burg growled. His light-grey, bushy eyebrows drooped and his walrus moustache twitched in indignation. Louise wondered whether Peter Burg would have booted her out six months ago too, had it been up to him.

He avoided her gaze.

"Can we take you anywhere?" Anne said.

Louise nodded. "To see Täschle in Kirchzarten."

"Isn't he called Däschle?"

"His name's Täschle, it's just Rolf who calls him Däschle."

Burg stayed to wait for the explosives experts and C.S.I., who were arriving at any moment. Wallmer led Louise through the narrow belt of woodland. When they stepped out onto the track where her car was parked, Louise instinctively looked up.

Yes, you could see the Flaunser.

They drove along the dirt track, parallel to the B31, then turned onto the road to Kirchzarten. Wallmer said she was glad to see Louise on the investigation team. Louise said she was glad to hear it. Much had been said in those few words, and she fell silent to avoid ruining the precious moment.

*

Before they went into Kirchzarten police station she took her mobile from her bag and reserved the second-hand white V.W. Polo she'd picked out at half past midnight. Thirty thousand kilometres on the clock, air conditioning, sunroof, tasteful leather upholstery, electric windows and wing mirrors, three doors, manufactured in 1999. A good choice, she thought. The right car for a divorced woman with no family, real friends or male acquaintances worth talking about. A little bit of luxury on the inside, but a rather modest exterior, just like herself. And conventional enough to support Louise in her attempt to remain dry, find her way back into middle-class life and maybe realise her suburban dream.

The police station was on the ground floor of a residential building close to the centre of town. Louise held open the entrance door for a woman with a pram, smiled at a barefoot child playing on the stairs, then went along a small hallway. Heinrich Täschle met her at the door. He was taller than she remembered – almost 1.90 m, she guessed – and lean and mistrustful. On the way to his office she saw one other uniformed officer, and otherwise nobody else seemed to be around. Once inside his office, Täschle pointed to a round table and said, "Please." She sat down. He opened a packet of biscuits, shook some onto a plate, fetched a thermos of coffee and filled two cups. Louise bit into a biscuit and said, "Mmm."

Täschle remained on his feet. "Ten o'clock," he said, towering over her. "That's when we rural police officers have our biscuit break."

"As do we in the city."

"Your boss never takes a break. He works round the clock. He's got so much on his plate that he can't even remember a simple name. Is that a Kripo tradition?"

"Is it just possible that you have a problem with Kripo?"

"You bet," Täschle said with a smile.

"Well, I'm glad we've sorted that out. You see, I need your help."

"Kripo needs the help of the constabulary?"

"For goodness' sake, Herr Täschle."

"That's *our* tradition. When Kripo turns up they get biscuits, but in return they have to listen to the complaints of the constabulary."

"Let me know when you're done with the complaining."

"I'm done." Täschle smiled again. He seemed to like smiling. He sat down and took a biscuit, smiling all the while. As he chewed he said, "Let me guess, you want me to accompany you to see Adam Baudy and Hannes Riedinger."

"Later."

"Later, of course. First you want to know what I've heard around here."

"Later. First I'd like some milk and sugar for my coffee."

They ate biscuits and drank coffee while Heinrich Täschle talked. Since yesterday morning he and five of his officers – the sixth stayed behind at the station – had been going around the town questioning the locals, but they hadn't garnered any useful information. Some had seen strange things or strange people, some had their suspicions, some had known all along. There were whisperings about asylum seekers on Am Keltenbuck, drunken Dutch at the campsite, neo-Nazis, and of course Riedinger, the failed farmer, husband and father.

Täschle shrugged. "Just village tittle-tattle."

"Like in the city."

He smiled.

Later they got into the patrol car. Täschle wanted to show her around town and Louise had no objection. Günter had abandoned her, she'd brought a handful of biscuits, there was water in her bag, so why not? In local parlance a section of the main street was known as "Pfaffeneck" – "the priests' corner" – while the administrative headquarters on the edge of town was called "Talvogtei" – "the valley prefecture". Almost ten thousand inhabitants, a C.D.U. mayor, Berthold Meiering, imported from the Swabian Allgäu years ago, had twice failed to get elected – which was down to his background more than his competence – and succeeded the third time. A short, rotund, upright man who was pleased that the city authorities with their Kripo officers, public prosecutors, professional fire brigade and logistics had taken over the case.

They left Kirchzarten to the south and passed the campsite on the way to Oberried, which like Stegen, St Peter and Buchenbach – together with Himmelreich – was part of the Kirchzarten police district. They turned off at Oberried and the road climbed a hill. Louise ate biscuits, drank water and listened with one ear to Täschle as she stared out of the window. Gently rolling hills, yellowy-green fields, mixed woodland, fruit trees, narrow roads on which two cars wouldn't be able to pass each other without tedious manoeuvres. Footpaths, farmhouses and barns with low-hanging, dark-brown roofs, higher at the front like a clipped fringe. A Black Forest idyll. At a sharp bend Täschle stopped in a lay-by and they got out. He pointed out the places below them   Oberried in the foreground, Stegen behind it and, between the two, Kirchzarten with Riedinger's pasture.

"Do you think Riedinger's got anything to do with the weapons?" Täschle said unprompted.

She shrugged. "There has to be some connection."

They went up the slope. Täschle had left his jacket and cap in the car, but large sweat patches sprawled from his armpits. Louise thought of Hollerer, the last chief of a local police station she'd asked for help. The next day they'd found him in the snow with two bullets in his body. She knew from Almenbroich that Hollerer hadn't gone back to work. After months in rehab, he'd moved to Konstanz to stay with his sister.

"Something wrong?" Täschle said.

She looked away. "No, nothing."

Täschle wasn't Hollerer and Kirchzarten wasn't Liebau. All the same she resolved to keep an eye on him.

They followed the road uphill and turned onto a wide farm track. The path led along a fence to a house, then on into the forest on the ridge of the hill. As Täschle made no move to return to the car, Louise stopped. He stopped too, then turned and stared at her.

"Why am I here?" she said.

Täschle shot a glance at the house above them. "We have a witness who might have seen something. But she's not the best witness. She's . . ."

"An alcoholic?"

Täschle dismissed the suggestion. Too quickly, too vigorously, Louise thought.

"No, she's just . . . peculiar."

"Peculiar." She nodded.

Täschle nodded too, wiping the sweat from his eyelids. "She sees more than we do. Things that don't exist."

"And yet sometimes they do?"

"Yes, perhaps. Please don't be judgemental."

"I know people like that."

Täschle smiled grimly. "You don't know anyone like her."

This house didn't have a fringed roof. Its window frames were painted green. A relief of grey stone was set in the centre of the front wall: a Madonna with child. A mailbox by the fence was marked LISBETH WALTER. There was no bell, so Täschle knocked. Louise was expecting an elderly lady, but Lisbeth Walter was in her mid-fifties at most. She didn't look "peculiar" or speak in a "peculiar" way; at first glance her behaviour was perfectly "normal". Louise thought she was beautiful, but beauty was relative. Lisbeth Walter came across as a confident and contented woman. She was tall, her grey, curly hair was tied up in a bun, she wore simple dark clothes and her fingers were adorned with a few silver, Celtic-looking rings, the most striking thing about her. She took them into a large, very sunny sitting room with windows on three sides. Endless books, plants everywhere, a shelf with hundreds of C.D.s and a grand piano in front of one of the windows. Cups and saucers were laid out on a coffee table and a pot of coffee stood on a warmer. Täschle had rung ahead.

"Please, take a seat," Lisbeth Walter said.

Louise sat in an armchair. She couldn't see any alcohol, she couldn't see an alcoholic. The coffee tasted like Täschle's; there was milk and sugar here too, but no biscuits. She began to relax. In any case, she thought, what happened to her, how she coped with her demons, had nothing to do with Lisbeth Walter, but with herself alone.

"Please tell us what you saw, Lissi," Täschle began.

Lisbeth turned to Louise. "He thinks it's important, I don't, but anyway. Not long ago I saw five or six men in the forest one night. That's all."

"Did you speak to them?"

"No. They walked past me, about twenty or thirty metres away. I barely saw them in the darkness."

"You didn't hear them either," Täschle interjected.

"That's right, I didn't hear them. They weren't talking and they hardly made any noise."

"Meaning?"

"Meaning they moved very quietly. Like . . . shadows. Ghosts." Lisbeth Walter forced a smile.

"How do you know they were men?"

"They could just as easily have been women. But I'm assuming I'm the only woman out in the forest at night-time."

Louise sipped her coffee and put the cup down. A large, robust cup for people with their own abyss. Not an immaculate filigree one like at Richard Landen's, which she hadn't dared touch. She nodded. "When you say 'Not long ago' . . .?"

"It could have been a few days or a few weeks ago. And by 'night-time' I mean it might have been eleven or three in the morning. I've lost all sense of time. I don't like clocks and I don't care what time it is anyway. But we don't want to discuss that now."

"Can you describe these people?"

"Goodness gracious." Lisbeth Walter sighed. "It was pitch black, the people were black."

"They were black?"

"Their faces were black. Everything was black. Faces, bodies."

"Are you saying they were black people?"

"What I'm saying is that it was so dark I could see almost nothing, not even anything light-coloured, and that could mean anything – that they were blacks, that they weren't blacks, that they were dressed head to toe in black. I'm happy to tell you what I saw, but please don't force me to interpret it using your categories. We have different categories."

"Oh?"

"You belong to the real world."

"And you don't?"

"Let's leave it at that," Lisbeth Walter said.

They left it at that. Louise asked questions, Lisbeth Walter answered. Täschle remained silent, looking from one to the other, ready to leap in, mediate or explain if they needed him to. They didn't.

Were there footpaths up there?

Not where Lisbeth Walter tended to go.

So the people had walked straight through the forest?

Yes.

Hunters, perhaps?

Possibly, but hunters had different associations for Lisbeth Walter.

Louise wondered whether she should explore these "associations" further. She let it lie.

Was there anything remarkable about these people?

The shape of their bodies.

The shape of their bodies?

The people were misshapen. As if they had humps. Hunchbacks of Notre Dame. Lisbeth Walter smiled. "Maybe they were just wearing rucksacks."

Five, six men or women with rucksacks walking through the forest in the middle of the night, a few days or weeks ago, before an illegal weapons depot exploded only kilometres away. Täschle raised his eyebrows; Louise just pursed her lips. It might be important, it might not.

She asked if there was anything else that stood out – posture, movement, size. Lisbeth Walter couldn't remember. Which rather suggested, she said, that nothing else had struck her as unusual.

Did anyone say anything?

No, not a word.

Haircuts?

"Haircuts? Oh, I see." Nothing out of the ordinary here either. In all probability the people were wearing headgear. As she'd said, nothing light-coloured. Not a shimmer of skin, no bald patches.

"Coming back to the date," Louise said.

"Try to remember, Lissi," Täschle begged. "What was before? Or after? You remember the glider incident. Was that before or . . ."

"Don't treat me like a fool, Henny."

"It might be really important, you know."

"He's got these ideas in his head." Lisbeth Walter threw her hands in the air. "That it might be *important*. Good God, I'm in the forest almost every night and I can't begin to tell you all the things I see there. Ghosts, souls, kobolds, a robot recently, or at least what I imagine a robot to look like. I see landscapes, cities, strands of memory, Ottilie from *Elective Affinities* and Mephistopheles on a regular basis. And then at some point a few days or weeks ago there were a few figures that seemed more vivid than the ones I'm used to. First I thought they were a hiking group, but nobody goes walking at night in that thinned-out bit of forest apart from me. Then I thought . . . would you like to hear what I thought?"

"Please."

"I thought, Heavens, the black hordes, Milton's hellish legions, how *interesting*!"

"Who's Milton again?"

"John Milton, the author of *Paradise Lost*. In Pandæmonium, Satan's capital, the hellish legions go about their work."

"Oh Lissi," Täschle said gloomily.

"Oh Lissi, oh Lissi," Lisbeth Walter imitated him. "That's how it is, Henny. In the forest you see the trees and I see the spaces in-between. Now you tell me what's more interesting."

Silence followed as they drank their coffee and exchanged glances. At length Louise said, "Take me there."

"Heavens," Lisbeth Walter sighed.

Louise and Täschle waited outside the house. Täschle called the station, informed his officer where he was and what they were going to do. Louise pondered whether she'd like to inform anyone – Bermann, Almenbroich, Günter – but in the end she didn't feel like it. She looked out at Oberried and Kirchzarten in the distance. Five or six women or men with rucksacks, wandering across the hills between Feldberg in the east and Schauinsland in the west. A weapons depot beneath a shed by the B31, without a single round of bullets. Was there a second depot with munitions? Is that where Lisbeth Walter's black hordes had come from, or gone to?

"What was that about the glider?"

Täschle didn't hear so she repeated the question.

At the beginning of July a glider carrying two people had taken off from the airstrip in Kirchzarten. Down draughts above Oberried had thrust the glider back to earth and it landed on the roof of a house. It was a close shave but there were no injuries. Like all the inhabitants of Oberried, "Lissi" had heard the loud noise when the left wing snapped off.

Täschle stopped talking as Lisbeth Walter approached them.

They followed the path up the hill and for a while walked along the edge of the forest. The air was thick with the smell of dry grass and dry cattle. "Please accept that I won't be able to find the exact spot," Lisbeth said, "just the rough area, O.K.?" Louise and Täschle said nothing.

A quarter of an hour later they entered the forest and snaked up the steep slope, Lisbeth leading the way. There was no obvious path. Twigs and dried leaves crunched beneath their shoes. Even though they were walking in the shade of the trees it was unbearably hot. The back of Täschle's shirt was dark with sweat, her T-shirt soaked through and her bare arms glistening. And yet she felt comfortable in this forest. For four months she'd been surrounded by woodland, a gentle protector against all distractions and demons. She'd gone walking for entire days, sometimes with Roshi Bukan, Chiyono or one of the other residents of the monastery, but mostly she'd gone alone or with the grey cat as her sole companion. As in the dark, cold monastery cells, it had been easier to resist her demons in the forest than during the last three weeks in Freiburg. In the city, life wanted to go on as if her time in Oberberg and at the monastery hadn't happened.

They crossed a clearing, then the forest floor became more uneven and the trees denser. There was not a breath of air. For a moment Louise wondered what Lisbeth Walter got up to here at night, but decided not to ask. She didn't want to know just how "peculiar" this woman was. Lisbeth Walter had seen unusual people at an unusual time in an unusual place, which was all that mattered.

Louise wondered what might connect Täschle and his witness. If she remembered correctly, on his desk stood a photograph of a blonde woman and three blond children. He and Lisbeth Walter seemed to know each other from a time before that picture had been taken.

Before she started going into the forest alone at night.

About half an hour after they'd set off they stepped into a small clearing. Lisbeth Walter said she knew it had been somewhere around here but she couldn't be sure exactly where. The group had been walking parallel to the clearing; she herself had been sitting against a tree right on the edge. Louise's eyes met Täschle's. He gave a sorrowful smile that was also a warning. "Where are we?" she asked.

"Between Oberried and Sankt Wilhelm," he replied.

"Are there any roads here? Footpaths?"

"Paths and a few forest tracks. A little way to the east there's the Three Lakes bicycle trail and to the west the road from Sankt Wilhelm to Oberrried."

"You don't get lost with Henny," Lisbeth Walter said. Louise thought it sounded a little sad. A "without Henny" resonated in there too. They walked around the clearing. Lisbeth Walter couldn't remember anything more.

Later Louise enlarged the radius around the clearing, even though she didn't know quite what she was looking for. Clues pointing to black hordes? It was better not to think about it.

Lisbeth Walter and Täschle followed her in silence. To the south of the clearing the forest floor sloped downwards. They worked their way with caution along the incline. "Down there," Täschle said suddenly.

Thirty metres below they could see a wooden hut between the trees. Louise climbed down. It was a small hut, the padlock on the door was rusty and the grass in front of it tall. She couldn't be certain, but it didn't look as if many people had stopped by over the past few months.

She was about to go back up to Täschle and Lisbeth Walter when she noticed a smell that didn't belong here.

Cigarette smoke.

Alarmed, she sank to her knees and motioned to the others to do the same. Lisbeth Walter whispered something and Täschle answered quietly. Crouching beside trees, they stared down.

Louise closed her eyes. The smell was still there.

Then came the doubts. The smell of one cigarette amongst the thousands that were being smoked this very minute in south Baden. A witness who was "peculiar", figures from a book. Not much had changed since the start of the year. She saw what other people saw, but fancied she could identify more in what she saw – connections, analogies, systems. Sometimes she was right, sometimes not. She'd seen the prints of children's shoes in the forest near Liebau and little

Pham in the monastery. The footprints and Pham had nothing to do with each other.

Everything else did.

She stood up and walked slowly around the hut. On the other side the smell was more distinct. She stopped. There was nothing to be seen except for trees, leaves and the odd patch of sky. A brook babbled in the distance. She turned around. Täschle was standing now, a pistol in his right hand, a mobile in his left. Louise raised a hand: Stay where you are. She hoped he wouldn't follow her. He had to look after Lisbeth Walter.

That morning she'd asked him what sort of offences his station normally dealt with. The list was astonishingly long: theft, fraud, bodily harm, coercion, traffic offences, environmental crimes. Once there'd been a murder, back in 1993, his first year at the station.

Freiburg Kripo had taken over the case.

This was both the advantage and disadvantage of police officers such as Täschle, Hollerer and Niksch.

She raised her hand again. When Täschle nodded she followed the smell.

A few metres further on the cigarette smoke became lost in the powerful aromas of the forest. She'd lost her trace.

The doubts returned, paired with listlessness. She thought of Günter, who'd vanished without explanation, of the strange phrase "helping out". It was redundant now, but it haunted her. She thought too of her growing desire for Richard Landen, and of Taro on the Flaunser.

Just as she was about to give up and return to Täschle and Lisbeth Walter, she came to the brook. It was narrow, carrying scarcely any water, and it coiled its way down from above in short twists, a deep, dark gash in the forest floor. She dipped her hand in. As she patted her face with lukewarm water she heard voices talking softly below her.

Two men.

They sounded relaxed. Once or twice they gave a restrained laugh. A lighter clicked. Cigarette smoke floated up to her.

The men were sitting with their backs to Bonì, less than fifteen metres further down the stream. One was smoking, the other drinking from a bottle. They were wearing dark-brown leather jackets. Hikers.

Hikers chatting in an eastern European language.

She carefully laid the shoulder bag on the ground and took out her mobile, I.D. and pistol. The life before, the life after. Half a year ago in Alsace, eastern Europeans who turned out not to be, and today real ones. That was the last time she'd fired a weapon. After her return Bermann had said it might be a good idea to spend the first few days on the range. She'd ignored him because she knew that he just wanted her out of the way.

A mistake, perhaps.

When the men laughed again she cocked the trigger of her Walther, then crept slowly downstream along the brook. Hearing her, the men broke off their conversation and leaped up. One spun around, then the other. She was staring at eastern European faces and thought: Croatia, Rottweil 1992.

Connections, analogies, systems.

The men spoke again, raising their hands defensively. The man on the left was shorter, slimmer, more nervous. "Police," she said. "Don't move. Do you understand me?"

The one on the right said something in a language she didn't recognise.

"Police," Louise said again, this time in English, holding up her police I.D.

The men nodded, their hands now above their heads. They muttered things to each other. "Don't do it!" she said in English.

At that moment the men turned and started running in different directions down the hill.

She went after the shorter man on the left, swearing and shouting orders, warnings, and finally firing a shot into the air. The men kept running, the gap between her and the shorter one grew, while the other man disappeared from view. Cursing, Louise put her mobile away. Täschle must have heard the shot and he would call for back-up.

Stooped and with her arm raised, she fought her way through the trees. Branches lacerated her bare arms and knocked against her legs, she tripped over roots. The slope became steeper and she had difficulty keeping a firm footing. Sometimes she looked up and caught sight of the brown leather jacket in front of her, dancing through the forest like a paper kite and getting ever smaller. Let the guy run away, she thought, we'll get him, we've got traces, cigarette butts, D.N.A.

But she didn't want to let him get away.

She wanted to do what she was doing. More tumbling down the slope than running, behind the kite, faster and faster, losing control of her footing, seized by a force she was powerless to resist, maybe a physical force, maybe an inner one. A force knocking her, dragging her into the abyss, at the bottom of which lay a lifeless body that could be Taro or Niksch or both.

She felt tears welling in her eyes and she laughed furiously.

A cry brought her back. The man had fallen and was lying on the ground.

When she reached him he was sitting leaning against a tree, breathing heavily. One leg was outstretched, the other bent. "Fuck you, police," he said in English. He was young, early twenties, and had a handsome, dark, angry face. Panting, Bonì asked him for his name, but he didn't respond. With her pistol she gestured to him to lie on his stomach. He obeyed and stretched out his arms.

At that moment a shadow appeared in the corner of her eyes. A body collided with Louise, sending her spinning. She lost her pistol and her left arm crashed into a tree.

Then she was lying on her back, trying to piece it together. The second man? But she hadn't heard or noticed anything.

Louise became aware of a stabbing pain. Pressing her right hand onto her left upper arm she felt blood.

She heard the voices again. The young one was groaning, the other man talking to him.

Louise sat up and they stared at her. The young one was on his feet, the other holding her pistol. "Drop the gun," she said in English. "Hands up, lie on your stomachs."

The men laughed in surprise.

Louise laughed too, then let herself fall backwards.

She could hear the men talking to each other. Once more the shorter, younger man groaned, then he seemed to move further away. The other one came a little closer, but not so close that she could see him.

Tears streamed down her face. She closed her eyes, shook her head. "Please don't," she said.

For a long time nothing happened, and by the time she opened her eyes and turned her head the two men had vanished. The Walther was on the ground a couple of metres away. She sat up and checked her wound, which was still bleeding, a gash that ran all the way from her shoulder to her elbow. She pressed her hand on it again and blood flowed out on either side. So much blood, and now she could smell it too.

Bonì sank back down. Exhaustion had spread through every inch of her legs, head, her entire body. Stand up, she thought, look for Täschle, she thought. Ring somebody, Bermann, Almenbroich, no, call Richard Landen. Take off your T-shirt and wrap it around the wound. *Do* something.

But all of that would have been far too strenuous. Lying on the ground was much more comfortable. In February she'd lain on the ground too, in Alsace. A dog had found her. There must be people with dogs in this forest as well. And there was Täschle and his witness.

Lying on the ground was much more comfortable.

*

She must have passed out briefly. When she opened her eyes a man was standing beside her, not Täschle or Bermann or another of her colleagues, nor was it one of the two men from earlier. Tears ran from the corners of her eyes, blurring the man who moved noiselessly behind a veil. Louise felt him remove her right hand from the wound. She blinked and now had a sharper view. The man wore a balaclava of black fabric and a camouflage jumper – Special Deployment Commandos teams looked like that, so did soldiers and counter-terrorism units. Perhaps Lisbeth Walter's black hordes by day. Perhaps she was dreaming.

Now the man was looming above her. He must have noticed that Louise was conscious, but he didn't look at her. His eyes lowered, he pulled her T-shirt tight. She kept still as he cut the material with a knife and helped him free her arms from the sleeves. Then he was beside her again, wrapping the material around her wound. She heard herself groan with pain and the man blurred again behind the veil. She felt him gently put down her arm and rest her hand on her bare stomach. When the pain became more bearable she thanked him. But the man didn't respond, he'd disappeared behind the tears, perhaps he'd already gone.

She heard a dog barking in the distance.

The life before, the life after.

4

Her encounter with the mysterious masked man was followed by a mysterious encounter with Bermann. Heinrich Täschle had found Louise and taken her down to the brook to clean and redress her wound. Lisbeth Walter had held her right hand and wept, perhaps for Louise, perhaps for herself – Louise couldn't say. Then Bermann appeared out of the blue, lifted her up and hurried down the slope with her in his arms. He didn't say a word or look at her, even though he'd never seen his colleague like this before – wearing only a bra up top. In his haste, his serious expression, she sensed the male gaze, coupled with concern and a new, yet to be defined form of affection. It occurred to her that there must be a Himmelreich in every Höllental, and vice versa. And that romance must be connected to the art of suppressing one's feelings. During those few minutes while she was being rescued by Rolf Bermann, she decided it was an art she was going to practise.

Later, wrapped in a blanket, Bonì lay in a St John's ambulance, staring alternately at Bermann and Löbinger, who were standing by the open door staring back. An Indian doctor with short black hair had given her an injection, cleaned the wound, dressed it again and was now attending to the scratches on her forearm.

Heinrich Täschle and Lisbeth Walter had been driven back to Oberried. As he was leaving, Täschle told her to pop by the station as soon as she could, because of Riedinger and Adam Baudy, and just generally. Lisbeth Walter said she should come for a coffee. Louise promised to do both, even though she found the idea of a coffee on her own with Lisbeth Walter rather unnerving.

"What was that?" the doctor said, tapping the scar below her left collarbone. For a moment the memory returned. Natchaya and the escape down to the Rhine at night. Her little, wicked friend that had come from the darkness and buried itself in her flesh. The eastern European who wasn't eastern European, who'd said, "The bitch is alive." Natchaya, who'd said, "You cannot save world, save your*self*," then deliberately shot to the side of her.

"Her appendix," Bermann said.

The doctor raised her eyebrows. "You're running out of space for wounds on your left side. Next time you should turn around before it's too late."

"Are you done yet?" Bermann growled.

"No."

"You're holding us up."

"Rubbish," Louise said.

Along with vehicles from other emergency services, the ambulance was in a car park at the entrance to the village of Sankt Wilhelm. The hunt for the two eastern Europeans and "other suspicious persons" had begun. Members of the investigation team, a canine squad, a helicopter crew from Stuttgart and Special Support officers were searching the area to the south-west of the locked hut for tracks, any other clues – and another depot. After all, there must have been some reason why the two men were sitting in the forest.

Evidently Bermann and Löbinger were trying to suppress how the "Weapons" investigation team had come across them. A witness who was peculiar, hellish legions from an ancient book, and in spite of all this a chief inspector who went looking in the forest . . .

Louise gave a weary smile.

"Are you in pain?" Löbinger said.

"Of course she's in pain," Bermann said.

The doctor looked at her. Louise shook her head. Out of the blue she wondered whether the doctor might be a Buddhist. Wasn't Buddha born somewhere in India, or nearby? Did Buddhists live in India? Or just Hindus and Sikhs?

The doctor gave her a pat on the arm and left the ambulance.

"Right," Bermann said. "Rottweil, 1992."

She sat up and arranged the blanket.

"Stay lying down, Luis."

"Tell me what you know."

Bermann started talking. Löbinger kept quiet.

In 1992 the Bureau were on the trail of around forty Croats in the Rottweil/Tuttlingen area, alleged to have been involved in arms dealing or arms smuggling. The chief culprit had acquired weapons illegally and sold them to compatriots of his in Baden-Württemberg. Some of the buyers drove the weapons to Croatia, clearly with the knowledge of the Croatian authorities, as written receipts prove. In 1991 the European Community, followed by the U.N., had imposed an arms embargo on the Balkan countries, and so at the beginning of the war the Croatian troops were poorly equipped. This must have been the reason for the arms purchases. Fourteen of the forty stood trial, four received suspended sentences and five were handed down fines.

In October 1992, more immigrants from the Balkans were arrested for attempting to sell uranium 235 and Soviet tanks.

Louise vaguely recalled this. She'd read the Bureau's report and a newspaper article, and at police H.Q. she'd seen videos from the regional television reports. But she couldn't remember how many weapons had been confiscated. Bermann told her: four Kalashnikovs, three machine pistols, twenty-five pistols and thirty-five hand grenades.

"Quite a difference."

"That's if our colleagues found it all."

Löbinger laughed. "How likely is that? The Croats were far too clever and the customs lax. And we know that the Croat exiles in Baden-Württemberg accumulated hundreds of millions of dollars . . ."

"We know that?" Bermann asked bitterly.

Löbinger ignored him. "Of course there were more weapons than our colleagues managed to find. I mean, the Croats were at war back home."

"*I* didn't know that," Bermann said.

"You'll find out about it at the next meeting."

Was there a link between Rottweil in 1992 and Kirchzarten in 2003? That was the big question. Louise knew that in spite and because of the weapons embargo, the Yugoslav War was a golden age for serious and not-so-serious arms dealers. Many had become rich, both smugglers and dealers – Germans too. That morning, after some research, Bermann had done a few calculations in his head. According to *Der Spiegel*, most of the weapons supplied to the warring parties had come from Germany and the C.I.S. countries. Roughly half of the weapons that went to Croatia came from Germany, with an estimated value of three hundred and twenty million dollars.

But the Yugoslav War was over.

Were they on the wrong track? Might the cache of weapons beneath Riedinger's shed have nothing to do with the wars or the Balkans? Despite the two eastern Europeans, despite the fact that the weapons had been manufactured in former Yugoslavia?

"And what does that mean, they were at war back home?" Bermann said. "Does that mean they were allowed to break the law here?" Although he'd rolled up his sleeves and taken his shirt out of his jeans, the sweat still ran down his forehead and cheeks. Transparent pearls hung from his moustache.

"It just means they were at war back home," Löbinger said in a friendly tone.

Louise got up. Bermann's moustache had reminded her of Pham, the little Vietnamese boy who Bermann, in his inimitably thoughtful–reckless way, had integrated into his private kindergarten and called Viktor. Bermann's moustache had been the greatest attraction for Pham after they'd freed him and the little girl from Poipet back in February.

She looked at Löbinger. "What are you going to do with Günter?"

"Suspend him."

"About bloody time," Bermann said.

"You can't suspend someone because they were *unwell*."

But Löbinger shook his head. Günter had left her in the lurch, Günter had put her in danger, Günter was out. He'd been getting on everyone's wick for months, years even, and was no longer capable of working in a team. He was "a psycho", he was *out*.

Louise froze. Had her colleagues whispered about her in exactly the same way a few months earlier? She decided she would appeal to Almenbroich on Günter's behalf. He deserved a little more patience.

"You look pale, Luis," Bermann said.

"What about the man who bandaged me up?"

"Later," Bermann said.

"Do you think I was making it up?"

Löbinger cleared his throat and gave her a tender smile. Louise understood. The strange witness and her hellish legions had already done his head in. There was no room for a masked saviour.

Oddly this did not bother Louise. It wasn't important and didn't have any bearing on the truth, irrespective of how it might look.

Bermann, on the other hand, seemed to have other reasons for avoiding a conversation about the unknown man. "Later," he said again, and from his expression she believed he really would discuss it with her. "First of all you're going home for a nice bath . . ."

"I need to see Riedinger."

Bermann shook his head. "You're going home."

Wait, she thought.

"I don't want to see you again before tomorrow, is that clear?"

She smiled. Good new Bermann. Good old Louise.

Outside she passed the Indian doctor and Bonì asked if she was a Buddhist. The doctor shook her head; she was a Muslim. Muslims in India? And not even 1 per cent of Buddhists? Astonishing. Louise gave an exhausted smile. Bermann, who'd placed his hand on her back, nudged her onwards. "Have you actually seen your Buddhist guy again?"

"No."

"That's for the best. He wasn't your type. Far too boring."

Somewhere behind them Löbinger chuckled.

Two uniformed officers were tasked with taking Bonì home. As nobody was wearing an extra shirt or a jacket in this heat, she had to make do with the St John's blanket she'd wrapped around her body, leaving her shoulders free. She sat motionless in the back. It was 2.00 p.m. In an hour the "Weapons" task force would be meeting. In an hour she had an appointment about the white Polo. In an hour, Louise decided, she'd be lying in bed thinking about the two men who'd done nothing to her when they'd had the chance.

They drove through the narrow valley along the River Brugga and entered the Kirchzarten basin via Oberried. On the right appeared Kirchzarten itself, ahead of them lay Riedinger's pasture, the B31 and, away in the distance, the Flaunser. Sometime soon she would ask Bermann to take her to where they'd found Taro. Sometime soon she would visit Niksch's grave. She felt that she needed to part company once and for all with last winter's dead.

And perhaps from the living too.

Later, in the tunnel, she thought of Anatol, who would be coming to see her that evening. Anatol, her midnight man. She suspected that this might be another parting of the ways. Sometimes the life lived before didn't simply continue. They had tried, everything was as it had been. But she could tell he no longer knew who she was. And that he couldn't deal with not yet knowing who she'd become.

As they came out of the tunnel into the white summer light, Bermann called. "Your masked man," he said.

"Yes?"

Bermann didn't want her to talk about the man for the time being. They didn't know who he was with. What if he was an informer? They couldn't put a search out on the guy if it might put him in danger. And if he was on the other side, it was better to try and find out what they could on the quiet. So not a word, Bermann ordered. Not even within the task force. Especially not there. "But we'll stay on the case."

"You mean: you and I?"

"Yes. Anselm thinks you were unconscious and just imagined this man."

"I thought he would."

"What Anselm thinks needn't interest us."

She laughed but said nothing. It was a strange feeling to be Rolf Bermann's confidante all of a sudden. Pleasant and unpleasant at the same time.

"O.K., then," Bermann said.

"O.K., then."

Keep quiet and stay on it: the classic rule. Given the issues of jurisdiction in this case, the intervention from outside, the diverse "emotions", Bermann's suggestion was sensible. And if at any point he happened to forget about staying on it out of respect for authority, she wouldn't hesitate to remind him.

As his confidante.

Bonì asked the officers to stop off at police H.Q., where she borrowed a blouse from a colleague's locker, summarised her conversations with Täschle and Lisbeth Walter on tape – without mentioning the masked man – and took the tape to one of the secretaries to type up. Then she went to see the arms and equipment officer to be issued with a replacement for her pistol, which C.S.I. had taken away for fingerprinting.

But the arms and equipment officer wouldn't give her a replacement. It hadn't been signed off.

She nodded. She knew it hadn't been signed off. But it was necessary.

The officer was intractable. What hadn't been signed off couldn't be necessary.

A short time later, as she was on her way home, Bermann rang again sounding agitated and harassed. She could hear voices and dogs barking in the background. They'd found a second depot. Plastic bags with lead crates of munitions, fifty thousand rounds at least. As well as several light machine guns, anti-aircraft missiles and mortar shells.

Louise remembered Brenner's comment. Someone was up for a war.

The only question was: where?

II

The Murder

5

Waiting at home were the bottles, the demons and an indescribable heat. Louise opened the windows, drew the curtains and got out of her jeans. There were three messages on her answerphone. Get cheap health insurance, translate a marriage contract into Estonian, call Günter.

Translate a marriage contract into Estonian?

She deleted the messages.

Louise sat for several minutes on the sofa, staring at the bottles and thinking: not today. Although the demons refused to give her any peace, today they were more feeble and unwilling to get into an argument.

Relieved, she went to bed with the investigation team documents she'd got from Hoffmann and Elly. She read without much concentration for a few minutes, then put the file on the floor. It was strangely quiet in her bedroom, in her apartment. Quiet in her world that still seemed to consist predominantly of memories, longing, struggles. Put all that together and it might add up to a life, but it wasn't the life she'd wanted.

Change it then, she thought. Call someone. Call Richard Landen. Get up and meditate. Do Tai-Chi. Go to the shooting range, collect the Polo. *Do* something.

But lying down was easier. Waiting for her out of bed were the memories, the longing, the struggles.

She curled up, listened to the ticking of the seconds the alarm clock was counting off and decided never to get out of bed again.

*

At around 6 p.m. she needed the loo. She made use of the opportunity not to go back to bed.

In the shower she thought of Richard Landen. At the mirror she thought of Landen's wife.

Tommo, the pencil wife.

The birth was only a few weeks away. Had Tommo come back from Japan? Had Landen flown out to be with her?

Part company, or telephone? Make a decision.

She picked up the hairdryer. Not today.

The second-hand car dealer was still there, as was the Polo, but there appeared to be problems with the part-exchange of her Renault. The dealer wandered silently around the red Mégane with its blue bonnet and blue driver's door. He got in, examined the steering wheel and dashboard, and ran his finger over the bullet hole beside the cigarette lighter. "The radio's brand new," Louise said.

The dealer, a shortish Pole in sandals, nodded and got out. He spent the next five minutes checking the engine compartment. When he closed the bonnet he was still nodding. He walked around the car, twirled the bunch of keys in slow motion around one finger and said, "Looks like a Renault Mégane."

"It is a Renault Mégane."

"Not inside," he said, pointing to the bonnet.

"Really?"

"No, someone's been tinkering around in there."

"The brother-in-law of a French policeman. An expert."

"The brother-in-law likes Japanese and Polish cars."

"He wanted the best of everything."

"He wanted the cheapest." The dealer gave a melancholic smile. He offered her two hundred and fifty euros for scrap. Louise looked back and forth between the two-tone Mégane and the Polo. Two hundred and fifty euros for a car that had saved her life. A car which, now that she thought about it, was the perfect match for her: colourful, dented, with an intensely varied inner life, with patina. A car which at some point might stay put because it didn't want to go on any more – just like her.

"The key, please," she said, holding out her hand.

Bonì drove back into the centre of town along Berliner Allee. When police H.Q. came into view she thought of Wilhelm Brenner, who'd wanted to ask her a question but never got round to it. She called his number – engaged. She turned left and drove towards the station, the low light of the sun glinting in her rear-view mirror. She had to speak to Riedinger, she had to speak to Adam Baudy, Günter, Richard Landen and tonight, Anatol. Brenner was on the list too, as were Täschle, Bermann, Almenbroich and right at the very bottom her father. After the months in the monastery, men had forced their way back into her life and she couldn't say whether she thought this was good, bad or just normal. But it lent a different light to the invitation from Lisbeth Walter.

Louise parked near the station and went to Enni's sushi bar, but he wasn't there. "Later," the elderly Japanese man behind the counter said. "Come later." She ordered and ate at the only free highboy table while skimming the documents from Hoffmann and Elly. She'd already read the notes from forensics, the conversation protocols and the witness statements. There was scant new material to go on as her colleagues were still working on the case. By now she also had the information about Rottweil in 1992 that Elly had obtained from the Bureau. From an article in the *Stuttgarter Nachrichten* on August 28, 1992, she learned – and this was something Louise hadn't known – that it hadn't just been Croats involved in arms dealing in Baden-Württemberg, but Bosnian Muslims too.

The names of the individuals involved were also new to her. The Bureau had drawn up a list of suspects, those accused and sentenced as well as their lawyers and countless witnesses. The list ran to several pages and contained a few Arab-sounding names of people from Bosnia-Herzegovina.

Louise thought of the two men in the forest. Croats or Bosnians? Or maybe Serbs? She had no idea. Zavodi Crvena Zastava, the manufacturer of the firearms, was based in Belgrade with a branch in Kragujevac, so Serbia. But that didn't necessarily mean anything.

A movement made her look up. The elderly Japanese man was standing beside her. He was holding a hand up to his ear to mimic a telephone call. "Enni more later," he said. "Come more later."

She nodded. "Thanks."

Continuing to leaf through the documents, Louise came across copies of articles from the *Süddeutsche Zeitung, Spiegel* and others. What she read was depressing, but the act of reading itself gave her a feeling of satisfaction. No witnesses with a maverick view of reality, no hellish legions or other figures from books, but numbers, facts, concrete information. A survey of human ruthlessness, but a framework of facts.

During those years half the world had become embroiled in the Balkans. The Serbs, she read, had obtained weapons, money and support from Russia and Israel, the Bosnian Muslims from Pakistan, Iran, the U.A.E., Saudi Arabia, the U.S.A., Nigeria, Sudan, Turkey and other C.I.S. countries, while assistance for the Croats had come from Germany, Italy, Austria, Poland, Hungary, the U.S.A., Argentina, Singapore and yet more C.I.S. countries. Apparently Slovakia and China had helped all the warring parties. At the beginning of January 1993, N.A.T.O. had captured a ship in the Adriatic containing Russian and Chinese anti-aircraft missiles. In Zagreb the C.I.A. had discovered an Iranian Boeing 747 with arms and munitions. More weapons and munitions were uncovered in a Budapest apartment, Soviet military helicopters at Prague airport (declared "civilian material"), and grenades, anti-tank missiles and machine guns in Graz.

The labour pains of democracy, if she understood it correctly.

Bonì ate her last piece of sushi and drank her last sip of water. She'd had enough of the framework of facts.

But two questions kept gnawing away at her. First, what did the Yugoslav War have to do with the two weapons depots in the southern Black Forest? Second, were they connected at all?

She wiped her mouth and hands with the napkin and took out her mobile. This time Brenner answered straightaway. He sounded tired; he clearly hadn't been spending much time at home.

"You wanted to ask me something."

"Did I?"

"Well, are you going to ask me now or not?"

"I'm not in the mood."

"O.K., let's talk about something else. How old are the weapons, Wilhelm?"

"Wilhelm!" Brenner mumbled. "Nobody calls me 'Wilhelm.'"

Louise put a lid on her simmering impatience. Forensic scientists could be overworked, overtired and overwhelmed too. "So what *do* they call you?" she said gently.

Brenner had regained his composure. "The weapons," he said. "Bermann asked me about them already today. Isn't it on file?"

She leafed through the forensics documents and found a recent entry she'd overlooked. "Sorry."

"That's O.K."

The pistols and the submachine guns had been manufactured in the Belgrade headquarters of Zavodi Crvena Zastava, the machine pistols in the branch factory in Kragujevac. The start date for production of the pistols was probably 1957 – hence "model 57" – the submachine guns 1970 – "model 70" – the machine pistols – "model 61" – 1961 or later, as the original Škorpion wasn't manufactured in Czechoslovakia until 1961.

"But the things aren't forty or fifty years old, are they?" Louise said.

"No, I don't think so," Brenner said. Even though his sources had told him that the machine pistols were probably manufactured prior to 1970, it was more likely that the pistols and submachine guns came from the 1980s. It would be a few days, if not weeks, before he could be more specific. The weapons were in such a bad state that it wasn't possible to reconstruct or analyse any traces of usage. They could no longer be fired, of course, and getting hold of the manufacturers' production lists was extremely difficult, if not impossible. "Your Almenbroich has asked us to send a request through to Belgrade about sales channels." Brenner laughed helplessly.

"He's under external pressure."

"External pressure, or pressure from above?"

"Both."

"Hmm." She heard Brenner light a cigarette and open a window. The machine pistols and munitions from the second depot, he said, were also from Z.C.Z. Thousands of rounds for the four types of weapon. The anti-aircraft missiles, "Strelas", were Soviet-manufactured and widespread in the former Warsaw Pact countries and Arabic states as well as Finland. They hadn't yet managed to glean more information as these weapons had only just been brought in.

Silence. Brenner smoked noisily and Louise tried to let what he'd just said sink in. But she wasn't able to focus. Too many types of weapons, too many nations, too many possibilities.

Some diners had now left and there were two empty tables. The elderly Japanese man cleared away crockery and glasses. "Come later," he whispered with a smile. She smiled back and swapped her mobile to her right hand because the wound on her left arm was aching again.

"What I wanted to ask you," Brenner said. She could hear him closing the window. Then finally he said, "Is Zen Buddhism dangerous?"

Further and more specific questions followed. Was Zen meditation dangerous? As in damaging? Did you lose your connection with reality? Your reason? Did a guru put you into a trance? Were drugs used? Sex?

"Sex?"

"Well . . ." Brenner laughed grimly. His seventeen-year-old son had decided to learn meditation from a Zen master. His wife found the whole thing worrying, Brenner thought it absurd. Their son didn't understand the objections. What was wrong with sitting crossed-legged and thinking about nothing for a while? "Thinking about nothing," Brenner said in horror, "and then he'll go to school the next day, think of nothing and fail his exams again."

"Maybe he'll fail if he *doesn't* learn meditation."

"Don't make it more complicated, Luis," Brenner said. "Just tell me what it was like with the Buddhists."

So she told him what it was like with the Buddhists.

When Louise stepped into the reddish-gold evening light, she wasn't sure if she'd succeeded in reassuring Brenner. He had been by turns astonished, fascinated, horrified and amused – she didn't know which of these had ultimately prevailed. Maybe it depended on what sort of concerns he harboured. Was it a father's concern? A policeman's? A Christian–Western concern? A concern born of envy?

This is what she'd missed at the Kanzan-an: questions about human behaviour, thinking, feeling. In Zen Buddhism – in Buddhism in general, perhaps? – it didn't seem to play any part. In Zen the aim was to eliminate your feelings, cast off the idea of an "I". The reasons behind these feelings were clearly of no importance. It wasn't about questions and answers, and for Louise that was the problem. Two decades with the police had left its mark, not to mention the four weeks in Oberberg. Where did one's feelings, thoughts, deeds come from? What was hidden beneath?

Asking questions was important, as it often resulted in an answer. Even if that answer wasn't always the right one, at least it led to further questions and answers. In the end you weren't a perfect individual, but you did know more. You could form a picture.

Questions such as: Why had she started drinking? Why had she fallen in love with a married man? Why hadn't she stopped being in love with him at the Kanzan-an? Why, why, why?

Questions like that.

The parallels with her career were clear.

At some point, she thought with a grin, she'd explain the parallels between police work and psychology to her confidant Rolf Bermann.

In the car she took her mobile from her bag. Anne Wallmer was chewing something as she answered and Louise apologised for disturbing her at this hour. "Just a bit of gum," Wallmer said. She was in the foyer of the police academy in Müllheimerstrasse, waiting for Bermann, Schneider and Hoffmann, with whom she'd been training in the gym.

"You got Alfons onto a fitness machine?"

"Not us, it was his doctor. Bowling isn't enough to keep you alive, he says."

They laughed. Then Wallmer asked about her arm. "It hurts," Louise said.

"You're not at home, are you?" Wallmer said cautiously.

"No. Did you see Riedinger this afternoon?"

"Relax, Luis. Have a rest. Everything else can wait till tomorrow."

For the first time in six years she was having something approaching a friendly conversation with Anne Wallmer. This morning, on the way to Kirchzarten police station, she had sensed that something had changed in their relationship. And Wallmer seemed to look at her through different eyes. With the men this was something to relish, albeit with caution. But with Anne? She remained elusive. Years ago a rumour had gone around that she was a lesbian. Bermann lost his rag and threatened everyone down to the porter with disciplinary proceedings. Ever since it had been quiet on that front. And ever since Wallmer had remained steadfastly loyal to Bermann. It had probably never occurred to her that he'd only protected her because he was repulsed by homosexuality. Anyway, people talked about other things in the gym.

"Don't exclude me," Louise begged.

Wallmer gave a tense sigh. Then she talked. Yes, they had been to see Riedinger – she'd gone with Peter Burg, Bermann, Löbinger and Marianne Andrele, the public prosecutor from Munich. They made a cursory search of the farmhouse and questioned Riedinger. They hadn't obtained any satisfactory answers, and he'd almost attacked them. Bermann and Burg believed he was involved somehow – he may have allowed other people to use the cellar. Löbinger and Wallmer weren't so sure. Marianne Andrele was keeping an open mind. But they all agreed that Riedinger posed a danger to his fellow man and they needed to keep an eye on him. Andrele was working on it.

"On what?" Louise interrupted.

"A Riedinger case."

Louise nodded. Marianne Andrele hadn't needed long to acclimatise. "Have you found out anything else?"

She heard Wallmer drink, swallow and suppress a burp. "Excuse me. Yes, we have." Now she spoke more rapidly. Berthold Meiering, the mayor, had sent his staff to the archive in Kirchzarten, where they'd dug out some information on Riedinger's shed and the cellar beneath it. Both had been built during the Second World War. At the time a house had stood on the pasture, the shed was used as a wood store and the cellar as a private underground shelter. The house was destroyed during a British bombing raid in November 1944, although the shed, only a few metres away, remained unscathed. The inhabitants had survived in the cellar. In 1950 Peter Riedinger, the father, had bought the field.

Wallmer lowered her voice still further. "Rolf's coming."

"Wait, Anne. Any Croats, Bosnians or Serbs?"

"Not yet." Then she said more loudly, "How's the arm?"

"Do you know what happened to Riedinger's family? His wife and children?"

"We didn't ask. Shall I take you to H.Q. tomorrow morning?"

"No, don't worry. Thanks, Anne."

"Hello Rolf," Wallmer said.

"Give her to me," Louise heard Bermann say.

She hung up and waited for a moment. When Bermann didn't call she put her mobile in the hands-free cradle and started the car. What connection could there be between Riedinger and the people who'd used his cellar as a weapons store?

This was the crucial question.

She slotted into the traffic and turned off to the east. In the B31 tunnel it struck her that she did in fact know a Bosnian. Zlatan Bajramovic, midfielder for S.C. Freiburg. But she knew only his name, not his face.

The Kirchzarten basin was bathed in the soft red light of the evening. The peaks of the Black Forest seemed to glow and the first shadows were creeping from the valley floor. She took the Kirchzarten road and found a dirt track that led eastwards to two buildings screened from the road and the town. Now she knew that the fields on either side of the track had been part of Riedinger's farm years ago, just like other arable fields and pastures on the slopes above Kirchzarten. In the 1990s Riedinger had disposed of almost all his land, reduced his head of cattle from more than one hundred to just ten, cut the number of chickens from three hundred to a dozen, gave away all his pigs, dismissed his employees and tore down the outbuildings. His daughter and both his sons went to boarding school in England in the 1980s and never returned, while his wife moved to north Germany. On the once-large farm there now lived only a man and a dog.

Lots of questions here too. What had happened within this family? Why had Hannes Riedinger abandoned what had been a flourishing farm business? Why had he not sold this particular piece of pasture?

Louise drove into the farmyard and trundled up to the house. The front door was open. Thirty metres beyond the house stood the barn.

And there, by the barn door, stood the man and the dog, eyeing her.

She stopped the car and got out. "The policewoman with different questions," she said. "Good evening, Herr Riedinger." She'd barely finished before the dog was on the move, rushing at her without barking or even growling.

Bonì stayed where she was, beside the open car door. Nobody even half in their right mind would simply stand by and watch their dog attack a police officer. Riedinger wanted to intimidate her, to toy with authority after everything that had happened that afternoon. In spite of everything, this was *his* realm. He would wait a moment before calling off the dog.

Bonì was suddenly gripped by fear. The dog was running faster now, she could see its bared teeth, its wide eyes, she could hear its panting.

But no command.

"What's going on, Riedinger?"

Riedinger said nothing.

She jumped into the car and slammed the door. Now the dog started to bark. It launched itself against the door, leaped up at the window as if out of its mind. She looked over in disbelief at Riedinger, who was still standing at the entrance to the barn. She couldn't make out his face in the shadow of the barn door.

Not a game.

Shaking with fear and anger, Louise started the car and put it into reverse. The dog barked and followed, stopping only when she was off the forecourt. After twenty metres she braked. The dog stood tensed, baring its teeth.

Not a game.

She switched her lights on full beam, shifted into first, put her foot down and aimed straight for the animal. It stared at her, but didn't move. What would it do? What would *she* do if it didn't get out of the way?

What would Riedinger do?

Not a game, she thought.

Neither man nor dog moved a muscle.

She accelerated. The dog cowered and tucked its head between its front paws. She thought she could hear it howl. Then it turned and ran to the barn.

She braked hard.

Riedinger hadn't moved. He stood in the beam of her headlights, five or six metres in front. His eyes were closed; it was as if he were waiting for her to keep driving. To put an end to everything – to what had already happened and what would happen in the future.

Louise deliberated. Perhaps she could talk to him now. But was that what she wanted? Nobody had ever set a dog on her before.

Tears sprang to her eyes. She'd thought that after her withdrawal, after those months at the Kanzan-an, everything would be better. That she would find her way back into normal life. A life with a simpler daily routine, simpler relationships, simpler emotions. Unspectacular, perhaps, but without shame, despair or humiliation. And now Riedinger had set his dog on her. Could there be anything more humiliating?

Step out of the fear.

Her eyes were burning. She cursed the equipment officer who'd refused to understand that sometimes rules were determined by necessity, then she put the car into reverse. She would return.

Surmount her fear, get some answers.

As Louise drove towards the red sun on the horizon, her entire body trembling, she dialled Günter's number. A telephone service voice, followed by the beep of the answerphone. "Pick up, Günter," she said.

Günter answered. "Nice of you to call."

"I'll be with you in ten minutes."

"Louise, I'm not sure I want that."

"I don't care. Just open the door."

Günter lived in the south-west of the city, in one of the Weingarten tower blocks. Decades ago Weingarten had been cheap and almost trendy, but now it was cheap and almost dilapidated. One of the city's problem areas – people in difficult social and financial circumstances, a high proportion of migrants, lots of Russian-Germans. Ethnic and social ghettos in high-rise estates on the edge of town – Weingarten in the south-west, Landwasser in the north-west – visible from afar, but not yet volatile enough close up to warrant intervention. The Russian-Germans were a particular worry. All of them permanently drunk, Bermann said, and they had zero desire to integrate. They would barbecue on the balconies of the high-rise blocks until a whole convoy of fire engines arrived to put out a non-existent fire. Löbinger's people complained that their criminal networks were almost hermetically sealed. But Freiburg was Freiburg. In Lahr, to the north, the picture was even more dramatic. There, around 30 per cent of the inhabitants were Russian-Germans.

Such were Louise's thoughts as she approached the entrance to the tower block. A massive, angular building with narrow horizontal slits for windows and graffiti on the exposed concrete. Did life get difficult because you ended up here, or did you end up here because it was difficult already?

But at the top and on the sides of the building shimmered aureoles of dark-red sunlight.

She rang the bell and Günter buzzed her in straightaway. As she waited for the lift she wondered how best to ask what she wanted from him. And, most of all, when to ask it.

The light went out and the lift door slid open. She gazed at the reflection staring back at her from inside the illuminated cabin. Louise Bonì, forty-three in a fortnight, flowing black hair, jeans, tight-fitting cropped T-shirt with the inscription YOU CAN LEAVE YOUR HAT ON.

The T-shirt was unnecessary, she thought.

Otherwise her reflection wasn't at all bad.

She got into the lift. Her ride was far too short.

She found herself on the tenth floor between two narrow corridors, both of them in darkness. Right or left? She'd just plumped for left when a door opened at the end of the right-hand corridor.

*

Günter's apartment consisted of a medium-sized room, a small hall-way with a kitchenette and a tiny, blue bathroom. The walls in the main room were bare, the furniture dark brown or black. A tele-vision, a hi-fi, no books, a small yucca with yellowing leaves. The tour didn't last long. The view from the window was towards the station, the minster and the Schlossberg. In the distance she could see the Dreisamtal with its undulations disappearing into the dusk. Oberried and the knoll behind Lisbeth Walter's house lay hidden beyond the foothills of Schauinsland. Boní thought of Riedinger, saw him before her, motionless and with his eyes closed as if hoping she would drive on and put an end to everything.

Then she thought of the masked man. Had she imagined him? Had she taken off her T-shirt and wrapped it around the wound herself? No. He did exist. He had been there. But who was he? Why had he helped her and then disappeared?

Louise turned away from the window. Günter was looking at the bandage around her left upper arm. He had apologised and she'd accepted his apology.

"I'm not skilled at diplomacy, but would you like to hear what I have to say anyway?"

From certainties to uncertainties, from questions to possible answers.

Günter nodded warily.

Louise turned back to the window and crossed her arms. She could make out the contours of her reflection in the glass. "I think . . ." she began, but then Günter said he'd rather do the talking.

He'd been plagued by nausea for a couple of years now, but it had grown worse over the last few months. Sometimes it came on while he was shopping, and he would have to abandon everything. Sometimes it came on during meetings at H.Q., in which case he'd try to struggle through or make a dash for the nearest toilet. He'd been to see a dozen doctors – internists, oncologists, surgeons – and had gastroscopies, colonoscopies and similar procedures. But no doctor had found the tumor or whatever else might be lurking in his stomach or colon – or wherever it was. Tomorrow he had another appointment with a specialist in Karlsruhe. Maybe she would find it. If not he'd been recommended an oncologist in Munich. But he was pinning his hopes on the specialist. Thirty years' professional experience, senior consultant, surely she would find something. In truth, he admitted, he was pleased that Löbinger wanted to boot him out. Because now the nausea was frequently accompanied by breathing problems. As he understood it, the tumor was pushing gastric acid into his gullet, obstructing his lungs, which was why sometimes he found it hard to breathe. Driving was also becoming more and more difficult, as the tumor was compressed when he sat down.

"What if it's something completely different?" Louise said.

"Something completely different!"

The reflection in the window gave a slight nod. She knew faces like Günter's from Oberberg. Nausea, difficulty breathing, hyperventilation, panic. She asked if he ever got panic attacks, but Günter said, no, no panic attacks. Just nausea and sometimes difficulty breathing. Angrily he added that he knew what she was getting at. And he definitely wasn't a psycho.

A tumor, Luis.

The reflection nodded again. No friendships with his colleagues. And yet he'd told her a lot, she thought.

"But that's not why you're here."

"Not just because of that, no." She turned around. "I need your gun."

Günter wasn't Justin Muller, they weren't in France, she wasn't ill anymore – these were the differences now, she thought as she drove back to Kirchzarten. If you lost your weapon or had to hand it over to C.S.I., you borrowed one from a colleague who wasn't on duty. This was usual practice, and obviously Louise could engage in usual practice too. She'd become Bermann's confidante, a colleague like any other officer, which made her work significantly easier. And yet she felt no less lonely and excluded than she had in February. Could this be because she was on the way to see a witness unaccompanied by a fellow officer – a witness who'd set his dog on her – and at nine in the evening rather than during the day?

Or was it because of René Calambert, who didn't dare creep up on her when there was no snow, but was still lodged inside her, an invisible shadow? The question of why had led to an answer with Calambert too, and this answer to more questions and answers.

Why wouldn't he get out of her head?

Because she had shot him dead.

Did this explain why she'd started drinking three years ago and still thought of him?

Of course it did.

Louise switched on the radio and caught the weather forecast. Still almost thirty degrees with some light rain during the night, the first in three weeks. She changed stations until her head rang with the hammering of bass and guitar riffs.

One of the psychotherapists in Oberberg had been close to probing further. To asking the right question in relation to Calambert. Louise didn't know why he hadn't in the end. She'd been waiting for it. She would have answered the question, answered both him and herself.

The question of why.

In the Dreisamtal the light had turned grey and shadows clutched at the house. She stopped on the track that led to Riedinger's farm. Fifty metres ahead of her a dark-yellow rectangle of light shimmered in the gloom. Riedinger was the key, but was it such a smart idea to visit him again on her own? No. Neither smart nor professional – for several reasons. One being that she was armed and still fuming with rage. The alternative would have been to ask Wallmer, Täschle or Bermann to come with her.

Or to wait at home for Anatol.

Approaching colleagues, waiting for a man – not exactly her strengths.

She drove on. First she focused on the barn. The barn door was closed and neither Riedinger nor his dog were to be seen. All the same she placed Günter's Heckler & Koch on the passenger seat.

The door to the farmhouse was ajar and a strip of light fell onto the forecourt. She drove the car into the light, came to a stop and glanced inside the house.

A hall, an open door, a table. At the table sat Heinrich Täschle. He was out of his uniform, with a bottle and a beer glass in front of him.

A colleague who didn't need to be asked, who came on his own.

A muggy summer's evening in the countryside, two men drinking a cool beer, peacefully discussing everything that needed to be discussed.

She would only be interrupting.

Täschle was looking in her direction, but he didn't signal whether or not he'd seen her. She took out her phone and dialled the number of his work mobile. Without taking his eyes off her he pulled the mobile from his shirt pocket. "I'm going to be a while yet, darling," he said. "We're nicely settled here."

She couldn't help laughing. "Oh, what a shame, honey. Shall I make you something to eat later?"

"Erm, no thanks."

"Maybe a nice little schnitzel?"

"No, darling, that's very sweet of you." Täschle's voice was soft and melodic. The aloofness had dissipated.

"Will you call me when you're done?"

"But don't wait up for me, darling, will you?"

"You know I can't get to sleep without you, sweetie."

"Yes – you too, darling."

She ended the call, put the car into reverse and turned. You too? Louise drove away slowly from the farm. Have a lovely evening, honey. Yes – you too, darling. Husbands, wives. From the tone of his voice she could tell the degree of his affection. The lights of Kirchzarten were ahead of her. Somewhere amongst them Täschle's wife sat waiting. She'd put the children to bed, left the door to their bedrooms ajar and occasionally she listened in the hallway to check that they were asleep. The television was on, tropical fish swam in an aquarium and puppies frolicked on the sofa. There were plants everywhere, yuccas with green leaves, cyclamen and – what were they called? – orchids on the window sills.

Bonì opened the glove box and rummaged in it, then stopped, aghast, when she couldn't find what she was looking for.

She'd been outwitted by her demons.

Waiting for Anatol wasn't an option so she took the investigation file up to her apartment and went back downstairs. There was a light on in the caretaker's kitchen and klezmer music drifted through the tilted window. Ever since Ronescu had realised that there wouldn't be any more bingeing together, he'd hardly spoken a word to her. Only now did she realise how important she was to him.

Young people were clustered outside student bars and nightclubs in the pedestrian zone. In Bertoldstrasse a tram had stopped and the driver got out. In his seat now sat a laughing Japanese tourist being photographed by three other laughing Japanese tourists kneeling beside the tram. The driver was laughing too. She had often met Mick under the clock at the corner of Bertoldstrasse and Kaiser-Josef-Strasse. They would go for lunch in the covered market, or to Café Atrium for a coffee. Mick had made puppy-dog eyes at her and sulked until she'd satisfied him in the ladies' toilet with everything she had. Those were clues too. Anybody who needed a public lavatory, the back seat of a car or a Black Forest meadow to get sexually aroused was way past their use-by date.

You expected heaven and you got hell's valley.

But you learned, and self-pity helped sometimes too.

A detective chief inspector who'd made a point of ignoring clues. She laughed bleakly.

On Augustinerplatz, Anatol appeared out of the blue. She didn't recognise him at first; his wild locks of hair were gone.

"Hey," he said softly.

"Hey." Louise ran both her hands over the stubble on his head. She had wanted to smile, but already she was in tears. Anatol took her in his arms and they stood like that for a while, the old woman and the young man. Then the young man said what had to be said, and although she didn't understand what he was trying to explain, and although he was someone she'd got used to rather than loved, she couldn't stop crying, not even when she sent him away and went home alone.

Later she sat on the sofa, staring at the bottles on the table, and thought: midnight without my midnight man, that's inconceivable. She looked at the clock: ten to twelve. Not today, she had sworn and she swore it again. Not today.

But maybe tomorrow.

The demons were silent. They knew why. They were lying in wait.

Nine minutes to twelve. Minutes could be so long.

The time passed more quickly when she stood up and wandered through the apartment. Putting on a C.D. helped too. Barclay James Harvest, of course, "Poor Man's Moody Blues" on a loop. In her bedroom she contemplated the fact that after detox, 95 per cent of people suffer a relapse if they have no further treatment. With further treatment the figures were between 30 and 60 per cent. Did her four months in the Zen monastery count as further treatment? As long-term therapy?

At least she would be in good company.

She stared at her reflection in the bathroom mirror. On the outside too beautiful for Anatol, who had been unable to relocate the "subterranean beauty" he'd fallen in love with.

A man who wanted to search rather than see.

Louise remembered. Back in the winter he'd said she wasn't immediately beautiful, at first glance, because she wasn't that slim and didn't look after her hair. But the longer he gazed at her, the more beautiful she seemed, because her expressions, her laugh, her smile, her look and her body all had their own particular beauty – something warm, wild, sad, unique, genuine. He couldn't keep his eyes – or hands – off her.

Now that she was slim and looked after her hair, he *was* able to keep his hands off her. Had her warmness, wildness, sadness, uniqueness and genuineness all vanished just because she looked after her hair?

She went back into the sitting room. What nonsense back then, what nonsense now. The way people classified their feelings.

"Poor Man's Moody Blues" started from the beginning. She looked at the clock. Midnight, even if the midnight man would never come again.

Louise sat on the sofa and gazed at the bottles. Vodka, bourbon, Jägermeister, more vodka. Not yesterday, she thought, but maybe today. If she wanted to – not because of anybody else or because of a dog. Only if she herself wanted to.

Did she?

Yes, yes, yes, the demons cried.

She was lying in bed when Heinrich Täschle called. He was breathing rapidly, pausing between sentences. Something was squeaking in the background. Täschle was on his bicycle, riding home four litres of beer and several glasses of schnapps. He laughed. His voice sounded as soft as it had during their charade earlier. Anatol-tears were running down Louise's cheeks and a Täschle-shudder down her spine. He had a name for her, Täschle said. She sat up. Ernst Martin Söllien, a lawyer from Freiburg, had wanted to buy Riedinger's pasture two years ago. At the time Riedinger was still using the pasture for his last few cows, and so he rejected the offer. Then about a year ago he rang Söllien because he wanted to sell. His call went through to a legal practice, and someone there told him that Söllien had died a few months earlier.

"Shit," Louise said.

"Shit indeed," Täschle wheezed.

She sank back onto the bed. "Thanks, anyway. How did you get him to tell you all this?"

"I must have asked the right questions."

"Which were?"

Täschle grunted, the bike squeaked. "If he still thinks about Kathi and his children."

"And?"

"Well, you can guess what the answer is, can't you?"

"Yes. First he batters them till they leave, then he weeps over them."

"Goodness gracious, you city types are so heartless."

Goodness gracious? She smirked. "Not heartless, Henny. It's just that we don't forget."

"Us villagers are better at that."

Louise laughed. "Will you take me to see Adam Baudy tomorrow?"

"Yes, but I've got to go now, I've got to . . ." He stopped.

"Out with it, Henny."

"I need to pee."

The name wrenched her from her sleep. Ernst Martin Söllien. Louise had heard the name before.

Twenty past four – outside, dawn was breaking. Ernst Martin Söllien. She got up.

Boni had dreamed of the masked man. Even though he hadn't revealed himself to her in the dream, she'd known that it was Landen. She had dragged him into the ladies' in Café Atrium and had sex with him on the floor.

"Poor Man's Moody Blues" was playing in the sitting room and it stank of alcohol. Had she or hadn't she?

No, she hadn't. She'd opened the bottles and emptied them into the sink. She went into the kitchenette, turned on the tap and rinsed the rest away.

Ernst Martin Söllien. Memory, or a figment of the imagination? Where had she heard the name before? Or had she *read* it somewhere?

Louise picked up the case file and sat on the floor. Ernst Martin Söllien, could he be a lawyer? She leafed through the information on those involved in the 1992 Rottweil trial.

And there he was. Dr Ernst Martin Söllien, a lawyer at Uhlich & Partners, Freiburg. Client: Halid Trumic, born 16/12/1949 in Tuzla, Yugoslavia, autonomous Republic of Bosnia-Herzegovina, he was fined in late 1992 for violating the gun laws.

Adrenalin shot through her veins. Ernst Martin Söllien, Halid Trumic. The first names.

6

The rain came at six o'clock. Louise stood at the open window in Almenbroich's office, watching fat drops smack onto the roofs. But the downpour didn't cool the air, which was still warm and stale. Almenbroich had been standing at the window when she came into the office a few minutes earlier. "Come, Louise, it's about to start." Together they'd waited for the rain, two exhausted, shrivelled Kripo officers who were getting barely any sleep, albeit for different reasons.

"How's the arm?"

"Better, thanks. And your circulation?"

"Oh." Almenbroich waved his hand dismissively.

The rain grew heavier, the air damper. In the east the clouds were breaking up and the odd ray of sunshine fell on the hills. They hadn't yet made it to the Flaunser.

"We've got two names," Louise said.

"Give me a few minutes," Almenbroich said.

She looked at him, shocked by the extent of his physical decline. Grey face, hollowed eyes, hollow cheeks, a stooped posture, mouth always slightly open, short breaths. Louise wondered how much longer he'd be able to go on. She really needed him.

"O.K., I'm ready," he said after a while. "Shall we go to your office for a change?"

"I haven't got an office yet."

"No?" Almenbroich smiled. For the first time in days there was a spark in his eyes.

He was still smiling as she followed him into the corridor. A father taking his child to see the presents under the Christmas tree.

*

The office was on the second floor. Bonì's colleagues in the drugs squad had made available a small meeting room, and Almenbroich had obtained a desk, two chairs, a telephone, a computer and two houseplants. On the wall was a poster-sized photograph. Children from the Far East in red monks' robes, laughing as they ran down some steps towards the photographer. She was moved even though she didn't know what the poster was alluding to. Her months at the Kanzan-an? That if she wanted children in this life it was high time she got started?

"The children from Asile d'enfants," Almenbroich told her.

Louise was dumbstruck.

Fifty-eight children from the Far East had gone missing, only two had been found at the beginning of the year: Pham and the girl from Poipet. There was no trace of the others; they'd been sold in Germany, France, Belgium and Switzerland.

And now they were running towards her in their red monks' robes.

"Is someone still looking?"

"Sort of."

They sat down. Almenbroich told her about the task force meeting the previous afternoon. It had been short and had thrown up little new information. Louise tried to concentrate but her eyes kept drifting to the poster above his head. The Asile children. She felt like howling. Looking at Almenbroich she wondered: Do I want to be looking at them every day? As if they'd come back, or had never been abused and sold?

The comforting illusion, the bitter reality. Forget, or remember. Decide which.

Not today.

Now that the jurisdiction issue had been settled, Almenbroich said, they'd expanded the task force with people from Löbinger's section and national security officers from D13. Löbinger was in charge, Bermann his deputy. He smiled meaningfully and Louise smiled too. A litmus test for Rolf Bermann, who was nobody's deputy but the prototype of the alpha male. So now Bermann was "helping out".

"Let's get to the names, Louise. What do you have?"

She told Almenbroich about Ernst Martin Söllien and Halid Trumic, and he tried to make the connections: "In 1992 a Freiburg lawyer defends a Bosnian Muslim accused of smuggling arms. In 2001 the same lawyer wants to buy some land from a farmer in Kirchenzarten, where there's an underground shelter dating back to the Second World War. Two years later an illegal weapons depot is discovered in the cellar or, more accurately, is blown sky high."

Silence. Almenbroich looked pensive, and Louise had become sceptical. It all sounded too flimsy.

"Well, it's a start, I suppose," she said eventually.

"It's more than that. It's the first lead that hasn't been whispered to us by some authority, a contact, an anonymous source. Do you trust this Täschle?"

"Yes."

"Good. Work with him. I'll add Täschle to the task force and then there won't be any problems. Both of you stick with this lead, no matter what Anselm and Rolf say. If you discover it goes nowhere we can think again. If you need any support, come to me and we'll find someone outside the task force." Almenbroich wiped the sweat from his forehead and cheeks with a handkerchief. His hand was trembling faintly.

"Someone from Kripo who would voluntarily work against Bermann or Löbinger?"

"If the order comes from me?"

"One of those two is soon going to be head of Division One."

"How do you know that? We've had seven applicants." Almenbroich smiled. "Well, we'll see how we can solve the problem. Have you got yourself a replacement weapon?"

"Günter's H. & K."

"The new H. & K.? Have you had any experience with it?"

"I know the differences. Thirteen rounds instead of eight, eighty grams lighter, automatically uncocks after every shot. It'll be fine."

"That's careless, Louise."

"I'll pop down to the range today."

"That's not enough as far as I'm concerned. The H. & K. is a magnificent weapon, but changing from a Walther isn't without its problems."

"I know. Some colleagues shoot too far to the left and too low."

"Go to the weapons officer, he'll give you a Walther P5."

"Yesterday he didn't think that was necessary."

"Well, I'll make sure he sees things differently today. Would you be so kind as to open the window?"

Traffic was building up on Heinrich-von-Stephan-Strasse heading into town. The rain had eased, the clouds were breaking up. Louise could see the high-rises of Weingarten on the other side of the railway line. She thought of Günter's nausea, the explanations, the tumor that the specialist in Karlsruhe was going to discover. She could only guess at how he felt, living in that tiny, black apartment, on his lonely, black path. No, not a psycho, not a madman, not someone who had problems with life. Just a man with a tumor, or whatever else might be sitting in his stomach or colon – or wherever it was.

She sat down. "You can't suspend Günter just because he feels unwell sometimes."

Almenbroich nodded; he shared her view on this. On the other hand, he said, Günter wasn't fit for Kripo work at the moment – he'd become a danger to his colleagues. He wouldn't suspend him, as Löbinger was advocating, but Almenbroich would ask Günter to get himself signed off sick. "Like you last winter." He put his fingertips together. The triangle became a circle and the circle became a triangle again. How familiar these movements had become. Now she knew what they were trying to conceal and project – uncertainty on the inside, determination on the outside.

She looked up. "You didn't ask me, you forced me."

"You're right," he said, smiling. "Sometimes undemocratic methods work best."

"Then 'ask' Günter to go and see a psychologist."

"I see we share the same suspicions. No offence, but could you recommend one?"

"Katrin Rein. For the initial conversations, at least."

"The lecturer at the Academy?" Almenbroich said.

"Young, pretty, a bit impulsive, but in it with heart and soul."

"Soul would be enough to begin with."

They laughed. Louise took four half-litre bottles of Evian from her shoulder bag and placed them in a row on her new desk. She offered one to Almenbroich and showed him how to open the sports cap.

He drank like someone dying of thirst.

"I need to go to the meeting," she said.

Almenbroich shook his head. The task force meeting had been postponed until ten – some Kripo officers were coming down from Stuttgart. National security officers. He shrugged. Neo-Nazis in Freiburg and southern Baden? Unlikely. They were based elsewhere.

"That brings us to our other lead," he said.

The other lead, neo-Nazi, was now a *Croatian*–neo-Nazi lead. Almenbroich had received more calls throughout the previous afternoon and evening. From their "friends" at the Bureau and F.I.S., as well as from a colleague of the permanent secretary. She had asked about the investigation and had been promised ample support in the fight against neo-Nazis, even if they came from Baden-Württemberg . . .

"Even *if*?"

"We're dealing with politics now, Louise. Don't forget that." Almenbroich's hands came together to form the finger triangle.

She nodded. There it was again – that inexplicable feeling from yesterday that there was something he wasn't telling her.

"Where were we?"

"The permanent secretary's colleague."

"That's right." The Bureau and F.I.S. had referred to the lists of names from Rottweil in 1992 and indicated that some of the Croats belonged to the nationalist right wing of the H.D.Z., the "Croatian Democratic Union", an opposition party. "They had, or still have, an office in Stuttgart, and at the time it was rumoured that they were calling on fellow Croats to smuggle arms . . . What do you know about Croatia?"

"Little or nothing."

He smiled. "I read up on it a bit at home."

"Last night?"

"Last night." He took a swig of Evian and said that the H.D.Z., originally a party of right-wing nationalists, had been formed in 1989 by Franjo Tudjman, later president of Croatia. Since Tudjman's death a few years ago the party had been reformed and was now more centre right than far right on the democratic spectrum. But some members were still refusing to distance themselves from the Ustaša state of the early 1940s . . .

Louise opened her mouth, Almenbroich raised his hand – the explanation was coming.

As far as he'd understood, the Croats had founded the so-called Independent State of Croatia, a one-party state under the fascist Ustaša following the invasion of German troops in 1941. He didn't know exactly what had happened there, but apparently there were concentration camps where hundreds of thousands of Jews, Serbs, gypsies and Croatian political opponents were said to have been murdered by Croatian fascists. "The Bureau and F.I.S. – let me repeat this, Louise – the Bureau *and* F.I.S. suspect that neo-Nazis in Baden-Württemberg and Croat migrants close to the H.D.Z. joined forces during the Yugoslav War in the early nineties . . ."

". . . and now they're planning to equip a private army?"

Almenbroich shrugged. "We know that European mercenaries, including German neo-Nazis, fought in the Balkans. The question is rather: What would these people be planning? But I have another problem with this story, as you know."

"Whether it's correct or whether we're being manipulated?"

"If you're being fed pretty much the same information at pretty much the same time from three sides, manipulation springs to mind. Or paranoia."

"And panic."

"Let's not exaggerate, Louise."

She smiled. "I'm not talking about you, I'm talking about whoever is disseminating this information, assuming it's one individual."

Almenbroich nodded. At any rate, he said, the task force would follow up the leads and check every name on the Rottweil 1992 lists. He looked at his watch and stood up; he had an appointment with Marianne Andrele in his office at seven. Six, seven, eight o'clock in the morning – the only bearable hours of the day. He gulped down the rest of the water. With a tired smile he pulled out his handkerchief and wiped the sweat from his face.

"Should I be worried about you?"

For a moment Almenbroich looked as if he wanted to be hugged and comforted. "No, no," he said gratefully. She knew he wouldn't show any vulnerability on duty. A fifty-five-year-old Kripo head collapsing in the summer heat during such an important case would be a nightmare.

"One more thing." Louise told him about the masked man.

Almenbroich sat down again. "That's not in any protocol."

"That's how Rolf wanted it." She explained why, and Almenbroich nodded. A reckless decision, he thought, but plausible. "For your information," Louise said, "Anselm thinks I was hallucinating."

"Rolf and Anselm," Almenbroich said. "It was a bad idea of mine to put them both on the task force."

"I imagine there was no other option."

"There's always another option. But this man . . . who, for heaven's sake . . ." Almenbroich said, shaking his head and looking perplexed.

She shrugged. There were so many possibilities. The less disagreeable ones were: a member of a Special Deployment Commando or counter-terrorism unit. Maybe a secret service agent, or an informer. Then at least he would be on her side.

"Describe him."

"Very fit, fast, focused, willing to take risks, silent, absolutely professional."

"And he didn't say a word?"

She shook her head.

Almenbroich pointed to his watch and got to his feet again. "We'll discuss this further."

"Just one more thing, Herr Almenbroich."

"Yes?"

"I have the feeling you know more than you're letting on."

Almenbroich hesitated before telling her she was mistaken; his paranoia must be infectious. He smiled and left, taking with him all that he was concealing from her.

For some moments Bonì sat at her new desk in her new office, far from her section and her colleagues, staring at the poster of the children and contemplating inexplicable feelings, and paranoia, and self-delusion. Almenbroich's voice had sounded as it always did and his smile as he left had been as it always was – friendly, serious, author-itative. And yet . . . feelings had both the advantage and disadvantage that they didn't necessarily concur with appearances.

She got the address and telephone number of Uhlich & Partners from directory enquiries and made the call. The legal practice was open, the answerphone explained, between nine and twelve.

Louise smiled as she rang Barbara Franke, who'd done so much for her over the winter. Baba from Terre des hommes, light-brown coat, blonde hair, laptop, so slim and beautiful that Anatol wouldn't have given her a second glance. What about Richard Landen?

"I don't believe it," Barbara Franke said, her mouth full. "You're alive!"

"Yeah, well, if you can call it that. Yesterday some guy set his dog on me."

"Report him."

"I'd rather shoot him."

"Shooting's good too." Barbara cursed – honey on her trousers. Louise expressed her sympathy and they laughed. "We should meet up sometime."

"How about later this evening?" Louise said.

"I'm in a meeting. Tomorrow morning? Come jogging with me, six o'clock at Kronenbrücke. We'll run along the Dreisam up to Ebnet and back, that'll give us plenty of opportunity to talk. You know I talk and listen best when I'm running." They laughed again. There was a rustling at the end of the line; Barbara Franke was taking off her trousers. She opened a squeaky door, walked across a parquet floor and said, "There was something you wanted, right?"

"Uhlich & Partners," Louise said.

"Never heard of them."

"A legal firm."

"Where are they based?"

"Here in Freiburg."

"Don't know them. I'll make some enquiries and call you back."

Then Boni was once again all alone, with the question of Almenbroich's secret and the children in their red robes. She went around her desk and carefully removed the poster from the wall. Illusion or reality, forgetting or remembering, one comforting, the other bitter – a difficult decision.

The weapons and equipment officer wasn't in yet. Louise went to the "data station", as section 43 was called. One of her colleagues at the computers checked both names: Halid Trumic and Ernst Martin Söllien. Files existed not just on Trumic, but on Söllien too – this she hadn't expected. Trumic had a record, from Rottweil 1992; the file had been put together by the local police. Söllien's file was in Freiburg. In late 2001 he'd been arrested for property fraud. There were photographs of both men and their fingerprints had been taken. The faces said nothing to her.

Louise left police H.Q. at a loss. Arms smuggling and property fraud. Were the two connected?

Half an hour later, for the first time since the start of the year, she was standing outside the little house in Günterstal with its wooden fence, stepping stones in the grass and its teahouse in the garden. The willow was now in leaf and no longer grabbed menacingly at the roof, but rather shaded it like a protective hand. It was daytime, so no lonely lights behind the small windows. A summer idyll, at least from the outside. A house in which she would surely sleep well at night.

Louise couldn't be sure why she'd come. To ring the bell and try her luck, or to take her leave of the house and Richard Landen.

She looked at the nameplate by the bell. TOMMO/LANDEN. Funny names, Niksch said in her head. Quiet, Nikki, she thought.

Yes, she would ring the bell, but there was no way she was going to step into that kitchen. In the kitchen sat the china cat, and Niksch. The living room was alright, in the living room sat Tommo, which wasn't so bad.

Bonì shuddered and rang the bell.

Nobody came to the door.

Waiting for a man was out of the question so she went for a walk. The fresh morning air of Günterstal would surely do her good after an almost sleepless night. She inhaled all the way into her stomach, as she had learned from Enni and then from Roshi Bukan at the Kanzan-an, sucking the fresh air deep inside to drive out the craving and the questions. The craving remained, and the questions returned. Where was he? In Japan with Tommo? Running to Ebnet, or wherever else Freiburg joggers went? Two children came towards her, then a woman with a dog. They each said hello and she greeted them back.

At a crossroads she stopped and turned around, cursing. She'd had enough of the Günterstal morning air, enough of not waiting for a man.

When Louise got to her car Barbara Franke called. She was on her way to the district court and in the background Louise could hear a tram, construction noise and young people talking. "Are you sitting down?" Barbara Franke shouted.

"One sec," Louise said, getting into the car. Almost simultaneously the background noise stopped; Barbara had gone into a building. For a split second the connection broke up. Louise opened the window and let her eyes wander across the house, the garden, the willow. Should she come back, or say farewell?

"Louise?"

"Shoot."

"Shoot – how apposite," Barbara said. Although Uhlich & Partners was a registered law firm, it operated almost exclusively as a lobbyist. Its clients were arms companies, both domestic and foreign.

"Well, well," Louise said. "Which ones?"

"No idea."

"Please find out for me."

Barbara groaned. "Alright, I'll look into it. *Shit.*" After a brief pause they both laughed. A *déjà-entendu.*

Barbara continued. Uhlich & Partners were Dr Horst Uhlich and Dr Christian von Leh, and at one time Dr Ernst Martin Söllien, but he died eighteen months ago. The firm had its headquarters in Munich and branches in Berlin, Stuttgart, Freiburg and Passau.

"Apart from Stuttgart, all close to the border, for whatever reason," Louise said.

"Correct," Barbara said. She asked whether this was about the weapons depot in Kirchzarten? Yes, Louise said and told her what she could. Barbara knew a little from the papers. The tabloids had pointed the finger at the farmer and the Croats, and to be honest so had she – a violent farmer, right-wing Croatian nationalists, it fitted perfectly with her view of the world. She laughed. What about Kripo?

"Following up several leads."

"No matter where they end up, the alternatives seem pretty ugly."

Louise turned to look at the house, the garden and green willow. The Landen idyll, fresh Günterstal morning air, a summer's day in southern Baden – and a weapons depot, the Yugoslav War, arms manufacturers . . . "It's hard to imagine," she said.

"Only if you're blind."

"The Yugoslav War, arms manufacturers – come off it."

Barbara spoke faster, more loudly, from her footsteps it sounded as if she was climbing the stairs. "We're the fourth largest exporter of arms in the world, Louise. In the nineties we exported weapons with an annual value of between one and three billion marks. So what do you mean by 'Come off it'?"

Bonì grinned. There she was again, the warrior she'd felt so comfortable with in the winter. She sensed that Barbara's fighting spirit would give her new life too. What was she doing in Günterstal? Apart from not waiting and feeding her self-pity? She turned the key in the ignition. "Who do you mean by 'we'? We Freiburgians?"

"We Germans. We Freiburgians don't live in Elysium."

"The Freiburgians in Günterstal do."

"No, they don't either. Filbinger lives in Günterstal."

"Could we stay in the present?"

"O.K., let's see what we've got nearby . . . Your friends Heckler & Koch are based in Oberndorf. H. & K. rifles manufactured under licence were highly popular with all sides in the Yugoslav War, that's a well-known fact – so there you are. Shall I go on?"

Louise smiled and pulled onto the road. "Yes, give me a little more."

"Last year the weapons nutters in Rottweil. There used to be a gunpowder factory in Rottweil too, producing a large proportion of German infantry requirements in the First World War. In Karlsruhe you've got Industrie-Werke Karlsruhe Augsburg A.G., who used to manufacture landmines and munitions. Then in Friedrichshafen there's the cogwheel factory that makes gearboxes and steering mechanisms for military vehicles, and M.T.U., who build engines for tanks and howitzers for countries like India and Korea. Not to mention, of course, DaimlerChrysler, they're everywhere thanks to their involvement in E.A.D.S., and they manufacture pretty much everything as well – nuclear missile launchers, mines, cluster munitions. Have I forgotten anyone? The Mauser factories used to be in Oberndorf too, and Ulm is the headquarters of Walther, who you know. At the nuclear research centre in Karlsruhe we furnished Pakistani scientists with nuclear know-how. Oh yes, and . . ."

"O.K., O.K., you're right."

"You wanted Freiburg. I'll give you Freiburg. At the end of the 1970s a Freiburg engineer sent chemical equipment to Pakistan which could be used to make or convert uranium compounds, or whatever it is. More than sixty lorries transported the stuff – just imagine that. Pakistan got the penultimate components for the nuclear bomb, and the engineer got an eight-month suspended sentence and a fine."

"I'm impressed."

"Pacifists on the warpath."

They laughed.

Louise drove through Günterstal scanning the road and the pavements. The not-waiting was over, the not-searching had begun. But nowhere did she see a tall, slim man with a friendly yet reserved expression, slightly reddish eyes and a small patch of grey hair in his right eyebrow either walking, standing or sitting. She drove through the archway of the former Cistercian monastery and accelerated onto Schauinslandstrasse. Should she come back, or say farewell?

"Don't forget the names of Uhlich's clients."

"Don't worry."

They ended the conversation.

Louise glanced in the rear-view mirror and decided to say farewell.
Decided to come back.
Decided on one, then the other.

In Herdern she decided to telephone instead. Nervously she called
Landen's number, and when the answerphone clicked in said, "I'm
back and I've got information about Taro, if you're interested." She
parked, got out of the car, pressed redial and said, "Louise Bonì, in
case you didn't recognise my voice."

Two calls within a few seconds. Landen would know it was urgent.
And surely the reason why, too.

As she crossed the road she tried to remember her last conversation
with Landen. She knew she'd asked lots of questions, but couldn't
remember what they were.

Questions she ought not to have asked – she knew that, at least.

Bonì peered across the street at the building which housed Uhlich
& Partners, an attractive, white, two-storey house with a small balcony
in front of the central window on the first floor. The corners of the
building were not rendered and resembled narrow grey columns.
Louise rang the bell and was buzzed into a large, panelled foyer with
indirect lighting and the fragrance of old wood. In the middle of a
thick carpet stood a smiling woman of about sixty. Her hands crossed
in front of her stomach, a discreet blue suit, gold-rimmed spec-
tacles – a young grandmother you wouldn't hesitate to confide in.

Uhlich & Partners were prepared for chief inspectors who turned
up unannounced.

Louise returned the smile.

At that very moment she remembered the questions she had asked
Landen. *Why are you flying to Japan? When are you back? Do you
love your wife? Why are you sometimes so likeable, and sometimes so
dull? When will I see you again?*

But the questions hadn't been the worst of it; she'd saved the worst for the end of their conversation. *That gives us plenty of time, then. You called me three times in one week, so I assume you want to spend some time with me. Am I right?*

Louise shook her head, aghast.

The grandmother raised her eyebrows, but the smile stayed in place.

"Relationship issues," Louise said, feeling comfortable with this phrase.

"Oh, you poor thing." The grandmother extended a hand. "Dr Annelie Weininger, office manager."

"Louise Bonì, chief inspector."

Annelie Weininger kept smiling. "What can I do for you? Would you like to talk woman to woman, or chief inspector to office manager?"

"We could switch as the mood takes us."

"Excellent! Let's makes ourselves comfortable then."

Annelie Weininger let go of Louise's hand and took her into some sort of fireside lounge with light-brown leather armchairs. She brought coffee, biscuits in different shapes, sizes and colours, and a carafe of water. Louise sat down and pushed to the back of her mind the embarrassment she'd caused Landen. A Gamma alcoholic in the prodromal phase, she told herself. He'll understand.

If he ever rings back.

Annelie Weininger closed the door and sat in an armchair opposite Louise. On the wall behind her hung posters of happy children playing and laughing together. On the wall above the fireplace were pictures of cities in the sunlight: Jerusalem, Rome, Berlin. "Let's start with the important stuff," Louise said.

"Your relationship issues."

"The crime."

"Oh." Annelie Weininger nodded.

They raised their cups and drank.

"Dr Söllien," Louise said.

*

Ernst Martin Söllien, Annelie Weininger said, had been dragged into a property fraud by a friend who worked for a bank. Inferior properties were offered to low- and middle-income earners as a provision for retirement, and then financed dramatically above their value. A few years later some of these properties were worth only 25 per cent of their purchase price. One of the buyers, heavily in debt, killed himself, and then the friend from the bank had a breakdown, confessed and gave Söllien's name. The inevitable happened: arrest, indictment, expulsion from the law society, social ostracism. His marriage collapsed, he had a heart attack and within two days he was dead. "I felt so sorry for him, in spite of all his mistakes," Annelie Weininger said. "A terrible time for us all, and especially for his family."

"I need the address of his ex-wife."

"Widow. They weren't divorced."

Annelie Weininger left the room and returned with a piece of note-paper and a photograph, the second picture of Ernst Martin Söllien Louise had seen. A chubby man in his mid-forties standing in the foyer of the practice, glass of wine in one hand, the other closed into a fist. Louise didn't like the face. No self-assurance, no attempt at poise. The expression reflected both servility and deviousness. Beneath the signs of middle age shone childlike features.

"He was a hard one to pigeonhole," Annelie Weininger said. Ernst Martin Söllien had many contradictory qualities, as if he'd failed to decide on who he really was at the critical age. He deceived systematic-ally, cheating simple people of their savings. On the other hand he was very kind to his colleagues, he never forgot a birthday. In court he was dishonest, and yet he donated to charitable causes and was a member of an association that supported projects in Pakistan. "In those six years I never managed to form a picture of him that still applied the following week." Annelie Weininger sighed. "Is there any reason to reopen the case?"

"Not yet," Louise said. "The crime I was referring to wasn't Söllien's property fraud. It's to do with illegal arms dealing."

"Illegal ..." Annelie Weininger was wide-eyed. "Kirchzarten?"

Louise nodded.

"But what connection could there have been between Kirchzarten and Dr Söllien?"

"There is one, and this leads on to the question of what connection there might be between Kirchzarten and Uhlich & Partners."

"None, of course!"

"Does the name Halid Trumic mean anything to you?"

"No."

"Which arms companies do you work with?"

"You know I can't answer that question."

"Can you tell me the ones you *don't* work with?"

"That's less problematic. So long as it doesn't go any further."

"Zavodi Crvena Zastava?"

"No."

"No means?"

"We don't work with them."

"You know the firm?"

"Of course."

"Let's assume you *were* working for them. What would you do, exactly?"

"We'd try to find interested parties or partners in Germany and other European countries for the products Z.C.Z. manufactures. We'd undertake lobbying work for the firm. Talk to politicians, place adverts in specialist publications, establish contacts at fairs, et cetera ..."

"What sort of interested parties? What sort of contacts?"

"Governments, armed forces, police authorities."

"Neo-Nazis, terrorists, guerrilla groups?"

"Of course not!" Annelie Weininger had turned pale. She took a sip of water, then clutched the glass in her lap. Louise believed her. If Ernst Martin Söllien or Uhlich & Partners had been involved in illegal arms dealing, Annelie Weininger had not been aware of it.

Louise's gaze wandered from the posters of children on the wall opposite to the sunlit cities to her left. Invisible tanks, bombers and weapons guaranteed their protection. She wished Barbara Franke were here; she could have torn down the slick façade with her fighting spirit. Louise herself was not the right person to lecture on morality. She had killed two people and in her bag was Günter's H. & K.

"Shall we talk about your relationship issues now?" Annelie Weininger said softly.

"Alright."

Louise left soon afterwards. The task force meeting was about to begin, but she decided to seek out Söllien's widow straightaway. She called Wallmer, whose reaction was as expected: Don't go on your own, you're so reckless, Rolf will be angry, and anyway, the meeting's compulsory. She was right on every point. "Don't wait for me," Louise said.

As she was driving she thought of Anatol for the first time since the previous evening. She asked herself why she'd been sad but had not wanted to fight. Why she was still sad and yet felt it was better this way.

Why suddenly she missed him nonetheless.

Marion Söllien lived in Zähringen, not far from Herdern. After her husband's death much had changed, according to Annelie Weininger. As a widow, Marion Söllien began to forgive her husband. She began to love him again and returned to the apartment they once shared. Occasionally she visited the law firm and chatted to Annelie Weininger about him, to try to get to know the dead man – with all his contradictions – a little better.

"She's a simple woman who can't cope with her fate," Annelie Weininger had said. "Be nice to her."

Louise intended to be nice. She rang the doorbell.

The second door that morning that remained closed.

*

The woman who lived in the apartment to the right said that Marion Söllien must be at home as she didn't leave for work until eleven, but she couldn't be of any more help as she'd been watching television. The neighbour who lived in the apartment to the left said Marion Söllien was definitely at home, because about an hour ago a man had rung the bell and was let in. He, the neighbour, just happened to be standing at the door, looking through the spyhole, which is how he'd seen him.

What sort of a man?

You know, a man.

Tall, short? Narrow, broad?

Tall, broad.

Blond?

Dark.

German?

More likely than not. But maybe not. Actually, more likely not. He'd only seen the man for a couple of seconds.

Louise knocked, rang the bell again, but still nobody opened the door. She went to find the caretaker and asked him to show her Marion Söllien's parking space in the underground garage. The car, a Toyota Corolla, was there. "What does that mean?" the caretaker asked, a short, sturdy old man.

She shrugged; she didn't know.

But she felt uneasy.

Ernst Martin Söllien wanted to buy the field from Hannes Riedinger. Why? What had a lawyer wanted with a cattle pasture if he didn't have any cattle? If he'd found out about the underground shelter and was looking for somewhere to hide the weapons, had his wife known about it?

They went back to the caretaker's apartment.

"What now?"

"Now I've got to start again from scratch."

But no matter how Louise looked at it, if Marion Söllien *had* known, then she was a threat to whoever was behind it all. Had they been watching the law practice to see if Kripo was on the trail of the Sölliens? Had the man who'd entered Marion Söllien's apartment come to Zähringen because Louise had turned up in Herdern?

She demanded the key to the apartment. The caretaker was horrified. He didn't know what rights, duties, options he had. And was she allowed to enter someone else's apartment without a search warrant? "By the time I get a public prosecutor or a judge on the phone Marion Söllien might be dead," Louise said, pulling the H. & K. from her bag and out of its holster. She held the pistol with the barrel pointing to the floor. "Anyway, it's not always a case of what you're allowed to do, but what's necessary. If you hear screams or shots, call 1–1–0. And now the key, please."

She telephoned the control centre and asked for back-up. The chief duty officer instructed her to wait until her colleagues arrived. Louise said nothing. If her hypothesis was correct, an hour ago a man had arrived who knew that Marion Söllien posed a threat. And if what the neighbours had said was correct, he was still in the apartment. Which meant that Marion Söllien might need help. If in the meantime the man had left the apartment unobserved, the same was true. She *couldn't* wait.

"Boni?" the chief duty officer said sharply.

"O.K., O.K., I'll wait."

She slid her mobile into her trouser pocket and went up to the first floor. Sometimes it wasn't a case of what you were allowed to do, but what was necessary.

She liked this phrase. She liked it so much that for the time being she ignored the question of who decided what was necessary.

On the landing she noticed how quiet it had become in the building. The neighbours were in their apartments, front doors closed. She thought she could sense their eyes on her, thought she could hear them holding their breath. What about behind Marion Söllien's front door? Was someone standing there, holding their breath too?

Louise approached the door from the side and stopped just to the right. She had to make do with the H. & K. after all, she thought, suddenly realising how light it felt in her hand.

Think of the differences. Some colleagues fire wide. Too far left, too low. But there were thirteen rounds rather than eight.

Louise slid the key into the lock and had to turn it twice. She shoved open the door, shouted, "Police," and waited.

Nothing.

"Frau Söllien?"

No answer.

Taking a deep breath, Boni entered the apartment.

A narrow hall, doors to the left and right, at the end an open door leading to a living room. In her mind she saw a shadow, a corpse, blood, she heard screams and gunshots.

In reality, not a sound, not a soul.

Proceeding slowly via the kitchen, bathroom, dining room and bedroom to the living room, she found nobody and heard nothing. In the living room the same. The apartment was empty.

The man who might have driven from Herdern to Zähringen hadn't killed Marion Söllien.

Not in her apartment, at least.

When the constabulary arrived she was sitting on a sofa, drying her sweaty face with a tea towel and swearing to herself that she'd slap the neighbour, slap the arms officer, slap Günter, and Bermann too if he uttered a single word out of place.

She'd slap herself as well, of course.

Louise let a few minutes pass before ringing the chief duty officer again. She needed two officers from surveillance to keep watch on the building and a few crime scene officers to look for fingerprints. She could deal with the search warrant herself – the public prosecutor would be at the task force meeting anyway. Then she went to confront the neighbour to the left and discovered that he'd been down to the cellar for a few minutes, during which time Marion Söllien and the man must have left the apartment.

She waited outside the building until the surveillance officers arrived and got into the back of their car. Matthias and Kilian, both young, barely older than Anatol, emphatically scruffy clothes, emphatically scruffy hair, the wild new generation of detectives. She placed her left hand on Matthias' shoulder – he was in the driver's seat – her right hand on Kilian's, and briefed them. The old woman, the young men. Perhaps, she thought, that explained Anatol – old and young – and the fact that she would have loved to stay young a while longer.

The stupid thing was that she'd never felt old before she got Anatol into bed to make her feel young.

7

When Boni arrived at police headquarters it was shortly after eleven. Hot, dry air filled the corridors. She went into her new office, washed her face and drank half a litre of water. Then she dictated onto tape what had happened at Uhlich & Partners and later at Marion Söllien's apartment block. She glanced up at the bare wall opposite and thought of the laughing children in their red robes and of the children on the posters in the lawyers' offices. The moment you placed something in a different context it seemed to lose its innocence. And how difficult it was to disaggregate all these contexts and return to the original one.

This was the core of Zen, if she'd understood it correctly.

And of police work, of course.

She took the tape to a secretary, asked her to type it up as quickly as possible and pass copies of the transcripts to Alfons Hoffmann and Marianne Andrele. Then she collected a Walther P5 from the arms officer. He didn't say much and nor did Louise. She signed, took the Walther and the holster and thanked him. He nodded without looking at her. As she came out of the lift on the fourth floor her mobile rang. A Freiburg number she couldn't place. Don't answer, an inner voice told her.

She answered.

Richard Landen.

Why now?

Louise stopped, thought, he's not ringing from Günterstal. It's a Freiburg number, but not his, not the Günterstal one. Where's he calling from? And why *now*?

"Hello," she said. She sat on the floor, leaned against the wall, thought, why now?

"Is this a bad time?"

His voice sounded different from how she remembered it. Wearier, sadder. More wintry than summery. Yet another Landen, that made five now. She smiled. The first didactic and boring, the second engaged and erotic, the third secretive and depressing, the fourth surly and even more depressing, and now a weary, sad, fifth Landen. What an indecisive man! But perhaps this was precisely why she felt so drawn to him. This was a man who required a painstaking effort to find, even if he was standing right in front of you.

"Louise?"

"I've got to go into a meeting."

"O.K."

"We . . . You were at the Kanzan-an. Why?"

Landen cleared his throat. "I'll tell you another time. Shall we speak later? Or tomorrow?"

Later, tomorrow, she thought – the stupid old game. "Taro's dead, he froze to death on the Flaunser," she said, standing up.

"I know, it was in the paper. Terrible. I . . . I thought of you straight-away."

"Good. Are you free this evening?"

"Er . . . yes."

"And your wife?"

"She's in Japan, she won't be able to make it for this evening."

In spite of everything she had to laugh. Landen laughed too, in his new, sad, wintry way and they agreed to speak again in the afternoon. When she was standing outside the task force room, she thought: My winter man will follow my midnight man.

At least that was the plan.

Between fifty and sixty bodies sat in the task force room, a good half of whom belonged to Löbinger's D23 or Freiburg Kripo's national security squad. A handful were from Bermann's D11. The remainder included the officers who'd been there the day before and Marianne Andrele. Louise didn't know the others. The windows were open, traffic noise droned from below. Movable partition walls had been pushed aside, and P.C.s and laptops sat on the tables. Ring-binders, clear folders, papers were scattered around. The productive chaos of a task force, which she loved so dearly.

She stood by the door for a moment. Two men she'd never set eyes on before were arguing about Rottweil 1992. One was defending the lenient sentences handed out to the arms-dealing Croats, the other was condemning them. Someone from the department of public prosecution and another from the police authorities – it wasn't hard to guess. A third man she'd never seen before, wearing a blue shirt and chunky glasses, said tartly, "They always turn a blind eye to Croats, it's unbelievable."

The other two were silent.

Louise went over to the chair that Anne had kept free beside her. Several pairs of eyes followed her. Almenbroich gave a dour nod, Hoffmann raised a hand and smiled, and Bermann looked at her absentmindedly. She sat down. Someone was missing.

Heinrich Täschle.

"Thanks," she whispered to Anne.

"We really need some answers," the man in the blue shirt said, "as to why Kohl and Genscher felt compelled to recognise Croatia in 1991, even though the E.C., the U.N. and the U.S. weren't ready to, and even though it was clear that the Serbs wouldn't just stand back and watch it happen . . . So you start to ask yourself if there are some relationships that the authorities always turn a blind eye to, but of course you can't say this publicly because you know what would happen if you did."

"Look, I don't understand a word," Löbinger said. "What are you talking about? What happens if you say whatever publicly? And what has it got to do with our case?"

For a moment there was silence. Then Thomas Ilic said, "It pisses me off when you talk about Croatia."

One of the secretaries laughed in shock.

"It really does, it *pisses* me off."

Louise looked at Bermann, who made no move to intervene. His arms were crossed in front of his chest, his legs stretched out and he was calmly watching what was happening.

Helping out.

"Would someone please tell me what all this is about?" Löbinger said, irritated now.

"The German–Croatian past," Almenbroich said. "Not a topic for this meeting."

"Not for *any* meeting," the man in the blue shirt called out. "It's high time someone got to the bottom of it all, but nobody has any interest in doing so, because . . ."

"Correct," Almenbroich interrupted sharply. "Not here, not now."

The man in the blue shirt shut up.

Anne Wallmer gently nudged Louise, pointed in turn to each of the external men and whispered who they were. The public prosecutor from Rottweil, not the one from 1992, but the successor of the successor, and his assistant. Kripo from Stuttgart, Criminal Investigation Bureau from Stuttgart, including the man in the blue shirt. Then two intelligence officers from Stuttgart, who'd come with Almenbroich, as well as two federal intelligence officers, who had arrived without prior warning. Wallmer turned to Louise and rolled her eyes. Louise nodded. Chaos on the tables, chaos in the task force.

"What about Täschle?" she whispered.

"Täschle? Why?"

Louise fixed her eyes on Almenbroich, waited until he looked over and mouthed "Täschle". Almenbroich brought a fist to his right ear and shrugged. He hadn't got through to Täschle.

She shook her head – how was that possible?

Almenbroich shrugged – no idea.

She shook her head – what do you mean, no idea?

Almenbroich shrugged – later, Louise, O.K.? He shot her a menacing glance, then took out his handkerchief and wiped his brow.

"We know," one of the Stuttgart Kripo officers said to Thomas Ilic, "that at least two of the Croats charged at the time had contacts within the German neo-Nazi scene . . ."

"And because of that all Croats are fascists? Are you a fascist because you're German?"

"What *are* you talking about?"

"Anselm!" Almenbroich said impatiently.

"That's enough!" Löbinger barked.

"Anyway, those contacts couldn't be proved," the state prosecutor from Rottweil interjected. "It may be that some of them were professional dealers or had some contact with German neo-Nazis, but the overwhelming majority were simple people, patriots. I mean, back home they were at war for goodness' sake. Their motives were idealistic, not financial . . ."

"Who says?" Bermann asked nicely.

"The trial records. They found the weapons in suitcases amongst nappies and underwear . . ."

Löbinger thumped the table. "*Enough!* We'll go on with Peter Burg and Anne Wallmer."

"No," Almenbroich said. "We'll have a break."

Almenbroich left the room with the Stuttgart officers, Löbinger and Bermann, while Louise stood up and went to the open window. Where was Täschle? She took out her mobile and called his number. Engaged. When she tried the police station she was put on hold. Memories flooded back. Hollerer drenched in blood in the snow, Niksch dead in her arms . . . She told herself to think rationally; not all village police officers were in mortal danger if she helped them.

Louise found some photocopies in her pigeonhole and took them to the window. Information from C.S.I. on the second depot. No fingerprints, but a few really good, really fresh footprints, all from the same shoes. A heavy man, around 100 kilos, size 46 shoes. Trainers, worn profile. Photographs and sketches too. This wasn't a chance visit, certainly no hiker – the man had been to the depot several times over the past few days.

She looked through the other photocopies. Analyses and sketches of further footprints, computer printouts of fingerprints – the two men she'd encountered in the woods. No names, no photos – they didn't appear on Kripo, Europol or Interpol records.

All of a sudden Marianne Andrele was standing beside her holding a piece of paper. Louise cleared her throat. The transcript of the tape, the missing search warrant. "Did you believe Marion Söllien was in danger?" Andrele asked, her eyes on the transcript.

"*Could* have been."

Andrele looked up. "Why didn't you call me?"

"Well, I couldn't, it was . . ."

". . . engaged? Yes, I was on the phone all morning." Marianne Andrele grinned. "Paragraph 102 or 103 of the criminal procedure code?"

"103. Marion Söllien isn't a suspect."

"Why did you call in C.S.I.?"

"Fingerprints. The man she left her apartment with."

"Who was present while the apartment was searched?"

"The apartment wasn't really searched as such. We just went in and when it became clear that nobody was there I left."

"*We* went in, *I* left?"

"C.S.I. and two surveillance officers are still there."

Andrele made some notes, then nodded. "We'll sort this out."

"Thanks."

Another nod. Nothing personal. A purely professional requirement. "We're starting again," Marianne Andrele said.

Almenbroich, the Stuttgart officers, Bermann and Löbinger were back.

*

Löbinger reconvened the meeting. When everybody was sitting down he said, "Peter and Anne have spoken again to Berthold Meiering, the mayor of ..."

"Wait," Louise said. "What about Halid Trumic?"

Everybody looked at her, nobody answered. Then Anne Wallmer whispered, "We talked about him at the beginning."

"She'll read the protocol," Bermann said.

A few in the room laughed, Almenbroich smirked and Löbinger shook his head in resignation. There was movement, people reached for their coffee, they relaxed. A secretary stood up to close the window; Almenbroich and Hoffmann begged her not to.

"Right then, if I may?" Löbinger said.

"What about Trumic?" Louise said to the state prosecutor from Rottweil.

"Why do you think he's important?" Almenbroich said.

She looked at him. For a moment she was unsure whether or not to speak. Too many agencies, departments, people, strangers – the task force was too confusing, the informers too strange. She eyed the outsiders. What interests were the C.I.B., Stuttgart Kripo and Domestic Intelligence pursuing? And what was Almenbroich keeping to himself?

Intolerable questions, intolerable thoughts.

"We're listening, Luis," Löbinger said.

"Ernst Martin Söllien is important – Trumic's lawyer in the Rottweil trial," she said eventually, then told them about her conversation with Annelie Weininger and her visit to Marion Söllien's apartment. She sensed she didn't sound convincing. She was talking too quickly, skipping some things. A voice in her head said: Keep it vague.

Another voice said: What happened to Täschle?

She concluded with a short assessment that was no more convincing. Curious associations and connections – Rottweil 1992, Trumic, Söllien, the underground shelter, weapons depots, arms firms. Marion Söllien, who *might* represent a threat to someone who *might* have taken her away against her will. And the coincidence of the timings – she went into the law firm and a few minutes later the man appeared at Marion Söllien's. The weakest link in the chain of argument.

"I hardly dare ask," Löbinger said, "but did you have a search warrant?"

"She didn't, but we're sorting that one out," Andrele answered for Bonì. The Kripo officers from Stuttgart muttered some scornful remarks. The joys of provincial policing; things weren't so easy in the state capital. You call that a capital? Bermann asked. The Freiburg lot laughed.

Louise asked again what the story was with Halid Trumic.

"Does she always cause so much chaos?" one of the Stuttgart intelligence officers said.

"Only when she's sober," someone murmured.

From the silence in the room Louise could tell that she hadn't misheard. Now Almenbroich and all the others were swimming before her eyes and a dull roar filled her head. Beyond this she heard Anne Wallmer say, "What a prick." Almenbroich said that if he ever heard anything like that again inside police H.Q. he'd personally draft the disciplinary letter. It's not important, Louise thought. Bermann asked whether the remark might not constitute a statutory offence – slander, harassment, whatever. Andrele said she'd have to think about it. One of the Stuttgart officers said no offence had been meant. Hoffmann said that if she wanted to press charges she could cite him as a witness.

Once again a deathly silence descended on the room.

"I'd just like to know about Halid Trumic," Louise said.

"He hasn't been in Germany for more than ten years," Löbinger said.

Halid Trumic had been handed a fine in 1992 because he'd bought a few pistols from a Croatian weapons dealer. As soon as the trial was over he left Germany for the Balkans. The German authorities heard nothing more from him.

Louise blew her nose. Trumic no longer in Germany. Chaos only when she was sober. She nodded. Everything quite simple.

"Hold on," Wallmer said. "If Marion Söllien is in danger, doesn't that mean Riedinger is too."

Bermann leaped up. "Shit! We're sitting here gabbling away and forgetting to do our job. *Shit!* Heinz, Anne, Luis – in my office. Alfons, ring Kirchzarten and tell them to send a patrol car to the farm."

As Louise hurried out with the others her eyes caught Almenbroich's. He'd turned a shade paler. She knew what he was thinking: if Marion Söllien and Hannes Riedinger were in danger, then so was Heinrich Täschle.

Täschle, who they couldn't get hold of.

She drove with Bermann, Wallmer went with Schneider. In Bermann's office she'd spoken to Täschle's deputy, "Andy" Liebmann, for the first time. Now she was calling him again. He didn't know where Täschle was either, he hadn't heard from him since late yesterday afternoon. But now he knew that Louise had called Täschle last night. His wife was with relatives in Bavaria and Liebmann didn't want to ring her yet. Some officers had gone to Täschle's house earlier, rung the bell and peered through the windows. But no Täschle, nothing suspicious, no bicycle. Liebmann was planning to drop in later himself. "Keep me in the loop," Louise said.

"Sure, sure," Liebmann said agitatedly and hung up.

She shot a glance at Bermann. He'd called Riedinger's number and was now shaking his head. Riedinger, who knew that Söllien had wanted to buy the pasture. Täschle, who'd discovered this. They couldn't get hold of either of them.

She closed her eyes. Wondered why she hadn't thought her hypotheses through to their logical conclusion. Had she made the mistake of failing to take a lead seriously?

*

They turned off the main road. An officer from Kirchzarten radioed them. He spoke in a deep, tense voice, his Baden accent had a Swiss twang. "*We're driving around the farm now.*"

"Anything unusual? People? Cars?" Bermann said.

"*No, nothing.*"

"Riedinger?"

"*No sign of him.*"

"Put the siren on."

The siren wailed for a few seconds before being switched off again.

"*Nothing,*" the police officer said eventually.

"O.K. Wait on the approach road."

"*Shouldn't we go in?*"

"Wait for us."

"*O.K., we'll wait.*"

"Ask about the dog," Louise said.

"Can you see the dog anywhere?"

"*No, no dog.*"

Bermann hung up. "I don't like working with village constables," he growled. "Village constables and the serious crime squad don't go together."

Riedinger's farm came into sight. The patrol car was parked at the end of the dirt track, the officers hadn't got out. Louise asked Bermann whether he thought she'd made a mistake. Bermann said, no, he didn't think so this time.

When they turned onto the track Bermann said that *she* wasn't the problem, it was the task force. The task force was a threat to the investigation. Too big, too disparate, too many competing interests. The task force was paralysing itself. He admitted he'd lost track of everything. The individual groups within the task force, the different interests and motives, the outsiders, most of whose names he'd already forgotten, and the quality of the leads. "Far too much politics, far too little real work," he said.

Louise nodded. She'd never seen him so helpless and depressed. But she understood what he was thinking. Task forces represented Kripo's strength in concentrated form. Its most important and efficient resource. Task forces were sacred.

And Bermann's real passion.

"If you want to be the big boss you're going to have to come to terms with this sort of politicking," she said.

Bermann gave her a dark look.

They drove past the patrol car and stopped. Schneider parked behind the officers from Kirchzarten. Everybody got out and Bermann gave instructions. Three teams of two: him and one of the village constables, Schneider and the other one, and Louise and Anne Wallmer.

They set off.

The farm looked deserted. No Riedinger, no dog.

The front door stood open, like the day before. On the gravelled forecourt Louise could make out the tracks of different tyres, now obscured by the rain. The tracks from her Mégane might well be amongst them, as well as those from the car in which Bermann, Andrele and the others had arrived yesterday afternoon. Tracks from bicycle tyres ran straight across those of the cars. Täschle arriving, Täschle leaving. She pictured him drunk, yawning, groaning. Then pulling out his mobile, calling her, cycling while still on the phone.

What if he'd simply ended up in a ditch? Slept off his drunkenness? If he'd . . .

"Wait," she said. Everyone stopped and turned to her. She called the station and asked Liebmann to send a car up to Lisbeth Walter in Oberried.

"I can't do that!" Liebmann exclaimed. He didn't have any cars or officers left. The two patrol cars and all of his officers were out on duty. Somebody had to stay at the station, the station had to be manned, *he* had to stay there.

"Will you sort it out?" Louise said, irritated, ending the conversation.

"Bloody village constables," Bermann said.

"They're not all the same," Louise said.

They entered the house and secured the hallway, kitchen and sitting room. Bermann always at the front, as if trying to make up for lost time, wasted energy. No Riedinger and no dog on the ground floor. Bermann ordered Bonì and Wallmer to stay downstairs while he worked his way upstairs with the others. Waiting in the sitting room, Louise couldn't shake off the odd feeling that this was still a room for five people rather than just one. On a dresser there was a vast amount of crockery, a cupboard with shelves full of glasses, two large sofas, a huge table. She saw five people everywhere. A pendulum clock struck noon. Louise went into the kitchen and the same thought crept up on her: cupboards, deep freeze, fridge – everything for five people. On the fridge were photographs of the four who'd vanished. The pictures had a green tinge, the colours had faded. Two boys and a girl, all about twelve or thirteen, and a plain-looking woman in her thirties. She couldn't see Riedinger in any of the photos. As if he'd never been part of these four people's lives.

She paused. All of a sudden she noticed the silence. No footsteps, no voices, no orders. Just silence.

Wallmer came in. "They've found him."

Louise nodded, stroked one of the photos and thought, Now he's vanished from your lives altogether.

Hannes Riedinger had been shot in his sleep. Two bullets had left his face unrecognisable and a third had torn a hole in his chest. He'd slid out of bed and was lying on his side. Flies buzzed around the wounds. Not a game, Louise thought. She went back downstairs. The Riedinger she remembered was standing outside a barn with his eyes closed. A brutal man, a lonely man. She decided not to forget either of these.

*

140

Bermann and Schneider found the dog lying at a distance from the farmhouse with a hunk of raw meat in his teeth. The murderer had lured the dog away from the house, then shot him.

They waited inside for C.S.I. and the paramedics. Löbinger, Andrele, Almenbroich and other Kripo colleagues were on their way too, as well as a Special Support squad from Lahr who would assist in the search for Heinrich Täschle.

Bermann outlined the evidence. No signs of a break-in or a struggle. The murderer probably entered via the front door at night, went up to the bedroom, walked over to the bed, fired three shots, then left. They wouldn't find much more in the house apart from a few footprints and the projectiles.

But Boni felt her suspicions had been confirmed. Riedinger's murder suggested that her hunch about the link to Ernst Martin Söllien and his widow was right.

"Unless it's something completely different," Anne said.

"Don't make it more complicated," Bermann snapped.

Louise took a few steps away from the rest of them and called Andy Liebmann. He hadn't left the station, hadn't sent anyone up to Oberried and didn't have any news on Heinrich Täschle. His people were searching everywhere, he said, and gradually running out of ideas as to where to look next. "In Oberried, for God's sake!" Louise said. "Why would Henny be in Oberried?" Liebmann said. He didn't ask about Riedinger and Louise decided to leave it at that. Evidently a missing boss was enough; Liebmann wouldn't be able to cope with a murder on top of that.

Bermann hadn't been wrong in his assessment of village constables.

But Kripo had its fair share of those sorts of people too.

When the first vehicles from Freiburg turned onto the track that led to Riedinger's farm, she asked Bermann to give her the two Kirchzarten policemen, to which he agreed.

The officers didn't know Lisbeth Walter and had no idea of Täschle's connection to her. She described the route there and got into the front of the car. They drove along the country road in silence, Louise picturing Täschle and thinking about Riedinger. How senseless his death had been. The very thing the murderer had been trying to prevent had already happened: Riedinger had mentioned Söllien's interest in the pasture. Something from that morning came back to her. Somebody had panicked. Somebody who was disseminating the same information in different places wasn't thinking straight. Especially not if they needed a day and a half to kill a man who needed to be kept quiet.

People who panicked made mistakes.

Which was both good and bad.

They had just left Kirchzarten when the Satie tune rang out. It was Alfons Hoffmann, who said he and Elly had been reading the report of her conversation with Annelie Weininger. Something had occurred to Elly. It said in the report that, according to Annelie Weininger, Ernst Martin Söllien had been a member of an association that supported social projects in Pakistan, or was still supporting them.

"And?" Louise said.

"Halid Trumic was also involved with Pakistan." They'd talked about it in the task force meeting that morning, before she'd arrived. Early in 1993, N.A.T.O. had found weapons, jeeps and other war material on a freighter in the Adriatic. The cargo had come from Karachi via Istanbul and Trieste, and was obviously meant for the Bosnian Muslims. Halid Trumic's name had also cropped up in this context, but no proof of his involvement had been found. Hoffmann gave a weary laugh, which sounded like a dog panting. "Quite apart from the fact that nobody knew where he was anyway."

"*Our* Halid Trumic?"

"It's a possibility."

"Could you find out via his birth date?"

"We can try."

Oberried appeared before them. Above the village and to the left stood Lisbeth Walter's house. Louise pointed and the driver nodded. She could hear Hoffmann breathing heavily. In the background Elly asked about the name of the Pakistani association. Hoffmann repeated the question. "No idea," Louise said, "ask Annelie Weininger." She stifled a yawn, suddenly feeling terribly tired. The nights spent half awake, the strenuous days, the heat. The news of Taro's death, her struggles with her demons. The chase in the forest, the injury, the masked man. The midnight man gone, the winter man back, Riedinger dead, Täschle missing . . .

Far too much for a few days with so little sleep.

She closed her eyes.

Despite the tiredness a vague memory stirred in her consciousness. Pakistan had been mentioned some other time in the last few days, but when? And by whom? She tried to focus.

Pakistan.

"Luis?" Hoffmann said.

She opened her eyes. "Sorry." She thanked him, hung up and put the mobile back in her trouser pocket. And then in a flash it came back to her: Barbara Franke had talked about Pakistan. In the 1970s and '80s, Pakistani scientists had been trained at the nuclear research centre in Karlsruhe. And she'd mentioned a Freiburg engineer who'd shipped illegal chemical facilities to Pakistan.

First the Yugoslav War, now the Pakistani nuclear weapons programme. First a neo-Nazi–Croatian lead, now a Muslim one.

Far too much for a few days with little sleep.

She decided she was too tired to think about either lead in the next few minutes.

She told both officers to wait in the car and walked alone up the path to Lisbeth Walter's house. From a distance she could hear the tinkling of the piano. Boni recognised the piece, something Romantic –

Chopin, Schumann, maybe one of the Russians. Nobody answered when she knocked,. In her mind she pictured Lisbeth Walter sitting at the grand piano with Täschle listening on the sofa. One of the few days *with* Henny.

She made her way round to the back of the house through an overgrown garden. The door from the terrace into the sitting room was open. Lisbeth Walter was sitting at the piano and smiled when she noticed Louise, but kept playing.

The sofa was empty.

"So you're alright, how wonderful!" Lisbeth said. "Do come in, I'll be with you in a mo."

Louise entered and sat where Täschle ought to have been. Lisbeth apologised; she couldn't break off in the middle of a piece. Louise sank back into the cushions. Get up, she thought, look for him. But she didn't budge. The music, the smell of the sun, books, peace and tiredness prevented her.

And a strange feeling of relief which told her: Even if you can't see him, he's here.

Lisbeth closed the piano lid. "Rachmaninov, prelude number five." She sat in an armchair opposite Louise. "Beautiful piece, isn't it? Perhaps a touch banal in its need to communicate, in its up-front beauty. But it's mysterious too, because the right hand at times plays the theme in the middle register while a second melody appears in the upper register. Hard to play, I'll say that without any modesty." She grinned. "Part of that world I set against your real one. Now you tell me which is the more beautiful."

"Yours, at the moment."

"So you're saying sometimes it's one, sometimes the other?" Lisbeth lowered her gaze. "You may well be right, but I hope not."

There was a pause in conversation and Louise felt her heart beginning to race. "Is he here?"

Lisbeth looked up. "It's not what you think."

Louise wanted to smile but didn't have the energy. Relief was exhausting. But perhaps it was exhausting just trying to stop yourself from bursting into tears.

Finally her heart slowed. "No? Pity."

Lisbeth Walter smiled.

Later Lisbeth went upstairs to fetch Täschle, who was in the "reading room". Louise heard voices, footsteps, doors. She called Andy Liebmann and asked him to inform his officers and Bermann that Täschle had resurfaced. Lisbeth came back down, pottered in the kitchen, and soon she heard the sound of a kettle. Then Täschle appeared in the room, pale, dishevelled, huge, and muttered, "It's not what you think." Louise got up and gave him a hug, just to be sure that she really had returned from Lisbeth Walter's world to her own – at least momentarily.

That life with Henny would go on.

Then for a few minutes she made Henny's life hell. What had he been thinking? Half the district was looking for him! Kirchzarten police station was in a total flap! Andy Liebmann was beside himself, panicking! Täschle frowned. He didn't understand because he was missing the vital piece of information – he didn't know that Riedinger had been murdered. Nor did Louise fill him in. He deserved to be confused, he deserved this roasting. She ranted at him, but not for long, as she lacked the strength for this too. "Are you quite finished?" Täschle said eventually, sounding peeved. "Can *I* say something now?"

"Be my guest, I can't wait," Louise muttered.

Early that morning Heinrich Täschle had woken up in a roadside ditch near Kirchzarten. As he watched the sun rise he tried to work out what he was doing in that place at that time. His memory returned, albeit in fragments, only when he clambered onto his bike again. He had ridden into Kirchzarten, then carried on to Oberried – from Oberried you had a wonderful view of the valley and the residual alcohol in his blood demanded a wonderful view of the valley. "The morning sun," Täschle said, blushing, "when it rises over the Black Forest, well, from here it's . . . for God's sake, it's not what you think, please stop smirking." Louise assured him that she was far too tired to think or smirk. Lisbeth Walter jumped up to fetch the tea and Täschle kept mumbling away. Once he'd reached Oberried he felt ill, had thrown up by the side of the road and was too weak to cycle back home. It seemed only obvious to . . . He broke off.

Lisbeth Walter came back with the tea and poured out a cup for them all.

"That's what friends are for." Louise could sense Täschle's frostiness. *This* friendship would have to begin again from scratch.

"Precisely," Täschle said.

At some point she would have to tell him that Riedinger had been murdered, would have to shatter this unreal atmosphere of Lisbeth Walter's other world.

But not just yet.

She told him a few minutes later, as Lisbeth Walter refilled their cups. Täschle was visibly shaken; Lisbeth had no idea how to react. There they were, two worlds that were incompatible. Täschle knew at once what Riedinger's murder meant, implied, required, what could have happened to him the night before. Lisbeth Walter, on the other hand, was manifestly unable to piece together the fragments of reality. A man murdered? That in itself was inconceivable. And she in danger herself? Lisbeth shook her head and laughed scornfully, defending her world against intruders.

Louise outlined the wider picture. The Rottweil weapons in 1992, some of which had also been manufactured by Zavodi Crvena Zastava. Trumic, who in 1992 had been charged with the illegal procurement of firearms and defended by Söllien. Söllien, who wanted to buy the pasture off Riedinger almost ten years later. Marion Söllien, who may have known something and had disappeared.

Täschle sat there, looking grim. She guessed what was going through his head.

He looked at Lisbeth Walter. "You're not going for your night-time wanders anymore. In fact you're not going walking at all, at least not on your own."

"Let's not go over the top, Henny, eh?"

He stood up. "I've got to go to the station, but I'll be back. Till then, don't leave the house."

"Goodness gracious, he's being serious." Lisbeth sighed.

"He's right to be," Louise said.

"From your perspective, not from mine."

"Tell that to Hannes Riedinger, Lissi."

"Let's not get silly, Henny. Now, go and do your work. If you like you can come back this evening and watch the sunset from Oberried too."

Täschle puffed up his cheeks and turned to Louise. "Shall we go?"

Louise yawned and shook her head.

"I think she's going to stay a while," Lisbeth said.

"It's not what you think, Henny," Louise said.

Lisbeth Walter suppressed a grin and Täschle growled, "Give us a call when you want to be picked up."

"It might be a while," Louise said.

While Lisbeth Walter showed Täschle to the door, Louise closed her eyes. Riedinger, Söllien and Trumic all faded, while her father and the Russians appeared. Rachmaninov, another mysterious name which had left its mark on her childhood and adolescence – Rachmaninov from the sixties, Filbinger from the seventies. She'd sat in her bedroom listening to the powerful, wistful sounds of the Rachmaninov pieces her father played. At the piano, with Rachmaninov, the other Russians, Chopin and Liszt, he was for a time the man her mother believed she'd married. The man who ought to have been a '68er. A passionate, romantic fighter who ought to have rebelled at her side against bourgeois convention and the politics of his home country, France, as well as hers, Germany. In the end, however, he'd only wanted to be one thing: boringly middle class.

Not an Alsatian Camus.

At the end of the 1960s he stopped playing Rachmaninov. Filbinger had replaced Rachmaninov; it was that simple. At least in her memory.

"Come, my child," Lisbeth Walter whispered.

Louise opened her eyes. Lisbeth was standing beside her, her hand on Louise's arm. She got to her feet, allowed herself to be taken upstairs on trembling legs to the "reading room", to the bed on which Täschle had slept, let Lisbeth take off her shoes, help her out of her jeans and tuck her in.

She fell asleep within seconds.

Two hours later she was awake. Riedinger, Söllien and Trumic had returned.

The sky was overcast, it was hotter and not even a mild breeze rose from the valley. Lisbeth Walter had opened all the doors and windows on the ground floor, but that didn't seem to help much. Louise drank an iced coffee standing up and checked her mobile. Seven missed calls, but she didn't have the heart to listen to her voicemail in Lisbeth Walter's house.

Outside, somewhere in reality, a horn sounded.

The two women stepped out of the front door. Below them, at the beginning of the track, stood a car from Freiburg South police station. A policewoman waved; Louise waved back. In the distance, to the left of the narrow, grey band of road lay Riedinger's pasture; to the right, hidden by trees, his farmhouse. Two patrol cars turned from the track onto the country road, while a civilian car turned into the driveway. She wondered who might still be observing the activity at Riedinger's place.

Not those who had panicked.

The others. Who had blown up the weapons depot.

She turned around. "Täschle's right."

Lisbeth said nothing.

"Do it for him."

Lisbeth smiled softly. A yes? A no?

They hugged.

Definitely a yes.

The policewoman was very young, very shy and very sheepish. Louise remembered her, Lucie or Trudi, maybe even Susie. They'd had talked briefly in the winter, before she'd driven with Bermann to Liebau and found Hollerer and Niksch in the snow. They shook hands. "Susanne Wegener," the policewoman said.

"Susie."

"Yes."

As they drove through Oberried Louise listened to her messages. Four from Bermann, and one each from Richard Landen, Enni and Alfons Hoffmann. In between, Hollerer crying in the snow and Niksch dead in her arms.

Bermann asking if she was O.K. Richard Landen giving her his new landline number, which she already had, and a mobile number she didn't have, then repeating both. Bermann saying he'd heard from Täschle that she was alright, but couldn't she call in herself? Enni saying, "I'm at the sushi bar this evening, Inspector, do you want to come past?" Bermann saying that in addition to the main task force there was now a smaller one; she was on it and the first meeting was at six that evening in his office. Hoffmann saying, we've got something on the Pakistani association, Luis. Bermann saying, we've got trouble – for Christ's sake, call me.

She dialled his number.

"At last," Bermann grumbled.

"What sort of trouble? Because of me?"

"What else?"

An increasing number of individuals in the task force, Bermann told her, were calling for her exclusion. Almenbroich had received complaints. She was impeding the investigation by creating chaos, some were saying; others had said that she was a potential risk, given her history. She was stubborn, she lacked discipline and self-control. She was a loner, not a team player.

Louise laughed; Bermann didn't. "It's not that simple, Luis."

"It just reminds me of what you said in the winter."

"Listen, in the winter it was completely different."

"Does that mean you lot are on my side? You, Almenbroich, Anselm?"

"In principle, yes."

"In principle?"

"Like I say, it's not that simple."

"So what makes it complicated?"

"What's more important: an individual officer, or solving a serious crime?"

"Who's asking such stupid questions?"

"Anselm, for example."

"What about Almenbroich? And you?"

"We need to find a solution we can all live with."

"And have you already thought of one?"

Bermann sighed. "We have a *suggestion*."

"Which is?"

"You remain a member of the smaller task force, but stay out of the big meetings. Because you're chaotic and you lack discipline, obviously."

Bonì didn't respond. It really was quite simple.

The life before, the life after – the differences were not that obvious.

When she felt major anger and major sadness brewing, Louise hung up. Time for a little self-pity she thought, turning to Susie.

They passed Kirchzarten and turned onto the B31. Louise talked, Susie listened and both had tears running down their cheeks. They laughed in the tunnel, at the lights they blew their noses. When they drove on, Satie rang out. Alfons Hoffmann sounded excited, he had to tell her what he and Elly had found out, especially Elly, the crime squad's networks were incredible, and Elly's were even more incredible, you gave her a lead and then she'd have thousands of ideas as to who you could call and e-mail and how you could search the net, because Elly thought laterally and made progress, while he thought vertically and found himself in one dead end after another, incredible. Elly gave a cheerful laugh, Hoffmann gasped for breath. "Anyway," he said, "the association."

The association Annelie Weininger had mentioned was called the Association for the Promotion of German–Pakistani Friendship, or A.P.G.P.F. for short, and was based in Offenburg. From 1999 until his death in early 2002, Ernst Martin Söllien was one of its four board members; now the board comprised a teacher, a former member of the state parliament, a businessman and a Pakistani professor. A.P.G.P.F. was founded in 1988 with the aim of fostering democracy in Pakistan by means of projects in the fields of culture, human rights, women's equality, and it also lent support to agricultural reforestation and irrigation initiatives. For some years now the association had been receiving money from the Baden-Württemberg government's budget for "development cooperation". "They've even got an office in Islamabad. And guess who runs that."

They'd just turned into Heinrich-von-Stephan-Strasse. Susie slowed down and stopped outside police headquarters. They looked at each other and smiled, both embarrassed. Susie's eyes were still glistening with tears.

They shook hands.

"Well?" Hoffmann said impatiently.

Louise got out and headed for the entrance. Who ran the office in Islamabad? She stopped. "No . . ."

Halid Trumic.

III

The Pakistani Lead

8

Boni went into her new office and sat down at her new desk. The new wall opposite her seemed terrifyingly empty. A few raindrops splashed against the window pane, then the sun broke through the cloud cover. She put on Anatol's rectangular sunglasses, pushed off with her foot and spun around. Enni first, or Landen? It took her ten minutes to decide.

"I'm here till midnight, Inspector," Enni said.

"O.K."

"Where have you been for such . . ."

"Later, Enni, please."

She dialled Richard Landen's strange Freiburg number, which wasn't for the house in Günterstal and which he'd dictated to her three times that day. He answered at once. His voice sounded fresher than it had in the morning, but still wintery. Louise told him they could meet at eight if that suited him. Landen said it did. Where?

"Where are you?"

He gave the name of a street in the Wiehre district. She refrained from asking why he was in Wiehre and not in Günterstal, and whether it had anything to do with his wife.

"I . . ." Landen said.

"Let's talk later," Louise said.

They hung up. Today or never, she decided.

Then she filled the white wall opposite with Hollerer, Niksch and lots of blood. Two lives that had been extinguished because of her, even if Hollerer had survived. Louise was briefly overwhelmed by the urge to visit him at his sister's house in Konstanz. She hadn't spoken to him since that Sunday in the snow, and she hadn't seen him since her visit to the hospital. First the serious gun wounds, then depression. After regaining consciousness he refused to allow anyone to visit him and had asked for the telephone to be removed from his room. As soon as Hollerer was fit to travel he had himself transferred to a hospital in Kaiserslauten, then to a rehabilitation centre in the Odenwald.

Clear messages.

She would ignore them.

Before Louise left the office she carefully stuck the poster with the children in their red monks' robes back on the wall.

The door was open to Alfons Hoffmann's office, where the task force's two chief case officers had set up their headquarters, but the room was empty. Louise checked the time. Half past five, another half an hour until the first meeting of the new, smaller task force. Lots of new things happening in the last few days, she thought – hopefully everything would be alright.

The door to Bermann's office was locked. As were Wallmer's, Schneider's and Thomas Ilic's.

She called Bermann on his mobile. He was with Almenbroich. She could hear Löbinger's agitated voice, then other agitated voices chipped in. "Come up," Bermann ordered.

In Almenbroich's office were around twenty Kripo officers from D11 – Bermann – and D23 – Löbinger – as well as the two task force members from D13 – national security – Almenbroich and Heinrich Täschle. Almenbroich sat deathly pale in his armchair, the Kripo officers were dotted in small groups around the room, while Täschle stood on his own by the wall. She smiled at him and he nodded back, visibly relieved.

"Fill her in," Almenbroich said to nobody in particular.

The others fell silent and Bermann said, "The Bureau has taken over the case. The task force is disbanded, it's Stuttgart's case now."

"No! Has this got something to do with me too?"

"There were complaints," Almenbroich said, "but we don't need to take them seriously. It's all political, they needed an excuse."

"It's a pretty good one," Löbinger said hoarsely.

Almenbroich raised his eyebrows. "I prefer the argument that the case is too big for Freiburg because of its international dimensions."

"And we're just going to accept this?" Louise said.

"As you know, the Bureau is a higher authority, which means we *have* to accept it. You could have left out the 'just'."

She apologised. "So what now?"

"The Bureau will assemble its own task force," Löbinger said. His eyes wandered from her breasts to the bandage around her left upper arm and back to her breasts.

"Which of our officers will be on it?"

Almenbroich answered this time. From D11 the Bureau wanted Rolf Bermann, Heinz Schneider, Alfons Hoffmann and Anne Wallmer; from Löbinger's D23 Peter Burg and a handful of others; and a few Freiburg national security officers as well. What about Anselm? Louise wanted to ask, but left it. Evidently the Bureau didn't want Anselm Löbinger. She looked at him and their eyes met. If he was disappointed or annoyed he didn't let it show; he had a good grip on himself. That's why, she thought instinctively, *he* would become head of Division One rather than Bermann. Only the external appearance counted, not what went on inside.

The bells of the minster struck six o'clock. "Going-home time," someone whispered.

"I've got an idea," Louise said.

They had a murder, so D11 would undertake a murder investigation. Nothing more, nothing less. In collaboration with D23, of course, because the victim may well have had links to organised crime. And obviously D13 would be involved too, because vague leads pointed to neo-Nazi and/or foreign persons. They couldn't leave out Kirchzarten police station either, because the victim had lived in Kirchzarten.

Bermann gave a weary smile and clapped her on the shoulder. Almenbroich muttered that he'd put the next call from the Bureau president straight through to her. Hoffmann said she really should apply for the Division One job too. Louise responded by saying she'd have to serve as section head first.

They all fell silent, in shock.

She laughed softly. "I was being quite serious. Maybe the Bureau would agree to it."

Almenbroich shook his head.

Bonì didn't let up. They knew that the Bureau's investigation would start off in the wrong direction. A day or two would be wasted until the Pakistani lead was taken seriously. And now they had a murder. "We *have* to stay on the case."

"She's right," Hoffmann said, and Bermann nodded thoughtfully. Almenbroich conferred with him and Löbinger for a few minutes.

"Alright then," he said. "I'll talk to the president of the Bureau again and suggest that we divide up the investigation somehow. If nothing comes of it I'll call the director, and if nothing comes of that, then . . . we're definitely out of it."

"It would help to have a few convincing arguments for the Pakistani lead," Löbinger said.

Bermann clapped his hands. "Guys, it's high time we called it a day."

Almenbroich shook his head. "No, we're not going to work like that. We'll keep going with those aspects of the case that are already up and running, such as the search for Marion Söllien. We'll wait with everything else until the areas of responsibility have been properly defined." He looked at Louise. She wasn't sure how she should interpret this. Was it "that applies to you too" or "that doesn't apply to you"?

Whatever. Sometimes it wasn't a case of what you were *allowed* to do, but what was necessary.

*

In the corridor she explained to Täschle how to get to her office and asked him to wait there for her. Then she followed Hoffmann. "The names of the A.P.G.P.F. board members," she said once they were in his office. "Who's got them?"

"We do," Hoffmann said, handing her a printout.

"For insomnia."

"Fresh air always helps."

They grinned.

Elly walked in. "Elly," Hoffmann said with a smile. D11 and D23 seemed to be developing a closer relationship. An ageing, childless, male chief inspector and a young, ambitious female inspector – those sorts of things did happen. But, Louise thought, no man could worship a woman more innocently than Hoffmann. An eager adoration, mainly paternal, only marginally romantic. Louise didn't begrudge him this enthusiasm. Hoffmann's wife was an uprooted dragon from Lower Bavaria.

Bermann was sitting at his desk and seemed to be expecting her. He pointed to an envelope, which she took and felt the photographs through the paper. Bermann said he would take her to the Flaunser now, if she felt like it; she said she'd go on her own at some point. Louise was about to leave when Bermann started up again. Why, he asked, was she giving herself all this trouble? Why had she come back, why was she still doing this job, after everything that had happened over the past three years? Surely she knew she wouldn't be promoted any further within Kripo, at most she might make pay grade A12, but she'd never be detective chief superintendent, not as an ex-alcoholic, so why had she come back? Why didn't she find herself a nice man, start a family, she certainly wasn't too old, she was "really pretty" and with her professional experience and understanding of conflict she'd easily find another, less dangerous and quieter job with the police, in recruitment, for example, or youth crime. No-one here would ever forget what had happened to her, so why all the stress, frustration, danger, those wankers from Stuttgart . . . ? "I really don't understand you."

"I don't want to hear all that, Rolf," Louise said and left.

Täschle was standing by the window, gazing out at the evening sun. "So this is how things work at Kripo?" he said when she came in.

"Not always."

He shook his head. "I'm glad I stayed with the constabulary."

"Did you want to join Kripo?"

"Who doesn't at some time or other?"

She put the list of names and the envelope with the photographs of Taro on the desk and slumped down on the chair. Bermann's gloomy monologue was still echoing in her mind. He might look at her differently now, but he himself would never change. For the first time in years he was perceiving her as a woman, which meant recruitment or youth crime, but not serious crime.

Bonì wondered why she didn't feel angry. Perhaps because, in a weird way, Bermann had been talking about himself too.

"Goodness gracious," Täschle said out of the blue. "I mean, we're not in New York or Kabul, we're in *Freiburg*."

"The world has changed."

Täschle shook his head.

"Could you have imagined that 9/11 was partly organised in Hamburg?"

"*Freiburg*," Täschle said.

"That Islamic terrorists keep popping up in the Ulm/Neu-Ulm area?"

"What?" Täschle turned around.

"We know that some of Bin Laden's people were in the Ulm/Neu-Ulm area. Like Mohammed Atta and a leading Egyptian terrorist."

"But *Freiburg*."

Louise shrugged and Täschle turned back to the window. She checked the time. Just under two hours until her meeting with Landen.

Enough time to drive somewhere, question someone, do something to keep her demons at arm's length.

She picked up the list. A teacher, a former member of the regional parliament, a businessman, a Pakistani professor. Ehrenkirchen, Freiburg-St Georgen, Lahr, Freiburg-Stühlinger. At that moment she was most interested in the Pakistani professor. To Stühlinger, then.

Louise looked up. The evening sun was slanting in on the children from the Far East. The monks' robes seemed to glow.

She knew Täschle wouldn't come to Stühlinger. He wanted to see Lisbeth Walter, to find a way of guaranteeing her safety. "Drive carefully," she said.

"I didn't get here by car," Täschle said. "Your boss had me picked up."

"There, see how much Kripo values the village police."

Täschle smiled. "What about now? Is Kripo going to take me back home too?"

Täschle didn't say much on the drive. She could guess what was going through his mind. A murder on his patch. A murder that could have been prevented, perhaps. That threw up some awful questions.

And one in particular: Was Lisbeth Walter in danger?

"Rolf Bermann has sent a patrol car over to her," she said.

"Me too," Täschle said.

They left the main road and passed Riedinger's farm, Riedinger's pasture. Täschle didn't look left or right and seemed not to notice that a man was walking across the field from the scene of the fire. The ghost they'd been waiting for on Monday evening?

"Who's that?" Louise said, indicating the man.

Täschle turned his head.

Yes, it was Adam Baudy.

She thought about stopping, but decided to talk to him later.

"What actually happened to Riedinger? Where are his wife and children?"

Täschle didn't reply straightaway. Eventually he said, "In the sixties his father had F.M.D. on the farm and . . ."

"F.M.D.?"

"Foot and mouth disease. The last major outbreak was in the sixties, when tens of thousands of farms were affected. It was especially bad in Baden-Württemberg and Bavaria, and old Riedinger's farm was one of those worst hit. It didn't last even two weeks but all the cattle and most of the pigs contracted it and had to be culled. I remember hearing the animals wailing all day long, the healthy and the sick ones alike, and not just at Riedinger's – other farms were affected too. When the whole thing was over, Hannes' mother hanged herself because she couldn't cope with the distress and then the father . . . the father went crazy. He was the one who cut his wife down from the beams . . . Somehow he . . ." Täschle shrugged. "He forced Hannes to rebuild the farm with him. Dragged him out of bed in the mornings, beat him all day long until late into the night, then it all began again the following morning. I helped out sometimes, me and a few other lads used to work on the farm in the school holidays for a few marks. And they actually did it, they bred cattle and pigs, hired farmhands again, but Hannes swore that he'd sell the farm as soon as his old man was dead. Only the old man wouldn't die. He became ever more senile and comic, but he refused to croak. Hannes got married and had children, and all the while the old man sat in his attic room, gibbering away to himself and refusing to croak . . ."

Täschle stopped talking. They'd reached the police station.

"Anyway, when the children said in the early nineties that they wanted to take over the farm at some point, it was Hannes' turn to go crazy. He packed them off to boarding school in England, started selling livestock and land, and got rid of his workers. That's why Kathi left. To begin with the children still came home in the holidays, but at some point they stopped."

"What about old Riedinger? The father?"

"He didn't die until he was alone again with his son." Täschle shook his head. "Just imagine . . . What some people do with their lives." He shot her a glance. "You have to do something to stop that from happening, don't you? Don't you think?"

"That's why I got divorced. To change my life."

"Yes," Täschle said. "That's exactly what I mean."

He got out and went over to his bike. She watched him cycle away up the hill.

Sunset in Oberried.

The ghost had gone; the pasture lay deserted. She looked at her watch. An hour and a half until she met Landen. Boni took out her mobile and got Adam Baudy's address from Hoffmann. A road at the edge of town near the "Talvogtei". She drove back to the police station and followed the road she'd driven along with Täschle the previous day. She thought of Oberried and would have loved to watch Täschle and Lisbeth Walter as they tried to deal with what was happening to them.

A pretty blue house, a front garden with flower beds, the joinery in the yard. She knew from the files that Baudy had been divorced for two years; maybe this was why she was struck by how well kept the house and garden looked.

Baudy wasn't at home or in the workshop, but as Louise was going back to her car, she saw him coming down the path. She stopped and felt for her police I.D.

He was wearing a simple blue suit and a white shirt. His nose and forehead were red, his eyebrows singed. His cheeks were sunken and dark rings lurked below his eyes. "It's not worth going into the house," he said. "I'm being picked up in a minute."

"No problem. I won't be long."

They stayed outside on the path.

"How's your daughter?"

"Fine."

"What about you?" She raised her hand and touched her brow.

"Not too bad."

"Terrible what happened to Lew Gubnik."

He waited. Kept his distance. Maintained an expression of aloofness. Both of them knew that there was no longer any reason for him to be questioned by Kripo. His actions at the scene of the fire were being investigated by the professional fire service and the state prosecutor's office. And Baudy didn't have anything to do with the weapons or the fire.

All the same, something about Adam Baudy still nagged away at her. He'd been one of the first at the scene of the crime, and for that reason alone he was significant.

She asked him a couple of questions about the morning of the fire and Baudy said, I've already answered this, it's in my report. She nodded. The wrong questions, because Baudy could hear only one: the question of his responsibility. The wheels of bureaucracy were unrelenting. He'd taken his four-year-old daughter out on an operation, the explosions had taken him by surprise, he'd lost a man.

But she couldn't think of any other questions.

"I heard on the radio that Hannes Riedinger's dead," Baudy said.

"That's correct."

"They're saying he was murdered."

Louise nodded. Maybe she'd get somewhere this way, by answering questions rather than asking them.

"They're not saying whether the murder's got anything to do with the shed. With the weapons."

"We're assuming it has."

Baudy nodded.

"You didn't have a chance, Baudy."

He looked away. A Mercedes Sprinter carrying a number of men had stopped on the other side of the road. A window was wound down and she heard a lewd whistle coming from inside the car. "We're here," the driver called out.

"One sec, Paul."

Paul Feul, Louise thought. The guy who'd been on the first hose with Lew Gubnik. She stared at Feul; he returned her gaze. His face was reddened too, and his expression was similarly aloof. "You didn't have a chance," she said again, turning back to Baudy. "You can't anticipate what you don't think is possible. Someone setting up a weapons cache under a field in Kirchzarten and someone else blowing it sky high with Semtex – that's not possible."

Adam Baudy didn't respond.

"You can't anticipate that, Baudy."

"Are you finished? I'd like to go bowling now."

She sighed. "Sure. But I have one request: please have a think. What was strange? What doesn't fit? On the morning of the fire, the days leading up to it. What was the first thing that went through your mind? What did you hear in town later? What did your colleagues think and hear?" She gave him her card. "You can talk to Täschle if you'd prefer."

"I'm not talking to anybody," Baudy said, and he walked away.

Louise sat behind the Sprinter until they hit the B31, then she let it race off. Still an hour before her meeting with Landen. Enough time to visit Stühlinger. She picked up Hoffmann's list of A.P.G.P.F. board members. Dr Abdul Rashid, professor of physics at Albert Ludwig University's Institute of Physics, born in Pakistan in 1950, married to a German, two children. Studied in Karachi, Paris, Essen, Heisenberg Fellowship from the German Research Foundation. Lectureships in Freiburg, Zürich, Karlsruhe, Heidelberg and Paris. Post-doctoral degree in theoretical quantum dynamics.

Hoffmann had written "quatnum" and Louise thought the word fitting. Quatnum, a new process of nuclear fission, discovered by Professor Abdul Rashid from Pakistan.

Louise switched on the radio and heard an unbelievably clear, melancholic jazz trumpet. The music was fitting too. For Richard Landen, for the evening atmosphere in the Dreisamtal and Adam Baudy's ghost.

One of those few moments in life when everything fitted. Even a word that didn't exist.

Her good spirits lasted until she arrived in Stühlinger. When she got out she was confused. The memorably chaotic task force meeting that morning, then Riedinger's body, her fear for Täschle, later in the afternoon Freiburg's provisional removal from the case, and an hour ago the Bermannesque career talk. Not to mention the events of the past two days and nights, the puzzles, Almenbroich's secret, the skulking demons. And yet she was bursting with silliness and jollity. With this overkill of emotions and events she felt as if the ground were slipping from beneath her feet. The centre was missing, the eye of the storm: a functioning investigation team. As she turned into the street where Abdul Rashid lived it struck her that she was used to working on the fringes of, or even outside, the investigation team. But this time something was different. She'd lost her blind trust in colleagues, superiors and police authorities in general. There was only one person she still trusted unquestioningly: Rolf Bermann.

And that was a really horrible thought.

Abdul Rashid lived in a building that would have gone well with Günter's arty get-up. A narrow, attractive, late-nineteenth-century apartment building with small windows, balconies with plants and bistro tables: an advertising agency on the first floor, what must be four people in a flatshare on the second floor, and on the third, ABDUL RASHID / RENATE BENDER-RASHID.

On the other side of the road, a café with a large window, next to it a bookshop. She crossed and entered the café.

"Luis," Bermann said.

He was sitting at a table by the wall, with a view of Rashid's building. Louise smiled and was about to say, so this is what happens when you obey Almenbroich's orders, but decided against it when she caught the serious expression on his face. She sat down.

"I've fallen into their trap," Bermann said quietly.

"What do you mean?"

"Rashid's being watched."

"What? By the Bureau?"

Bermann shook his head. A white Audi A3 with French plates. No German authority would assume a French disguise. Bermann looked edgy; his eyes were narrow. They'd spotted him before he'd spotted them. They'd observed him, recognised him. How did they know who he was? When he noticed them, they drove off.

"How many?"

"Not so *loud*, Luis. Two men."

"Did you see their faces?"

"Only vaguely, the sun was in my eyes."

"So how do you know they were watching you?"

"I can't believe you're asking me that."

"Well, I'd like an answer."

"You get a hunch."

"Well I never!"

"Kiss my arse, Luis."

"Not in this life."

They took a moment to compose themselves, then Bermann filled her in. Having been dropped off by a patrol car nearby, he wandered past Rashid's house and stood by the bookshop window for a while. Then he went in, bought a book and came out again. Which is when he spotted the Audi.

"Have you got the reg.?"

"Like I told you, the sun was in my eyes."

A young waiter arrived. Louise ordered an espresso and tap water, Bermann a beer. He said, "This is something you're going to have to deal with now, Luis."

She gave him a poisonous grin. Such was living and working with Rolf Bermann.

*

They tried to make sense of this latest development. An Audi with French number plates, two men inside who *probably* had Abdul Rashid under surveillance and *probably* knew who Bermann was. Who *possibly* belonged to the group that had blown up the arsenal, simply because Rashid *possibly* belonged to the group that had stashed the arsenal. Bermann groaned. "Come on," Louise said, "let's go and pay Rashid a visit." He shook his head. They didn't know who they might bump into. No move tonight, Luis, we're going to wait.

Wait? Rolf Bermann?

They agreed that Louise would call the Franco-German Joint Centre for Police and Customs Cooperation the next day. Their French colleagues might be able to get some information on the Audi. They had to find out if the men in the car were with the French police.

"You know that they're in Kehl now?" Bermann said.

"Kehl? Not in Offenburg anymore?"

"They moved in February." Bermann sipped his beer. "You weren't with us in February."

"Really?"

"Yes."

She shrugged. "So if we're not going to knock on Rashid's door, what are we going to do?"

"I'm going home," Bermann said, nodding at the window. Rita Bermann was standing outside, waving. They waved back and Bermann stood up. Kindergarten parents' meeting. It was his turn as chair, so he couldn't miss it. And it was in his living room. "I'll be back around ten to relieve you."

Louise shook her head. "I'm meeting someone."

"Oh?"

She nodded. "Wait, Rolf. I'd really love to see Pham again."

Bermann sat down again. "Viktor."

"Viktor."

"I'll think about it. Are you meeting your Buddhist man later?"

"Yes."

Rita Bermann pointed to her watch and made dithering signs. Louise asked how she managed to stay so slim and beautiful, after four pregnancies. Bermann said, we work at it. "No move tonight, Luis," he reiterated.

She promised. Even though for a second she thought he was referring to Richard Landen rather than Abdul Rashid.

Heinz Schneider arrived soon afterwards. He was in a dark evening suit, which for him meant nothing more than the fact that it was evening. Bermann had told him only the essentials; Louise filled in the gaps. "So just sit here and see if anything happens?" he said.

She nodded.

"What if something *does* happen?"

"Call Rolf. Or me."

"I thought you had a date."

"Don't think, Heinz."

"Let me get this straight. If anything happens I call, otherwise I do nothing."

"Well, it depends on *what* happens."

Schneider rolled his eyes. When he was with Bermann he was a good policeman, but without him he was adrift, everyone knew that, you could adapt to it. But she'd never seen him as lost as now, struck down by the virus of uncertainty.

Placing a hand on his shoulder, she stood up.

As Boni left the café she instinctively looked around. No Audi A3 with French plates, just Schneider peering at her through the window.

9

She drove to Wiehre and parked near the street Landen had mentioned. She didn't know if she really wanted to look at the photographs of Taro's corpse. In her imagination he sat leaning against a tree with his eyes closed, overlooking the valley, monitoring her path. He was dead yet went on living.

That's how she wanted to think of him.

On the other hand, as Bermann had said a couple of days ago, you can't change it. It's the reality.

She opened the envelope and paused. The comforting illusion, the bitter reality. But this time in both cases it was about remembering, not forgetting.

This time it was an easy decision.

She closed the envelope.

A few minutes later she was standing face to face with Richard Landen and had to make another decision: should she throw her arms around him straightaway, or leave it till later?

"You've changed, you and your car," he said with a smile.

"We spent a bit of time in France, and look what happened."

They shook hands.

He had changed too, visibly affected by the winter, thinner and with more grey hair. Tommo in Japan, Landen here, even though they would be parents in a few days or weeks. It allowed for all sorts of interpretations.

He pointed to her arm. "Were you injured?"

"Ran into a tree."

"That suits you somehow."

They laughed.

"What now?" she asked.

He suggested a restaurant around the corner. But not Japanese, she said. No, Landen said, Italian.

They walked there, neither saying a word. She sensed that their silence was a good sign. It meant that they were beyond small talk. No *How are you?*, no *Oh, not too bad, what about you?* Just silence, taking a run-up to get to the important stuff right away.

She switched off her mobile.

Landen pointed at a restaurant with a terrace.

"Fancy sitting outside?"

"I'd prefer it inside." Inside would be darker, fewer people, more intimacy, maybe candles and music. Inside was better to get to the important stuff right away.

Inside was perfect: they were the only customers.

They were handed menus, they ordered, were brought mineral water, toasted each other, were brought bruschette and began to eat. Once or twice Landen cleared his throat, and Louise sensed his unease. What does this woman want? What is she planning? Is she going to throw herself at me? *When* is she finally going to throw herself at me? She suppressed a smile. Give him time, she thought, spearing the bruschetta with her fork, give *yourself* time. Months had passed, both of them had changed, did she still want him? "So, how are you?"

"Oh, not too bad, what about you?"

Yes, she did still want him.

A waiter cleared away their starter plates while another brought small portions of pasta. That looks *fantastic*, Landen said, a little too cheerfully. Time to get to the important stuff, Boní thought. Putting her fork down, she said, "There's something I have to ask you. Why are you here rather than in Japan? Why are you in Wiehre rather than in Günterstal? And why were you at the Kanzan-an?"

Landen raised his eyebrows. "Why were *you* at the Kanzan-an? Did you have an alcohol problem? Do you still have one?"

"Those are tough questions . . ."

He smiled pugnaciously. "Let me start with a simpler one then. Tell me about the case you're working on at the moment."

She sighed. Evidently the path to the important stuff led via banalities.

Landen was impressed all the same. He'd read about the weapons discovery in the newspaper, but hadn't taken it very seriously. Not gun obsessives, but an international network and now even a murder? He wanted to know what they had found out, which leads they were pursuing and, more generally, how you set about an investigation such as this. She told him what she could, remaining vague when she had to. But she was pleased that he was interested. "So how are you going to manage that?" he asked. "How will you cope with such burdens? Murder, arms dealing, stress . . ."

They stopped eating and looked at each other. A fairly harmless question, Louise decided, so a harmless answer would suffice. "Oh, you get through it somehow. For a few days I'm wired, then hopefully the case is solved." She shrugged.

"In winter I had the impression that you . . ."

"Impressions can be deceptive."

"You don't want to talk about it?"

"What?"

"You know what I mean."

"Somehow you were more discreet in the winter."

"A lot has happened since."

"Such as?"

Landen pushed his fork around his plate. "This and that."

Louise smiled. "You don't want to talk about it?"

"Eat up, the pasta's getting cold." Landen was smiling too.

She puffed her cheeks. A nice game, but it didn't get you to the important stuff, not now nor later. "Surely the question," she said, "is why are we here? What do we really want? Food? No. Then what? And how do we get to what we want? Do we have to spend hours eating before we do what we want? Do we have to start by doing what we don't want so we can then do what we do want?"

Landen cleared his throat. "What *do* we want?"

This *wasn't* a harmless question, which was probably why she found it so difficult to answer. "I think you know what I mean," she said after a moment.

"In the winter you were less discreet."

"Are we going to start this all over again?"

Landen smiled dully. "Alright then, let's talk candidly. In a few days' time I'm flying out for the birth ..."

"That's not what I want to hear, Rich."

"... for the birth of our ... Where does the 'Rich' come from?"

"That little punk girl back in winter. Selly."

"Oh, yes. Well, she's the only person who calls me that."

"By the way, how are Selly's mother and the lama in India?"

Landen started eating again. With his mouth full he said, "So I'm flying out to Japan at the beginning of August for the birth of my son, and ..."

"A son? How sweet. Have you chosen a name already? Kawasaki? Harakiri?"

"... and at the beginning of September I'm coming back. Without Shizu and without our son."

"Without? Meaning?"

"Meaning the two of them are going to live in Japan and I'll be in Germany."

"Sounds like a fabulous, modern, multicultural solution." She laughed.

"It's more like a multicultural separation," Landen said.

A simple, neat story – no humiliation or disasters, as in Boni's case. After a few years in Germany Tommo had realised that she wasn't coping with the life here. And Landen realised he felt surprisingly comfortable with the idea of a separation. The only complication was the fact that Tommo was pregnant. One's own child at the other end of the world? "I'd imagined my life would pan out differently," Landen said. One's life plans in ruins, she thought, unspectacular disasters.

One waiter removed the empty pasta dishes while the other brought the *secondi*. "What do Buddhists do when they separate?" Louise asked. "I mean, how do they deal with it?"

"I don't know."

They gazed at each other in silence. It occurred to Louise that Landen's ideas about crisis management were likely to be different from hers. No distractions, just conscious mourning. If not the Buddhist way, then the psychological one. Which also meant: no new relationship until the old one had been properly processed.

She groaned inwardly. She'd hit upon the wrong man.

But there remained the question of whether the wrong man might not, in a weird way, be the right one.

Buddhism, the next unspectacular disaster. They were now on their espressos. Louise had abandoned her plans for the evening, suppressed her disappointment and switched her mobile back on. Landen told her that over the past few weeks he'd been wondering to what extent all the Buddhist and Japanese interest in his life was connected to his wife. What did it mean to him beyond being together with her?

"But it meant something to you before."

"Now it's inextricably linked to Shizu, though, which is why I'm wondering what's going to happen when we're no longer married."

"Because it reminds you of her?"

"That too, but not only that. I can imagine myself seeing it through different eyes when we're no longer together. Sounds a bit like an academic problem, doesn't it?"

"Certainly does."

"It's still a problem, though."

"Is that why you're living in Wiehre rather than Günterstal?"

"Partly." He'd been finding Günterstal uncomfortable. Too much Japanese and Buddhist stuff, the failure of this part of his life perceptible in every nook and cranny. All those questions, those unexplained elements. The past, the future. He slept badly in Günterstal and didn't enjoy the waking hours there either. Günterstal fuelled bouts of depression.

Louise talked about Niksch and Günterstal. About the kitchen she hadn't been able to enter after Niksch's death.

"That's why you didn't want to eat with us that time."

She nodded.

"Which means you'd never visit me there?"

"Let's just say I'd never cook anything for you in Günterstal."

They laughed.

Louise felt for her mobile and switched it off again. A waiter was at their table, talking to Landen with animated gestures. Landen said something, the short man said something and turned to her, grappa from Bassano, sheer poetry. She nodded, only she could be the judge of that.

"*Salute*," the man said and left.

She stared at the glass in front of her. What now?

Drink it, a voice in her head replied. A glass between romantics, what harm could that do?

No harm, she thought. A tiny glass of grappa with Richard Landen – really nothing wrong in that. On the contrary, it loosens the tongue, eyes, hands. It helps you get to the important stuff. And after all it's only *one* glass.

Not even that. A *thimbleful.*

Today yes, she thought, but not tomorrow, that's a promise.

Don't worry about tomorrow. She knew about not drinking. She had not drinking under control. She'd prove it for the thousandth time tomorrow.

Louise leaned back and looked at Landen. But because of a man?

Not *because* of a man, the voice in her head said, but *with* a man.

She nodded. At least there was a distinction.

Landen said something, Louise raised an index finger – not now, she couldn't speak now, she needed to concentrate. She had to make this decision on her own.

Landen kept talking, his voice sounded insistent, but the voices inside her head drowned him out. A *tiny* thimbleful, she said. The first and last.

She closed her eyes. The last glass. When had she drunk her last glass of alcohol? Louise couldn't remember. In the end she'd just drunk straight from the bottle.

Opening her eyes, she said, "Right, back to your difficult questions."

Later, after she'd told him about her addiction, about Oberberg and her lonely battles at the Kanzan-an, they left the restaurant. It was dark outside but it hadn't cooled down. The heat hung in the tranquil streets of Wiehre. They walked to Anna-Platz and found themselves amongst pedestrians, couples, children out late. Landen looked thoughtful and anxious, which she was pleased about for the long term, but not now. He asked whether Zen had helped her "with it".

"With it?" she said. Why was it that whenever she was in his presence she felt grubby? In winter it had been Landen's pure teacup she hadn't been able to touch, in summer Landen's pure language . . . The man as a whole was too *pure* to sully himself with words that described her state.

To sully himself with a woman like her.

But perhaps that was what made him so attractive. Richard Landen, Elysium, salvation for Louise Bonì, swimming in the filth of her soul, her job, her life.

"With stopping," Landen said.

She frowned. "I was, I mean, I *am* an alcoholic – get used to it."

"I've understood that."

"Then spell it out."

"O.K., did Zen help when you were trying to give up drinking?"

"Well, sort of. No, it didn't. Or maybe a bit."

"Did you practise *zazen*?"

She laughed. "Far too demanding. And it puts pressure on your joints."

"You could always meditate in other ways."

"I'm too lazy and too impatient to meditate."

"So what did you do all that time at the Kanzan-an?"

"I went for walks, chatted to the roshi and Chiyono, drank tea, stroked the cat, slept, wrote letters, ripped up the letters, felt angry, froze, wept, felt homesick, and so on. Time passes. Now it's your turn. Why were you at the Kanzan-an?"

Landen hesitated. "I can't remember precisely."

"Imprecisely will do."

"Well, you had vanished from the face of the earth. And there was far too much that was still . . . unresolved."

"With regard to Taro?"

"With regard to Taro, to you, to me."

"My idiotic phone call."

"Oh, it wasn't so idiotic. You asked me questions I was asking myself too. Why was I flying to Japan? Did I still love my wife? Why did I . . . ? Those sorts of questions."

"Idiotic questions."

"I didn't find them so idiotic."

"Well I did, Rich."

"I'd rather you didn't call me that."

"Only if you don't call me 'Luis'." She told him about Bermann and how he pronounced the "u" with all the power of a bodybuilder. Landen laughed softly. He remembered Bermann, his virility and lack of politeness. His intimidating look, his thigh muscles, his moustache. "Pham loved the moustache," Louise said. She told Landen about Bermann and Pham, who was now called Viktor and in good hands amongst four other children.

A bit too much Bermann, she thought, for a conversation with Richard Landen.

Landen admitted it had crossed his mind that he and Shizu could have adopted Pham themselves. If she hadn't had her problems he would have asked her. Now Louise was having to fight back the tears, remembering the image that had come to her at some point over the winter: Richard Landen and Pham in a garden, looking at Louise as if they'd been waiting for her.

They crossed the Holbein district and stopped at a junction. Landen took her arm and pulled her to the right. Left took you to the road that led to Günterstal, right didn't. To the left, anything might happen; to the right Landen's hand was on her arm.

They walked back via Mercystrasse. Landen asked about Taro. What had happened to him at the Kanzan-an, why had he run away? Louise shrugged. They didn't know, they never would. He'd seen things he shouldn't have seen – Natchaya having sex with two men. He was discovered and beaten, then he escaped. He hadn't trusted anyone, not even the roshi. Why, they couldn't say. Not even the roshi had been able to answer this question. Perhaps Taro had run away from himself, too, Landen said. Doubts, questions about the meaning of life. Louise nodded. *In Taro doubt*, the Roshi had said. *Many questions.* Taro had been searching. Perhaps he'd found something inside himself that shocked him. Perhaps *that* was what he'd run away from that night.

"It begins with desire," Landen said.

"Yes," Louise said. "But what would life be without desire?"

*

A few minutes later they were back outside the house where Landen was currently living, subletting from a university colleague. His hand had gone, but the closeness was still there. She began to believe that they might get onto the important stuff after all. At some point, one day in the distant future, when everything had been processed and overcome, and a new space had opened up in his heart.

Landen said how impressed he was by her strength and persistence. Louise thanked him. This was followed by kisses on the cheek, some holding of breath, some clearing of the throat, some unavoidable small talk and a vague arrangement to meet again before Japan. And then they went their separate ways. Was it the right way or the wrong way? She couldn't yet say for sure.

Boni got into her car and followed the road to the next junction, then turned right. A major compliment each time they met – not bad. Last time it had been the *special gift of emotional sincerity*, today it was the *impressive strength and persistence*. And next time? How about *a body that even Kali would have envied*?

Elated, she took the next right turn and found herself in a small street parallel to Richard-Landen-Strasse. She slowed; some kids were playing football on the pavement. Just as she was about to accelerate again she caught sight of a white car parked by the side of the road.

An Audi A3 with French plates.

A cold shudder ran over her head and down her neck. She stifled the instinct to stop. Don't do anything out of the ordinary, she thought. Don't lose the slight advantage you have.

She drove a little faster, repeating the registration number silently to herself as she kept the Audi in her sights in the rear-view mirror.

Nobody approached the car, nobody got in.

How many white Audi A3s with French plates might there be in Freiburg right now? Her reason said: could be two or three. Her instinct said: only one.

Had she and Landen been followed on foot? Did they know where he lived?

And who were they?

Bonì turned onto the main road and lost sight of the Audi. She stopped at some lights. No Audi in the rear-view mirror. Where were they? At Richard Landen's? She would have to go back and make sure he wasn't in danger, even if that meant squandering her slight advantage.

The lights turned green.

At that moment the Audi appeared in her mirror.

10

Bermann was back, Schneider had gone home. On the small table stood five empty beer glasses and a full one. Boni sat down and pushed over the scrap of paper on which she'd jotted down the registration number. It took a moment for him to understand. "Did they follow you?" She nodded. Bermann slammed his fist onto the table. "And now they're back here?"

"I guess so. At some point I lost sight of them."

Bermann took out his mobile. Louise told him she'd already passed the registration on to the chief duty officer. "O.K. So what happened?"

She told him when and where she'd seen the Audi and they sat there in silence, staring at each other. Bermann's eyes were tired and reddened. Parents' meetings must be torture for him; the unsolved investigation did the rest. Heinz Schneider drank incredibly slowly, so four of the five empty glasses must be Bermann's. His voice didn't give anything away, only his eyes and shoulders that were hunched forwards a little.

"And here?" she said.

Abdul Rashid had come home by bike with a woman – probably his wife. Nobody watching, at least no-one visible from the café. Bermann laughed grimly.

"Do you think they know we know that they're here?"

"Maybe," Bermann said. "I'm no actor, they'll have realised I spotted them." He drank and burped.

"I'll drive to Kehl," she said. "Who knows how long it'll take if I just call them."

"That's not how it works. You can only do it over the phone. You . . ."

"This time it's going to work a bit differently."

" . . . call the Joint Centre, tell a German colleague what you want, he compiles a dossier, which he passes on to a French colleague, who processes the dossier, contacts the relevant French authorities, relays the results back to his German colleague and then he rings you back. Nobody drives there in person."

"Except me. I've always wanted to know what they do. Have you ever been there?"

Bermann shook his head.

"There you go. Freiburg Kripo wants to take a look at the Centre and so sends one of its experienced representatives. Should I pass on your regards?"

"At least take Illi with you, then."

"No, I'm going on my own."

Bermann's eyes glowed with sudden anger. "You *will* take Illi with you! You're not going there on your own!"

"They're colleagues, Rolf, not killers."

"We're not talking about Kehl, Luis."

She understood. Even before she had it clear in her own head, Bermann knew what she would do.

Pop into A.P.G.P.F. in Offenburg on the way to Kehl.

She rang Thomas Ilic and arranged to meet him outside police H.Q. at eight o'clock the following morning. Bermann gestured for her mobile and she gave it to him. Looking at Bonì, he said, "Be polite, cautious and undemonstrative, Illi. If nobody wants to talk to either of you, then leave. If they're only prepared to talk via lawyers, leave. Not a word about the weapons. You're just there to get an impression. If they complain to Almenbroich afterwards, we're fucked." He gave her back the mobile. She wiped it on her jeans; it reeked of beer. "Go home, Luis. Get a decent night's kip."

"I don't want to go home."

"And I don't want you here." He nodded towards the window and she followed his gaze. Standing outside was an unbelievably beautiful, unbelievably slim and unbelievably sexy blonde woman. "Keep that to yourself, understood?"

"Let me see Pham, then I'll keep it to myself."

"He's called *Viktor*, for fuck's sake."

"When we've got the guys with the weapons."

"Yeah, yeah, O.K."

Louise waved at the unbelievable blonde to come in.

"Go home," Bermann said again with a grim smile. "Unless you're interested in a threesome."

"Where's the man?" She laughed, stood up and walked past the blonde. The laugh caught in her throat. The woman was so unbelievable that she could understand Bermann, Mick and every other adulterer.

For a moment at least.

Boni drove north-west and waited in a small, unlit side street in Hochdorf, before driving back into town at around eleven. The Audi didn't reappear, nor any other suspicious vehicle. Where were they? She called Landen's Wiehre number; his university colleague answered. "Oh, it's *you*," he said, sounding oddly upbeat. Landen was sitting in the kitchen drinking red wine, deep in conversation. Buddhologists talking shop, you understand. Landen's colleague laughed. Now Landen was asking for the receiver, wanting to speak to her, and before she could refuse the colleague had taken the phone into the kitchen. "I'm not at my sharpest," Landen said apologetically.

She sighed and pulled over. Half-cut men sat everywhere, thinking about women, sexy blondes and sexy brunettes.

"What's she saying?" Landen's colleague asked in the background.

"Nothing," Landen said.

"Oh. Is she a Buddhist?"

"*Shunyata*, you remember," Landen said.

"No. Are you free tomorrow evening?"

"*Shunyata*, emptiness. Roshi Bukan ..."

"Let's speak tomorrow, then, Rich."

Bonì hung up. She hadn't stared into the grappa abyss a couple of hours ago only to talk to a sozzled man now.

She drove on. What now? She didn't want to go home; home was where her demons were waiting and she was far too exhausted for another battle today. Her eyes drifted across the city, alighting on tiny, illuminated rectangles that hovered high up in the darkness. One of them might be Günter's apartment, where perhaps at this moment he was sitting at his black table thinking about a woman too, the specialist from Karlsruhe who may have discovered what was going on inside his body, assuming it was in his body and not his soul.

She dialled his number; he didn't pick up.

In the end Louise went back home after all. She opened the windows, drew the curtains, got out of her jeans. There were two messages on her answerphone. Katrin Rein, the police academy psychologist, had a timid, minute-long rant about the fact that Louise had disappeared for three months, hadn't been in touch since her return, wasn't attending the A.A. meetings or seeing the therapist the clinic had recommended, or going to ...

At that point the answerphone had taken pity on her and cut off.

The second message was from an Estonian, wanting her to translate a certificate into Estonian.

When she sat on the loo in the bathroom she realised how exhausted she was. And when she looked in the mirror she could see it too.

She spent a moment or two peering down at the street through a gap in the curtains, looking out for an Audi, shoes protruding from an entranceway, the red glow of a cigarette, a masked man – but she saw nothing.

Nobody was watching her, nobody was keeping her company in her exhaustion and in the darkness.

*

At some point the telephone rang. She was sitting on the kitchen floor beneath the window, a full bottle of water between her knees, an empty bottle of water beside her, listening to the sounds of the city at night and the electronic melody of her mobile giving a rather harsh rendition of Vivaldi's "Spring". It was about midnight – maybe her midnight man was calling, but she thought that unlikely. It could be her winter man wanting to apologise for being drunk, he never usually drank, never drank too much, he didn't want her to get the wrong impression, in Elysium you drank for pleasure, not to forget, you drank with your nose, not with both hands, you were strong and pure, not weak and filthy . . .

Louise reached for her mobile on the work surface.

Günter.

"Did I wake you?"

"No, no."

Silence.

"So? How was Karlsruhe?"

Silence.

"Come on, Günter, tell me. What did they do in Karlsruhe?"

No answer.

O.K., she thought, I'll say nothing.

"I wasn't in Karlsruhe," Günter said.

The nausea. He had felt so unwell that he'd stayed in bed. Then the breathing problems started. The tumor had forced gastric acid up into his gullet, which had restricted the workings of his lungs. For an hour or two he hadn't been able to breathe properly, so he'd stayed in bed.

He'd go to Karlsruhe tomorrow or the day after.

If he could make a new appointment.

"Someone called," he said. "Left a message."

"Katrin Rein?"

"I don't know what that's about."

"Listen to what she has to say."

"She wants to come by tomorrow. I don't want strangers in my apartment."

"Listen to the message."

"I need an oncologist, not a psychiatrist."

"Psychologist."

"You know each other, don't you? She says she knows you."

"Yes."

"What's she like?"

"Very nice, very pretty, very young. Very competent. You just mustn't work her too hard or she'll curl up on your sofa and fall asleep."

"Did you meet her over the winter?"

"Yes."

"And? What did she do?"

"She showed me a way to, er . . . well, to get out of it."

"But you were a different case."

"Talk to her, Günter."

"What use to me is some psycho queen?"

"She helped me back then. It all started with her."

"The stopping?"

"Yes, the stopping started with her."

They laughed.

"I don't want it to start," Günter said.

"But you want it to stop."

The bells of Pauluskirche struck midnight and were joined by the bells of other churches. Today was coming to an end. Today was beginning.

Bonì lay on her side and drew her legs up. The skin of her bare legs was warm and soft; beneath her T-shirt it was damp with sweat. She closed her eyes and pictured the black apartment, Günter on the sofa, invisible in the darkness in his black outfit, apart from his face. A midnight man, as filthy and impure as she was, as close to the abyss as she was. With whom everything was so different, and yet somehow not so different either.

"Do you want to come over, Günter?"

Louise rolled onto her back. Was this a good idea? Sympathy, desire, the heat . . . Sex, to cool off and not to be alone with her demons.

Hers, his.

"I can't," Günter said. "I can't *go out.*"

He couldn't leave his apartment. He had tried – for Karlsruhe. But whenever he opened the door he found he could go no further. As if he were facing a wall. As if he *were* a wall. That's why he hadn't gone to Karlsruhe, he said. Because of the wall.

Louise sat up. She'd heard stories like this in Oberberg. Stories of people who, once on the street, were suddenly unable to take another step. Who couldn't leave their apartment until someone had given them a telephone number or a name, or had brought them to some-one or brought someone to them.

That's how it began. With a telephone number, a name, a person.

She stood up. "Please listen to what she has to say."

"Katrin Rein."

"Yes. Goodnight, Günter."

She put the telephone back in its dock. That's how it began. With a name, a person. Then other names, other people came. Then you were alone again, still fighting demons, still feeling alone, still calling midnight men.

The life before, the life after; not much had changed.

But she couldn't tell Günter that.

At around half past midnight she went to bed, and at around half past one she fell asleep. She woke up at four, drenched in sweat, and recalled lustful dreams in which she'd undressed in front of Richard Landen, Günter and Bermann's unbelievable blonde. They'd drunk bourbon with ice, grappa with ice and four or five ice-cold beers, and had licked and kissed each other along endless bodyscapes.

She got up. Her skin was red from the heat. As if the demons had taken possession of every fibre in her body.

She had ice, but nothing to drink.

Louise tried water, drank half a bottle. Water didn't help.

As she put down the bottle she glimpsed the activity plan, intended to help her combat the loneliness, the demons, the urge to drink, and sometimes it did actually help. She skimmed it. Already too late for most things. And none of the others would be any use.

The simplest way, she thought, wasn't written on the plan.

Drinking.

Somewhere she found an open packet of Mon Chéri with two chocolates left, two months beyond their best-before date. She placed the liqueurs on the kitchen table and stared at them, then threw one out of the window and ate the other.

The heat remained, the desire remained. She opened all the windows and got into the shower. She began to feel better beneath the cold water. She sat down, the water still running. In her head a thousand voices were screaming over one another. The demons were rejoicing, the other voices crying in horror. In her mind Louise saw the pure Richard Landen, her father, Rolf Bermann, dour, pale Almenbroich, and at a stroke she calmed down. Yes, she'd allowed herself a moment of weakness. She had done it.

And now she'd never do it again.

At least not today.

11

Boni was woken by the telephone. A quarter past six and she was lying naked on the sofa, the curtains billowing in the morning breeze. She was freezing. Everything looked the same, everything had changed.

"Shit," she said.

"Shit," Barbara Franke said.

"I can be with you in fifteen minutes."

"That's too late, let's do it another time."

"Don't be angry."

"I'm not, it's just that I've got an appointment. Are you in a bad way?"

"Don't know. No. How's my info coming along?"

"I'll fax it to your office. But I can tell you now there's not much, I've got the names of only three Uhlich clients." Barbara Franke listed them – large arms manufacturers, one German, one British, one French. Getting any more information was tricky. The firms themselves didn't want to say much, while Uhlich & Partners wouldn't say anything at all. "What's wrong with you?"

"Let's do that another time too."

"O.K. And I'll keep on at Uhlich." Barbara Franke was going to delve further but she couldn't promise anything. Louise was on the verge of telling her that the leads were now taking them in a different direction, but she simply nodded; she felt sick from talking.

The nodding didn't help either.

Louise took another shower, dragged herself to bed, then back into the bathroom and onto the sofa again. Her limbs felt heavy from the disappointment and exhaustion, and there was fear in the mix too. What would happen now? What biochemical substances had been coursing through her body since last night? What were they doing to her? Did it mean that all the battles she'd won over the past few months were now lost?

By seven o'clock she felt able to face breakfast. She had closed the windows, put on two jumpers and a hot-water bottle sat in her lap. But still she was freezing.

Bermann called when she was on her second cup of coffee. He was already at H.Q. No news, he said. Ilic had been in a car outside Rashid's apartment since four, and in the café since six, but nothing had happened. Abdul Rashid was reading the *Badische Zeitung*, Renate Bender-Rashid was out jogging.

No white Audi, no other suspicious-looking cars or people. But Bermann was convinced they were there and that something was going on at Rashid's place. The question was: what?

Bonì finished her cup. Bermann's furious energy fortified her against the disappointment and fear. She asked whether Hoffmann and Elly had found out any more about A.P.G.P.F. No, Bermann said. Hoffmann was spending the day at home, recovering from stress and the heat; Elly was out with colleagues. Löbinger had assigned his officers to other investigation teams until Stuttgart came to a decision. "I mean, he's looking to be chief of Division One and he doesn't want to get his fingers burned again before then." Bermann sounded both impressed and bitter. Anselm Löbinger knew what was important.

"He'll get the job, too," she murmured.

"Oh, really?"

"Because the truth is, you don't want it."

"Oh, really?"

"It's just a hunch. You're not a chief officer."

"You've made my day, Luis. Thanks for that," Bermann grunted.

But Bermann's day had been pretty lousy as it was. Since late yesterday evening he'd been trying to get hold of an acquaintance who worked at the Federal Criminal Police Office. If the F.C.P.O. had a liaison officer at the German embassy in Islamabad they could be put on the trail of A.P.G.P.F. and Trumic. But Bermann's acquaintance wasn't picking up any of his damn phones.

"We know someone else at the F.C.P.O., Rolf."

"Aren't you meeting Illi at eight o'clock? It's eight now, time you went."

"Do you want *me* to call her?"

No answer.

"Come on, give me her number."

Louise heard rustling. Bermann read out a number.

"Oh, Rollo," she said, then hung up.

She called on the way to police H.Q. "My heroine!" said Manuela Lang, one of Rolf Bermann's many old flames, the number of which was no doubt growing by the month.

"What do you mean 'my heroine'?"

"You must be the only policewoman in Freiburg who hasn't shagged Rollo."

Louise gave a hearty laugh.

The F.C.P.O. did in fact have a liaison officer at the German embassy in Islamabad and Manuela Lang promised to get in touch with him. Louise was grateful; the laughter had helped. "What time is it there now? Are they all still asleep?"

"They'll just be going to lunch."

When Louise told her it was urgent, Manuela Lang said it would be better to go via the Foreign Office. F.C.P.O. liaison officers tended to be overburdened with work and rather slow to respond. It helped if the call came from the Foreign Office.

"I don't know anyone there," Louise said.

"I do." Martina Lang chuckled. She'd married into the Foreign Office a few months earlier. A long-distance relationship with a politician – could you wish for anything better? When he had time for his wife he was with her. When he had no time for her, he was unbearable anyway. In Berlin he was a politician, in Wiesbaden a husband. "The others get the exterior, I get the core. I think I've done rather well for myself."

"Assuming he's a nice husband."

"He's robust. You know I like robust men."

Thomas Ilic was smoking outside H.Q. Jeans, blue shirt, jacket over his shoulder, crew cut and an expressionless pale face – a nondescript, silent man in the narrow strip of shadow; he didn't like the sun. "Sorry, the car wouldn't start," she said as he got in.

"We've got plenty of time now," Ilic said, putting a folder on the dashboard.

The half-Croatian Ilic and the half-French Bonì, she thought as she pulled away. Although they had a number of things in common, she found him slightly spooky. Those dark eyes with their aloof yet vigilant gaze. Nobody knew what was going on in his head. His outburst yesterday in the task force meeting had come as a complete shock to all.

They drove beneath the railway bridge. No white Audi in the rear-view mirror, or at least not one with French plates. But Louise wasn't surprised; the Audi must have been removed from the streets.

"Luis, the heating's on."

"I've got a cold."

"And you need the blower on too?"

"Well, maybe not the blower."

Without the blower it was very quiet and very cold.

They drove past Rieselfeld and Hohenzollernscher Wald and turned onto the motorway at Freiburg-Mitte. From time to time Ilic wiped his face with a tissue, but Louise was still freezing. The biochemical substances were transporting the cold into every fibre of her body. What else? Weakness? Addiction?

Fear.

"By the way," Ilic said, taking a sheet of paper from the folder. "Marion Söllien." He held out the black-and-white copy of a photograph. A short, laughing woman with a perm and another short, laughing woman with a perm, plus a dachshund.

"Which one?"

Ilic shrugged. It didn't really matter; you couldn't tell the two apart.

"Where did you get the photo from?"

"Her apartment." Bermann had sent Wallmer there yesterday evening and she'd found the photograph in the kitchen. Marion and her twin sister Heidi, the caretaker had said. Lives in Canada. They come for Christmas every year, Heidi and the dog. But why don't you ask the parents? They live just around the corner.

They exchanged glances.

Because in Stuttgart the Baden-Württemberg minister of the interior, the head of Freiburg Kripo and the president of the Baden-Württemburg Criminal Investigation Bureau were discussing the issue of jurisdiction.

Bermann called when they were near Emmendingen. "Can Illi hear me?"

She put her mobile in the hands-free cradle. "He can now."

The footprints C.S.I. had found at Riedinger's farm, on the stairs and in the bedroom, matched those at the second depot. The man with size 46 trainers who'd been in the forest above Lisbeth Walter's house had also been to Riedinger's farm. He'd gone up the stairs and into the bedroom.

No proof, but a clue.

Boni thought of the vague description of the man who'd taken Marion Söllien: tall, broad and dark. The same person?

"Call me," Bermann said and hung up.

They stopped at a service station near Lahr. Louise filled up and Ilic went into the restaurant. On the other side of the motorway lay the

Rhine, some way beyond the river was Sélestat. In the winter she'd set off from there into the mountains with Reiner Lederle, to watch their French colleagues storm the house belonging to Steiner, the Asile d'enfants doctor. Sélestat, St Dié and the Vosges – in her mind they were inextricably linked to the events of last winter. Other memories were overwritten, they faded out. Such as the fact that her father's family came from Gérardmer, and how for her the Vosges used to be inextricably linked to her father. How Germain had loved the Vosges, and until his death in 1983 had always spent a few days or weeks with their uncles, aunts and cousins in Gérardmer.

Is Germain with Auntie Natalie again?

Yes, *ma chère*, he's with Auntie Natalie.

Louise replaced the nozzle and her fuel cap. As she made her way to the till she glanced around discreetly. Half a dozen cars at the petrol pumps, a dozen in the car park. None that could be deemed suspicious.

She entered the shop, which was arctic from the air conditioning. Ilic waved to her from the restaurant and she pointed to the till. Her father, Germain, the uncles, aunts and cousins in Gérardmer – people from another time, another life. As if where they lived had been erased from her memory.

At the till her hands hovered for a second over the Mon Chéris. How absurd, she thought. How shocking, how shockingly absurd.

It occurred to her on the way back to the car that although the places might vanish, the people remained – while they were still alive.

"I'm going to need ten minutes in Kehl for a private matter."

Ilic nodded as if he'd been expecting this. Their mothers German, their fathers not – evidently that created a bond. She smiled, but felt uncomfortable at the sudden intimacy. An understanding between two people that needed no words was more intimate than sex.

They sat in the service station restaurant, drinking coffee and eating croissants.

"By the way," Ilic said, taking another sheet of paper from the folder.

Another photograph and a smattering of information. "Abdul Rashid," Louise read, rubbing her bare arms. A man with a bright, narrow face, bright, narrow eyes, narrow lips, and short, grey hair. A good-looking, distinguished, reserved man in his mid-fifties. His eyes stared pensively past the viewer.

Photographs, invisible faces, their opponents remained elusive. A lobbyist for the arms industry who'd died a year and a half ago. A convicted arms dealer who'd disappeared from the Balkans years ago, and had then resurfaced in Islamabad. Footprints on a staircase, traces of D.N.A. on beer bottles in the forest.

A masked man. A war that was over seven or eight years ago.

She looked up. Ilic was looking at her.

"Do you want to visit your father?"

"Well, we don't see each other that often, and last time, back in the winter, we argued. It's time I talked to him again."

Ilic nodded.

"Seeing as I'm in Kehl."

He was about to say something, but didn't. Keeping quiet eloquently, he was good at that, Louise thought.

Later Ilic rang their colleagues at Offenburg Kripo and told them what they were up to. No, they didn't need support, they weren't planning on interrogating anyone, just an informal chat with a secretary from the association, or whoever. "Another coffee?" Louise whispered, her teeth chattering. He nodded. She fetched more coffee, went back to the counter to get some sugar, then went back again to get milk. When she sat down she didn't feel quite so chilly. She clasped her hands around the cup and the warmth travelled as far as her wrists, where it petered out in the cold.

Ilic put his mobile away. "What's wrong with you?"

She shrugged and blinked away the tears forming in her eyes. "Could I borrow your jacket?"

"Are you cold?"

"Bloody frozen."

"They've got sweatshirts here."

"Sweatshirts?"

He nodded towards the shop. Louise went over to the F.C. Bayern sweatshirts, took a small and a medium, plus an F.C. Bayern scarf, and then her hands hovered over the Mon Chéris. How shockingly ridiculous, she thought, but her hands didn't hover over the spirits: a sign, perhaps, that she was through the worst.

On her way out of the shop she glimpsed the reflection of a face in the window. Eyes that appeared to be looking in her direction. A moment later the face was gone. She turned around: fifteen or twenty customers by the shelves, in front of the drinks coolers, at the two tills.

Ilic, peering over from the restaurant.

She returned to their table. One face amongst many, a fleeting, unintentional glance, movements behind glass, perfectly normal toing and froing . . .

But Bonì decided to trust her instincts. She'd noticed the face, which was all that counted.

She tossed the sweatshirts onto the table, ripped open the packaging and put on the small one followed by the medium one.

Why was she freezing so miserably? What was happening to her?

In Oberberg she'd read in an Alcoholics Anonymous handbook what the first glass – the first one *afterwards* – could mean: losing your job, home, health and perhaps ultimately your life.

"I watched the game in Belgrade; I was in Belgrade at the time," Ilic said, his eyes fixed on the sweatshirt.

"What game?"

"Red Star v. Bayern Munich, European Cup semi-final, return leg, April 24, 1991. Bayern were leading 2–1 till the ninetieth minute and had booked their place in the final. Then Augenthaler and Aumann managed to fabricate a truly comical own goal and Bayern were out. A few weeks later . . . We ought to go, we don't have a huge amount of time."

They abandoned their coffees and went outside into the heat and the cold. Ilic took off his jacket; Louise wrapped the scarf around her neck. The sweatshirts had a pungent reek of material and dye, and perspiration was accumulating beneath the scarf. Somewhere inside her body, at least, a hint of warmth had begun to materialise. "What happened a few weeks later?"

They got into the car.

"War," Ilic said.

Storm clouds had gathered to the west, over France. To the north-east, above the Baden wine road and Offenburg, hung a white haze. The only blue sky to be seen was in the rear-view mirror. The heating and the sweatshirts were doing their job; Bonì wasn't freezing anymore, and as her warmth returned so did her confidence and determination.

Maybe the thought of war had put everything into perspective.

"I'd seen the first leg in Munich and was planning to watch the return one in Belgrade," Ilic said. "I wanted them to lose."

"Who?"

"Bayern." He put the folder on the dashboard and folded his hands in his lap. "What a result that would be, I thought, to beat the great Bayern team. My father loved Red Star, but in 1990 the Krajina Serbs proclaimed autonomy, which is why he wanted Red Star to lose . . . but in a way he wanted Red Star to win too." He laughed. "Every goal made him angry."

"Who are the Krajina Serbs?"

"The Serbs who live in Krajina. Or lived. Many didn't come back."

Where was Krajina?

In Croatia, which was the problem. One of many. The enclave problem. The Serb enclaves in Croatia and Bosnia, the Croat enclaves in Bosnia.

Louise nodded. She had a vague memory of the enclaves. Safe areas and enclaves: key words from a European war.

Ilic said his father believed the war had begun in 1990, when the

Croatian Serbs established the Republika Srpska Krajina. Others said it had started as far back as 1980, when Tito died. Or with the Croatian Spring of 1974. With the Ustaša in 1941. In 1918 with the founding of the Kingdom of Serbs, Croats and Slovenes.

With the Battle of Kosovo in 1389, when the Christian Serbs were defeated by the Islamic Ottomans.

"1389? Please!"

"Or in 1054 with the schism between the Catholic and Orthodox Churches." Ilic shrugged. "It's complicated, there are so many different stories."

She nodded even though she didn't know the stories.

"Switch the heating off, would you, Luis?"

She smiled and turned the dial to zero.

"It's complicated," Ilic said again. "If you don't know who you want to win or when something started, then it's complicated."

"And if you don't know when something finished," Louise said.

They arrived in Offenburg and Illi navigated them to the centre. When they were at a traffic light he said it had been complicated in June 1991 too: parents in Stuttgart, sister in Belgrade, aunts, uncles and cousins in Zagreb and Banja Luka, and he, the "German son" on dirt tracks somewhere in Serbian Vojvodina with his Serb brother-in-law, heading for the Serbian–Croatian border at Vukovar.

Banja Luka, Vukovar, other key words from the Yugoslav War. Dubrovnik, Sarajevo. Gradually the memories returned.

But she couldn't remember what had happened in Banja Luka, Vukovar and Sarajevo.

Then Louise recalled those other names and terms that had really stamped these wars with their identity: ethnic cleansing, mass rape, mass graves, Milošević, Karadžić, N.A.T.O. bombardments. Genocide. Srebrenica, the failure of the U.N., the West. Later, The Hague.

They didn't form a complete whole. Not today, not back then either.

The lights went green, she drove on.

In the late summer of 1991, five or six elderly Croatian men sat in Ilic's parents' Stuttgart kitchen, cleaning even older pistols. On the Friday lunchtime they set off in his father's transporter for their homeland, where they fired their pistols until the magazines were empty. They were back in Stuttgart on the Monday morning, recounting tales of atrocities committed by the Croatian Serbs, Bosnian Serbs and Belgrade Serbs.

At some point they swapped the old pistols for newer ones.

"Rottweil 92," Ilic said. "Our colleagues didn't seize all of them."

In spite of everything, Louise couldn't help laughing.

It didn't get any less complicated. His sister came to Stuttgart, her husband went to Bosnia to join the war and later they divorced. In Banja Luka and elsewhere Croats fought with Muslims against Serbs, Croats with Serbs against Muslims, and Serbs with Muslims against Croats. His relatives fled, some died, the rest were expelled. Long before that, in December 1991, Germany recognised Croatia and Slovenia as sovereign states, earlier than had been agreed with the U.S., the U.N. and most other E.C. countries. Croatian radio stations played the song, "Thank you, Germany", cafés called themselves "Genscher". The old men in his parents' kitchen cried, "You see, we are right! The Germans know this and they're going to help us!"

Soon afterwards one of them was shot dead in Bosnia–Herzegovina. The others continued to join in the war at weekends. The Germans didn't help. Nobody helped.

Then the weekends weren't enough for the elderly men. They took holidays, home leave, leave of absence, Ilic's father joked. He urged his son to join them on holiday. But Ilic stayed in Stuttgart. He was a policeman, a German policeman. In the canteen at his station he talked of the atrocities committed by the Croatian Serbs, the Bosnian Serbs and the Belgrade Serbs.

They were beyond the town centre. Ilic was holding the map and looking out of the window.

Then, he said, things got even more complicated. People started saying that the Croats were committing war crimes too. They were breaking ceasefires, closing the borders to Muslim refugees from Bosnia, organising massacres of Krajina Serbs. One German newspaper wrote, "Croatia, the dangerous foster child." Tudjman and Milošević met in secret, allegedly to discuss carving up Bosnia–Herzegovina between them. Dreams of Greater Croatia, Greater Serbia? The same paper wrote that Croatia was increasingly becoming an ethnically pure state. Good old Franjo Tudjman and Milošević – "Spiritual twins"?

This didn't mitigate the Serbs' guilt, but now there was guilt on the Croat side too.

And ever more questions.

"I didn't want to listen," Ilic said.

"I can understand that."

"Sometimes you're German, sometimes not."

She looked at him.

"Sometimes you're German, sometimes not," Ilic said again.

Now they had passed through Offenburg and there were no more houses on either side of the road. For a few seconds a blue dot was visible in the rear-view mirror, then it was gone. They drove as far as Zell before turning around. "Straight ahead," Ilic said when they were back in town.

Sometimes you're German, she thought, and sometimes not. She'd always felt herself to be German, never French. Her father was French, and she'd avoided having anything in common with him.

A short time later the blue dot was for a split second back in Boni's rear-view mirror, somewhere on her retina, but her reactions were too slow, she saw only the recollection, the image in her memory, a blue dot which had moved behind them, one of many in the traffic, and yet she was certain that she'd seen this one twice in the past few minutes.

12

The A.P.G.P.F. office was to the south of the town centre. A narrow, treeless street, a light-blue building opposite a public car park. On the pavement a couple of passers-by and a jogger who from a distance reminded Louise of Richard Landen, because of his height and upright poise. Did Landen jog? Unlikely. It made you dirty, you *sweated*.

But thinking about him made her feel good.

She drove into the car park and turned to allow them a good view of the office. A glass door with a wooden frame, a display window with posters of Pakistan, a sign on the door. Louise screwed up her eyes to read it – TEMPORARILY CLOSED DUE TO ILLNESS.

"Shit."

Ilic leafed through the folder and dialled a telephone number. "Answerphone."

"Let's call Andrele."

"Pointless."

Louise looked at the sign, then at the posters. Desert landscapes, mountain landscapes. An old man with a beard and a white turban. A beautiful woman in a red dress with mirror embroidery. Beneath this, BALUCHISTAN in big letters. "Looks like a travel agent's. Call Andrele, Illi."

"She's not going to let us in there."

"Try."

He tried. It was a short conversation. "No," he said. "Come on, let's go to Kehl."

As Louise started the engine, Satie rang out on her mobile. A man with an incomprehensible name and a distant, stern voice. "What?"

she shouted, switching off the engine. The man repeated his name, still incomprehensible. All she could make out was "embassy".

"The police liaison in Islamabad," Ilic whispered.

"That was quick," Louise said.

"Don't expect too much," the man said through the ambient hissing. "I haven't got what you're after. But I do have something else. I assume your phone is secure?"

She grinned in surprise. "Of course."

"All the same, I can't give any names down the line."

"I understand."

"Yesterday lunchtime a Schengen visa was approved here at the embassy for a Pakistani couple. Both of them are scientists, geologists. The names and digital copies of their visa applications and declarations will be sent via encrypted e-mail to your station, and copies to the Foreign Office and the Federal Criminal Police. Have a look at the address of the person who's issued the invitation – Freiburg. I thought that might be of interest."

"Freiburg?" she repeated.

"Yes."

Ilic was scribbling on the back of a piece of paper. Louise's eyes followed the words in blue ink. "Have you got the name and address in Freiburg?"

"Not over the phone."

"When was the visa application made?"

"Yesterday morning."

"Are you telling me it was submitted yesterday morning and approved in the afternoon?"

"With scientists it's sometimes quick."

Ilic muttered something she couldn't quite hear. "But not *that* quick."

The liaison officer didn't reply.

"How long does it usually take for a visa application to be approved?"

"Upwards of three weeks."

"Is it possible to speed up the process? Does it help if you've got connections?"

No reply.

"I need the Freiburg name," Louise said.

"You'll get it by e-mail."

"Not good enough, I need it now."

Ilic touched her shoulder. Keep calm, remain polite. The man in Islamabad is our friend. We need friends in Islamabad. Shaking her head, she said, "The first name begins with 'A', the surname with 'R', the street begins with a 'G'."

No reply.

She looked at Ilic, who had raised his eyebrows. The invitation had been issued by Abdul Rashid.

"One more thing," the liaison officer said.

The Pakistani couple were booked on the 14.00 flight to Amsterdam. From there they were flying with Lufthansa to Frankfurt – scheduled arrival: 21.30 central European summer time.

This evening, Louise thought.

The Audi, Ilic wrote. They know.

They know the two are coming, she thought. How's that possible?

"I'll e-mail you the photos so you can identify them," the liaison officer said.

Ilic pointed his pen at the A.P.G.P.F. window. She understood. The posters. "Where do the two of them come from? Originally?"

"Just a moment."

They waited.

"Both from a place near Panjgur. South-west Pakistan."

"Baluchistan?"

"Baluchistan."

Louise thanked him. "Seeing as it's for Germany," the man said, before the connection was interrupted.

*

Bonì rang Marianne Andrele, while Ilic called Bermann. Once Andrele had spoken to her counterpart in Offenburg the search warrant was approved. Her colleague would be there in an hour, and Bermann was on his way too. They got out of the car and Louise pointed to a park on the other side of the main road. Ilic looked at his watch and nodded. Louise led the way, needing to talk, to recap. The more they uncovered, the more confusing the case became. An underground shelter, an arms depot that was blown up, a second one in the forest. Two men who had fled, the murder of Hannes Riedinger. The Yugoslav War, a Pakistan association. Halid Trumic in Islamabad. Abdul Rashid's address on the Schengen visa, two men in an Audi outside his house. Posters of Baluchistan, a married couple from Baluchistan travelling from Islamabad to Freiburg.

Zwingerpark was laid out with trees, fountains and flowers beside a narrow river. Ilic headed for a bench, but Louise shook her head. She needed to keep moving.

They walked in silence along the towering city wall. A white haze filled the sky. It was muggy, and finally Bonì felt warm. She removed first one Bayern sweatshirt, then the other. "The key figure in all this is Halid Trumic," she said eventually. "He was convicted in the '92 arms trial, where he was defended by Söllien. Later he was involved in arms dealing in the Balkans, and now he's running the A.P.G.P.F. office in Islamabad. He's the key figure."

"Yes," Ilic said.

"Let's turn to Rashid."

"Yes."

"Don't you like talking about cases?"

"I'm better at listening."

"I need to talk about it."

"It's perfect then."

She smiled. In the winter she'd seldom had the opportunity to discuss the case with colleagues; there had seldom been any around. Colleagues who'd wanted to talk to her.

Bonì went on. "Abdul Rashid, board member of A.P.G.P.F., professor of physics. Under surveillance by two men in an Audi with French number plates, and then his name crops up on the Schengen visa of a Pakistani couple arriving in Germany this evening. We're assuming that Rashid's being watched because they're coming."

"Yes."

"But we're not sure."

"No."

"No?"

"No, we're not sure."

"Because we don't know if they're actually coming to Freiburg."

"Yes. No."

"Don't say anything, Illi."

Ilic chuckled.

"If Rashid is under surveillance because of the couple from Islamabad, how do the people in the Audi know they're coming? What's the connection between them?"

"How do *we* know they're coming?" Ilic sucked his upper lip between his teeth. He was walking to her right, in the shade of the trees. Louise thought of 1991, saw the old men in the kitchen, Ilic's father begging him to come to Croatia to fight. She saw Ilic in the canteen of his Stuttgart police station, talking about Serb atrocities.

Sometimes you were German, sometimes not.

"And the connection?"

"We still don't know who the weapons were meant for."

"A Pakistani couple?"

"Why not? Weapons for a Croatian fruit importer, weapons for a Pakistani couple."

They turned back. Louise scanned the paths ahead. An old woman feeding pigeons and ducks, a few passers-by, nobody out of the ordinary. "Does your father import fruit?"

"He went bust when the embargo was put in place. He specialised in fruit from the Balkans . . . cherries, plums, raspberries, blackberries.

When the fruit stopped coming, that spelled the end for his business." Ilic stopped walking. "But it had its good side too."

The cherries, plums, raspberries and blackberries had been imported from Serbia.

They crossed the bridge and made for the light-blue building. When they were almost there Bermann called Ilic's mobile and said, are you already in? Well, *don't* go in. The plan's changed, move away. We mustn't arouse suspicion, mustn't scare anyone. We don't want the Pakistanis to turn back halfway because Kripo turned up at A.P.G.P.F. We want them to come to Freiburg, we want to know why they're coming and what they've got planned.

Louise shook her head. Waiting, waiting, waiting. First involuntarily, now voluntarily.

"He's right," Ilic said.

"Illi, we're looking for a *murderer*." She called Bermann herself. "We're looking for a murderer, we're looking for Marion Söllien, we've *got* to go in, Rolf."

"We're going to wait, Luis."

"I'm going in now."

"No, you're going to wait," Ilic muttered to her right.

"Wait!" Bermann screamed to her left.

The chorus of ditherers.

She bared her teeth and stopped at the A.P.G.P.F. window. Waiting, waiting, waiting. Of course Bermann was right in some way. But at the same time he was wrong.

The old man in the turban stared at Louise with his black eyes. The beautiful woman gazed past her into the distance.

Baluchistan.

Weapons for a Pakistani couple? For Pakistani terrorists? For Islamists? Who had wanted to stop the weapons getting into the hands of their intended recipients? Who was the masked man?

"Let's go back to the park and wait in the shade," Ilic said. He called Bermann and told him where to find them.

Through the window Bonì could make out shelves, more posters, a desk. The desk was in a mess. The illness must have struck like a bolt out of the blue.

What did A.P.G.P.F. do? They knew so little.

They sat on a park bench, Ilic silently leafing through his folder.

Louise rolled her eyes. Waiting and keeping quiet – not exactly her strengths.

She tried to relax. Breathed into her stomach, watched a mother pushing a pram, a jogger, two elderly men, two elderly women. Three girls, possibly students, sat on a patch of grass. A dog peed against a tree.

Plus pigeons and ducks, pigeons and ducks everywhere.

"Musharraf was in Germany recently," Ilic said. "But in Berlin, not Freiburg."

"Hmm," she said dozily. Musharraf in Germany? She tried to remember. Couldn't.

"Maybe there's a connection."

"When was that?"

"Beginning of July. You weren't back yet."

She nodded. She had still been at the Kanzan-an. Excited about Freiburg, dreading Freiburg, postponing her return over and over again. On one occasion Roshi Bukan had said, "We drink tea, we talk." But he hadn't said a word, just prepared tea in the ceremonious, long-winded Zen way and drunk it with her. She was convinced he'd sensed her excitement and her dread, yet he had said nothing. When Louise went to bed that night it crossed her mind that the excitement and dread might be both present and absent. But this thought didn't seem to be of any help to her. A few days later she drove away, still feeling the excitement and the dread.

Satie wrenched Bonì from her thoughts.

The distant voice, the incomprehensible name. She made signs to Ilic.

"The Baluchistan thing," the liaison officer said.

The consulate in Karachi was responsible for Baluchistan, not the embassy in Islamabad, so he'd called Karachi. Karachi said that three men from somewhere near Panjgur had applied for Schengen visas at the consulate yesterday morning and been issued them soon afterwards.

At 12.15 local time the men were on board Emirates flight EK 601 to Dubai. From Dubai an Emirates plane took off for Frankfurt at 14.10 local time. All three men were booked on that flight, which was due to land in Frankfurt at 19.00.

Not geologists this time, but irrigation experts.

And this time not a Freiburg address, but one in Emmendingen.

"I think you've got a problem on your hands," he said.

"I need *names*, for Christ's sake."

The names would only come via e-mail. Bonì cursed under her breath.

"One more thing," the liaison officer said. The three men and the married couple were all from the Jinnah tribe. "Heard of them?"

"Help me out."

The man laughed paternally.

The Jinnah were one of the many tribes of Baluchistan. Head of the tribe and the man who gave it its name was Khalid Jinnah, not related to the first president of Pakistan, Muhammad Ali Jinnah. The Jinnah settled near Panjgur in a desert fort and surrounding villages. Like the Bugti from Quetta they regularly skirmished with government troops. Musharraf's Pakistan was too America-friendly for their liking.

And Pakistan was unstable. A synthetic state, established in 1947 to keep Muslims and Hindus separate. The "land of the pure", and yet as artificial as its name: P was Punjab, A Afghan Province, K Kashmir, I Islam, S Sind and TAN Baluchistan.

She shook her head. The things you learned on a park bench in Offenburg on a day of waiting, waiting, waiting. She yawned.

"Am I boring you?"

"I assume you're getting at something specific."

"Indeed I am."

In Pakistan conflicts broke out repeatedly between the government and Islamic parties, tribes and regions. The fact that American soldiers and secret service agents were hunting members of the Taliban and Al-Qaeda in Baluchistan and elsewhere didn't make things any better. The Jinnah were traditional Muslims – not extremists, but fundamentalists.

"And that's where we come full circle," the liaison officer said. The Bosnian T., the Pakistani Jinnah. Like fellow Muslims from other countries, Jinnah also fought on the side of the Bosnian Muslims in the Yugoslav War.

The sky had grown dark; clouds had edged into the white. They got up from the bench and walked on. Louise told Ilic about the irrigation experts, the Jinnah in Baluchistan and in former Yugoslavia. She told him that they'd come full circle. Finally their opponents were tangible. Finally a story had materialised. Weapons from former Yugoslavia for the Baluchistani Jinnah. The weapons had been destroyed in a depot in Germany, the Jinnah were coming to Germany. Intersections in this network of contacts were Ernst Martin Söllien, Halid Trumic and individual members of A.P.G.P.F., or all of them.

"That's *one* story," she said.

"Yes."

"The other story is: someone takes Semtex to the weapons depot and blows it sky high. A masked man gives first aid. Two men in an Audi with French plates watch Abdul Rashid, recognise Rolf, follow me in Wiehre, then vanish without trace."

"Maybe not *the* other story, but one of many others."

"How about Riedinger's murderer? Which story does that belong to?"

"What stories?" Rolf Bermann asked behind them.

*

It was agreed that they would wait. In spite of the Jinnah, in spite of Baluchistan, in spite of Musharraf, or perhaps because of them. Their colleagues at Frankfurt Airport would monitor the aircraft from Dubai and Amsterdam, keep an eye on the Pakistanis and do nothing. Freiburg would wait for information, monitor the people from the association and likewise do nothing.

But Bermann was restless. He was finding the waiting difficult too, Louise thought. Bermann most of all.

They were heading for the park entrance.

"Is the guy trustworthy?" Bermann said.

Louise sighed inaudibly. "Which guy?"

"The liaison officer."

"We'll worry about that later."

"What's his name?"

"Impossible to make it out with all the crackling on the line," Ilic said.

"You don't have his name?"

"No," Louise said.

"It was a long-distance call, Rolf. The line was bad."

"And there was a storm in Islamabad."

"Shit," Bermann said. "You don't even have his *name*?"

"Call Manu, she can get it for you," Louise said.

"Talking of Manu," Ilic said, "we need to inform the F.C.P.O. and the Public Prosecutor General. And Domestic Intelligence."

"And Stuttgart," Louise said.

"Yes, yes, and Stuttgart." Bermann wiped sweat from his brow. His dark T-shirt was soaked through. Now she could smell it too.

"Have you heard from Almenbroich?"

"Stop jabbering on about Stuttgart and Almenbroich, would you Luis? I need to *think*." Bermann stopped, raised a hand, stared into the distance and outlined the situation. A couple from Islamabad, from the Jinnah tribe of Baluchistan, were on their way to see Rashid in Freiburg. Three men, also Jinnah, were on their way from Karachi to Emmendingen. The couple would land around half past nine in Frankfurt, the three men two and a half hours earlier.

She nodded even though he couldn't see her.

If the three men from Karachi took the intercity express from Frankfurt, Bermann said, they'd probably arrive in Emmendingen or Freiburg sometime between ten and eleven o'clock. The couple from Islamabad were unlikely to make the last intercity from Frankfurt Airport – if Bermann remembered correctly it left at 21.50.

Maybe they would hire a car.

Maybe they would all go in the same hire car.

Maybe they weren't going to Freiburg or Emmendingen at all. Maybe they were going somewhere quite different.

They walked on.

The surveillance squad was being assigned to deal with A.P.G.P.F. With immediate effect the four board members would be under twenty-four-hour observation – the teacher in Ehrenkirchen, the former member of the regional parliament in Freiburg St Georgen, the businessman in Lahr and Abdul Rashid in Stühlinger. By now they'd also discovered the identity of the remaining members of the association. There were three of them: a retired couple from Freiburg and the politician's mother. The retired couple had been living in their Mallorcan holiday home for several months, while the politician's mother was in a care home near Stuttgart.

"Stooges," Louise said.

"I don't know," Bermann said. "Last year the Mallorca pensioners were in Panjgur."

"Still, I mean, a retired couple on Mallorca."

"Rashid flies to Panjgur once a year. That politician . . ."

"Dr Johannes Mahr," Ilic said.

"He goes to Panjgur three times a year."

They stopped again at the entrance to the park. The wind had dropped completely. Louise was now sweating too. She looked up and saw the dark rainclouds still glowering in the white haze. But it wasn't raining.

Bermann had asked the Baden-Württemberg government foundation about A.P.G.P.F. Since 2000 the association had been receiving grants for projects in Beluchistan. Cultural projects, social projects, agricultural projects. "Versatile people," he said. "Women's equality, schools, reforestation, irrigation. Lots of irrigation. Panjgur and the surrounding area must be under water by now."

Nobody laughed.

"Do we know who set up A.P.G.P.F.?" Louise said.

Ilic leafed through his folder. The seven founding members were Johannes Mahr, Aziza Mahr, Wilhelmine Mahr, the couple on Mallorca, the teacher and Abdul Rashid.

"Who's Aziza? Mahr's wife?"

Ilic read on, then shook his head. Mahr's wife was called Susanne. They had two sons, but no daughter. Wilhelmine was Mahr's mother.

Aziza, Louise thought.

"Maybe he's been married before," Bermann said.

They went over to the car park.

"What now? Is there any point in still making enquiries at the Joint Centre?"

"No idea, Luis," Bermann said. "Find out. We've got plenty of time. Nothing's going to happen until ten this evening."

Ilic and Bonì looked at each other. Mothers German, fathers not – the children seemed to know what the other was thinking: let's hope Rolf is right.

13

O n the short drive to Kehl they hit thick traffic and were at a stand-still for several minutes. Individual raindrops as large as marbles splattered onto the windscreen. Louise's eyes darted between the rear-view and wing mirrors. One blue car after another, shadowy faces. Were they there? Unlikely. Why should anyone follow them to Kehl?

And yet . . . she felt she was being watched.

After-effects of the Mon Chéri? She smiled grimly.

"May I?" Ilic said, pointing to the cassette player. She nodded. It was new, but the cassette wasn't – Beethoven's "Für Elise" ground out of the speakers. Boni switched to the radio – French pop music. "Thanks," Ilic said with a grin.

By the time they got moving again the rain had stopped.

In Louise's memory Kehl was grey, inconsequential and stuffy. The German appendage to the French bijou city of Strasbourg on the other side of the Rhine. Maybe it was the circumstances – Kehl, her father's town.

Today she found it green, not unattractive and quite lively.

The last time she'd been here was nine years earlier, when Mick had wanted to meet her father. One year before the wedding, six years before the humiliations. They had got on well, the grey, inconsequential, stuffy father and the courteous, charming, relaxed fiancé with a "von" in his name. One wanted to get closer to his daughter, the other wanted to generate cast-iron trust. One failed in his goal, the other succeeded.

And that handsome young chap next to Lou in the photos – is that Germain? the fiancé said.

That's Germain, Herr von Kyburg, the father said.

I'd have *loved* to meet him, the fiancé said.

"Left up there," Ilic said. He'd taken a photocopy of a map of Kehl from his folder. Louise smiled. You didn't get lost walking with Henny, and you didn't get lost driving with Illi.

Just so long as no memories resurfaced to interrupt his navigation.

They were in a car park between two imposing four-storey buildings from the nineteenth century. "If they're so big, how come I know so little about them?" Louise muttered as she gazed at the sandstone-coloured façades.

"It's not just the Joint Centre in there."

"We could have done with them over the winter."

"You only had to ask."

"We could really have done with them."

Ilic pointed to the smaller of the two buildings and they headed for the entrance. "It's part of the Archduke Friedrich barracks. A hundred years ago the Baden engineer battalion was housed here."

"You've been doing your homework."

Ilic laughed. A few years ago he'd toyed with applying to the Joint Centre. The first binational authority in *one* building, day-to-day, cross-border cooperation – a nice idea, he'd thought.

"But?"

He shrugged. "The wrong border, the wrong country."

Ilic had arranged a meeting with a detective chief superintendent. A young female chief inspector took them to an office with two desks, two computers and two houseplants. "Oh, he's not here," she said, confused.

They waited in the corridor.

Louise closed her eyes. She knew she wouldn't be able to keep going for much longer. Far too much had happened in these past few days for her to cope with the restless nights she'd been having. She thought of Lisbeth Walter's "reading room" and the cosy bed with Täschle's warmth, of Rachmaninov and her father, of the 1960s, before she'd started to avoid his company. Of Germain, who'd ridden around the dining table on his new yellow bike.

How she longed for a rest in the 1960s. And if that wasn't going to be possible, then at Lisbeth Walter's.

She opened her eyes. "Why *does* the Joint Centre exist?"

"Good question," Ilic said, smiling. "If it weren't coming from the mouth of a police officer."

She nodded and yawned at the same time.

"It's because of the Schengen Agreement. With no borders any more, cooperation between police forces needs to be optimised. It took a while for the politicians to understand that. The border between Germany and France disappeared in 1995, but the Joint Centre wasn't set up until 1999."

Thomas Ilic seemed to be enjoying his little speech.

All in all, he said, around fifty officers from the border force, customs and police of both countries worked at the Centre. Their tasks were to facilitate a better flow of information, to assist with police investigations, demonstrations and the transport of radioactive waste, to coordinate surveillance and other operations, and to co-operate with the judiciary.

Team work in the border area.

"Sixty years ago you were still killing each other; now your security agencies are under the same roof. That's what you call coming to terms with the past. In the meantime we've started killing each other again."

Louise stifled a yawn and fixed her eyes on the window that looked out onto the larger of the two former barracks. The Europe Bridge was visible in a narrow gap between the houses. Far in the distance, on the other side of the Rhine, the sky was blue, the sun shining on her father's homeland.

She thought of Rachmaninov, of Germain on his yellow bike.

Is Germain with Auntie Natalie again?

Yes, *ma chère*, he's with Auntie Natalie.

When she stood beside Germain's grave in 1983 she swore she would never visit Auntie Natalie in Gérardmer again.

"Coming to terms with the past – that's a lesson we could learn from you," Ilic said. "But it's difficult when there are so many stories and questions and you don't know what's true and what's false. If you don't know what began when and what finished when . . ."

"Illi, I'm too tired for this kind of chat."

"When it's *complicated*," Ilic said. "It's not a chat, Luis, it's a monologue. When I'm hungry I need to talk."

"Would you like one of the broken biscuits from Kirchzarten police station?"

Ilic shook his head and went on talking.

Ten minutes later they were sitting in the little office, eating French biscuits, drinking still water and engaging in friendly small talk with Commandant Bertrand Allehuit, who'd "taken on" the meeting because the German colleague he shared the office with had an external appointment.

"Are you going to translate?" Ilic whispered. Bonì nodded.

"*Je vous en prie!*" Allehuit said with a smile, before switching to German, which he spoke flawlessly and without an accent. His voice was warm, earnest, wonderful. A gaunt man, early fifties, totally focused. Each time he peered at her over the top of his glasses, Louise could have sworn that the entire organisation, Allehuit included, existed for her alone.

"Great," she said. "Let's begin."

Allehuit was informed, was expecting her questions, knew the background, had answers ready. French police officers carrying out surveillance in a stolen car on German territory? No – that was very hard to imagine. And completely unnecessary, at least in the border region. After all, that's what the Joint Centre was for. He smiled.

"Stolen?" Louise said.

"Last Monday. The car belongs to an insurance rep from Marseille, who's since been interviewed by our colleagues from the Gendarmerie Nationale." Nothing suspicious, no obvious connections, no journeys to crisis areas, and no contacts that would link him to Pakistan. A victim, no perpetrator. A dead end.

Allehuit handed them copies of the documents from Marseille, which they skimmed. "What about the French secret service?"

"Anything's possible, but it's unlikely."

"The French secret service wouldn't steal a car with French number plates," Ilic said. "They'd nick one with German plates. They don't want to stand out so they steal a German car."

"I don't think they'd steal *any* car," Allehuit said gently.

"Pakistani spies?" Louise said.

Ilic and Allehuit both turned to her.

"That's a possibility too," Allehuit said eventually. I.S.I., Pakistani military intelligence, didn't have a great reputation. It was said that some of their number were close to the Taliban and Al-Qaeda, deliberately fanning the flames of the Kashmir conflict, and in the 1980s and '90s had – with the acquiescence of the C.I.A. – encouraged the production of heroin and opium in Afghanistan and Pakistan in order to finance the Afghani Mujahedeen struggle against the Soviets. "Now, what's true in all this and what's not . . ." Allehuit said, holding up his hands.

Louise frowned. "What interest could Pakistani or French intelligence have in a Pakistani . . ."

"Or German intelligence," Allehuit interjected.

" . . . or German intelligence have in a Pakistani national who lives in Freiburg?"

"What do you know about the Pakistani national?"

"Not a lot. We're still gathering information."

"It's just occurred to me that Musharraf was also in *Paris* in July," Ilic said. "He flew from Berlin to Paris. He was in Washington, London, Berlin and Paris."

"Are you thinking of a terrorist attack?" Allehuit said. "A plan that wasn't carried out?"

"What was Musharraf doing in Paris?" Louise said.

"Mirage jets," Ilic said.

"Amongst other things," Allehuit said.

"What else?"

Allehuit leaned back. Something had changed in his bright eyes. Sometimes I'm French, she thought, and sometimes not. So what am I now? "International recognition, closer economic ties, investment . . ." Allehuit said.

"But first and foremost Mirages," Ilic interrupted. "It's always the same."

Allehuit stared at him. "What's always the same?"

"Arms deals with dodgy heads of state."

"A large chunk of Pakistan's nuclear knowhow comes from Germany," Allehuit said.

Ilic raised his eyebrows. "How about India? What are you doing with India?"

"What about India?" Louise asked.

"This isn't going to get us anywhere," Allehuit said.

Ilic nodded. "You're right. I'm sorry."

"Is anyone going to tell me about India?"

Allehuit looked at her.

India, Pakistan's arch enemy. Like the U.S., France maintained military relations with both countries. A defence agreement with New Dehli provided for French military technology, investment by French arms firms and joint military exercises. Pakistan had fighter planes, submarines, anti-ship missiles, minesweepers and helicopters from France.

"You've also got the Russians, the Chinese, the British," Ilic said charitably.

Allehuit nodded. "And a few others."

"Reminds me of Croatia and Bosnia and suchlike," Louise said.

"And a few others," Ilic said.

"Yes," Allehuit said. "But that's not what we're here to discuss."

"Isn't it all connected somehow?" Louise said.

Allehuit accompanied them to the main entrance. He said goodbye to Ilic, then offered Louise his hand and said softly in French, "Four years ago I was at the same point you were at a few months back, Madame Bonì. I know how hard it is, but now I also know how much it's worth persisting. That's what I wanted to tell you. It's worth it."

She nodded, but said nothing. Word had got as far as Kehl.

Allehuit gave her an encouraging smile, kissed her on both cheeks and left.

They ate curry sausage with chips at a stand in the pedestrian zone. On the back of his photocopies Ilic jotted down the questions and answers that had arisen in the conversation with Allehuit. Louise followed the blue scribbles with her eyes, but her mind had returned to the Archduke Friedrich barracks and made itself comfortable in Allehuit's little office, listening to his wonderful voice, sensing his intense eyes on her, watching him deal with the German–French border issues, while also addressing hers.

14

When they were back in the car Ilic said he'd take the train to Freiburg so she could have more time with her father. "Nonsense," Louise said. "I need ten minutes, no more."

"It might take longer."

"It bloody well won't."

"Is he even there?"

"No idea."

"Give him a call."

"No, I'm *not* going to call. We'll drive to his apartment and if he's there you can wait ten minutes. If he's not, we'll drive on."

"What if you need more time?"

"We won't, for God's sake." She turned on the ignition.

Ilic persevered. They hadn't seen each other in months, hadn't even talked to one another. There was so much to say. They were father and daughter. They needed time.

"For *what*?"

"For you both."

They looked at each other, then burst out laughing at the same time. The half-Croat officer and his half-French colleague. They had a lot in common, but only the half-Croat was cheesy.

At least during the daytime.

Now she was standing outside the apartment block in which her father had lived for thirteen or fourteen years, and spent two of the ten minutes wondering whether she should actually ring the bell. What they needed to say to each other could be done over the telephone too.

Assuming it needed to be said at all.

Then came the anger at her father, who'd rewritten the family history because he wouldn't look the truth in the face. Arguments, insults, hysterical scenes between him and her mother? *No, no, Louise. You might say we had differing opinions.*

Ten ugly years erased, and with them all the suffering. Germain's despair, her despair.

No fisticuffs. No disasters.

No marital problems, just health problems.

Your mother was ill, Louise. Mentally ill.

Rubbish.

Very, very ill.

Such rubbish, Papa.

A different history, a different family.

She frowned. Telephoning would be better. They'd only quarrel.

But since she was already in Kehl . . .

She rang the bell. The door buzzed open, the intercom remained silent. Should she, or shouldn't she?

No, she thought, entering the hallway.

The door to her father's apartment was ajar. A boy leaned against the frame, eyeing her. "Hello," she said, surprised.

"Hello," the boy said.

Louise looked at the nameplate on the wall – BONÌ. Then she looked again at the boy. He was eight at most, with dark, curly hair and dark, sceptical eyes. He looked strangely familiar, but she was certain she'd never met him.

"I know who you are," the boy said.

"Oh really?"

He nodded.

"Go on then, tell me."

"You're Louise."

All of a sudden she felt queasy. Now she knew why he looked familiar. She knew that dark, curly hair and those dark, sceptical eyes.

She'd seen them on a different boy, in a different life.

She sat on the top stair, one hand on the banister. Her heart was pounding. From the remoteness of her memory she heard her father's voice. Germain? the voice called out. Germain's with Auntie Natalie, she wanted to reply, but no words came.

"We've got photos of you," the boy said.

She nodded. She and Germain by the banks of the Rhine. Germain on her father's shoulders, she on her mother's shoulders. She and Germain in Gérardmer. Photographs from a time before the disaster that had been erased.

Germain? her father said in her memory.

The boy blurred before her eyes. It was better this way; she didn't want to see him.

Louise felt a gentle touch. The boy had sat beside her.

"Don't you want to know who I am?"

She shook her head.

Then her father's voice again, much closer now, he spoke French, you mustn't tell him, for heaven's sake, you mustn't tell him, I beg you, don't tell him!

Later she stood at the window in her father's little kitchen, looking down onto a small park with pruned trees and colourful flowers, and listening to the silence in her head, the silence in the kitchen. He had remarried, had another son, he'd called this son Germain too, he'd never told her about his second wife and second son.

That was the whole story. A simple story. And at the same time very complicated.

Far too complicated.

"I've got to go, my colleague's waiting outside," she said.

"Chérie, please ..." her father said.

She turned around. They were sitting at the kitchen table, holding hands and staring at her: a little, grey, old man and a little, pale seven-year-old. Her father, her brother.

A *different* brother.

Too complicated for today, for these days. For this life. "I've got to go."

She sat at the other end of the table.

"Chérie," her father said. The boy said nothing. She couldn't look at him. The hair, the eyes ... Still, the rest was different.

Louise looked at her father instead. The disasters erased, death erased. Germain erased. And replaced just like that, seven years ago.

Louise was struck by the realisation that she liked her father in a rather indefinite way, and hated him in a very definite way. I've got to go, she thought, and stayed in her chair. *"Est-ce qu'il le sait?"*

Her father shook his head. Panic had flooded his eyes. *You mustn't tell him!* So that's what he'd meant. The other brother didn't know that she'd already had a brother called Germain. The lie was being spun further. The bogus history was being retold; the true one no longer existed.

Her history no longer existed. Everything had been erased. *She* had been erased.

Louise got up.

"Chérie," her father muttered.

In French she told him she didn't want to live like this, with all these secrets and lies; they would only give rise to further secrets and lies. Unsayable things, taboos, we're creating taboos, Papa, about our past, us, our identity. What good can ever come of this? Nothing, absolutely nothing. The lies and taboos will end up destroying us – no, I don't want to live like that. You've got to decide, Papa, either *our* history with me, or *your* history without me.

"Please sit down, Chérie."

"I've got to go now." She sat.

"Ask your brother what he's called, Chérie. What *else* he's called."

"I don't want to know."

Her father bent down to the boy. "Germain, tell your sister what else you're called. What your middle name is. You remember it, don't you?"

A strange glint was now in her father's eyes, his lips twitched into a smile. A vague memory stirred inside her. It was how he looked when he was proud.

Louise felt the eyes of the young boy on her. Reluctantly she looked at him. He seemed unsure; he'd stuck out his lower lip. Suddenly she felt sorry for him.

"Come on, Germain, tell her, please."

Now she understood what her father was getting at.

She nodded to the boy. Say it quietly. I'll be able to cope with that.

"Luis," the boy said.

Germain Luis Boní. Here they all were, reunited in the new, bogus history. All erased.

She covered her eyes with her hands and began to cry.

Ilic came to the rescue. "I'll take the train."

"I'm coming down." She put away her mobile, blew her nose and stood up.

"But Chérie," her father said, "you can't leave now. There's so much still to talk about. You have to meet Karin, Germain's mother, and I bet Germain would like to show his big sister his toys . . ."

Germain.

Louise shook her head. "It's too complicated, it's all too complicated for me." She eyed the boy, whose bottom lip slid left, then right, his gaze fixed on her all the while. She sighed. "Will you take me to the door?"

He nodded.

"Bye-bye, Papa."

"Bye-bye, Chérie."

"Chérie, Chérie, for God's sake drop this bloody 'Chérie'!"

"I'm sorry."

"Chérie, Chérie – Jesus!"

The boy took her into the hallway and opened the front door. She tapped him on the shoulder. "Now you know what it's like to have a big sister. Not so great after all, is it? All they do is scream and howl."

The boy shrugged.

Louise turned around. Her father had followed them, fear in his eyes. *You mustn't tell him.* A bitter smile was on her lips. He'd made his decision. The bogus history would be maintained.

She tapped the boy on the shoulder again. "See you."

He nodded.

"Bye-bye," her father mumbled.

As Louise went down to the ground floor she thought of the dark, curly hair and the dark, sceptical eyes. She felt a brief, painful longing for the original, the *real* Germain.

When she stepped outside, her father's voice said in her head: but he's here, Chérie. He's back, thank God.

"Well?" Ilic said.

"Well," Louise said.

She started the car and drove off.

"I've got some news," Ilic said with a grin.

Almenbroich had rung Bermann and Bermann had rung him. They had reached an agreement in Stuttgart. The turning point had been the information from the liaison officer in Islamabad, whose identity had been verified by the F.C.P.O. and the Foreign Office. The areas of responsibility had been allocated as follows: Freiburg would focus on Baden and Pakistan, Kehl on Marseille, and Stuttgart on the rest of the world. Bermann, Löbinger, Hoffmann and Elly, plus four officers from the Baden-Württemberg Criminal Investigation Bureau and four from Stuttgart Kripo would form a contact group – the fulcrum between the individual authorities. They would report to Almenbroich, the president of the Bureau and the head of Stuttgart Kripo.

"Great," Louise said.

"Sounds reasonable to me."

"Sounds totally bureaucratic. In any case, by tomorrow morning the F.C.P.O. will have taken over the case and all this effort will have been in vain."

Ilic didn't respond.

"What else?"

"There's nothing else, Luis. That . . ."

"Illi, my name's 'Lou-*ise*', for Christ's sake. 'Lou-*ise*', with the stress on the 'i'. I'm a woman and women aren't called 'Luis'. At a pinch they might be called 'Luise', but not if it's the French version, as in my case. Only *men* are called 'Luis', O.K.? Men and little boys."

"O.K. I'm sorry."

She snorted. "So what's Stuttgart doing with the rest of the world?"

The Bureau and Stuttgart Kripo were now trying to pin down the sources of those sources that had attracted the attention of the Bureau, F.I.S. and the permanent secretary to the Croatian–neo-Nazi lead in the first place. Maybe the trails to these sources went in the same direction – to someone who'd panicked after the weapons depot had exploded.

"And Almenbroich?"

"He's on his way back to wait with us."

"Fantastic."

They drove along the Strasbourg road close to the Europe Bridge. Louise grumbled that she'd love to know who'd come up with this bloody "Luis"; she bet it was Rolf Bermann, right? Ilic sighed. Yes, Bermann was responsible for "Luis", it came from another time and had stuck. And now nobody was aware that she actually . . .

From another time?

When she was different. More difficult. The thing was . . . Bermann's father's Dobermann was called Luis. He was difficult too. Moody. Snappy.

"What a bitch of a day this is turning out to be!" she said.

"I did offer to take the train."

"Such an *arsehole* . . . What's *that* got to do with it?"

"You'd have had more time, and maybe you wouldn't have got so worked up."

"I didn't need more *time*, Illi, just a different father."

Instead of that, she thought, she now had a different brother.

Illi's mobile rang just before they got to Freiburg. Bermann again. Ilic said "No" and "Fine" and "Fine". Bonì said, "Give him to me." Putting his hand over the microphone, Ilic whispered, "Just calm down, would you? Now is not the time for a row with Rolf." She nodded wearily and said, "Just give him to me."

"Louise wants a word," Ilic said into the mobile, and slotted it into the hands-free cradle.

"Rolf, I need the afternoon off."

"Are you crazy? Today?"

"You can wait without me quite happily. I'm absolutely knackered and I need to *sleep*."

Bermann sounded more and more irritated. She'd been assigned to the A.P.G.P.F. observation team, only she had contact to the man in Islamabad, she had to look at the documents he'd e-mailed her, it was . . .

"But Illi can do that."

. . . *broad daylight*, she couldn't bloody well go home and sleep in *broad daylight* . . . Bermann cursed and ranted as if he'd been waiting for this moment. Ilic tried to calm the situation by saying, why not, nothing's going to happen till ten o'clock this evening anyway. Bermann cursed again and said, "I want you at H.Q. at five o'clock sharp."

She checked the time. "At five I'll still be asleep; I'll come at six," she said, and ended the call.

Ilic sighed, Louise shrugged. For a few days Bermann had been almost nice to her, but since yesterday the old Bermann had been in evidence again.

"He's stressed," Ilic said.

"I'm stressed too, but at least I'm polite."

They exchanged glances.

"Now and again, at least," she said.

Louise dropped Ilic off at H.Q. "We should do that again sometime," he said. She nodded; she knew what he meant. Make a team. Work together. Talk about fathers. The complicated things in life.

"If you're ever hungry give me a call, Illi."

Ilic smiled. "When we've got the Pakistanis."

"When we've got the Pakistanis."

At home she opened the windows, closed the curtains and got out of her jeans and T-shirt. She was clammy all over; the biochemical substances had been sweated out. There were three messages on her answerphone. The first two were from her father. Both began with "Chérie" and she skipped them both. The third was from Katrin Rein; she had paid a visit to her "colleague" and said, "It was good that I saw him. I think I can help, I can give him a few names and addresses to get him back on track, you know."

"Excellent," Louise said with a yawn as she took off her bra.

"It was a bit tricky to begin with, but I think I managed to convince him . . ."

"I bet you did."

"But what's happened to *you* . . ."

"What do you mean?" She removed her knickers.

". . . you're not going to your A.A. meetings, you're not having any more therapy, you . . ."

"Oh, that," she said, pressing the stop button.

In the shower she thought of the last thing Thomas Ilic had said: When we've got the Pakistanis. It struck her that other words lurked behind these. But she was too tired to think about it.

The biochemical substances she had sweated out stuck doggedly to her skin. It was some time before she'd washed them down the plughole.

Standing at the mirror she thought about her other brother and wondered how she was going to deal with him.

But he's here, Chérie. He's back, thank God. That's how her father had erased his own despair.

Then she thought of Ilic's words again. When we've got the Pakistanis. She yawned as she went into the sitting room and the words followed her. She went over to the C.D. player. "Shine on You Crazy Diamond" on a loop.

In the bedroom she put her mobile and cordless phone on the bedside table, set the alarm for a quarter past five, then half past five, then a quarter to six.

When Bonì was in bed, Ilic's words increased in tempo. When we've got the Pakistanis when we've got the Pakistanis. An earworm of five words. Again she sensed that behind these, somewhere in the depths of her exhausted mind, other words were lurking.

She closed her eyes.

Then the words behind the words were there, and more words too.

It wasn't about the Pakistanis.

It was *only* about the Pakistanis.

Then she was asleep.

IV

The Night of the Murderers

15

She was woken by the telephone. She opened her eyes but didn't move. Vivaldi's "Spring" – the call couldn't be that important. Only Katrin Rein, Günter, her father and the Estonians still used her landline. Louise glanced at the alarm clock. Four p.m. She hadn't been asleep for even fifteen minutes. She closed her eyes.

But in that fifteen minutes something had changed. The music, the Pink Floyd loop, had been paused. Boni sat up with a start and stared at the bedside table. Only her cordless handset was there; the mobile had gone.

Vivaldi cut out and then started again. She grabbed the handset. No number on the display. An unknown male voice said, "We need to talk, Frau Boni." The voice sounded friendly and very close. "Just a chat, Frau Boni. Don't be afraid, O.K.?"

A shiver ran down her spine.

They were in her apartment.

As she got dressed she forced herself to remain calm. They could have killed her in her sleep if they'd wanted to. But they hadn't.

Just a chat, Frau Boni. About what? About the other story? The explosion of the depot?

She put the telephone to her ear. As expected, the line was dead. Even if they just wanted to talk, they wanted to do it alone.

Louise looked around for a weapon. In the drawer of her bedside table she found a corkscrew – thank God for Boni chaos! Suppressing a hysterical urge to laugh, she slipped the corkscrew into her trouser pocket. Keep calm, she thought, taking a deep breath. She'd survived her father's invasion in the winter, and what could be worse than your father picking up your dirty underwear from the floor, washing it and hanging it up to dry?

Strangers standing beside her bed while she slept.

There were two of them. A man in the sitting room to the left, another in the hallway to the right. She had a good view of the man in the sitting room, whereas the hallway was obscured in shadows. "Don't be afraid, Frau Bonì," said the man in the sitting room, the one who'd telephoned. He raised his splayed fingers reassuringly. He was wearing white gloves and she couldn't see a weapon. All the same a cold fear crept over her body. They'd closed the windows.

She turned to the other man. "Either come into my sitting room, or get out of my apartment. For God's sake, I want to *see* you!" She reached for the light switch.

"Don't do that," the man whispered in English.

"He'll leave, Frau Bonì," the first man said. He nodded to the man in the hallway and a few seconds later she heard the front door close. She tried to memorise what she'd seen of him. Slim, no taller than 1.70 m, jeans, dark jacket, maybe brown. Small head, short, dark hair. White gloves. There had been an American twang to the "Don't do that".

"And you, don't move," she said to the man in the sitting room.

"No problem."

Louise's eyes scanned the galley kitchen, then she went towards the bathroom on the right, nudged open the door. Empty. Her fear subsided as her anger grew. They were in her apartment.

Keep calm, she thought. He just wants to talk.

So let's talk.

"Are you armed?"

"Yes," the man said.

"Did you take my weapon?"

He nodded.

"Put it on the table. My mobile too."

The man reached into his jacket pocket, put the pistol and phone on the coffee table and stepped back. When she picked them up, both mobile and gun were lighter than normal. No battery, no bullets.

"Later," the man said.

Bonì nodded.

She sat in one of the two armchairs and studied the man. Slim, 1.80 m, her age, jeans, blue shirt, black jacket. Longish, light-brown curly hair. His face gaunt, sombre, serious, his gaze penetrating. He looked the efficient type. She couldn't see or hear him breathing; his movements were precise and inaudible. One of those men who didn't exist. Who inhabited a different world. Lisbeth Walter's world, perhaps.

Now they had come into her apartment.

What she failed still to understand was why he was showing her his face.

The fear returned. *Just a chat, Frau Bonì*. She believed him. Perhaps because she sensed that they knew each other from the forest to the south of Oberried.

"I assume we're colleagues of some sort."

He nodded. "F.I.S."

"Department?"

"Five."

Operational reconnaissance and analysis. Organised crime, arms dealing and proliferation. Terrorist hunters. She nodded slowly. "I need proof."

No proof. No I.D. No call to Foreign Intelligence. She wouldn't find out anything there, not from anybody, because virtually nobody knew anything about him. The team didn't exist, *he* didn't exist. His voice was deep, soft, steady. He spoke slowly and with a gravity that made her shudder once more.

"What about your American friend?"

He shook his head.

"Do you have a name at least?"

"No name."

She sighed. "O.K., let's talk."

"Five passengers from Baluchistan," the man said. "One of them's a key figure for me, for you, for our country. If we find out what he knows, we'll be able to prevent terrorist attacks in Europe and the Middle East. If we don't, innocent people will die."

"Will he give up the information voluntarily?"

"Yes."

"What about the other four?"

"They're on the other side."

"Islamists?"

"That too. But first and foremost terrorists."

"Are they coming to Freiburg?"

"Yes."

"Why? Because of A.P.G.P.F.?"

The man nodded. "There are more deals planned." He knew when the two Pakistani groups were arriving in Frankfurt and that they'd be under Kripo surveillance. He knew that the Freiburg surveillance squad were keeping tabs on the A.P.G.P.F. board members, including Abdul Rashid.

And that was the problem.

If Rashid or any of the others became remotely suspicious, the Pakistanis might not come. And the F.I.S. informer's life would be in danger. "Pull your people out. Just until tomorrow afternoon. By then we'll have spoken to our man and got him to safety. Then you can bust A.P.G.P.F."

"Nobody will get suspicious."

"It's too great a risk."

She felt the corkscrew in her trouser pocket and pulled it out. The man smiled fleetingly. "Nobody will get suspicious," she insisted. He said nothing and she let him think. About cooperation, support. You give me something, I'll give you something in return. Sooner or later he'd have to make her an offer, if he was serious.

Her eyes roamed the sitting room, kitchen, hallway. The fact that they had got inside her apartment, had stood beside her bed, had changed something fundamentally. It had made her feel vulnerable and violated. In some way the apartment was a place inside her; the men had got inside *her*. Their shadows would stay inside her. She would have to learn to live with them.

"I need a name."

"What?"

"I need a name for you."

"You're a complicated woman, Frau Bonì."

"Come on, a name, that's not so difficult."

The man shook his head. "No name."

"Without a name there's no deal." She smiled.

"O.K. then – Marcel. So we can make some progress."

"My neighbour's called Marcel."

"I know."

She nodded, disappointed. "So let's go from the beginning again."

They began with the weapons. Yes, Marcel and his "team" had known about both depots for some time. Yes, the weapons had been intended for the Jinnah. No, they didn't know who'd blown up the depot in Riedlinger's field. Yes, they did have their suspicions – rivalries between Islamic fundamentalists. The Jinnah, the Iraqi Shias, Al-Qaeda. Bound by mutual antipathy. None of them liked to see the others becoming too powerful. From time to time they fought, or sabotaged each other's efforts. Even now.

Marcel paused. The "even now" echoed in her head, together with a voice that said the guy was mad.

He seemed to detect her scepticism. "Two years ago the world changed, Frau Bonì. Your world too. Your city, your work. You see it and you sense it, every day. In all those things, large and small, which are now different. The security measures, the media reports, the discussions, the F.C.P.O.'s terror warnings. In your attitude towards Arabic-looking people."

He paused again. Louise said nothing.

"All of a sudden people from a different culture, with a different religion and a different concept of civilisation are playing a fundamental role in your life. In your *future*. Your little, seemingly cosy world has changed, Frau Bonì."

"I know, I know – the defence of Germany begins in the Hindu Kush."

"And here, in your apartment."

"That was a joke."

"A joke about 9/11?"

She got up with a sigh. "Coffee?"

"No, thanks."

Corkscrew in hand, she went to her galley kitchen. She knew he wouldn't accept a coffee. He wouldn't drink anything, touch anything, wouldn't leave a single trace.

She switched on the coffee machine and thought, no proof, no I.D., no call to F.I.S. . . . but there was a dictaphone in the kitchen drawer.

The light streaming through the curtains into her apartment was golden. The air was getting sticky, ever hotter, and in it hung an unfamiliar smell she couldn't identify. Louise had sat down and was blowing on the coffee which she wouldn't drink, because it was far too hot for coffee. She was in a permanent sweat. T-shirt and trousers stuck to her skin and drops of perspiration ran from her armpits to her waistband. Dark sweat patches had appeared on Marcel's shirt and his face was shining. "Ernst Martin Söllien," she said, hoping their voices were loud enough for the dictaphone to pick up.

"An A.P.G.P.F. agent. Unscrupulous, money-grubbing, dead."

"Hannes Riedinger."

"Knew nothing."

She nodded. She thought of the living room for five people, the kitchen for five people. The photographs that showed only the wife and children. A man waiting, his eyes closed, in the glare of her headlights.

"He didn't need to die," Marcel said. "You weren't paying attention, we weren't paying attention."

She pursed her lips. "Who killed him?"

Another A.P.G.P.F. agent. A young Bosnian Muslim, barely twenty years old. Nicknamed "Bo". A heavy man, Louise added, around one hundred kilos. Size 46 shoes. Trainers, worn profile. Marcel smiled. They hadn't looked at the bottom of his shoes.

Louise put her cup on the table, picked up the bottle of water and drank. "The two men in the forest."

"Bosnian Muslims. They were guarding the second depot. Harmless cannon fodder, two brothers whose family and entire village were bombed to bits in the war. They don't even know which country they're now in."

"You've been observing them?"

"Them and the others."

"Since when?"

"For a few months."

"Are there other depots?"

"No. But two years ago there was a weapons delivery to the Jinnah, and there's another order. They're arming."

"Wouldn't it be much simpler via Afghanistan?"

"No. The Americans are on both sides of the border. It may be a longer route via the Balkans and A.P.G.P.F., but it's less risky."

"How did the weapons get here?"

"In the nineties there was a route from the Balkans via Hungary, Slovakia, Poland, Rostock, Hamburg, Karlsruhe and then via Dunkirk to Africa. We suspect that A.P.G.P.F. has reopened this route. There was another route via Trieste and then across the Alps in lorries. That's assuming the weapons have come from the Balkans rather than anywhere else."

"And what do the Jinnah want? Is it about Musharraf?"

"It's about Musharraf, about power. Their aim is to plunge Pakistan

239

into chaos, get rid of Musharraf and install a new Islamic fundamentalist leadership that will end cooperation with the West and stop supporting the International Security Assistance Force in Afghanistan."

"Do they plan to assassinate Musharraf?"

"We can't say for sure. There's evidence that they were going to try in Paris, and now we have intelligence that they may try to kill him in Islamabad."

"And that's what you want to prevent?"

"We *have* to prevent it. If we don't want to lose the battle for freedom, democracy and justice, we need Musharraf. If we want to prevent Pakistan being dominated by Islamic fundamentalists. His predecessor was trying to establish Sharia as the sole principle of law. Musharraf averted this by taking over the government. The West needs him."

Louise leaned back, trying not to forget all the questions she needed to ask. Why had Marcel helped her in the forest? Because "the Kirchzarten policeman" had gone the wrong way. He had the woman with him and didn't know what to do. Marcel hadn't known how badly injured she was. And since they were colleagues ... He shrugged. In any case he saw it as part of his duty to help, to protect.

She smiled, she felt touched.

He asked if the wound was healing well. She nodded.

Then she thought about a word Marcel had just uttered: "Kirchzarten". He'd stressed the first syllable, he'd said *Kirch*zarten like the locals, not Kirch*zarten* like the rest of the world.

Whatever that might mean.

She asked more questions. Yes, his people had "procured" the white Audi and had followed her to Wiehre as well as to Offenburg. *He* had followed her. In a blue car? No, not blue. She thought of the service station, the face in the car window, the eyes fixed on her. Had he been there? He nodded, looking momentarily surprised. "You're not invisible, you know," Louise said.

"With time you believe that you are."

They'd followed everyone – Bermann, "the Croat", Heinz Schneider, her. They wanted to maintain control, keep track of things. So they could intervene if necessary.

"Like now."

"Like now," Marcel affirmed.

"Why did you come to me?"

"Because you know I exist."

"Even though you *don't*."

Marcel smiled.

"There's one thing I don't understand," Louise said.

"I'm glad to hear it."

If they'd had A.P.G.P.F. under surveillance for months, how could they not know who had planted Semtex amongst the weapons? Marcel shrugged. Quite simple. They hadn't kept the shed under observation round-the-clock. There weren't enough of them.

He came to the table and put the battery and magazine beside the mobile and pistol. "Now you have to make a decision."

"Do I have a choice?"

"Of course. But it won't be a hard one. We're on the same side, after all."

"Sometimes that's not enough."

"That's why I'm going to make you an offer."

It was an enticing offer. They would get the name and whereabouts of Riedinger's murderer, the two men from the forest and Marion Söllien. And tomorrow morning they would be given photographs, documents and snippets of conversations or telephone calls between A.P.G.P.F. members and a weapons smuggler from the former Yugoslavia. All this in exchange for an immediate withdrawal of the squad keeping Rashid, the A.P.G.P.F. people and the Pakistanis under surveillance – nothing more, nothing less.

"And how in God's name am I going to sell that to my boss?" Louise said.

Marcel reached into his inside pocket, pulled out a digital recording device and placed it on the table. "With this," he said.

Then came the nitty-gritty – when Kripo would learn the details, when they should strike, at what time tomorrow they would get the material. She didn't bother trying to remember it all; the recorder in the drawer was still switched on. Instead she stared at Marcel, memorising his facial features, the shape of his nose, eyes, ears, the style of his hair, his physique. The way he spoke, his pitch, his voice. The tiny but significant distinguishing features – two liver spots on the right cheek, rather patchy facial hair, pronounced worry lines on his brow. There might come a time when it was crucial for her to be able to describe him accurately. No name, no I.D., no official authentication, she thought, just the memory of a bizarre half hour in her apartment, on an unbearably hot day in July 2003, during which the defence of Germany took a step forwards.

16

"And then?" Bermann said.

She shrugged. "He left."

"You just let him *go*?"

"Yes, I let him go."

"You should have detained him. You should have brought him here—"

"Rolf!" Almenbroich interrupted hoarsely.

Bermann fell silent. She stared into his wide, reddened eyes and thought of the Dobermann. Luis, the Dobermann.

Dog days. One dog went for her, another acted as her namesake.

Bermann looked away.

Detain Marcel? She had certainly considered it. When he was on his way to the door his back was turned for a few seconds. Enough time to load her pistol. But he would have known she wouldn't shoot. He would have walked on regardless.

"She did everything correctly," Almenbroich said.

They'd assembled in Bermann's office – Almenbroich, Löbinger, Ilic, Bermann, her. Almenbroich was sitting at the desk, the others leaned against the walls as if they no longer had the strength to stay on their feet without support. The blinds were closed and it was oppressively hot. Louise was holding a bottle of Evian, which was passed around from time to time.

"She did everything correctly," Almenbroich repeated, more to himself this time.

Bermann put his hands over his face. "I think I'm going mad."

"Nobody's stopping you from getting a transfer," Almenbroich said.

For a few moments silence descended on the room.

Then Bermann said, "I'm sorry?"

"He doesn't mean it like that," Ilic said. "We're all . . ."

Bermann took a step forwards. "What the hell is that supposed to mean, Christian?"

"We're all a bit irritable and . . ." Ilic said.

"Pull yourself together, Rolf," Löbinger said.

"You keep out of it!"

Almenbroich raised a hand to nip this exhange in the bud, then apologised to Bermann. The heat, the virtually sleepless nights, the exhausting meeting that morning in Stuttgart. His face was grey and he was squinting, even though the light in the room was dim. When he'd passed her earlier Bonì had detected an unpleasant odour of sickness, old age, neglect. She suspected that everyone in the room was asking themselves the same question: how long is he going to last?

"I'm sorry, Rolf," Almenbroich reiterated.

Bermann nodded, but the anger remained in his expression.

"Come upstairs later and we'll straighten things out."

"And now you're going to pull yourself together," Löbinger said.

"I'd like to hear the tape again," Ilic said.

They listened a second time to the conversation between Louise and Marcel, followed by the description of the two men she'd committed to tape as soon as Marcel had left. "So what do we do?" Löbinger said, tapping his watch.

A quarter past six. Marcel would be calling any time now.

"I suggest we give him what he wants," Almenbroich said. "Fifteen hours."

"No Christian!" Bermann said. "If we let F.I.S. stick its oar in too . . . I mean, this is *our* investigation for God's sake! *Our* responsibility! We're going to look like right bloody chumps if we . . ."

"Rolf!" Löbinger warned him.

Bermann walked to the desk and propped himself on his hands.

"We're closing in on this one, Christian! For the first time in this case we've got almost everything under control! We know when the Pakistanis are arriving, we're on to A.P.G.P.F. . . ."

"And we'd be jeopardising an intelligence operation that's been in the planning for months, maybe even years," Löbinger said. "Quite apart from the fact that we'd be endangering the life of an informer."

Almenbroich looked at Bermann. "These are weighty arguments. Let's take a vote and then decide. Anselm?"

"Call off the surveillance."

"Illi?"

Ilic shrugged. "Tricky one. We need more information and more time."

"We don't have either. Louise?"

She took a sip. It was a risk. A lot could happen between this evening and tomorrow morning. Quite apart from the fact that Bermann's objections were justified. And that she didn't know what role the American in her hallway played in all this. An American with the German Foreign Intelligence Service?

But she felt that the potential gain justified the risks. She nodded.

"That's exactly how I see it," Almenbroich said. "What al—"

"I don't fucking believe it!" Bermann said, slamming his palm on the table.

"What alternative do we have, Rolf?"

"We stay on the case!"

"What's your problem?" Löbinger asked. "That D11 has to share its authority again?"

Bermann looked at him and wrinkled his nose as if an unbearable stench were emanating from Löbinger's body. Then he said, "Do you mind if I have my office back now?"

"Once Marcel has called," Almenbroich said. "But if you'd like to sit down . . ." He made to get up, and to Louise it seemed that he might not manage it.

Bermann flapped his hand at Almenbroich and went back to

the wall. Nobody spoke. Almenbroich had put his fingers together in a triangle and was staring at the desktop. Ilic's eyes roamed the room. Löbinger's arms were crossed and he was peering at the calendar on the wall, as if counting down the days to his holiday.

The team was falling apart and everybody knew it, Louise thought.

She glanced at the clock. Twenty-five past six. Nervousness had gripped them all. In half an hour the three Pakistanis from Karachi would be landing in Frankfurt. At this very minute their colleagues were moving into position, while they were standing here arguing, making themselves dependent on one man who used her neighbour's name and who otherwise didn't exist.

She had no doubt that he would call. But Bermann's objections were gnawing away at her. Triggering further questions and objections. Could they afford to relinquish control again? Satisfy themselves with just waiting – again? Trust a man with a false name?

And what about the American?

"And what about the American? An American with F.I.S.? Or is he with one of the U.S. secret services? I—"

"Oh *please!*" Löbinger interrupted with a groan. "When did we last have American spies here, Louise? In the fifties?"

"—can't get this American out of my head."

"Maybe he was speaking dialect." Löbinger laughed. "Maybe he said, '*Doan der dat,*' or something."

"What sort of dialect is that?" Ilic said.

"I don't know. Franconian? Certainly not Texan."

Nobody reacted.

Then the waiting began.

An uneasy waiting. She couldn't get the American out of her head. Hadn't there been mention of an American over the past few days? But in what context? She couldn't remember.

Then the other brother stole his way into her thoughts too.

*

At 18.32 her mobile played the Satie melody. She looked at the display and said, "Täschle."

"Keep it short," Bermann ordered.

Boni took the call. "I'm in a meeting, Herr Täschle."

"I'll be brief," Täschle said. One of Hannes Riedinger's sons had turned up. In case they wanted to talk to him, he'd be at the farm during the day and was staying at Hotel-Restaurant Fortuna, in the pedestrian zone. "I mentioned you," Täschle said.

"What about Kathi and the other children?"

"They're not coming."

She thanked him and ended the call.

Almenbroich smiled weakly. "Kathi?"

"Don't forget to switch on the loudspeaker," Löbinger said. He hadn't finished his sentence before the mobile rang again.

Marcel did the talking, Boni listened.

Bo – the man who'd murdered Hannes Riedinger – the two Bosnians from the forest and Marion Söllien were holed up in a country house south-east of Heuweiler. Only Bo was armed. And he was dangerous, Marcel said, a ruthless killer. There was a landline in the house, and Bo and Marion Söllien both had mobiles. But the house was in a dead zone; mobiles only worked a hundred or so metres away so they could ignore them. But they would cut off the landline just before they carried out their raid.

Marcel paused, then said, "You know how important this is for us?"

"Yes."

"No word to the press before tomorrow morning. No lawyers before tomorrow morning. You know what's at stake."

Bermann came over holding out a note: *Marion Söllien – hostage?* She asked the question. No, no, Marcel replied, Marion Söllien was in on it. Once again: no press, no lawyers before tomorrow morning. Could she guarantee that?

Almenbroich nodded.

"Yes," she said.

"Good."

Louise saw Almenbroich nod to Löbinger, who then left the room. He would tell their colleagues from surveillance to withdraw and put in a request for the S.W.A.T. team in Umkirch.

Marcel described the house: living room and kitchen on the ground floor, three bedrooms, a bathroom and loo upstairs. Bo was sleeping in the room to the left, Marion Söllien in the middle and the two Bosnians on the right. No neighbours, at least none within a radius of three hundred metres.

"Who does the house belong to?" she asked, looking at Ilic. He'd opened his folder and was scribbling some notes. Bonì felt she would have been swamped by now were it not for this folder. The words in blue seemed to guarantee that nothing would get lost in these days that passed so quickly.

"We don't know. All we know is that A.P.G.P.F. are using it. Mahr and Busche meet there once or twice a month, and others sometimes turn up too. Middle men, weapons smugglers, couriers."

Mahr, the ex-member of the regional parliament, Louise thought, but who was Busche? Then she remembered. The businessman on A.P.G.P.F.'s board. Mahr, Busche, Rashid – that left the teacher, the couple on Mallorca and Mahr's mother, Wilhelmine. You can forget them, Marcel said. Puppets, the lot of them. Mahr, Busche and probably Rashid were the ones pulling the strings; the others had no idea what A.P.G.P.F. was really up to.

"*Probably* Rashid?"

"He hasn't yet been to any meeting we've observed. But he's a Pakistani, he's got contacts in Panjgur, he's a physicist and he used to work in nuclear fission. Reason enough to keep a close eye on him."

"The changed world."

"Yes," Marcel said.

"Who is Aziza Mahr?"

Ilic looked up. *We know that now*, he mouthed silently.

"You don't know? Mahr's first wife."

"Is she significant?"

"No. She died years ago."

Ilic nodded and drew "90" in the air with his finger. "So what's going to happen tomorrow."

Marcel would call her at around ten and give her a meeting point. Come alone and come by car. You'll get plenty of documentation – everything you need to bust A.P.G.P.F. We've spared you a lot of work. He laughed ironically; a joke between colleagues.

"I need a phone number," Louise said.

"You know I can't do that."

Bermann jotted something else on the piece of paper and held it out to her: *Get him to call you at 22.00.*

"Can you call me again at ten this evening?"

"Why?"

She looked at Bermann and improvised. So that she could tell him how things had gone with Bo and his chums. So they could check whether everything was proceeding satisfactorily on both sides. There might be things they needed to discuss. After all, Kripo and F.I.S. didn't always work smoothly together. Marcel laughed softly. He had laughed a lot over the course of the conversation. "O.K.," he said.

Bermann nodded.

"O.K.," Louise said.

They swiftly sorted out what needed to be done before the operational meeting in twenty minutes. Bermann and Almenbroich were especially businesslike. Löbinger, who'd come back into the room, was being especially affable.

Louise and Ilic exchanged glances. The team was falling apart.

The core was falling apart.

Almenbroich would consult with Stuttgart and activate his F.I.S. contacts, Bermann would notify their colleagues in Frankfurt and talk to the telephone company. Lobinger would assemble his team from

D23 and Ilic the D11 officers, while Louise would write up her encounter with Marcel and the American. Löbinger left the office and a member of the technical staff arrived to fetch the recording device. With the help of speech diagnostics and voice analytics they would get a little bit closer to Marcel than he'd like – psychological and sociological behaviour, linguistic idiosyncrasies, traces of dialect; they would find something. He had spoken high German, but he could have been trained. He'd said *Kirch*zarten.

"Would you leave the door open, please?" Almenbroich said.

"Is that going to help?" the technician said.

"They're forecasting warm rain for tonight," Ilic said.

"Warm rain, right," the technician said, and left.

Ilic was about to follow the man, but Louise held him back. The e-mails from Islamabad – anything unusual about them? He shook his head. Pakistani names, places, faces. Five scanned visa applications together with declarations. Information about Pakistan, Baluchistan, the Jinnah. Everything was printed out on the desk in his office, the pile with the Post-it marked "Louise". She was touched. A "Louise" pile. She'd never had that in ten years with Kripo. Not even in Reiner Lederle's time, and he was known for assembling legendary piles.

"By the way," Ilic said. The man from Emmendingen who'd issued the invitations was a Pakistani student.

His eyes stayed on her. The half-Croat man, the half-French woman. Once again they seemed to be thinking the same thing: the couple from Islamabad were coming to Rashid in Freiburg; the three men from Karachi to Emmendingen – and not a single Kripo officer was watching.

After Ilic had left the room Almenbroich got up with some difficulty. "We'll talk again later, Rolf. I don't want anything left unresolved."

Bermann raised his eyebrows.

Almenbroich walked around the desk. Louise wanted to help him, but he rebuffed her without saying a word. At the door he said to

Bermann, "Things are slipping from my grasp. I'm losing track, I'm too exhausted to concentrate. If I'm not feeling any better by tomorrow, you take over." And then he left.

Closing the door behind him, Bonì turned to Bermann. He looked pale and expressionless, "What?" he said.

Not a great time to be making a secret pact with him.

All the same. "What F.I.S. knows is incredible. Marcel knows the house, the people, he knows where they sleep. He knows what they've done, what they're planning. He knows about the weapons deliveries, the dealers, the middle men."

Bermann leaned against the edge of the desk and motioned to her to go on.

"He observes, photographs, listens in on conversations and telephone calls, lets these people do what they want. He watches while they commit crimes, neither intervening nor notifying us."

"He's notified us now."

"Because we're endangering his operation."

"An important operation with an important informer."

"I thought you were against us pulling out."

"And you were in favour." He shrugged. "What do you want from me, Luis?"

"I want . . . Rolf, my name's *Louise*. Not Luis like your father's Dobermann, O.K.? Can you remember that? Shall we have a little practice?"

Bermann tried not to smile. "That's it?"

"I want us to put someone on the train."

"The train from Frankfurt to Baden?"

She nodded. They would post an individual, unofficially, at Frankfurt Airport. Someone Marcel and his people wouldn't know, and who would be inconspicuous. An older man, an older woman. Maybe one of the airport detectives. If the three arrivals from Karachi took a train, that person could get aboard with them. If they waited in Frankfurt for the couple from Islamabad, the detective could wait too. At least that way they'd know what was happening, rather than relinquishing control altogether. Nobody needed to be told anything – not Almenbroich, not Löbinger. Nobody from Freiburg, and certainly not anyone from Stuttgart.

Bermann breathed in and out heavily, then nodded.

Waiting in her office were the Buddhist child monks, and now her other brother too. The monks were laughing, but not the brother. She hadn't behaved in a very sisterly fashion, she thought. It wasn't his fault that he was the wrong Germain, that the right one had been gone for years. Now he's back, Chérie, her father said to her amidst the silence, the heat, the exhaustion. As far as the other brother was concerned, she didn't know what was worse: what she was doing, or what her father was doing. All of a sudden she felt the urge to tell Richard Landen about her brothers, right ones, wrong ones, ones who were here, ones who had disappeared. A worrying sign, in every respect.

She picked up the dictaphone. She would tell the dictaphone about her brothers.

Afterwards Bonì wrote up the events that had taken place in her apartment, then embarked on the "Louise" pile. Ilic was right; there was little new material apart from the faces of the Pakistanis. Dark, closed faces she couldn't evaluate. Two of the men had moustaches, one had a beard. She liked the look of the woman, possibly a few years younger than she was. She looked proud, cultured. The men from Panjgur were in traditional costume, whereas the couple from Islamabad wore Western clothing.

None of them looked like a terrorist.

But that must be true of many terrorists.

Prior to 9/11, the liaison officer wrote in an e-mail, the Jinnah may not have been called "terrorists" in the West either, but "freedom fighters". The C.I.A. and Musharraf's people called them "terrorists". They engaged in political resistance and were active in the large Muslim opposition to Pervez Musharraf. A more radical grouping within the tribe, centred around a grandson of its leader – the man with the beard – was also launching attacks against military facilities, barracks of the Bambore Rifles frontier corps, police stations, infrastructure and state officials.

And they'd announced they were going to kill Musharraf.

Whether they're terrorists or freedom fighters, they're murderers.

Not a Pakistani offshoot of Al-Qaeda, the liaison officer wrote.

But murderers.

But of course they're criminals, the liaison officer wrote. Despite this he was "advocating" differentiation. You couldn't understand complex political problems by generalising, and Pakistan was a complex political problem. Baluchistan was a complex political problem. Around sixty tribes, most of them strictly Muslim and organised along mediaeval power structures, plus the army of the American-friendly Musharraf (a highly controversial figure in his own country), all the Afghan refugees, the proximity to Iran – quite apart from the poverty, drought, hunger, drug cultivation.

There followed several pages outlining the complex political situation in Pakistan. With a mental promise to the liaison officer that she would refrain from generalising, Louise put these to one side and looked through the visa applications. All five Jinnah had put three days for "length of visit" (point 25) and for "purpose of visit" (point 29) they'd placed a cross in the box marked "other". When asked for more details about the purpose of their visit, the answers had all been similar: to develop social and cultural projects with A.P.G.P.F. Offenburg. She made a note of the name and address of the Pakistani student in Emmendingen, who appeared on three of the applications.

The telephone rang. "Where are you, Louise," Bermann said. "We're waiting."

"See you later," she said to the children and brothers, and left her office.

*

The task force room contained a handful of colleagues from D11 and D23, Bermann and Löbinger, Almenbroich, the head of the S.W.A.T. team plus his squad leader and a secretary. Also present was Hubert Vormweg, the Freiburg police commissioner, a small, squat Swabian with a steel-grey beard. He wore cords and a casual shirt. He had already been home. "How's the arm?" he said.

"Better, thanks."

"Are you having the bandage changed regularly?"

"If I get round to it."

Wallmer signalled to her that she would do it later. Louise raised her eyebrows. Wallmer grinned. Trust me, I'm good at that sort of thing.

"Are we ready? We're in a hurry," Bermann said.

"Before we begin . . ." Almenbroich said.

He now looked even more exhausted. For the first time Louise thought he might give up. Might have no choice.

Almenbroich told them that he'd called an acquaintance who was in a "let's say, rather high" position in the operational reconnaissance department at F.I.S. His acquaintance had said he knew next to nothing about the activities of other departments. Pakistan? Well, he "wasn't going to deny" that the service had been keeping particularly close tabs on Pakistan for a while now.

Bermann grunted and a few others chuckled.

Nor, Almenbroich continued, "would he deny" that since 9/11 special units had been dealing with the problem of Islamic fundamentalism in a way that befitted the new "circumstances".

You mean over there, on the ground?

I don't have that much detail.

What about here in Germany? Months-long surveillance of arms dealers, secret talks with Pakistani informants, turning a blind eye to crimes.

No, I can't imagine *that*!

"So it's true," a D11 officer said.

Somebody laughed again, after which there was silence.

So it's true, Louise thought.

The chief purpose of the meeting was to inform their S.W.A.T. colleagues about the house in Heuweiler and its inhabitants, and to fill them in on the background to the case. A request had also been put in via the Ministry of the Interior for the Special Deployment Commando from Göppingen, but it was involved in a large-scale operation against suspected Islamists in the Ulm/Neu-Ulm area and wouldn't be available until the following morning. If they could contain the situation in Heuweiler, however, they shouldn't need the Special Commandos. The house in question was isolated and the likelihood of outsiders being put in danger, or a hostage-taking situation, was low.

Vormweg nonetheless asked whether they couldn't wait until the morning and in the meantime gather further information about the house's inhabitants, draw up an accurate picture of the situation and carry out the raid in tandem with the Special Deployment Commando.

"We have an ad hoc situation," Bermann said. "We *can't* wait."

Vormweg frowned. The two men didn't get on. Vormweg the old student revolutionary, Bermann the old macho. Unlike many of her colleagues, Louise rated Vormweg. She valued the fact that the boss asked one too many questions rather than one too few. That he weighed things up, even hesitated on occasion. Ultimately Vormweg was smart enough to leave the decision-making to the practitioners. And to assume responsibility for their decisions.

"We believe there's a danger they may escape," Almenbroich said. "We shouldn't wait until tomorrow morning, Hubert."

"What if we sealed off the area and . . ." Vormweg paused as Bermann was already shaking his head.

"There are fields, hills, woods. You can't just seal off the area." Bermann exchanged glances with Pauling, the S.W.A.T. boss, a tall, grey-haired man.

Pauling nodded. "We've only got two more hours of daylight."

"If that," the squad leader said. "It's supposed to rain soon."

Everyone glanced out of the window, everyone apart from Hubert Vormweg. "How big is your team?"

"Ten men. We haven't yet been able to bring in more," the squad leader said.

"We've also got a dozen Kripo officers, and an S.S.U. is on its way from Lahr," Löbinger said reassuringly. Louise suppressed a smile. Löbinger usually referred to Special Support officers as "the button mob". Vormweg loathed such derogatory police slang; the individual gets lost, he liked to say. But Löbinger was canny enough to ensure that when he spoke with Vormweg, nobody got lost.

"We've got enough, Hubert," Almenbroich said confidently.

"But without the commandos, we don't have any snipers," Vormweg said.

Bermann rolled his eyes; Vormweg didn't notice.

"We don't reckon we'll need any," Pauling said.

"But you can't be certain."

"Of course we can't be certain."

"The only thing that's certain is that it'll be dark soon," Bermann said.

Vormweg nodded. But he had further questions. Had arrest warrants already been drawn up for "this Bo and Frau Söllien"? Marianne Andrele would sort that out in the morning. What did they know about Bo? Nothing yet. Didn't Interpol have anything? Or the authorities in Bosnia–Herzegovina? S.F.O.R.? Europol? Those E.U. police in Bosnia – what were they called again?

"E.U.P.M.," Ilic said.

"Maybe something will come in yet," Almenbroich said.

Vormweg nodded once more. "Alright then," he said in conclusion.

17

They hurried to the vehicles. Louise was about to get into Ilic's car, but Bermann took her arm and dragged her along with him. His car smelled of cigarettes. Bermann loathed smokers, but he seemed to allow for exceptions. "The blonde from last night?" Louise said.

Bermann didn't respond.

As they approached the junction with Heinrich-von-Stephan-Strasse they slotted into the middle of the convoy of civilian vehicles. In front of them was a Skoda, behind them a Renault. The S.W.A.T. team set great store by using inconspicuous cars.

Two patrol cars moved to the front and headed northwards. With their flashing lights and sirens they cut quickly through the evening traffic. "Listen," Bermann said eventually.

The Frankfurt colleague who would get on the train with the three Pakistanis was called Turetzki. Bermann had given him his own and her mobile numbers. Turetzki was with the airport police and officially had the evening off. His boss knew, and nobody else. Apart from him and her, of course.

And Almenbroich.

"You—"

"He's the boss," Bermann grumbled. "You keep bosses in the loop."

Boni frowned. Soon she would have to speak her mind again. However stressed Bermann was, she wouldn't be able to put up with his intolerable mood for much longer. From confidante to necessary evil – Louise was finding the change in Rolf Bermann too abrupt.

Then she thought about how Almenbroich might know more than he was letting on. That the unbearable Rolf Bermann was the only person she trusted 100 per cent, apart from Ilic since their excursion to Offenburg and Kehl.

But not Almenbroich any longer.

They sped along the B3 at 120 k.p.h. In the west the razor-sharp contours of the Vosges rose from the horizon. In the east, above the Black Forest, sat the mild evening light. It struck Louise that she barely knew the Vosges or the Black Forest. She had never been up the Schauinsland, never to the top of the Feldberg. She had been up the Schlossberg a few times because someone had wanted to go there with her.

Someone who was no longer important.

Boni had no idea why these thoughts had entered her head. She didn't care for them much; they told her that something fundamental was wrong with her life.

That she'd failed to establish anything in all these years.

No connections. Not even geographical ones.

And they threw up fundamental questions. Which people and which places meant anything to her? With whom and where did she feel at home?

"There's something else you ought to know," Bermann said.

The Bureau was taking over the case tomorrow. The file had already been prepared, completed, copied.

She nodded, disappointed. They'd got to grips with this case, committed themselves, and now it was over. That was the way things went. A case of this magnitude had to be handed over to the Bureau. "So that's why Vormweg wanted to postpone the raid," she said.

Bermann shrugged.

They passed Gundelfingen, and at Denzlingen turned off towards the Glottertal. She asked whether anyone from Freiburg would be on the Bureau's investigation team. Bermann nodded. He and Hoffmann from D11, Löbinger and Peter Burg from D23. "Finally, some sleep," Louise said.

Bermann didn't look at her and didn't say anything. She sensed that something was still weighing on him. Something crucial.

He didn't tell her until they'd driven through the village of Heuweiler and its smaller neighbour, Hinterheuweiler. They passed the last farms and houses on a single-track road, before it ended in a turning circle. Above the houses to the left was the edge of the forest; to the right horses grazed on pasture. The cars at the front of the convoy came to a stop and they watched the S.W.A.T. team gather around Pauling and the squad leader – menacing shadows in the twilight. "Listen Louise," Bermann said. "I expect my team to stand by me rather than stab me in the back, do you understand? If you're not willing to support me and the department, then at the very least keep your trap shut, like Illi. The department speaks with *one* voice only, and that's *my* voice. If you don't like it, you can join another department or force whenever you like. Understood?"

Having said his piece, Bermann got out without waiting for an answer. Louise stayed in the car and tried to grasp what had got into Rolf Bermann yesterday evening, and had been troubling him ever since.

The S.W.A.T. team had put on their protective vests and helmets with headsets, and slung their submachine guns around their necks. Now the shadows had acquired edges and points. They were still studying maps and discussing the operational plan. Bermann was with them, while Louise was a few metres away with Löbinger, Wallmer, Schneider, Ilic and other Kripo colleagues. They were going to stay in the background during the raid. Although Kripo was nominally in charge, the planning and execution resided with the S.W.A.T. team, trained for operations such as this one.

The preparations had not gone unnoticed in the village; some youths were approaching across a meadow. Laughing raucously, they were heading for the S.W.A.T. team. Wallmer hurried to intercept the posse and send them back. "Boom, boom," they said, bursting into laughter again. But they obeyed. A handful of villagers stood at the end of the driveway to the nearest house. The S.S.U. from Lahr stood with them. More people were gathering beyond the last patrol car. Even the horses seemed to be watching. Heuweiler in a state of emergency. They could only hope that nobody followed them into the forest.

That Bo didn't get wind of this.

Louise checked the time. Eight o'clock. She thought of Turetzki who might now be on the intercity to Freiburg, or perhaps still at Frankfurt Airport. Of the five Pakistanis who might not be terrorists, but were killers nonetheless.

And who were coming to the area.

They could only guess at why these people were making the trip. New business with A.P.G.P.F., as Marcel had said, and perhaps some old business too. If you'd ordered hundreds of weapons and these weapons had been mysteriously destroyed, you would jump on a plane in Pakistan and fly to Germany.

Bonì gazed at the fields, the hills, the forest. Was Marcel out there somewhere? Of course he was. Marcel and F.I.S. were pulling the strings; the Pakistanis and the investigating authorities were dancing to their tune.

Apart from Turetzki. Turetzki was their trump card.

She wiped the sweat from her forehead. Her thoughts became slower, more sluggish. The words like treacle.

Just one last thing, she thought. Just Bo. Then it's home time.

A movement shook Louise from her torpor. Bermann came running over and said, "If we need an interpreter, Illi, can you do it?"

Ilic nodded and the two hurried away.

Then the squad were on the move.

Bonì climbed the hill beside Wallmer and they entered the forest. The house Marcel had described stood in a small clearing about three hundred metres from Hinterheuweiler. In front of them, scarcely visible in the gathering gloom, the S.W.A.T. officers made their way between the trees. The gap soon grew bigger. Wallmer began to run and Louise quickened her pace too, all the while thinking of Marcel who was pulling the strings. Who knew so much and yet had got in contact with Kripo so late. And she thought of Almenbroich's decision to grant Marcel fifteen hours. The old reservations about F.I.S. bubbled up again. They do their own thing, they're not really interested in cooperation. They always exaggerate. And at the critical moment they'll turn up too late.

Her mobile vibrated and she dug it from her trouser pocket without slowing. Her friend from Islamabad, but the reception was terrible. She retreated a few metres, back towards the edge of the forest. "Now," she said, panting. From the corner of her eye she could see that Wallmer had stopped and was waiting for her. It occurred to her that it must be around midnight in Islamabad. A friend doing overtime. Was that responsible, or suspicious? Louise tried to shake off her burgeoning mistrust.

"The man you were asking about?"

"Yes."

"He's gone."

Halid Trumic had left the A.P.G.P.F. office at noon and hadn't returned. As far as they could tell he wasn't in his apartment. One of the embassy's Pakistani contacts was still out looking for Trumic's car and unobtrusively asking questions. The liaison officer said he had not yet checked all the airlines, but so far the name hadn't cropped up. Perhaps he was travelling under a false identity. "You should assume he's on his way to you, Frau Bonì."

Louise was silent. Was Halid Trumic coming to Freiburg too?

She glanced at Anne, who was frantically gesturing to her to get a move on. Their S.W.A.T. and Kripo colleagues were no longer anywhere to be seen. She raised a hand. One sec.

"Any more questions?"

"Not just now."

"I'll call again."

Louise jogged back to Wallmer. The Pakistanis, she thought, and maybe Halid Trumic now too. And somewhere Marcel and F.I.S. were waiting. The focus seemed to be shifting away from the weapons, A.P.G.P.F. and Bo, and towards the Pakistanis, Marcel, and perhaps Trumic.

To somewhere where there would be no Kripo officers for the next fifteen hours.

The hill grew steeper, the forest thicker. Bonì developed a stitch and stopped to blow her nose. Wallmer stopped, and she raised a hand: one sec. Wallmer nodded sympathetically. Louise gripped her knees, closed her eyes and took deep breaths, in, out. The stitch was still there. Sleep, she thought, finally some sleep, sleep for ever, sleep *now*. She wouldn't take another step in the next fifteen hours, she told herself. She'd give in to the exhaustion, lie down on the forest floor and not get up again until tomorrow morning. Relieved, she fell to her knees and sat down. She had no desire to return to her apartment in any case. Marcel and the American were in her apartment. The American from Franconia.

Louise couldn't help laughing.

All of a sudden Wallmer was beside her.

"The American from Franconia," she said, laughing again. Maybe she was crying too. Why me? she thought. Why me, again? Why do they come to me? Will it never end? Why is it always me?

"Come on," Wallmer said.

"No."

Wallmer lifted her up gently, but implacably.

"I've got a stitch," Louise said.

Wallmer nodded. "We'll take it more slowly, Luis, O.K.?"

"Luis the Dobermann." She laughed or cried again. For a moment she thought she might be drunk. That at some point she'd drunk something without realising. Or had forgotten. The same feeling in her head. The weakness in the legs.

But it was just exhaustion.

"The Dobermann?"

She nodded. Wallmer looked blankly at her. "Alright then," Louise said.

They hurried on. Blood rushed through her brain, impulses sent information, individual words surfaced, thoughts coalesced. This is important now, Luis, her thoughts said. This is an absolutely critical moment. You need to be awake now. She nodded. She wondered why the thoughts in her head were saying "Luis" too.

They were alone. Their colleagues were nowhere to be seen. It couldn't be much further. Just a few hundred metres and they'd come out in the Glottertal.

In the Glottertal, her thoughts echoed.

Think, Louise, *think!* her thoughts screamed.

She stopped. Now she remembered where she'd heard mention of Americans over the last few days. In Adam Baudy's report. Americans in the Grosse Tal.

Which began only three or four kilometres from Riedinger's pasture.

Ilic was waiting for them. He put a finger to his lips and they went on together. Thirty metres ahead there was a clearing, in the middle of which stood a little white house. Beyond it a track led back into the forest – the only access to the house. It ran along the hillside, and after many twists and turns it emerged into the Glottertal.

Bermann, Pauling and two S.W.A.T. officers were hiding behind trees, the others had disappeared with the squad leader. Ilic pointed to their Kripo colleagues standing a few metres behind Bermann. They approached as silently as possible.

Nobody spoke. It smelled of sweat, peppermint chewing gum and coffee.

"Have you got *coffee* here?" Bonì whispered excitedly.

Ilic smiled. There was the crackling of a sweet wrapper – Pocket Coffees. He dropped one into her hand, she looked up and said with her eyes, just one? Are you mad? Alright, then, Ilic's eyes said, and a second one followed. More, her eyes said, I'll buy the rest off you – a hundred euros for the remaining two, come on, Illi, this is business, you come from a family of traders, where's your trader soul now?

"Someone's greedy," Ilic whispered.

"You come from a family of traders," she whispered back.

"What?"

She shook her head and he gave her the last one of his Pocket Coffees, which she unwrapped and stuffed into her mouth all at once.

"By the way," Ilic whispered. Chewing, she held her ear towards his mouth. News from Wilhelm Brenner. He had called Schneider – Bermann's mobile was switched off – Schneider had called Löbinger, and Löbinger had told them all just now. In Riedinger's bedroom forensics had found a partial footprint from a shoe that wasn't Bo's. Someone had stepped into the pool of blood with the edge of their heel. Someone had been in Riedinger's bedroom after the murder. Not so long afterwards, but a while – an hour perhaps, Brenner's people reckoned, given the clotting and consistency of the blood on the floor and the characteristics of the footprint.

Ilic looked at her, waiting for her to say something. She swallowed, felt the chocolate slip down into her stomach and the caffeine go to her head. It's helping, she concluded.

The footprint. There weren't that many possibilities. Someone from A.P.G.P.F., someone from F.I.S. But Marcel had said: you weren't paying attention, we weren't paying attention. Surely that meant that F.I.S. *wasn't* nearby when Riedinger was murdered? But why would someone from A.P.G.P.F. – the probable client here – have come to the farm so soon after the murder?

She shrugged. "A.P.G.P.F. or F.I.S.," she whispered through the gloop.

"Or whoever blew up the depot."

Bonì had forgotten about them. She nodded. The people Marcel knew nothing about.

She told him about the Americans in the Grosse Tal. Ilic said nothing. She sensed he had his doubts.

A hand touched her arm. Wallmer, her face glistening with sweat and a flake of bark sticking to her forehead. "This afternoon . . ." she began. Louise picked off the bark and Wallmer ran her hand across her brow in surprise. "This afternoon, while you were asleep, we got a call from a colleague at the Bureau."

The Bureau had located the source of the source of the source which on Monday had first suggested a neo-Nazi lead, then a Croatian–neo-Nazi one. The source's informer said he'd been rung up by a contact on the "political scene" and was instructed to pass on the message to the Bureau source. When they paid this contact a call he'd summoned his lawyer and had been silent ever since. But they'd discovered that he did regular work for a former member of the regional parliament in Stuttgart.

"Johannes Mahr," Louise said.

Wallmer nodded.

The Bureau had also run some checks on the permanent secretary who'd issued the warning about Baden-Württemberg neo-Nazis. He appeared trustworthy and had obtained the information from an equally trustworthy colleague who'd been rung up by an informer. This informer had likewise received his instructions from the "contact on the political scene".

"Mahr panicked," Louise said. Wallmer nodded. They stared at each other in concentration. More and more leads were pointing in the same direction. The depot had been blown up and Mahr had panicked. To give himself and A.P.G.P.F. breathing space he'd fabricated rumours about neo-Nazis. But rather than use the time this bought him to get away, he had stayed.

Why? she thought. Did Mahr believe he would get through this unscathed?

Then, far too late, the murder of Hannes Riedinger, who'd been contacted a couple of years ago by Ernst Martin Söllien, an A.P.G.P.F. member, about the pasture and the shed. Even then Mahr must have suspected that he might *not* survive unscathed. But still he hadn't made his getaway; he'd stayed in his house in Freiburg St Georgen, where the surveillance squad had been watching him now for a few hours.

Why hadn't he disappeared?

They needed to talk to Mahr.

But they couldn't. They would have to wait.

"And there's something else," Wallmer whispered.

"I shouldn't have gone to sleep."

Wallmer smiled.

They'd seen the list of all the calls to and from Marion Söllien's landline over the past few days. She had called Mahr several times a day, including on Wednesday morning, just before she'd vanished from the apartment. Had Mahr sent Bo to fetch her while Bonì was chatting to Annelie at Uhlich & Partners?

Whatever the case, the fact remained that the informers and telephone calls were threads that converged at A.P.G.P.F. and Bo rather than Marcel. Maybe the focus was shifting again – to where they were.

Or perhaps, she thought, it just looked that way.

The minutes passed. The waiting, the silence, the wonderful forest air were all poison given the state she was in. Louise couldn't stop yawning. She thought of the coffee in the chocolates she'd just eaten, the aroma of coffee, thought, that's got to be helping now, dammit. Clouds were moving in from the south-west, twilight was descending fast. A light went on inside the house, then another. A window was tilted open, a lavatory flushed upstairs. Louise saw four shadows flit to the rear of the house, then two of them appeared at the side she was facing.

Her mobile vibrated again.

The display showed an unknown number. She was about to switch it off when she remembered Turetzki. As Bonì hurried away from the clearing she put the mobile to her ear.

"Turetzki," a man's reedy voice said. "I can't get hold of your colleague, Bermann."

"I know."

The line was poor but Louise understood what he was saying. The three "friends from the east" had landed on time. Rather than wait for "the couple" they'd boarded the next intercity to Freiburg. They were sitting at a table in an open carriage; he was a few rows behind. Right now he was in the "bathroom". "So do I get off when they do, no matter where it is?"

"Yes."

"And then I follow them wherever they go?"

"Yes."

Turetzki had spotted two men, both travelling alone, who might be trailing the Pakistanis too. One had just got off in Mannheim, the other was in the restaurant car two carriages further down. Although she doubted that Turetzki would be able to pick out Marcel's men, she said, "Keep an eye on him. But be careful."

"Don't worry. People don't notice white-haired old men with walking sticks." Turetzki laughed; it sounded melancholic. Arthritis in his right hip, he explained. The pain and the stick were for real. "Nobody ever notices me."

"Because you're experienced."

"Am I sounding maudlin?" he said. "At any rate, I won't be able to run after them."

"You won't need to."

"That's true, the younger ones can do that."

Louise said nothing.

The moment their conversation finished, loud voices came from the clearing. The raid had begun.

*

But it wasn't going according to plan. As Louise raced back to Wallmer and Ilic she saw two S.W.A.T. officers backing out of the house, their submachine guns aimed at two men who came out after them – the same men she'd pursued in the forest between Oberried and Sankt Wilhelm. Then came two more S.W.A.T. officers, also walking backwards, but nobody else.

Silence had descended on the clearing, the edge of the forest and everyone waiting there. Nobody spoke; all eyes were fixed on the house.

Bo and Marion Söllien had not emerged.

Louise went to Bermann and Pauling. "He's holding her hostage," Bermann whispered without looking at her. Rubbish, Louise thought, she's in on it. Marcel said she's in on it. "Downstairs left, in the living room."

Bo had a pistol and a combat knife.

Rubbish, Louise thought again.

A ruthless killer, Marcel had said.

The voices were becoming entangled in her head: Bermann, Marcel, then Pauling whispering something into his microphone, giving Bermann updates, Bermann replying, Pauling whispering instructions, saying, "First floor," Bermann saying, without looking at her, that the hostage seemed to be unharmed; what hostage, she thought, she's in on it!

All of a sudden another voice, an angry, high-pitched man's voice issued from the house, unintelligible words in a foreign language, a pause, then more shouting.

Then silence.

Bermann waved Ilic over.

"He's swearing," Ilic said.

Pauling raised a hand. Now they heard it too. A woman was crying. Pauling whispered again, listened, ran a hand over his short grey hair and said to Bermann, "They're coming out."

Bo was shouting again.

"More swearing," Ilic said.

Now Marion Söllien appeared at the door and, right behind her, Bo. He was so tall that he had to stoop to step outside. His left hand clutched Marion Söllien's hair, as if he were holding her head out in front of him; a pistol in his right hand was pressed to her temple. They moved to the middle of the clearing, Bo bellowing with rage, Marion Söllien screaming in pain and fear. That can't be right, Louise thought, she's in on it. But it was obvious that Marion Söllien was panic-stricken.

"Swearing," Ilic said.

"Are you sure you're understanding him right?" Pauling said.

"He's saying: 'Fuck you, you shitheads, you arseholes, fucking hell, fuck your mothers, fuck your . . .'"

"We get the picture," Pauling said.

Marion Söllien had raised her hands and made a grab for Bo's fingers. Now he shoved her forwards without letting go, shouting even louder.

"Do something," Louise muttered.

Pauling turned and stared at her. His gaze seemed to come from a great distance, and yet it was full of intensity. As if they'd once been very close, many decades ago, and not since. But they hardly knew each other.

At least that was true as far as she was concerned. Did Pauling know more?

He turned away.

Marion Söllien had dropped to her knees and was leaning against Bo's leg, her back arched and hands holding on to his fingers. Bo, quiet now, kept the pistol pressed to her head. For a moment they were still, as if frozen into a gruesome sculpture in the porous evening light.

The executioner and his victim.

"It's like he's going to kill her," Ilic whispered.

Louise nodded. "Pauling . . ."

"He won't shoot," Bermann said.

"No," Pauling said.

Ilic took her aside and whispered in her ear. "Watch how you go with Pauling," he said. "He's an uncle of Theres, you know, *the* Theres." She nodded, horrified. The Theres who went rally-driving. Who had been engaged to Niksch.

"Take a deep breath," Ilic said.

She nodded again. Theres and Niksch would have to wait.

They joined Bermann and Pauling.

Bo was now animated again, they could see a shudder run the length of his massive body. He wrenched Marion Söllien from the ground and began to shout again, drowning out her screams with his furious, high-pitched voice.

"What's he saying now?" Pauling said.

"He's swearing," Ilic said calmly.

Pauling ran a hand through his hair and whispered something into his microphone. Louise fancied she could hear a distant voice and some static, but maybe these were inside her head. "O.K.," Pauling said. "Let's go."

"Wait," Ilic said. "I'll talk to him."

Bo burst out laughing when Ilic addressed him in Croatian from the edge of the forest. They exchanged a few words. Bo nodded, laughed, and talked a little. The delight in his face made his features seem childlike Louise thought. He'd strayed into a war in a foreign country, and now he had met someone from back home. This made a war more bearable.

He motioned for Ilic to join him.

Ilic turned to Pauling and Bermann.

"Your man," Pauling said.

Bermann hesitated, then said, "O.K., Illi."

"You're mad," Louise said, unsure of whether she meant Ilic, Bermann or both. She glanced at Bo. "Both of you are mad."

Ilic stepped into the clearing. Bo said something and Ilic took his service weapon from its holster and placed it on the ground. Bo allowed him to come within a couple of metres. He laughed again, before pushing Marion Söllien away and aiming the pistol at Ilic. Marion Söllien fell to the ground and sobbed. Bo was talking again.

"We need two chairs," Ilic said.

"Chair, yes, yes!" Bo cried keenly.

"This is our chance," Pauling said into the microphone. "Otto, send—"

"*My* man," Bermann interrupted him.

Pauling hesitated, then nodded.

"I'll go," Louise said. Her heart was thumping, the tiredness had dissipated. She stepped forwards.

"Pistol!" Bo shouted.

She put her gun on the ground. Bo laughed and gave another nod. He seemed to be relaxing. A foreigner in a foreign country, but the communication was working rather well. Now she could see him better. In truth he was little more than a child, a big, overweight child with bumfluff, dark moles, tiny eyes. A war orphan, Marcel had said. She guessed he was about eighteen. He'd been sucked into war as a child, and at some point had turned into a murderer.

Louise glanced at Marion Söllien, who lay where she'd fallen. Where else could she go? Behind her the executioner, before her the judge.

"Chair! Chair!" Bo said, laughing.

Inside the house she went into the living room, where she found chairs around a dining table. The smell of beer and fried onions hung in the air, there were empty plates on the table. Beer had spilled from an overturned bottle.

When she came out, Bo was laughing animatedly. She put the chairs near him and pointed to Marion Söllien. "Yes, yes, yes," Bo said, waving her away.

Marion Söllien looked hardly anything like the twin sisters in the photograph. The perm was gone, her hair was mousy and lank, her face puffy and spotty. She stank of cigarette smoke. "I don't want to," she said, reluctantly allowing herself to be helped up.

"I know," Louise said.

She walked around Bo and Ilic.

"Do you speak his language?"

Marion Söllien shook her head. She put a hand to her mouth and swallowed.

"I know," Louise said, picking up her pistol.

Bo and Ilic had placed the chairs facing each other and sat down. They were talking, Bo nodded, smiling broadly. The hand with the pistol rested on his leg, the barrel pointing at Ilic. Then out of the blue he leaped to his feet, shouting. Ilic translated calmly: Are there more of my countrymen out there? A Slovene, or another Croat? Or a Kosovan? Bo laughed. A Kosovan would be good, but a Slovene will do. Best of all would be a Bosnian, maybe someone from Jajce, lovely Jajce? Come on, come and join us. We'll talk about home, we'll sit and talk about how life used to be back home, then we'll see.

This isn't happening, Louise thought.

"Have you ever seen anything like it?" Pauling said. Then came more whispering, listening, whispering. "Peter? Really?" Pauling ran a hand through his hair and whispered, "O.K., send him out."

A S.W.A.T. officer appeared on the other side of the clearing, short, dark-haired. She had never seen him before. He called out to Bo in his language. Bo laughed again and stood up to answer him. Wearing his protective vest but without a helmet, the officer stepped into the clearing.

Pauling turned to Bermann. Peter from Lahr, his parents born in Germany, his grandmother a Serb from Banja Luka in Bosnia.

Peter had fetched another chair from the house and now sat at a similar distance from Bo and Ilic. Bo gestured to him to speak, and when Peter spoke Louise saw him hesitate, as if he were grasping for words. Serbian wasn't his mother tongue. Bo laughed, asked questions. Peter answered him, then Ilic joined in the conversation. Now all three were talking at the same time. Ilic and Peter laughed, they looked relaxed. Bo seemed calmer, less hysterical. But his pistol was still pointing at Ilic. And somewhere, Bonì thought, there was a knife.

Ten minutes had passed. The three men in the clearing were still laughing, and sometimes they all spoke at the same time. Fellow countrymen abroad – talking gave them a touch of home. Bo talked and laughed the loudest.

The clouds had closed in and it was almost dark in the forest. In a few minutes they would barely be able to make out the figures in the clearing. Darkness, she said, would be a nightmare. An unpredictable murderer, two unarmed policemen. Who could say how he would react? Would he try to escape? Would he panic? He wouldn't be able to see anything either.

Pauling, by contrast, seemed to be willing the darkness on. As soon as it was dark the S.W.A.T. team would move in. He had worked it out, given orders and produced a sketch on a scrap of paper. Four officers would creep up on Bo from behind. It would take them between five and seven minutes to cover the thirty metres. The light from the living room meant they couldn't crawl past the house; instead they would come from the forest, midway between the house and Bo. For the first few metres they would edge their way perpendicular to the clearing, then approach Bo from an obtuse angle. Once on their feet they'd have their man, job done. The moon, Pauling had whispered, wouldn't be a problem. Even if Bo turned around he wouldn't see the officers; the moon was behind the clouds and far too low even if the clouds broke.

Everything thought out, everything calculated, the angles, the time it would take, the probability of success, which could never be 100 per cent, especially if you had no snipers. "Otto, if you . . ." Pauling whispered into his microphone – then fell silent.

Something had changed.

Louise took a step forwards. Pauling's chatter was buzzing in her head when something happened in the clearing, but she couldn't work out what. Her body knew, her pulse was racing, the pain throbbed in her head.

And then she knew.

Ilic was talking, Peter was talking – but Bo had been silent for a while. He sat there motionless, a huge, crooked shadow in the twilight, the war orphan abroad.

Now only Ilic was talking. His voice sounded as if it were meant to be reassuring, but it didn't conceal his own fear.

"Have they persuaded him to give himself up?" Pauling said.

"I'm not sure," Bermann said. He sounded tense.

She shook her head. Bo wouldn't give himself up. It was either logical reasoning or fear that induced people to surrender. Bo wasn't the kind of man who reasoned, he certainly wasn't logical and fear didn't even come into it. Her mind might be drained, but at least she could process these thoughts.

Bonì's eyes were on Bo, but her thoughts were with Ilic.

"They've talked him round," Pauling said. He'd raised a hand, as if this could prevent any unforeseen incidents in the clearing.

Louise was now beside him. "We have to . . ." She stopped. Bo was on his feet, aiming the pistol at Peter's head.

"Now!" Pauling cried.

A gunshot tore through the silence.

Bo dropped the gun and sat down.

Peter was still alive when they got to him. Pauling held his blood-soaked head while the S.W.A.T. paramedic tried to staunch the bleeding. Other S.W.A.T. officers knelt beside him. "Light!" Pauling yelled. "We need light!" Torches flashed on and in their beams Louise could see Peter moving his fingers, very slowly, as if playing a *larghissimo* without a piano. She turned away and threw her arms around Ilic, who stood beside her, who was unharmed, who would stay alive. He was trembling. Louise stroked his hair and back, but the trembling didn't stop, not even when the torches were switched off and nobody said another word.

Later Ilic told her they had spoken about "home", about Jajce and Sarajevo, the Croatian island of Mljet and Zagreb, about Banja Luka and Belgrade. They'd shared stories from their childhood, but also spoken of the present, of the destruction you still saw when driving down the coast through Krajina to Dubrovnic, or through Bosnia. The war had been present in the stories, but more as an event that had concerned generations other than their own. As if they were the generation whose only contact with the war was through stories. Bo had been happy, and after a while Ilic believed he was more interested in swapping these childhood stories than saving his skin. A few minutes more and he might have surrendered, Ilic said. But then Peter had started talking about how difficult the 1990s had been for him and his family in Germany because of their background and surname. Bo asked what he was called, and Peter said, Mladic, you know, like Ratko Mladic, and then the war caught up with them.

Bermann assembled his D11 colleagues. He was going to stay here, wait for C.S.I. and take a look at the house; the others should return to H.Q. Ilic said he wanted to stay too. No, Bermann said, go back to the office, write up your conversation with Bo, then go home and rest. Ilic shook his head. He didn't want to go home and rest, he wanted to stay. He gazed across the clearing. "I have to stay here now," he said.

Bermann hesitated, then nodded. "In that case, Louise . . ."

She raised a hand defensively. "I'm going home, Rolf, I *can't* any more, I'm going home."

She promised to leave a message on his voicemail if Marcel called. Or anyone else.

Bermann told Wallmer to head back to H.Q., where Bo and Marion Söllien had already been taken, and to have them photographed and fingerprinted and get everything ready for the interrogations the next day.

"Will you give me a lift?" Louise said.

"Sure," Wallmer said, the first time she'd opened her mouth since the raid.

Louise glanced at Pauling as they were leaving. His eyes fixed on the ground, he stood beside the squad leader who was talking frantically at him. Pauling ran a blood-spattered hand through his hair. Louise thought of Theres and Niksch, of Peter Mladic, and of how she and Pauling were quits now, in a way.

She despised herself for this thought.

The darkness of the forest was pierced by numerous shafts of light. Special Support officers with torches were coming and going, and forensics technicians too. Bonì spotted Almenbroich by the cars, but he was heading for the house and didn't notice her. They got into Wallmer's car and drove back through Hinterheuweiler, then Heuweiler. Every-where stood groups of people, watching, talking. Constables kept the road clear. Everything was the same as before, everything was different. The life before, the life after. In the seam joining the two a shot had ripped through the silence. They had to wait at a narrow bend in the village; a fire brigade rescue vehicle with a lighting tower was manoeuvring slowly around the corner. Louise got out and told the man in charge that they wouldn't get to the clearing via Heuweiler, only via the Glottertal. As they were leaving the village Wallmer broke her silence. She asked who the man was that Ilic had spoken about, Ratko Mladic. As far as she could recall, Louise said, Mladic had been in the Bosnian Serb army during the Yugoslav War and was one of those responsible for the massacre at Srebrenica. Massacre of who? Bosnian Muslims, Louise said. Wallmer just nodded.

Louise thought of Pauling. He would go. After a disaster like that, police officers in positions of responsibility had to go. Perhaps she should have gone voluntarily too, back in the winter. Officially, nobody had held her responsible for Niksch's death, but she could have shouldered the blame, just as Pauling would shoulder the blame for Peter Mladic's death.

When Marcel rang they had just turned onto the B3.

"What happened?"

"Were you there?"

"Near enough to hear the shot."

"Bo shot dead one of our S.W.A.T. colleagues."

Marcel paused, then said, "I did warn you."

"Yes. It all got . . . confusing."

"So what now? Are you going to stick to our agreement?"

"In theory, yes."

"In theory, Frau Bonì?"

"I need a phone number. My boss has his doubts."

Wallmer gave her a look of weary surprise. She shrugged. Intuition, or exhaustion perhaps. The memory of Peter Mladic's fingers playing piano without a piano, round and round inside her head.

"Your boss has his doubts?"

"He wants to be able to ring a number and know that you exist."

Marcel sighed, and then gave her a number with a Munich prefix.

She called from her office and spoke to a man with a grumpy voice and Bavarian accent from department 5 of F.I.S. Yes, yes, the man she knew as "Marcel" did work for the service and was with an undercover unit that included agents from allied countries too. As she knew, he said, since 9/11 the service had "modified" its working methods – this operation was an example of the new approach.

So what are they doing?

Establishing contact with a Pakistani informer, if you don't muck things up.

Wallmer gave the thumbs up.

"Is that enough for you?" the man asked.

Louise said yes.

"Never call this number again," he said.

She ended the call and thought, "What utter crap!" Information from mysterious sources – were those stupid games going to start all over again? She pressed last number redial and it rang over the loudspeaker. Nobody answered.

"Well, that's all clear then," Wallmer said. "Even that thing about the American guy. It's all clear now, isn't it?"

"Yes," Louise said. But nothing was clear.

She asked Wallmer to tell Bermann about the calls with Marcel and the man in Pullach.

Anne nodded. "But now you're coming with me."

"Where to?"

"To my office. You need a fresh bandage."

There was so much they should have discussed, Louise thought. Why hadn't Marcel given her the number until now? Why wasn't she to call again? Who was the man with the Bavarian accent? And what sort of unit was it, exactly? What assignments did it have? Why did it resort to methods outside the law if it was part of F.I.S.? And was it conceivable that Marcel, who seemed to know virtually everything, had no idea who'd blown up the weapons depot?

But Louise was far too exhausted to talk about these things now.

At the door she glanced back at the laughing children in their red robes. But all she could see was Peter Mladic's fingers playing piano without a piano.

Wallmer bandaged her arm in silence. Louise was surprised how gentle her strong hands could be. Hands that lifted weights every day, pinned down people in judo holds and held on to detainees without giving them any chance of resistance.

Their eyes met.

"We'll do this every day now, O.K.?" Anne smiled. She looked as if she'd been wanting to cry, but hadn't allowed herself to.

Louise nodded and moved her arm up and down. "Perfect, thanks."

"Say 'Kirchzarten', Anne."

Wallmer was from Cologne. For her it was Kirch*zarten*. "Same as everybody."

Louise nodded. Same as everybody who wasn't from the Breisgau area.

In the car she listened to her voicemail: two new messages. The first was from Turetzki. The three Karachi Pakistanis had got out at Freiburg, where a man had picked them up in a car with Offenburg plates and taken them to Emmendingen town centre. Turetzki gave the car registration and the street name, and repeated both. Boni knew the address already – it was where the student lived whose name was given on the visa applications. Turetzki had followed in a taxi from Freiburg and was now waiting in a side street for "further instructions". No surveillance, no unusual incidents or behaviour, nothing. Three harmless tourists from Asia in beautiful Emmendingen.

And in a side street a forgotten, arthritic old man.

He laughed grimly.

She saved the message and looked at her watch. Half past ten. The couple from Islamabad must have arrived by now too. They would be on their way to Baden.

The second message was from Richard Landen. His voice sounded thoughtful and intense. Listen, I thought I'd drive out to Günterstal to try to deal with those ghosts in my head. Do you fancy coming with me? *Cough. Cough.* I just thought, because of Niksch and the kitchen, we might try and deal with them together. Hmm? He laughed, surprised. Well, it was just a thought. I'm heading off now. Call me.

She groaned. "I want to go home, Rich, I *can't* anymore. I want to go home."

She called Turetzki, thanked him and suggested he spend the night in a hotel in Emmendingen. She dealt with the forgotten old man more cursorily than he deserved so that she could call Richard Landen and tell him that she really *really* wanted to go home, but then again ... well, that she wanted to sleep with him now too, but unfortunately, or thank goodness, she was far too exhausted for that, unless ...

It went to voicemail and she hung up, cursing.

Inside her apartment it was quiet, dark and muggy. She could sense Marcel and the American with every breath. There was a message from Günter on her answerphone.

He told her about Katrin Rein. She was nice. She was pretty. But she wanted to send him to a *therapist*. She thought it was all "psychological". That there was no tumour. He laughed helplessly. He didn't know what he was going to do.

He hung up.

Louise resolved to tell him the stories she'd heard in Oberberg. About the nausea, the breathlessness. The wall which stopped you from being able to leave your own apartment. When he was strong enough to deal with it, someone else could tell him that these were stories about anxiety and depression.

She would tell him that people could be rid of their addictions, but also of what was sitting inside them. And that surely it was better if the tumour turned out not to be a tumour.

But not now. Now she would deal with her ghosts. The dead and the living.

She threw some underwear, trousers and a T-shirt into a holdall, followed by a washbag, a new novel by Nora Roberts and some Barclay James Harvest C.D.s, in case she ended up spending the rest of her life in Günterstal.

She would have liked to take a shower, but put it off till later. Showering in Günterstal seemed like the perfect beginning to the rest of her life.

18

In the hectic summer evening's traffic Louise crossed the Dreisam and turned into Günterstalstrasse. For a brief moment she wrestled with the temptation to turn around and drive to H.Q. Wallmer was there now; Bermann and Almenbroich would be there later. And Ilic, who they'd almost lost this evening. Everyone would be there. They would confer, process what had happened. Determine strategies for tomorrow when they would arrest Rashid, Busche and Mahr, and search the A.P.G.P.F. offices in Offenburg. She ought to be there, she was part of it. But she wouldn't last ten minutes. She needed sleep. She needed someone to lie beside her.

Turning into Schauinslandstrasse she passed the sign that showed her speed: sixty. The limit was forty. She took her foot off the pedal only briefly. A kilometre or so up ahead she saw the twinkling lights of Günterstal, with heavy clouds beyond. It could be one hell of a deluge … Seconds later the red light by the former Cistercian monastery loomed above her and a frantic tram horn blared. Boni braked hard. The tram glided past, bright, unfamiliar faces peering through the windows. She couldn't remember the kilometre between Wiehre and Günterstal.

She'd been asleep for an entire kilometre.

Louise drove on, locking her arms straight and squeezing the wheel to keep herself awake.

The Volvo was parked outside the house with the weeping willow. She pulled in behind it and got out, leaving her bag in the car. She didn't want to terrify the man.

On the dashboard of the Volvo was a mobile, and on the passenger seat Bonì saw scrunched-up paper bags, tissues, plastic bottles and books. Evidently the Landen sense of order had gone. Maybe it had just been a Tommo sense of order.

Light streamed from every window of the house. She could hear fast, rhythmic music she somehow recognised. At the garden gate she thought of Niksch. But the music drove the memory away.

She rang the bell, Landen opened up. With a smile he said, "I knew it."

Then you know the rest too, she thought.

He showed her into the living room. The windows to the garden were open, as was the door to the terrace. Nothing had changed since her last visit at the beginning of the year. The dining table in light wood, soft beige cushions rather than chairs or a sofa in the sitting area. In a windowless alcove stood a vase with three flower stems, with a calligraphy hanging above it. It came back to her: *tokonoma*, the picture recess.

Only the music was new, and it changed everything.

"Santana?"

"*Moonflower*, the album of all albums."

Louise had to smile. Culturally they had been shaped by the same decade, and sometimes it showed. She began to feel more comfortable. The music gave her a sense of home. She'd never been up the Feldberg or Schauinsland, but there was such a thing as a home in time.

And there was music like Santana.

"Alongside Pink Floyd's *Dark Side of the Moon*," she said.

"And *The Doors* at the end of the sixties." Landen's eyes were blazing. He was unshaven and wore jeans and a T-shirt. She could see and feel that he was on the verge of beginning a new life. But he was finding it hard to say goodbye to the old one.

His own child on the other side of the world.

"Not forgetting Genesis, *Seconds Out*," he said.

"We could go on and on."

"Would you like a drink? I've got mineral water, apple juice, orange juice, pear juice, plum juice, blackcurrant juice, carrot juice, tomato juice."

She laughed. He'd been shopping for her. "I'd been expecting a tea."

"Sure, you can have tea too."

"I'll go for pear juice. Then I'm going to have a shower. And after *that* I'm going to sleep. Is that O.K.?"

"Of course."

She yawned. "Or should I have my shower before my drink?"

"Whatever you like."

She yawned again. "Maybe I'll have a coffee first."

"Espresso?"

Louise was still yawning. "Make it a double."

He glanced at her. She shrugged. That was the problem with words when they lost their innocence: they kept on referring to *it*.

"Will you come into the kitchen with me?"

The kitchen was unchanged too. The black china cat on the window sill, the furniture in light wood, the maize-coloured walls. The table where they'd sat in the winter: she, Landen and Niksch.

It wasn't half as bad as she'd expected.

"I visited his grave in the spring," Landen said.

She looked at him in astonishment. "Why?"

"I don't know. Perhaps because we sat here together." He filled a shining chrome espresso machine with water.

"I'm going to go this weekend."

Landen nodded.

The espresso cup was like the filigree teacup from the winter. Boni held it by the rim, fearful of snapping the handle.

They drank standing up.

Niksch was and wasn't there.

The only reason, perhaps, why the memory of him was so painful was because she'd been the one to find him in the forest. Because she'd held him in her arms just minutes after he'd died. If she hadn't found Niksch she would have remembered him in a different, nicer way.

If she hadn't sent him to his death.

But she *hadn't* sent him to his death. She'd asked him to keep an eye on Taro, that's all.

Louise wondered where responsibility began and where it ended.

"He was a sweetie, and good fun. He went rally-driving."

"Rally-driving?"

She nodded and thought of Theres, who also enjoyed rally-driving. Of Pauling, Theres' uncle, who'd hoped for the dark and had made the wrong decision. She thought of Peter Mladic, the German with Serbian heritage. Of Calambert, who she'd shot dead two and a half years ago. But it had been different with Calambert.

Where did responsibility begin, where did it end?

She wanted to talk about it with Landen. She would spend the rest of her life in Günterstal discussing the fundamental aspects of human existence. About words that had lost their innocence, and responsibility that began somewhere, but had to end somewhere too.

They went back into the living room. Santana's "Let the Children Play". She loved this song and hadn't heard it in years. The sentimentality of people in their forties. All of a sudden you would remember the detail of your youth, as if you'd left something precious by the side of the road and were now hurrying back to gather it up. You began to like the pimply, immature, precocious, messy creature from back then. Maybe you began to understand it too.

Louise went to fetch her holdall and followed Landen up to the first floor. The lights were on up here too, and the doors to the rooms open. "Bedroom, guest room, study, bathroom," Landen said with a sweep of his hand. Up here there was an impressive sense of order too. No carpet out of line, no shirt hanging outside the wardrobe, no book jutting out from the rest. She had to smirk when she thought of how this house would look the next morning.

"What's so amusing?"

"Everything's so . . . unbelievably neat and tidy."

"That only started when she got here. She became so unbelievably neat and tidy. She came with me to Germany because she thought that was what was right. The wife goes where the man goes. She thought she would come to like it here, eventually. But she never did. She always felt an outsider. Hence the order amongst the chaos. She clung to it. To straight lines, to what appeared to be perfect. The simple beauty of a view disturbed by nothing." He opened his arms. "Zen."

"I'll soon bring disorder to your Zen," she said.

"We've already done that," Landen said.

The bathroom smelled of Tommo. But apart from that she'd vanished from it. No little bottles, jars or tins that only women used. Was Zen not emptiness too?

And was emptiness not the perfect order?

Louise sighed. Her thoughts were becoming treacly again.

She undressed but resisted the temptation to toss her clothes in a corner, only to return in a week to see what had happened to them. Maybe Tommo would come back from Japan to wash and iron them.

She laughed. It was O.K. to be a little bit mean.

But at the mirror her smile vanished. Even a week's sleep wouldn't come close to being enough.

The lights in the living room had been switched off. The music was off. She stood by the door, looking for Landen in the darkness. She went barefoot across the room and sat on one of the cushions. What a wonderful place to sleep together. Surrounded by the silence and beauty of this sparsely furnished room with no distractions.

But she wouldn't sleep with him in this room. Not in this house.

They had to find a place where it would only be a little bit mean to Tommo. Somewhere else in time or space.

He was out in the garden at the back of the house, sitting on a chair in the darkness. Glasses, bottles and an unlit candle stood on a small wooden table. He smiled when she appeared, a meaningful smile. She sat facing him on his lap and they kissed. Louise felt the first drops of warm rain on her arms. Unfamiliar warm hands on her breasts. Landen could be lustful too.

She felt as though she had come back to some sort of home after many years. She thought of Tommo, who'd returned to a home of a different kind.

At some point she sensed that Landen had opened his eyes. "We've got time," he said to her lips.

"Right now," she said, putting her arms around his neck and laying her head on his shoulder.

The rain became heavier for a few minutes, then stopped abruptly. But the low-hanging black clouds still rumbled and growled.
Louise was sitting on a second chair, drinking pear juice and fighting the tiredness. Don't fall asleep now, she thought. Not now.

The air was warm, damp and heavy.

She placed a hand on the table between them. Just in case Landen's hand was there, but it wasn't.

She wanted to talk about the child that would be born in Japan and would live in Japan. About her two brothers, the dead one and the living one. But she felt it wasn't the time. And after all, she hadn't come to talk.

"Would you make me another espresso?"

"Of course." He went back into the house.

Louise looked out at the garden. As far as she could make out there was no order here. The garden looked as if everything was allowed to grow up as it pleased, until someone came to chop it back. Then it would grow again as it pleased.

When Landen returned with the espresso, she said, "Is the garden your domain?"

"Is that so obvious?"

"No Zen."

They laughed. She heaped sugar into her coffee and saw that he was watching her. Unfamiliar hands, unfamiliar movements. He looked interested. She sensed that he liked her hands and movements.

She thought of his hands. Of his lust.

"Why do you wear a ring on your thumb?"

She shrugged and knocked back her espresso.

"Silver suits you. But how about gold? Don't you like gold?"

"No."

Louise stood up to take off her T-shirt and bra and went to him. She felt sexy, eroticised. Everything was warm, damp, heavy, everything swollen. Landen followed her with his eyes. Even before she sat on him his hands were there. His hands were warm, damp and heavy.

She rested her elbows on his shoulders as they kissed. It struck her that she was kissing Tommo's husband, being caressed and unbuttoned by Tommo's husband.

She turned around so he could slip a hand inside her trousers. When the hand had been inside her trousers for a while, Tommo's husband whispered, "Not here, Louise. Not now."

She sat on his lap for a moment longer in the hope that he might change his mind.

And because his hand was still there.

"Do you understand?"

Louise had dressed again and was sitting on the other chair. "Depends," she said with a yawn.

"On what?"

"On when." She hadn't understood him while sitting on his lap, but now from the other side of the table she could understand.

He nodded and looked away. His fingers stroked hers. "Even though we're separating, this is her place," he said. "She's here. The house is part of her, it belongs to her . . . I don't know how to put it. It would hurt her deeply. It would wreck something that was once important to her, and to me. God knows you can't live without being considerate towards someone you once loved."

Louise yawned again. She didn't know what she could and couldn't do. Whether she'd be able to stop at that stage again. Despite her scruples, she had started.

But she believed she understood Landen. For him, consideration, restraint and self-denial were, in a way, a passion. A very personal passion that fulfilled him.

Her self-denial was accompanied by regret, his by commitment.

"Fine," she said. "But at some point a new life has to begin."

"Shizu and my son will be a part of my new life too."

"Yes, but there will come a time when you won't be wrecking anything by having your hand in my trousers. Except perhaps my trousers.

He laughed in surprise.

"I mean, one can take things too far," she said.

"That's true."

"Even being considerate and having one's doubts."

"Do I though? Hmm, maybe sometimes."

"I'll help you find the right level."

He smiled. "But for now, leave the T-shirt on."

At some point Louise's eyes closed. She felt his hand in hers, the warm, heavy air, the warm, heavy tiredness. Sleep, at last. But at the very back of her mind, a word had appeared that would not let her rest.

Marcel.

She opened her eyes. Marcel, who was everywhere. Here too?

Louise found this thought absurd. Why would he be spying on her here? All the same her eyes scanned the dark, low hedge that divided the garden from the neighbouring property. He'd been inside her apartment.

She saw nothing, and yet . . . Marcel was here. If not out there in the darkness, then somewhere inside her. "Let's go in."

In the living room they lay facing each other on the cushions. Their bare feet were touching. Louise closed her eyes briefly. Marcel had been joined by the memory of Mladic.

Peter Mladic from Lahr, his grandmother a Serb from Banja Luka in Bosnia.

Bonì realised that she was missing a second or two of her memory, like the entire kilometre she'd missed on the road to Günterstal. She was missing the moment when Mladic was shot and had collapsed, and she realised she hadn't witnessed it. She'd closed her eyes just before Bo fired. She'd opened them just after Mladic fell. That wasn't a microsleep. She'd obeyed an instinct; she hadn't wanted to witness it.

Automatic protection mechanisms that controlled the body.

Landen was staring at her. She smiled fleetingly. Don't say anything, Rich, I'm thinking.

She knew what trauma could do. How deeply it ate into the subconscious, what it could give rise to years later. Calambert was a kind of trauma, but there were worse. One of her colleagues, a young officer at the time, had been taken hostage by a bank robber and not freed for hours. For years not even his wife noticed that anything was wrong. Then, on holiday fifteen years later, he'd collapsed in tears and ended up in a trauma clinic.

Bonì was glad that she closed her eyes sometimes.

She thought of Pauling, who wouldn't have closed his eyes. Of Bo, who'd been a child during the war in his home country. Of the countless people in Croatia, Bosnia and Serbia who had suffered the most dreadful experiences and had no trauma clinics.

She thought of Ilic, who hadn't wanted to let his fear show. Who'd trembled for some time after everything was over.

"I have *no* idea where your thoughts have taken you," Landen said.

"You could be anywhere. Maybe you're asleep?"

She smiled again. How she'd missed moments like these. "What do you know about the Yugoslav War?"

"Which one?"

"The one in 1991."

She told him about Heuweiler and Bo, Ilic and Peter Mladic from Lahr.

Landen sat up. "Christ, that's . . ."

They looked at each other. My profession, she thought. That's my profession. You have to get used to stories like this.

To crimes.

He shook his head. "That's horrific."

"What do you know about the Yugoslav War?"

Landen said nothing. He looked away.

"Yes," she said. "Truly horrific."

"And bloody irresponsible."

"You weren't there, Richard. It could have gone fine."

"He was a Serb. Surely it was predictable, what would happen."

"He wasn't a Serb, he was German."

"Then he'd still be alive, wouldn't he?"

She nodded slowly. Sometimes you were German, sometimes not.

"What about you? You must be . . . You watched a man being killed. A *colleague*. How can you be so calm?"

Now Louise sat up too. It was happening early on, the not understanding each other. Maybe that was a good thing; they would suffer no illusions.

"I was there and I'll never forget it. Maybe that's all there is to it."

Landen had gone to the kitchen to make himself an espresso. She assumed he was mulling things over. Wondering whether he wanted to be confronted with such stories. She lay on her back. My profession, my stories, she thought. Part of my old life, part of my new one. When you take on someone, you take on their stories too, Rich.

When he came back she said, "You have no right to criticise me for how I deal with what happens in my life."

He sat beside her and put down the cup. "I know. But how should *I* deal with it?"

Good question. They needed to find an answer if this evening's developments were to have any future. She thought of Mick. Mick's answer had been simple: I don't want to know, Lou. I want you to give up that fucking job. Come on, let's have a shag, Lou.

Landen's hand was on her tummy, half on her T-shirt, half on bare skin. But it seemed to want only to rest there, nothing more.

All the same, the fact that it rested there was an answer of sorts.

To whatever was the question.

"The Yugoslav War, Richard."

"Hmm, that might take a while."

"We have time."

He pulled away his hand and rolled onto his back. Well, he said, in fact it was all quite simple. The Slovenes and Croats wanted to leave the Serbian-dominated federation; the Serbs wanted to prevent this. The Slovenes and Croats declared independence; the Serbs started a war.

"But . . ." Louise said with a yawn.

"The 'but' is the problem," Landen said.

"As always," she said, and she fell asleep.

Louise dreamed of Yugoslavia. A chaotic dream, bloody, incomprehensible, a total mess, and yet very precise. The Second World War made an appearance too, as did the First, Austria–Hungary, the fascist Croat Ustaše state with its concentration camps, murderous Serb Chetniks, and Tito partisans who killed Croatian and German fascists along with many civilians. The old red-and-white chessboard, the Ustaše emblem, the emblem of the new, independent Croatia. Krajina Serbs, who'd once been a constituent people, were then declared a minority and proclaimed their autonomy in what had suddenly become a foreign country. Serb militias and bands of Serb butchers, Serb massacres, Serb refugees. Muslims suffering, ethnic cleansing. The early recognition of the new states by Germany and Austria, which proved counterproductive, and the at times biased reporting in the Western media. The propaganda of nationalists on three sides. Three deluded old men. Srebrenica featured in the dream, the massacre of Muslims before the eyes of a world that sat back and did nothing. And Bonì kept dreaming of questions. What was true, what was not? What was propaganda, what was not. What had really happened? Everything that had been reported? What role had religion played? How was reconciliation possible if there was no real coming to terms with events? Was it too early for this? What was the future for the artificial construct that was Bosnia and Herzegovina, with its two constituent parts and three ethnic groups? When would an international, objective evaluation of the events take place? Could it simply be left to the International Court of Justice? Could states be admitted to the E.U. without achieving reconciliation with each other? Why didn't the Western media review its reporting? Surely democracy was objective reporting too. "The thing with us", Louise, she dreamed, might become something, but it'll take time. The but, she dreamed, is always the problem.

Hours later she woke with a start. It was lashing down outside, and the air was damp and stale. She could hear a soft, familiar melody coming from somewhere.

Landen was asleep on his side, facing her. His arms crossed over his chest, his mouth slightly open, his eyebrows slightly raised. Even in his sleep he seemed to be thinking. She laid a hand on his cheek. Stop worrying about things, don't always worry. It's just how it is.

Louise got up to close the door to the terrace and heard the music again. Erik Satie.

She found her mobile on the hall table. "Illi" on the display.

It was just before three o'clock.

"We've been had," Ilic said.

19

She left without waking Landen, closing the front door as gently as possible. At the garden gate she looked back. The branches of the willow bobbed up and down in the heavy rain. The house itself was dark and silent. More than ever it was Tommo's house. She felt like going back in and waking Landen, to take him from this dark place, but she knew that this was ridiculous. It was his house; he would have to leave it of his own accord.

And was this really what she wanted? Did she belong in the same house as Landen?

By the time she got in the car she was soaked through, and she realised she'd left the holdall with her dirty clothes in the house. With Nora Roberts and Barclay James Harvest. She pictured Landen opening the bag and taking out her things. He would find out a lot about her.

She liked the idea.

Boni returned Ilic's call when she was on the road. Earlier he had outlined the essentials; now he filled in the details.

It didn't change anything. They'd made a catastrophic mistake. They had been duped by Marcel. Marcel wasn't a colleague. He was . . . They didn't know who or what he was. Who he was working for. Not for F.I.S. – that much, at least, seemed to be clear now.

Rather than go to a hotel, Turetzki had sat on a bench by a stream in Emmendingen and observed the house into which the three harmless tourists from Asia had gone. Bermann had called him and said, thanks for everything, he should finish up now and find himself a hotel. But Turetzki didn't want to go to a hotel. He didn't know why, exactly, but for the time being he wanted to stay on the bench and watch the house. "He explained it was because of his hip joint," Ilic said calmly. "The pain in his hip was so strange, totally different from normal, so he guessed something was up." Ilic stopped talking. Bermann was shouting in the background. Someone else shouted too.

She sped through the Cistercian gate. The rain had let up. Bricks were rattling around inside her head, their corners and edges digging into everything that was soft and sensitive. "What then?"

"Wait," Ilic said. A door was closed and the voices were no longer audible.

Then, at around half past two, four cars had driven up to the house in Emmendingen: three black 4×4s and a black Mercedes. Half a dozen men leaped out and disappeared into the house. When Turetzki took out his mobile a man's voice behind him said, "No!" He felt the gentle pressure of a hand on his shoulder. "O.K.?" the voice said, in a very friendly tone. "O.K.," Turetzki said. He'd had to give the man his mobile and pistol, and move away from the house. Which was why he only heard rather than saw what happened a few minutes later: the footsteps of lots of different people, a man groaning, car doors slamming, the vehicles driving off. Then Turetzki was alone.

"They were after the three Pakistanis and the student," Ilic said. "That's what it was about all along. They weren't interested in talking to an informer, they wanted the Pakistanis, the Jinnah grandson in particular, I expect. That's what it was all about. They've got nothing to do with F.I.S., they've got nothing to do with us. They're bounty hunters, or . . ." He broke off.

She nodded. Despite her headache she was beginning to understand. "They blew up the depot themselves, Marcel's lot."

"Yes."

"Because they wanted to lure the Pakistanis to Freiburg. The Jinnah grandson."

"Yes."

She tried to picture the man with the beard – the Jinnah grandson – but couldn't. "That can't all be true, Illi," she said.

"No. Yes."

And yet, she thought, somehow it was entirely logical.

Louise had reached Wiehre. The streets were dry. As so often, the
rain had stayed in the valleys. She thought of Tommo's house in
the pouring rain, of Landen who would feel lonely when he woke up.
Without Tommo, without the lustful chief inspector who came at
night and left at night.

"What about the others? The couple from Islamabad?"

"They're gone too." They had arrived at Rashid's at around half
past midnight, and vanished without trace at half past three. "And
someone else has disappeared," Ilic said.

"I know. Trumic."

"Have you read the e-mail!"

"Which e-mail?"

During the evening another e-mail had arrived from Islamabad.
Trumic's wife had reported her husband missing. Missing on the way
from his office to his apartment. Louise nodded. That seemed sort of
logical too. The Pakistanis in Freiburg and Emmendingen, the Bosnian
in Islamabad.

Marcel had cleaned up.

Police H.Q. was brightly lit. Constables and Kripo officers were hurrying along corridors, S.W.A.T. officers loitered. She met Löbinger on
the steps but he ignored her. Ilic was suddenly at her side. She touched
his arm, eager to sob with relief that nothing had happened to him
in Heuweiler, but if she remembered right she'd already done that
back then in his arms.

As they ran upstairs he filled her in.

Abdul Rashid and his wife had been arrested by Pauling's team.
The wife had suffered a nervous collapse and they'd rung the emergency doctor. They were still in the apartment. Rashid was now at

police H.Q., having been brought there by Pauling himself. Vormweg had enforced the highest level of security. Rashid might look distinguished and harmless, but for now he was to be regarded as a terrorist.

A search had been put out for the three Pakistanis from Karachi and Marcel. Two helicopters were on their way from Stuttgart, several S.S.U.s from Lahr, as well as the F.C.P.O. from Wiesbaden.

But they could be anywhere.

"Maybe not," Bonì said.

"What?"

"The American. If Americans were involved . . ." She stopped. She had been thinking of military bases, but then she remembered Baudy's report – Americans in the Grosse Tal.

But there they would be trapped.

"Are you thinking of an American military base?"

"You know, you hear and read things."

Ilic didn't respond. He seemed to be pondering what it was you hear and read.

"Söllingen, near Baden-Baden," she said.

"It was abandoned in the early nineties."

"Really? Then maybe Ramstein, or Spangdahlem."

"Those are two or three hours' drive away, Louise."

"They can easily evacuate them from there."

Ilic nodded. "Anyway, the Grosse Tal."

"They'd be trapped, Illi."

Ilic had been reading Adam Baudy's report. When Baudy had speculated who might have set fire to Riedinger's shed, he'd thought of the asylum seekers in Keltenbuck, the Dutch at the campsite, and the American students camping in the Grosse Tal.

For a moment they were silent. American students – that sounded far-fetched. But the same was true of Ramstein and Spangdahlem.

Bonì remembered that Marcel had said *Kirch*zarten. That perhaps he knew the Grosse Tal because he'd once lived in the region.

She couldn't get the Grosse Tal out of her head.

"We need to speak to Baudy," she said.

"Later," Ilic insisted.

She nodded. She felt that Baudy had been right. It's all in my report, he'd said.

All was quiet in section D11 on the third floor. No-one was to be seen apart from Vormweg and Almenbroich, who were standing in the corridor and looked at her. Almenbroich's hand rested on the handle to one of the offices. He seemed to be supporting himself.

She stopped. For the first time since Ilic had telephoned, the question of responsibility came to mind. Marcel had been in *her* apartment. She was the only one who'd seen him, the only one to have spoken to him.

She had believed him. She'd told the others about him.

Boni scrutinised the faces of both Vormweg and Almenbroich for any sign of recrimination or reproach. But all she saw was helplessness, horror and torpor.

"How's the arm?" Vormweg said.

"It's a disaster, Louise," Almenbroich said.

A door opened and a woman she didn't know stepped into the corridor. She was short, pale, nondescript, and she smelled of cigarette smoke. Her suit from a cut-price department store, her haircut straight from a woman's magazine. At first glance one of those sad, overlooked souls who sat at the tills in discount supermarkets. But Vormweg and Almenbroich stood up straight. "My colleagues will be here in an hour," the woman said.

Vormweg nodded.

"F.C.P.O.," Almenbroich explained to Louise.

Vormweg seemed to pull himself together. "We have a meeting in the task force room in five minutes."

"Where's that?" the woman said.

"On the fourth floor. Come with me." Vormweg and the woman walked off.

"What a disaster," Almenbroich said again. He looked greyer, feebler, sicker than on the previous evening, and all at once she was struck by the consequences of the disaster. Almenbroich would be saddled with the responsibility. As soon as the file was closed he would go, would be removed from the firing line, which for high-ranking officers meant promotion to the district administrative authority or state police headquarters. If that didn't appeal, he would be transferred to some college, maybe the police training college in Villingen-Schwenningen, maybe the outpost of the police academy in Wertheim, where few went voluntarily.

Not a good moment for confrontation, but she stepped close to him. "I'd like to know what you're keeping from me."

"I'm sorry?"

"I *have* to know. I can't go on like this, with the feeling that you . . ."

Almenbroich straightened his back and took his hand off the door handle. She expected him to fall, but he didn't. At a stroke his strength seemed to have returned. Perhaps, she thought, there was still hope, in every respect.

They headed towards the stairs.

"When all this is over, I'll tell—"

"No," she said. "*Now.*"

They stopped.

"Fine." Almenbroich's voice and expression were stern and resolute. This is the Almenbroich she knew, feared and admired. "I don't care what's on your file. You had a crisis, you got over it. You showed you're strong enough, stronger than most of us. But when I'm no longer around, my opinion isn't going to count anymore. Then you—"

"I don't think I want to hear this," she said in horror.

"—then you're what it says in your file. A difficult, quick-tempered, intelligent, highly demanding colleague with an alcohol problem. An *alcoholic.* And that's how you'll be treated unofficially, irrespective of whether you drink again or not. You won't be promoted again, you'll never head up a task force, you'll always have your past thrown in your face, like at the meeting yesterday."

Almenbroich paused for breath.

"I don't want to hear this, Herr Almenbroich," she said.

"When I'm no longer here I won't be able to protect you, Louise. Then you'll pretty much be on your own. *That's* what I've been thinking about these past few days. *That's* what I've been, well, keeping from you. Do you want to apologise now, or when this disaster is over?"

She said nothing and they went to the lift. Almenbroich pressed the call button. "Did you really think I was withholding information from you?"

"I . . ." She broke off.

"There's no need to apologise," he said. He seemed grey, feeble and sick once more. "We've all been . . . this terrible heat. This terrible case."

The doors slid open and they entered the cabin. Almenbroich pressed "4". The doors closed. "Now I'm going to fling my arms around your neck and have a good cry," Louise said.

Almenbroich pressed "STOP".

The meeting began at three fifteen and lasted barely ten minutes. Bermann spoke for most of it. Nobody asked critical questions regarding the events of the past few hours. No blame, no discussion, no argument. This was not the time to review matters. "We're going after A.P.G.P.F. now," Bermann said. There were heavy bags under his eyes and he was sweaty, impatient. He didn't look at anyone while he spoke.

Löbinger and a few of his team were there, Pauling was there, Vormweg and the two F.C.P.O. members were there. Schneider, Wallmer and Ilic were there. Pauling's squad leader wasn't there. For a moment she was confused, then the penny dropped.

Pauling would *not* be going.

Unlike Almenbroich. In the lift between the third and fourth floors, the disaster in plain view, his howling problem child in his arms, he'd confirmed all that she had feared. Of course he would be going.

"Anselm and his team will get Busche," Bermann said. "Anne and Heinz will get the teacher from Ehrenkirchen, Illi and Louise will get Mahr, and I'll start interrogating Rashid, Marion Söllien and Bo. Our colleagues in Spain will look after the couple on Mallorca. Questions?"

Vormweg raised his hand. "Is Mahr the former member of the regional parliament? That's a really tricky one. Maybe we should . . ." He broke off; Bermann was already shaking his head.

"Illi and Louise will arrest him."

Vormweg looked at Ilic. The tiredness in his face had momentarily given way to worry. Think about it. A politician. Really tricky. Ilic gave a reassuring nod. Don't worry, we'll take him with kid gloves on. Tricky politicians are our speciality. The half-Croat officer, the half-French officer: a good team.

Good man, bad woman.

In spite of everything she had to smile.

"Alright, then," Vormweg said.

"No more questions?"

"Yes," she said. Rashid – what was he saying? Bermann shrugged. What people say when they're arrested. It's a mistake. I haven't done anything wrong. I'll cooperate. I want a lawyer. I'm German.

German?

Naturalised through marriage.

"Is that it?" Bermann asked.

Nobody said anything. Bonì looked at the faces of her colleagues. Tired faces, most of them apathetic, bewildered, at a loss. Faces in the mirror of disaster. She realised that nobody wanted to think about the Pakistanis abducted in Emmendingen, or Marcel and his "unit". Terrorists in the Breisgau district? Extra-legal terrorist *hunters* in the Breisgau? We're not equipped for that. It's not our responsibility. We're out of our depth. Anyway, how can it all be true? I mean really, in the Breisgau! Let's get the A.P.G.P.F., the tired faces said, then we're done.

"No, not yet," she said.

The apathetic faces turned to her.

The three Pakistanis from Karachi. Marcel and his people. What about them?

Bermann's eyes widened. In them was a spark she couldn't interpret, but she knew it meant nothing pleasant. The search was underway, he replied; they could do no more for the time being. In any case it was the F.C.P.O.'s responsibility.

Now she understood. You should be bloody happy that this poisoned chalice is passing us by, the spark said. Terrorists and terrorist hunters in the Breisgau, Christ, what can we do? "If one of Marcel's men is an American . . ." she began.

"We'll take care of that," the F.C.P.O. woman said.

"If one of them is American, there might be more too."

"I said we'll take care of it."

"And they might head for Ramstein or Spangdahlem and within a couple of hours they're gone for ever."

The F.C.P.O. woman sighed.

"We've got vivid imaginations down here in the Breisgau."

"And we've got the experience."

"*Please*," Vormweg said.

"Americans, Luis . . ." Löbinger said, adjusting his glasses. "Do you understand the implications of what you're saying?"

"You hear and read things."

"Oh really? What, for example?"

Louise signalled to Ilic to let her answer. She didn't want him to stick his neck out. She was responsible for rebellion, he for integration. That was important. Let's not confuse our roles and tasks, Illi, but thanks all the same. Guantanamo, she said, C.I.A. abductions, dragging prisoners off to states that sanction torture. You didn't need much of an imagination to start believing that other stories were possible.

Löbinger took off his glasses, rubbed his eyes, put the glasses back on. "Look, I don't understand a word she's saying. What *is* she talking about?"

"Let's leave the Pakistanis and Marcel to the F.C.P.O., shall we?" Almenbroich said.

Bonì shook her head. She had more questions. The couple from Islamabad – they had disappeared, but was that all they knew? Or did they know more? Ilic said they didn't know *much* more, and this only thanks to the initial information from Rashid. Apparently he'd been woken by the telephone at half past two. He said he'd heard animated voices and the sound of the door closing. When he got up to check he realised his "guests" had gone. Shortly afterwards he went back to bed and within minutes he found himself surrounded by a S.W.A.T. team. "But whether he's telling the truth . . ." Ilic shrugged.

While the others stood up Louise tried to grasp what Ilic had said.

Marcel's people had been to Emmendingen, but not to Rashid's in Freiburg. The couple from Islamabad had been tipped off; they'd left Rashid's apartment about an hour ago and hadn't been kidnapped.

Louise wanted to say something, but left it. Bermann had already gone and the others were thronging towards the door. She stood up and followed Ilic into the corridor. A man and a woman from Islamabad, she thought, roaming around Freiburg, maybe on the run, maybe on the hunt.

The rain had not yet reached the city by the time she left the building at 3.30 a.m. An oppressive mugginess hung over Freiburg because the low, heavy clouds – this, at least, was her explanation – kept the air trapped. She decided that later on, after they'd arrested Mahr, she would take a drive in the rain and then stand out in it. It would wash away the tiredness, the headaches – everything that didn't belong in her head or in the Breisgau. "If you were them, where would you go?" she asked Ilic.

"Hmm?"

"They don't have that many options."

"No."

"Busche, the teacher, Mahr."

"Yes."

"Marcel said the teacher's not part of it. Maybe that's true at least."

"Yes, maybe."

They got into Ilic's car. "I'd go to Mahr," she said.

"Why?" He put the folder on the dashboard. They wouldn't get lost then, she thought with a smile.

"Because of Aziza."

"Aziza's been dead for thirteen years."

"Maybe she's a link."

"You mean another key figure?"

"Maybe, yes."

She leaned her head back and yawned. As Ilic started the car she asked if they had a recent photograph of Johannes Mahr. Yes, he said, pointing to the folder. She didn't have the strength to look. Boni's thoughts returned to the man and woman from Islamabad who were either on the run or on the hunt in Freiburg. But when she closed her eyes she saw Bo and Peter Mladic and Thomas Ilic. They were sitting in the clearing near Heuweiler, and they had stopped talking.

Louise opened her eyes and touched Ilic's arm. Caress or sob, she thought, and she'd just been sobbing.

"I'm alright," he said.

"Good."

But she didn't believe him. His voice sounded breathy, his face shone white in the darkness. It seemed as if he was only gradually becoming aware of what had happened in Heuweiler.

Cars glided past, pallid faces behind the windows. Louise waved to Wallmer, she saw Löbinger – he ignored her – in a passenger seat, with the nervous, young blonde officer from his section in the back. His nose was pressed up against the window and he gave her a coy smile.

She smiled back maternally. Her young men phase was over. Now it was time for more seasoned ones.

*

Boni's eyes closed and she fell asleep, her head against the window. She awoke with a start when the car stopped. She was surrounded by orange neon light – a petrol station. Ilic was outside. She saw a woman step out of a French car in the darkness of an early morning and enter the shop. A little Sunday gathering, little Wednesday gathering, little birthday gathering. On the counter: orange juice, coke and the rest. Half a dozen bottles, sometimes more, three bags, a few pages from Ronescu's *Badische Zeitung* to muffle the clinking and clanking. Then slowly back to the car where the bags with their soundproofed bottles were zipped into an overnight bag. Always the same, a ritual, a habit. Only the places changed; sometimes she'd driven to Lahr or Bad Krozingen. Sometimes she could tell from a particular look or gesture that she had already been there, even though she'd thought it was for the first time. The woman having the little party, three bags, yes, she'd forced herself to hold the gaze. Ilic came back to the car and a shudder ran down Louise's spine. What a life, a life full of lies, shame, humiliation. But she had done it, she thought; she'd finished that life and begun a new one, all of that was practically over, the life before, the life after – there were in fact substantial differences. All that remained was the memory of the shame, the suffering, a feeling in her skin that would never go away. But it was a good feeling, and it definitely helped with the complicated undertaking that was life.

Later, to stop herself from nodding off again, she asked about Bermann. What was up with Rolf? From confidante to necessary evil – surely she couldn't be responsible this time.

"Rolf?" Ilic muttered.

"Do you know anything?"

"We . . . we had a little chat yesterday."

"While I was asleep."

He nodded.

Rita Bermann wanted her husband's career to go places. In her eyes he ought to become chief officer and, in the long term, get a promotion into the upper echelons of the force. One year at the police college in Villingen-Schwenningen, one year at the management academy in Münster. It didn't have to happen straightaway – she felt she was being reasonable about this – but at some point. The main thing was that it was and remained the plan. It was all well and good, his being an outstanding section head, but what use was that if he progressed no further? Salary grade A14 sounded better than A13, and A15 was a worthy goal. Give me status and I'll shut my mouth, Louise thought. Then I'll look after your many children and turn a blind eye to all your women. She couldn't help smiling. Everything really did have its price, and not even all those pretty, slim, sexy blondes came for free.

"What does Rolf say?"

"That he'd rather stay where he is."

"So now he has to become something he doesn't want to be."

Ilic said nothing.

"And all for love." She laughed.

"Ha ha. Talking of Rolf," Ilic said. He'd also spoken to Bermann about Pauling, who had relieved his squad leader of all duties. He'd said that as the S.W.A.T. boss he needed to be able to rely on the judgement of his men and the information they gave him. You couldn't make the right decisions if you got the wrong information. There was no doubt his squad leader was a good man, but perhaps he was better suited to a different position.

"Democracy." She yawned. "The big cheeses survive." Democracy and love, she thought, what hypocritical words, what slimy words – surely their original meanings were different.

"But in a way he's right, don't you think?" Ilic said.

She yawned again. "The 'but' is always the problem."

"Have a little snooze."

She smiled. That was a real partner.

20

When Ilic woke her they had stopped in a dark, narrow street, perpendicular to the one in which Mahr lived. Louise was about to get out of the car, but he held her back. He'd driven twice past Mahr's house, he said. It was light in the room to the right on the ground floor and light in the kitchen to the left, but he hadn't seen anyone.

She checked the time. A quarter to four. Even politicians were asleep at a quarter to four in the morning.

They considered requesting back-up.

"But how long is that going to take?" she said with a yawn.

"They come pretty quick," Ilic said, taking out his mobile.

But not today, today it was going to take a while. The hunt for Marcel and his team, the arrest of the teacher in Ehrenkirchen and of Busch in Lahr – every officer available at this time of the morning would be out on duty, the rest were being woken now.

"Come on, then," Louise said.

But Ilic stayed behind the wheel. The man and woman from Islamabad, she thought, and lights on at a quarter to four in the morning. And Heuweiler. Heuweiler was catching up with him.

"We'll just take a look around, Illi."

"That would be contrary to your reputation."

"It's something I'd like to shed."

"At four o'clock in the morning?"

"When else?" She laughed. "Come on."

They got out of the car.

*

Ilic went ahead of her, in the wrong direction, but she followed him in silence, thinking of her reputation. They climbed over a fence, wandered along the wall of a building and wriggled their way into a conifer hedge. Through the branches they saw the bright glow of a lit-up room. Ilic put a finger to his lips. They were there.

Shielded by a garden shed they emerged onto a closely mown lawn. In the darkness they took a few steps towards the house, which was old and welcoming, three storeys, balconies on the first floor and a bay window on the second. It stood in the middle of a large green garden. Louise liked the look of it – a house for a new life. After all, they would need a new house, she and Landen.

Ilic stopped when they had a good view of the lit-up room about thirty metres away. A large living room, a dining table, chairs, coffee table, an armchair. A man was sitting in the armchair at the coffee table. As far as she could make out he was around sixty years of age, tall, slim, almost bald, glasses, and wearing a suit and tie.

"Mahr?" she whispered.

Ilic nodded. She nodded too.

They sat back to back on the lawn and for about five minutes observed the man in the living room, the house, the garden and the hedge. Mahr didn't move, nobody came or went. The man and woman from Islamabad weren't there. Marcel wasn't there.

"By the way . . ." Ilic whispered right into her ear.

The Bureau's forensics team had listened to the recording of her conversation and come up with some initial hypotheses. Childhood here in the region, adolescence in northern Germany, probably the Bremen area, but dialectal colour almost completely eliminated through years of elocution training. Early forties, high social standing, academic education. Decisive, calculating, clever. Cold-blooded. Passionate. She pictured Marcel and nodded.

The details would follow.

"What do forensics say about me?"

"They're still puzzling over which species you belong to."

They laughed silently.

Bonì looked again at Mahr. For the first time she wondered how he would react to the accusations. What sort of person he was.

Who he was waiting for.

"Illi…"

"He's waiting for someone."

"Yes."

"The question is: who?"

She shook her head. She knew the answer.

The conifer hedge extended around the entire perimeter of the property, interrupted only by the gate and the entrance to the garage, where there was an unobstructed view of the house.

By the bell a yellow clay sign with four names: JOHANNES, SUSANNE, TOBIAS, FLORIAN MAHR. Susanne and the children lived in Stuttgart, Ilic had said.

They checked their weapons and took out their police I.D.s. She thought of Hannes Riedinger, who'd lived alone in rooms for five people. Of Richard Landen, who would be alone when he awoke this morning. Of Johannes Mahr, who was alone in his living room at four in the morning, waiting to be arrested. Ultimately life boiled down to being alone.

Thoughts in darkness and tiredness.

Ilic looked at his watch. "Three more minutes."

She raised her eyebrows.

"Paragraph 104, criminal procedure code."

"Really?"

"Between nine p.m. and four a.m. we are only permitted to enter and search a property if we catch somebody committing an offence, or in the case of imminent danger."

"I didn't know the criminal procedure code had so many sections. I stopped reading after paragraph 1."

Ilic smiled feebly. "The substantive jurisdiction of courts is determined by the Courts Constitution Act."

"No novel could have a more thrilling opening line. I've been wondering what that means for twenty years."

"I'll explain if you like."

"Next week, Illi."

"Two minutes," he said.

They waited.

"O.K.," Ilic said at length, but didn't move. She felt that he was at the end of his tether, his self-control.

"It's got to be now, Illi. Just this last thing."

He nodded.

Bonì opened the garden gate and walked up to the house, her I.D. in one hand, the Walther in the other. Her eyes darted from the door to the windows, the corners, back and forth – you never knew. Out of the corner of her eye she registered fruit trees, a basketball net, a small football goal, a washing stand. A garden for four people, she thought, and wondered why these things always occurred to her.

Ilic caught up with her.

She rang the bell and heard slow footsteps. Mahr opened the door and they introduced themselves. Mahr glanced at the I.D.s and nodded. Stepping aside, he said simply, "Come in."

Nothing more.

Mahr was back in the armchair, Louise and Ilic sitting opposite him. Ilic explained that an arrest warrant had been issued, that they were here to carry out the arrest and that he would be given a copy of the warrant at the police station in the morning. "Yes," Mahr said, nodding, but he refrained from looking at either Bonì or Ilic.

"Would you like to call your wife? Another family member or a friend? One of your sons?"

"No," Mahr said. "No, I've rung my lawyer, but he's not there, he hasn't called me back." He raised his hands and stared at his fingers. Mahr had small hands and small fingers; overall he looked a fragile person even though he was very tall, as tall as Täschle, Louise reckoned. But he sat hunched. He had a white, trimmed beard and short hair above his ears, but nowhere else. His eyes were red and he wore teardrop-shaped glasses. A harmless-looking backbencher who'd taken a circuitous route into the regional parliament, an expert in some complex international legal issues. Voters liked to have experts dealing with such matters in their regional parliament.

Mahr dropped his hands and, without looking up, said, "I suspect he's on holiday, so now I don't really know what to do."

"You don't have a huge number of options," Louise said.

"No." Mahr took out a cloth handkerchief, awkwardly lifted his glasses and dried his eyes. "I'm glad that—"

"This isn't an interrogation, Dr Mahr," Ilic interrupted him gently. "You don't have to comment on the charges now or during an interrogation. Do you understand?"

"Yes." His hands trembling, Mahr folded the handkerchief and slipped it back into his jacket pocket.

They waited. The battery in the ceiling lamp buzzed, for a moment the only sound in the house.

"I'm glad it's over," Mahr said. "The fact that two people died is—"

"Dr Mahr," Ilic said.

"Three people," Louise said.

Mahr looked up "Three?"

"Dr Mahr, this isn't an interrogation."

"Leave it, Illi." Their eyes met. "Let's just chat, O.K.?"

Illi's expression was wan, unsettled. Keep going, Illi, she thought, just a few more minutes. He nodded. Go on, then, tell him. I'll cope.

She told Mahr about Heuweiler, Bo and Peter Mladic.

Lew Gubnik, Hannes Riedinger, Peter Mladic. Three deaths.

Ilic was looking away. Mahr rubbed his thighs. "I wanted to do a good deed, but then three people had to die."

"A good deed?" she said.

"Yes, of course. I—"

"You wanted to help kill Musharraf," Ilic said.

"I wanted to help Pakistan become a democratic state. An outpost of democracy in Asia. Not a democracy by the grace of America, dependent on America's interests. A democracy which would meet the complex demands of the region and yet still be a democracy. This can't happen with Musharraf. As long as he's in charge, Pakistan will remain a dictatorship – and a powder keg. As you know, Pakistan is a nuclear power. The country's internal politics is a combination of different interests. At some point the centrifugal forces will be so strong that . . . But you're not interested in that. You're interested in three dead people."

"And the other dead people," Louise said.

"Musharraf would have been killed," Ilic said. "Maybe others, too. There might have been civil war."

"Yes, that would have been the price. A civil war. A short, bloody uprising by the majority against the minority. Now this rebellion may never happen, but there will be other wars instead, wars between competing interests when the centrifugal forces reach breaking point. Everyone against everyone else. Without the uprising I was going to support, Pakistan will sooner or later become a new Lebanon. Nobody could want that. Democracy or chaos – we have the choice, see? And in either case there's a price to pay, no matter what we choose." There was resignation in Mahr's voice. He had no desire to press his point or try to convince them.

"Let's go," Ilic said. "I can't listen to this anymore. You're talking too casually about other families' tragedies."

"No, no, I'm not being glib," Mahr said. "Please believe me. The price is horrifically high, I know that. But democracy is worth it. It's the price of democracy. Democracy costs lives."

"Let's go," Ilic said.

"You understand me," Mahr said, almost softly, raising a hand as if to touch Ilic. But he was sitting too far away. "You have a Yugoslav name, don't you? You have a Yugoslav name."

"I don't understand at all. I don't understand, for example, why you're so shocked by the murders of Hannes Riedinger and Peter Mladic when you were ready to incite complete civil war in Pakistan."

Mahr withdrew his hand. "Murder and civil war – there is a difference. Murder is . . . murder is dictatorship. One person takes a decision about the life of another. Deprives them of sovereignty over their own life. That is the difference. Do you understand?"

"And you only knew that in hindsight?" Louise said.

"No, I knew it beforehand. I thought it necessary for the greater objective. But I was misled."

"Because you panicked?"

"*Misled?*" Ilic said in disgust.

"I thought . . . Yes. I suppose you have to call it that. I panicked."

"Come on, let's go now," Ilic said.

Mahr stood up. He was a head taller than Ilic, but he walked with a slight stoop. In the hallway he reached for a travel bag that was beneath the stairs. Ilic took it from him, rummaged through the contents and gave it back.

Louise opened the door.

"Have you arrested them?" Mahr said.

"Who?"

"Shahida and Jamal."

She stared at him. Again her thoughts were treacly. Mahr's voice and choice of words implied that they *ought* to have arrested them.

Take it slowly, she thought. Shahida and Jamal, the faces in the photographs, the couple from Islamabad. Someone had warned them. They'd called Mahr just before or after fleeing Rashid's apartment. They'd believed, of course, that the *police* had been in Emmendingen and arrested their fellow Pakistanis. They had fled from the police.

Have you arrested them?

She closed the door. They had the answer at last.

Shahida and Jamal had been on the run.

*

Mahr had sat down again, Louise and Ilic were on their feet. "Not the police?" Mahr said. "Not you?"

"No," Louise said feverishly.

"Well who then? Who in heaven's name?"

She tried to get Ilic's attention, but his head was bowed. Beads of sweat stuck to his brow and his face had turned white, deathly white. It seemed to be happening very quickly now. "Are you alright, Illi?"

He looked at her with tiny eyes, nodded and blinked reassuringly. I'm alright, just give me a few minutes, it'll pass soon. But he didn't look as if it would pass soon.

"Who then?" Mahr repeated.

She looked at him. A man who'd assumed the name of her neighbour. A man who might be American, but maybe not. Others she knew even less about.

Boni said nothing.

So they had been after Shahida and Jamal too. Then, earlier that morning, something had gone wrong – someone had warned the couple. They'd fled Rashid's apartment, called Mahr and asked him for help. Someone's after us, Shahida said. I can't help you, Mahr said. Don't come here, whatever you do don't come to my place. It's all over. I can't help you. We're going to kill you, then, Shahida said. Tonight, in a week, in a month, in a year. We're going to kill you.

Boni glanced at the terrace door. Behind it the garden, the conifer hedge, the darkness. Were they outside?

Were Marcel's people outside?

Ilic said, "You were going to have Musharraf assassinated in Berlin or Paris."

Louise turned to him and said, "There's plenty of time for this, Illi. Let him tell it to Andrele and the Bureau, it's of no interest to us now. Now we have to . . ." She paused. What did they have to do now?

They had to ask Adam Baudy about the Grosse Tal. Find Marcel and his team. Save Shahida and Jamal.

Save the murderers.

Ilic cleared his throat, rubbed his nose, rubbed his face with his hand. "Do you know what war is?"

Mahr frowned. "I don't understand—"

"You wanted to help spark a war. Do you know what war is?"

"Illi, please, I need to think. Help me *think*!"

"You wanted to help kill Musharraf in Berlin or Paris. You planned an assassination in a major European city, hazarding hundreds of deaths. You wanted a war in Pakistan. Do you know what that is, war?"

"For Christ's sake, Illi, this isn't getting us anywhere!" Louise said.

Mahr shook his head vigorously. "No, no, that's *not* what we wanted – we *prevented* it! They were going to kill Musharraf in Berlin at the beginning of July and we said, no, we can't allow that. Then they wanted to do it in Paris, but we couldn't allow them to do it in Europe. You've got to do it in Pakistan, we said, the conflict must be contained within the region, it has ... For goodness' sake, because of Paris they'd already established contact with the Algerian Armed Islamic Group, but here we refused outright, we weren't going to work with *terrorists* ... we didn't want a terrorist attack on western European soil ... and then the depot was blown up and all of a sudden . . . the whole situation had turned critical . . . They refused to believe that we had nothing to do with the explosion, they thought we had deceived them, they wanted to come here and they demanded that I got them visas and . . ." He slumped into the armchair, put his hands in front of his face and said in a muffled voice, "But who was it then, if it wasn't you?"

"Do you know what war is?" Ilic said.

Louise took her colleague's hands. They were clammy and very cold. She couldn't feel any strength left in them. The shock wasn't coming fifteen years later, but that same night.

"Come on, let's go," he mumbled.

"Yes, we're going now, Illi. But we can't go back to H.Q."

"No."

"We have to visit Adam Baudy."

"Yes."

"We'll just see Baudy, and then it's home, Illi. We'll leave the rest to Pauling and his team."

"What sort of team?" Mahr cried.

"But we've got to be careful, Illi," she said. "They may be here, or they're following us."

"Either one or the other," Ilic said.

She nodded. Either one or the other.

They walked outside: Ilic in front, Mahr in the middle and Louise behind. The night was even darker and quieter than before. Her eyes flitted across the garden, the hedge – everything dark and quiet, all she could hear were her footsteps, her breath and a voice in her head: we're going to kill you.

But nobody was there.

21

Ilic drove while Louise sat in the back beside Mahr, who had acqui-
esced without a word as she put him in handcuffs. Now he was
staring out of the window, seemingly oblivious to everything, oblivious to the fact that it was raining, that they were trying without success
to contact Adam Baudy, that they were redirecting their back-up to
Kirchzarten, and that they were arguing with Bermann, who was in
the middle of a serious interrogation and, as expected, didn't want to
know about Shah-whatever and Jamal. Mahr seemed only to register
the darkness outside and that this was the end.

When they went into the tunnel he gave a start.

"Tell me about Aziza," Louise said.

Mahr lowered his head and began to cry.

They'd met in Karlsruhe in 1975. He was a lecturer at the Centre
for Applied Law and she was the secretary to a Pakistani scientist
training at the Nuclear Research Centre. She went back to Pakistan
and he followed. A year later they were married in Germany. They
moved to Bonn, then Stuttgart and finally to Freiburg, spending a
few months in her home town of Panjgur in between, Mahr said.
You wouldn't know it, it's a town in the desert, the province is called
Baluchistan.

"Yes," Louise said, "I've heard of Beluchistan."

"Our home," Mahr said.

She nodded.

Aziza kept wanting to leave her home town; he kept wanting
to return there. Mahr adored the people, those simple, poor, wild

people, you might call it ethno-romanticism, he said. He had fallen for ethno-romanticism. He'd wanted to become a Muslim, a Muslim desert person, but Aziza had knocked this out of him. We need you, she said, but not in a tent in the desert.

"We?"

"We Beluchistanis, we Pakistanis. We Muslims."

"I see."

"But she didn't rush me," Mahr said. "She allowed me to go through my ethno-romantic stage, spend a holiday in a tent in the desert, ride through Beluchistan with a turban and a beard. There are photographs of me from that time, I look like one of Bin Laden's horde."

He gave a desperate laugh.

As if you were so different, she thought.

But Mahr wasn't unlikeable. He knew he'd lost and was prepared to admit it, marking him out from all those other politicians who never lost, who always won, no matter what happened. But there was no getting over what he had done.

Ilic said something. She leaned forwards. "What?"

"And then?" Ilic said.

Then the ethno-romantic period was over and they became pragmatic. Mahr took the institutional path, climbing up the greasy pole of the party. Aziza worked independently, first against Zia ul-Haq, who carried out a putsch in 1977 and Islamicised the country, then in the eighties for Benazir Bhutto, whose father had been hanged by Zia. A brief dream of democracy and freedom ensued when Benazir was first elected as prime minister in 1988, but hers was a hapless time in office. She soon found herself under suspicion of corruption and two years later was deposed. The dream was shattered and they went their own way, without Benazir. "We founded A.P.G.P.F. in December 1988 after Benazir became prime minister," Mahr said. "We wanted to back agricultural projects and support the democratisation of the country . . . But I assume you know all that."

She nodded.

"We wanted to create a Pakistani form of democracy. We thought it would be possible. And it *is* possible."

"Then she died," Louise said.

"Then she died."

Low, heavy clouds hung over the Dreisamtal too, but there was no rain there either. They turned off the B31. Nobody was following them. Mahr's head was turned to the left and he gaped into the darkness towards Kirchzarten, where Riedinger's farm was, where two days ago a young Muslim from Jajce had committed a murder because he, Mahr, had panicked.

"Then the Yugoslav War began," Louise said.

Mahr nodded. The genocide against the Muslims.

Ilic said something. Once again she had to ask him to repeat it.

"Not now, O.K.?"

She nodded. "O.K."

Boni's eyes met Mahr's. She knew this expression. Almost every criminal she'd spoken to after arrest had looked at her like this at some point. I need to talk now, the look said. I need to tell you my story. Their personal story was so important that they had committed a crime because of it. But the crime hadn't brought redemption. Only telling the story brought redemption.

"Not now, Mahr," she said.

Adam Baudy's blue cottage lay in darkness, but there was a light on in the workshop in the yard. Someone else who couldn't sleep at night. Ilic got out of the car. She tapped on the window and gestured to him, one minute, Illi, O.K.? He didn't notice her; he just stood beside the car.

"The Yugoslav War," she said. "But keep it short."

The Yugoslav War, Mahr repeated, the war against the Muslims. The Croats received credits worth billions from the Vatican, and weapons and money from the West. They even got weapons from F.I.S.

via Hungary. The Slovenes bought their independence. The Serbs had the weapons from the Yugoslav People's Army. So the Muslims, who had neither weapons nor money to begin with, had to die. And that was the goal, wasn't it? This was a war by Europe and the U.S. against the Muslims.

Louise said nothing. What should she have said? Just one thing. That this war was different every time, depending on who was talking about it.

Ilic stood outside, doing nothing.

This was the crux of it, Mahr said. The Catholic Croats, the Orthodox Serbs and the West had a common goal: to prevent an Islamic state in Europe. You want proof? I'll give you proof. The U.S. knew early on about Srebrenica, they knew that the Serbs were going to attack the city – Amnesty International has the documentation on that. The Croats destroyed the bridge at Mostar, fought against Muslim troops and stopped Muslim refugees from returning. The U.N. imposed a no-fly zone to prevent Iranian aircraft carrying weapons from landing in Tuzla. The mosques, the bazaars, the Islamic institutions, Mahr said, everything Islamic in the Balkans was destroyed, and we were sitting there, unable to do a thing . . . Louise thought, we Baluchistanis, we Pakistanis, we Muslims, us, Aziza and I.

"That's where it began," she said. "In the Yugoslav War."

He nodded. Yes, that's where it began. Irrigation projects, gender projects, cultural projects for Baluchistan – all well and good, but what if one day the Americans came or the Indians or the Iranians? He flew to Panjgur, went to Aziza's home in the desert, asked, could you defend yourselves? Old Jinnah was dismissive – they won't come; young Jinnah was a firebrand – they only won't come if we're strong. Old Jinnah said no. Then there was the Kosovo War, the next conflict against the Muslims, but old Jinnah still said no. Then in 1999 Musharraf came to power and everything changed. A network formed: young Jinnah and his activists in Beluchistan, Shahida and Jamal in Islamabad, Halid Trumic in Bosnia, Busche, Söllien and Mahr in

Germany. It took a while for things to get moving, then the first weapons from former Yugoslavia arrived in Baden, although Mahr didn't know by which route. Trumic and Busche dealt with the vendors, the transporters and the routes while he, Mahr, kept in communication with Islamabad and Beluchistan. The weapons went to Pakistan and the armed Jinnah started mobilising politically, forging a political opposition against Musharraf, demanding democratic elections and Musharraf's resignation as commander-in-chief of the army if he were going to remain as president . . .

Then came 9/11 and after that Afghanistan. The Americans arrived in Beluchistan and Musharraf clamped down in Pakistan. For the sake of our great friend America, everything Muslim and Islamic was now suspected of being linked to al-Qaeda. "That's why it must continue," Mahr said agitatedly. "They need more weapons, now it's between democracy and freedom or dictatorship and oppression. Do you understand?"

She wondered whether to tell Mahr about Marcel. Marcel who'd used the same words, had the same goal but was just taking a different route. Democracy, freedom, justice, Marcel had said. To achieve these we need Musharraf.

She shook her head.

"No, you don't understand," Mahr said.

Bonì imagined this tall, stooped man amongst a group of adolescent Pakistanis, saw him walk awkwardly through a bazaar, saw him sitting on a horse in the desert, gangly and fired up with enthusiasm. Utterly grotesque images, one big, grotesque misunderstanding.

What about Aziza? Did she join in? Weapons, an attempt to assassinate Musharraf, civil war? Would the new dream of democracy and freedom have appeared the same to her? Full of blood and violence?

She asked the question. Mahr looked away without answering it. The question of all questions. Louise thought the answer was clear. In his dreams Aziza came to him and said, what are you doing? You murderer! And Mahr said, but I'm doing it for you, for our vision,

320

it's the right thing, you'll see! No, Aziza said in his dreams, you're a murderer, you're no better than those you're fighting against, and Mahr said, no, don't talk like that, please don't talk like that.

Louise's hunch had been correct. Aziza was the link, the key figure. The beginning and end.

"We've got that sorted out too, then" she said, and stepped out of the car.

Boni closed the car door and closed her eyes. For a moment all was quiet, still, dark.

She went to Ilic, who was pursing his lips and shaking his head. You ought to have gone straight home from Heuweiler, Illi, she thought. Now you're here, damn it, and I need you. "Could you keep an eye on him for a few minutes? Our colleagues should be here soon, then you can go home."

"I'm sorry. I'm . . . I just can't concentrate."

"I know," she said, placing a hand on his cheek.

"I ought to have gone straight home."

She nodded and thought, what am I going to do with you, Illi? I need you – why are you all abandoning me this fucking summer? Günter, Almenbroich, now you, and Rolf is aiming to become something he doesn't want to be, and Löbinger's being smarmy and poisonous, and neither of them wants to hear about terrorists or terrorist hunters in the Breisgau. For Christ's sake, what is *wrong* with you all?

"You're here now." As she stroked his cold cheek she realised she'd placed her hands on the cold cheeks of her colleagues rather more often than usual in the past few days. Then she thought of Landen's warm hands on her breasts and smiled: what strange thoughts one has at four in the morning when everything's going belly-up.

Adam Baudy was sitting at a table, screwdriver in hand, fiddling with a casket of dark wood. He jumped when she pushed open the door. "Jesus Christ!" he exclaimed.

"I need to talk to you," she said.

He turned his attention back to the casket.

As she went over to him she breathed in the scent of wood, then other smells the closer she got: cigarettes and beer – pub odours that lingered in his clothes.

She sat beside him on the bench. He was bent over the casket, running a finger along one of the edges, unbelievably slowly, as if he had all the peace and time in the world. Perhaps that was true, she thought, at four o'clock in the morning.

He glanced at her. "What's happened?"

"The American students in the Grosse Tal."

He nodded. "Paul saw them. Paul Feul."

"Not you?"

"No."

Anything but that, she thought. Please no more driving off to talk to someone else. She had no energy left to tune into yet another person, to start from the beginning again.

She placed a hand on Baudy's shoulder. What she needed now was to hold on to Adam Baudy, who'd been called out to an innocuous fire and had ended up in an inferno, and who in spite of this allowed himself all the peace and time in the world.

He glanced at her. "You look so tired."

"It's all been a bit much."

He didn't respond.

Louise took her hand away. "Where does Paul Feul live?"

"He's here."

"With you?"

"He's been sleeping here ever since the fire. If he sleeps at all. Which is to say not much, he was on the first hose with Gubby."

"Yes, I know. It's in your report."

He nodded.

"How about you? Sitting in your workshop at four in the morning."

"It's peaceful. No telephone, no people to deal with. Just the occasional exhausted ghost." He smiled.

And the dead, she thought.

"Do you want me to get him?"

"Just give me a minute. I need a break."

Baudy went back to his work, ran his palm over the casket, opened and closed it. Screwed the hinge, wiped away some wood dust with his thumb. Boni put her hand back on his shoulder; that's where it belonged in these strange moments, she thought.

They sat there like this, silent and immersed, Baudy in his work, Louise in his deliberate movements.

Paul Feul arrived in jeans and a blue T-shirt, both crumpled as if he'd slept in them. His eyes were swollen slits, he reeked of cigarette smoke and pub, of beer and vomit. Baudy handed him a glass of water, he drank, refilled the glass and drank again. Feul looked at her silently, grimly, with suspicion.

"The Americans in the Grosse Tal, Paul," Baudy said.

Feul nodded.

"Tell her."

"I saw two Americans in the Grosse Tal."

"And?" Baudy said.

"What do you mean, 'And'?"

"You said they were students. What made you think they were students?"

"Oh, you know." A cautious nod, intense thinking.

While she was waiting she thought of Niksch, who had died at Feul's age. Early twenties and already savaged by life in all its cruelty. One dead, the other's friend burned to death.

"Because one of them had the word 'university' on his T-shirt. In English," Feul said.

"Was there anything else on it?"

"Virginia. Of Virginia."

"Paul," Baudy said softly.

"Sorry. My head," Feul said, putting his hands to his temples.

"The hangover," Louise said with a fake smile. "We'd best stick you in a bath of cold water."

"No, no, please!"

"Good idea, let's do that," Baudy said.

Feul belched, frowned, then mumbled, two Americans, students, one with a University of Virginia T-shirt, somewhere in the Grosse Tal, no, not just somewhere . . . wait . . . they were near the car park by the stream, not the Reichenbach, but the one that comes down from the Rappeneck. When was that? Must have been a few weeks ago, he'd been out with his father and brothers, they went walking together occasionally, the last time was around the end of June, and that's when he saw the Americans.

"Did the others see them too?"

"No, just me. I needed a pee and that's when I saw them."

"What were they doing?"

"Standing in the stream."

"Paul," Baudy said.

"Sorry. Well, they were having a wash . . . you know, like when you've been camping, except that it was the evening, not the morning."

"Did you hear them say anything?"

"I think one of them said, 'Fucking warm!' The other one said 'Yeah.'" He shrugged. What did Americans say? "Then I'd finished my pee."

"Did you see anything else? Apart from the T-shirt and the two men? Hear anything?"

Feul thought about it, then cautiously shook his head.

"Let's put him in the bath," Baudy said.

"No, please don't. It won't help," Feul mumbled.

She handed him her business card, just in case. "Look after him," she said to Baudy.

*

Baudy accompanied her outside. The back-up had arrived. Behind Ilic's car stood a patrol car, a policewoman leaning against the wing. Shy Susie Wegener, who she'd wept and laughed with sometime during these oppressive, hot days on the way from Oberried to Freiburg.

She was one of the young ones too.

Susie smiled and Louise smiled back as best she could. "Anyone else coming?"

"Maybe later."

Bonì glanced at Ilic, who was back in his car.

She took a deep breath and exhaled. A Kripo colleague who was in shock, a police constable, barely twenty years old, whose two green shoulder stars were hidden in the folds of her jacket, and an overtired chief inspector who'd barely slept more than ten hours in the last four days and nights.

"What are you going to do now?" Baudy said. "Drive over there?"

"Yes."

They shook hands.

"If you want I'll get my men. I could get together a team of ten or twelve."

Bonì declined the offer. More young men, unarmed ones at that, even though they'd probably turn up with their fire brigade axes. A dozen volunteers with axes versus terrorists and terrorist hunters who didn't exist in the Breisgau.

"Think it over."

"Thanks for the offer, but no thanks."

Baudy nodded.

"What about you?"

He shrugged then jerked his head towards the workshop. A bit more work. Waiting for the ghosts of the night and the dead.

They sat in the patrol car to confer: Louise and Susie Wegener in the front, Ilic in the back, a white, shining face in the light of the streetlamp. Louise spoke, Ilic said yes and no and yes, Susie nodded and thus their plan of action was agreed. They couldn't take Mahr with them into the Grosse Tal, she said. Because of Shahida and Jamal it was far too dangerous. He would have to be taken back to H.Q.

"Yes," Ilic said.

Susie nodded.

"O.K., then . . ."

"Wait." Ilic rubbed his brow with his fingertips, mustered what remained of his strength and recapped. Shahida and Jamal, who had vanished, were probably being pursued by Marcel's team, may already have been captured and he was taking them to the Grosse Tal, you say, where Paul Feul saw two Americans back in June, who could have been camping, you think, and somewhere around there Marcel's people had their camp too. Is that right? In the Grosse Tal?

She nodded.

Ilic's fingertips left red marks on his white forehead, but he kept rubbing. Bonì wanted to grab hold of his hand. But what made her think that the three Pakistanis from Karachi had been taken to Ramstein or Spangdahlem, Ilic asked, whereas the couple from Islamabad were in the Grosse Tal, assuming that Marcel had actually abducted the former too?

"In Emmendingen he had a head start – he's lost that now. He has to get through all the cordons, all the road blocks. If he doesn't want to risk that, his only option is the Grosse Tal."

And a thousand other valleys, she thought, a thousand other hiding places.

But this was the best lead they had. They could hunt for Marcel and they could sit and wait in the Grosse Tal. There was nothing else they could do.

"No, there's nothing else," Ilic said, finally taking his hands from his brow.

"And it's not *that* improbable, is it?" Lisbeth Walter had seen Marcel's people to the south of Oberried that night; Paul Feul had seen two men one evening in the forest above the Grosse Tal. Perfectly good witness statements. They were on the move at night, withdrew to the forest before sunrise and slept during the day. Why not?

"Yes, why not?" Ilic said.

"We'll take your car, Illi, and you drive Mahr to H.Q. in the patrol car. Let's go!"

"Hang on, what, me?" Ilic said. Louise saw a storm brewing in his face and then the storm broke. What if somebody actually *is* there? came his anguished cry, if Marcel and his team actually *are* there as well as the couple from Islamabad, and I'm not with you, how are the two of you going to detain them? For God's sake, Louise, what are you going to do then?"

"I . . . I—"

"What the hell are you going to do then?" Ilic shouted.

"I don't know!" Louise shouted.

"I'm coming with you," Ilic said, now calm again.

"No!" Louise screamed, and then she kept screaming because once again Ilic was saying nothing with great eloquence. For a few seconds she gave vent to an untempered fury, a murderous combination of indignation, disappointment, fatigue, and a longing to sleep and chuck it all in.

"Don't make such a fuss, Illi!" she screamed. "What the fuck do you think *you* could do if they *are* there and you're standing in the forest, thinking about Heuweiler and Peter Mladic. How is that going to help us?"

Ilic said nothing.

"You are *so* fucking stubborn!"

They stared at each other, the half-Croat officer, the half-French officer, and again she guessed what was going on inside his head. She'd hurt him, she had made him stubborn, she would lose the battle.

"Then we're agreed," Ilic said.

"No."

"We'll come to a compromise."

"I hate compromises. But alright then."

Susie Wegener would accompany them as far as Kappel, where they would call Bermann and then decide who would bring Mahr to H.Q., and who would go with her into the valley.

Louise got out of the car feeling shattered. How complicated it was to work with colleagues. How nice it was to work alone.

To be alone.

They drove out of Kirchzarten and into the darkness, Susie Wegener in front in the patrol car, Bonì and Ilic with Mahr behind. To the right lay Riedinger's pasture, a black abyss, to the left humped hills with pastures, farms and barely visible summits. It started drizzling. About halfway between Kirchzarten and Kappel, Mahr interrupted his silence and started up again about Baluchistan and his Yugoslav War, his fight for democracy and freedom. It was a generational problem, he said, that she couldn't understand his ideals, that her generation didn't understand the ideals and visions of his generation. That is our *trauma*, he said, the trauma of the 1968 generation, we keep fighting as we did in the sixties and seventies, while our sons and daughters, who grew up in the miracle years of West German democracy, look at us with a combination of astonishment and ridicule, as if we were exotic creatures. But they forget that *we* fought for these miracle years, *we* made them possible, and they don't understand that we need to fight again, that our legacy is in danger, democracy and freedom, they just don't get it, and so they abandon us, betray us if we resume the fight and start throwing stones again . . .

"You mean bombs," she said. "You're throwing bombs."

"I'm speaking metaphorically for God's sake . . . That's exactly what . . . That's the unbridgeable cultural divide between generations that I'm talking about, between our visions and your everyday pragmatism, between our metaphors and your literalism. We read the wider context, you read the word." Two patrol cars were approaching. To the east of Freiburg they saw a helicopter and blue lights flashed in the dark distance. We read the word, she thought, perhaps that's true. We read "democracy" and this word has nothing to do with murder. That makes us slightly limited; we don't think *beyond*. "1968," Mahr said, "for you that's *history*."

"You're not a sixty-eighter, you're a criminal, *that's* the nub of the problem. Murder isn't a metaphor, Herr Mahr, no matter which generation you belong to. Now kindly shut up."

Mahr obeyed.

In Kappel she got out into the rain and walked away from the cars to ring Bermann. As anticipated, his reaction was incendiary. "No! No more officers, no helicopters, no fucking Grosse Tal, you get back to H.Q. immediately! I just don't believe it, Louise," he screamed. "I actually can't take any more of your nonsense, your madness, your solitary crusades, why do you always have to make everything so much *worse*? The trouble you're stirring up again now, I mean, for fuck's *sake*!"

"I'm following leads, you arsehole," she screamed, then hung up and dialled Almenbroich's office number. When nobody answered she dialled his mobile number, and finally his home number. If you need support, come to me, Almenbroich had said. Well, here she was.

"Oh, Louise," Almenbroich said, his voice a wreck.

He was sitting at his kitchen table, supping camomile tea and chewing vitamin C tablets. Sleep was out of the question.

"Don't go," she said, close to tears.

Almenbroich said nothing.

"Don't leave."

"Oh, Louise."

Seconds passed without a word. She could hear slow, laboured breathing.

"What do you need?" he said eventually.

She told him about Mahr, Paul Feul, the couple on the run, the Americans in the Grosse Tal, that they were there without back-up, that they didn't know what awaited them. She needed a thermal imaging camera with a helicopter attached, of course – Louise laughed briefly – there was one over Freiburg anyway, surely it could make a little detour to the south, fly two or three times over the eastern part of the Grosse Tal, then they would see if Marcel and the two Pakistanis were there or not.

"Or someone else," Almenbroich said.

"Isn't there always?"

She heard him drink, swallow and breathe. "I'll sort it out."

Bonì updated Ilic and Susie, who were standing by the cars in the rain. Come with me for a sec, Illi, she said, pulling her colleague to one side. She linked arms with him and said that she'd never get over it if anything happened to him, she couldn't deal with losing another colleague, it was only a few months ago that she'd lost Niksch – and Hollerer too, after a fashion – Lederle had gone and Almenbroich was going soon too. Ilic said nothing. Illi, she said, we both know that you . . . that you . . . Oh say something, for God's sake, Illi. It's not your decision, Illi said.

22

Trees drifted past and beyond lay an elongated cornfield. Then more houses, a few farms, then nothing. The road glistened in the rain and became narrower, with dense shrubs on either side that were a black wall once the headlights had swept past them. They had reached the Grosse Tal.

"Can you hear that?" Ilic said.

She nodded. The helicopter.

As they made their way slowly along the winding, untarmacked road, she wondered whether she was doing the right thing. Whether it was responsible or irresponsible.

It wasn't her decision. But did she bear the responsibility?

They stopped at the car park at the foot of the Rappeneck and got out. Now it was pouring, but despite the clatter of raindrops they could hear the rotors quite clearly. Louise looked up at the black sky. The sounds weren't changing; the helicopter seemed to be high above them. Once or twice she fancied she could see the navigation lights. But that was nonsense, of course. They would have dimmed the cabin lights and turned off the external ones, while the searchlight was switched to infra-red. They didn't want to be visible from the ground. Didn't want to offer a target.

Ilic stood beside her with a colourful umbrella. "What now?"

"We wait to see if they've found anything. If they do, then . . ." She stopped. The noise was moving away.

Call me, she urged. But they didn't call.

A thousand other valleys, a thousand other hiding places.

Then there was the fact that the thermal-imaging camera couldn't penetrate foliage. Leaves produce warmth. The forest was more or less a uniformly grey surface. The camera couldn't see what was beneath the leaves, even if the helicopter dipped below the minimum safe height of five hundred feet. Deciduous trees in winter were good. Clearings, cuttings, gaps in the trees. Then the camera could capture a human being even from a height of one thousand metres. Here, above the forest by the Rappeneck, they barely had a chance. Even if Marcel and his people were in there somewhere, they might go undetected.

"What then?" Ilic said.

She shrugged.

They were back inside the car, waiting and listening to the rain which was now hammering down on the roof. They shared a muesli bar from Ilic's glove compartment. Boni's clothes were wet, they stuck to her body and smelled of sweat and damp. She had her mobile in her hand, but that didn't help either: no call came from the helicopter. Marcel in the Grosse Tal – what a silly idea. The students were students, if that; a T-shirt didn't make you a student. She shook her head and was about to laugh out loud in anger when she heard the helicopter. She opened the door and cocked her head to listen. Again the chopper appeared to be hovering somewhere above the slope of the Rappeneck. Call, for God's sake, she thought, closing the door. Don't let this be just another obsession that's got the better of me.

And then they called. A man by the name of Schober said that they'd spotted a person lying almost directly beneath them in a narrow clearing by the stream.

"*Lying?*" Louise said.

"Yes, lying." Schober went on talking but his young, high-pitched voice was drowned out by the noise of the rotors and the rain.

"What?" she yelled.

"If they're dead then they haven't been dead for long," Schober shouted. Measuring the temperature with the camera was only accurate to within plus or minus five degrees. The body temperature of the person was around five degrees below normal. The rate of cooling was one degree per hour, Louise thought instinctively. Maybe a little more due to the rain. If there *was* a corpse up there, it had been dead for three, four hours at most.

As she got out she could hear the helicopter but couldn't yet see it. "Where's the body?"

"About halfway up the stream."

"Have you picked up anyone else?"

No, they hadn't.

Only one person, she thought. Who could that be? Louise looked at the dark wall of trees that rose before her. Then she asked Schober to call the control centre and notify the chief duty officer. Explain that there was a dead body on the Rappeneck.

And then do one more circuit.

"We really ought to be getting back," Schober said.

"Just a quick one, Schober." There must be more people down there. If there's one, there will be others. Even if they couldn't see them.

Schober said nothing.

"Please, Schober."

"Hans," Schober said.

"Please, Hans."

She heard the helicopter moving away.

"One," Ilic said.

She nodded.

They were sitting in the car, staring at the windscreen. Torrents streamed down the glass; all they could see was water, nothing beyond, not even the blackness of night. After days of paralysing heat and dryness had come the deluge, in the valleys at least.

Marcel in the Grosse Tal, she thought, plus Shahida and Jamal. Pakistanis from Islamabad in the Grosse Tal – what an idiotic thought.

But someone was lying on the slope of the Rappeneck.

"Illi, I'm going up there now."

She looked at him and he nodded. "I'll come with you. I'm feeling better. I'm feeling fine." But he didn't return her gaze.

"Fine," she said, turning away.

It wasn't her decision.

On the other hand, she would have taken the same decision had she been in Thomas Ilic's shoes. The decision she'd taken time and again, even with too much alcohol in her blood. Even though often she hadn't felt fine.

So it *was* her decision.

Ilic opened the umbrella and Louise took his arm. Their laughter was fraught with tension – the half-Croat officer and the half-French officer on an operation, strolling leisurely through the rain beneath a large, colourful umbrella. For a moment the old feeling returned, the Offenburg feeling, the Kehl feeling. The assurance that, professionally, something significant was developing between them, that the circumstances in which they found themselves were forging a team with a promising future. A team with elements in common as well as useful differences.

Then she thought of Heuweiler and remembered that Ilic ought not to be here, didn't want to be here. The assurance evaporated.

The car park resembled a landscape of lakes and muddy potholes. They made better progress along a dirt track that sloped gently upwards, with water running down ditches on either side. They could make out waterlogged tyre tracks and vague footprints: a large car, several people. Ilic had noticed the marks too. He shrugged and she knew what he was thinking. Forestry workers, hikers, whatever. And the tracks could be hours old. Who knew when it had begun raining here?

On they went.

One person, she thought. Who could that be? Who was lying on the Rappeneck in the rain?

Straight ahead was the dense forest, and a few metres further on they saw the stream. It was narrow and contained less water than they'd expected.

Ilic closed his umbrella and leaned it against a tree. She grinned. If they needed back-up, their colleagues would surely find them.

They checked their torches and mobiles. They still had reception.

"Let's go," Louise said.

"Wait." Ilic tapped a number into his phone, then fixed his eyes on her as he spoke to the chief duty officer. But it was too dark to gauge his expression. He held the mobile away from his ear. The chief duty officer had promised to arrange back-up. A dead body changed the situation. But it didn't make the task of mustering additional officers any easier. "We don't know if there *is* a corpse up there," Ilic said.

"This isn't the time for citing the rule book or hair-splitting, Illi."

"Yes," Ilic said. "No." He looked at his mobile and pressed a few buttons. "While we're at it . . ." He put the phone to his ear, said, "Hmm," and listened. Again his eyes were on Louise, and again she couldn't identify what was in them. She heard a loud voice. Then Ilic said, "There's a dead body up there, Rolf." She heard Bermann bellow, "Bullshit!"

"Just so you know where we are," Ilic said and put his mobile away.

"What's happened to Susie and Mahr?"

"They've just arrived at H.Q."

"You still have the choice, Illi. You can stay here and keep watch. It would be good to have someone down here."

"O.K.," he said, staring blankly at her.

Boni thought that he should have closed his eyes too in the forest clearing. Watching someone being murdered changed everything, whether you were a police officer or not.

You should have shut your eyes, Illi.

It was an arduous climb; there was no path alongside the stream. The ground was covered with sodden leaves and slippery. They moved towards the edge of the forest, more sheltered from the rain, and held on to tree trunks and branches, and each other. Where they had to they went on all fours, first Louise in front, then Illi, mostly in the dark and sometimes in the harsh light of a torch. The air was humid and warm, it smelled of soil, damp, forest, fungi and occasionally of wild garlic. She began to sweat. Her trainers were drenched, her jeans wet from her ankles to her knees, and her T-shirt was soaked anyway. She thought of Shahida and Jamal, who came from a region she thought of as parched and desert-like. She visualised the two faces on the visa documents; Shahida was clearer in her mind. A proud, cultivated face, a proud, alert expression. It was strange how familiar this face and this name were now, even though she knew them only from a photograph. Even though Shahida was evidently a murderer and a terrorist. The sound of the name, the exoticism of the face? Ethnoromanticism, she thought, amused. They were *both* hopeless romantics, the former member of the regional parliament from Freiburg St Georgen, and the Kripo chief inspector from Gartenstrasse.

"Wait, Illi," Bonì panted after ten or fifteen minutes. She squatted on her heels and wrapped her arms around her knees. Ilic stayed on his feet, hands on hips, breathing rapidly.

"How much do you think we've done?"

"Maybe half?"

"Half of halfway?"

He nodded.

"Only halfway there." Louise leaned back her head and closed her eyes. Raindrops fell onto her warm face and ran down her temples, her cheeks, her neck. She listened to the sounds of the stream and the rain. There were no other sounds, human sounds, to be heard. If her hunch about the Grosse Tal was correct, there must be half a dozen people on the slope of the Rappeneck. Half a dozen people who must have come here by car. They hadn't seen any cars. They hadn't seen or heard anything. They'd only discovered one person, who was lying beside the stream somewhere above them.

When Louise opened her eyes, Ilic's face was turned in her

direction. She sensed his eyes on her. She had no idea how he was feeling, whether he was suffering and, if so, in what way. Whether he was afraid of what might be awaiting them up above.

"Say something, Illi."

"I'm feeling better, really I am. I'm fine now." He placed a hand on her shoulder, just the fingertips. They stayed like that for a moment, looking at each other without seeing anything.

Then Louise got to her feet. "Would you like a broken biscuit courtesy of Kirchzarten police station?"

"Yes."

"And water?"

"Yes."

When they'd finished Täschle's biscuits and drunk from their last bottle of water, they resumed their climb.

A few minutes later they heard the helicopter on its way back. They changed direction and walked along the slope to the stream so Schober could see them. He called soon afterwards. You're almost at the body, he said. Another thirty or forty metres and you'll trip over it.

"What about the others?"

"I'm sorry, I can't see anyone else, Louise."

"Will you do one more circuit? Please Schober, just one more!"

A pause, then he said, "Hans."

"Hans." She grinned. Hans and Louise.

"But then we'll have to head back. We're only on loan," he said, then laughed uneasily.

She put her mobile away. "Thirty, forty metres, Illi."

Ilic nodded, but did nothing.

Bonì pulled out her gun and they kept climbing.

There was the body. A foot appeared in the beam of Ilic's torch, a leg in soaked jeans, a torso. A dark-skinned, wet face, eyes closed. She knew this face.

They'd found Shahida.

"They're here, Illi," she murmured.

Blood was flowing from Shahida's right temple. A small calibre gun, the wound had hardly done any damage.

But it had brought death.

Her gaze scanned the lifeless body. A dirty denim jacket, a dark shirt. Her chest was full of blood too. To the left, near the heart, the jacket material was shredded. A bullet in the chest from the front, a bullet in the head from the side. They'd wanted to be sure.

What had happened? Why had they shot Shahida? And where were they? Where was Jamal? Louise looked up, let the beam of her torch sweep both sides of the stream. All she saw were trees, shrubs and rain.

Ilic was still staring at Shahida. She touched his arm. "We have to call Rolf." He nodded.

She knelt beside the body and put a hand to Shahida's cheek. The skin was warm; she couldn't have been dead for longer than an hour. Only now did Louise notice the blood beneath her left eye and the blue marks on her left temple and cheek. They'd beaten Shahida before shooting her twice.

She lifted the hem of the jacket. The denim and the shirt beneath were drenched with blood. Her chest seemed to be moving.

"She's alive," Ilic mumbled.

Louise looked up in horror. Now Shahida's eyes were half open. Carefully she laid her hands on the dark cheeks and stared into the dark eyes. "Call Rolf, Illi," she whispered, as she began stroking the warm cheeks. She thought of Shahida's desert-like homeland, and of how she was going to die in a foreign country in the rain. She felt sorry for this woman, even though she was a murderer and terrorist.

She heard Ilic talking to Bermann and then shouting. They needed back-up, they needed a rescue helicopter, they had found Shahida, and she was seriously injured. Marcel and his people were here, please, for God's sake send some back-up now . . .

Calm down, Illi, she thought, she's dying, calm down.

"We need help, Rolf!" Ilic cried.

"Calm down, Illi."

The dark eyes were still fixed on her. She tried to smile, but felt the tears running down her cheeks. "Shahida, help is on its way," she whispered in English.

"Now listen, Rolf!" Ilic shouted.

"Illi, please!"

"They're all here," Ilic said.

"Shahida," Louise whispered.

She felt the last, long breath. Then the dark eyes slid almost imperceptibly to one side.

They sat side by side in the darkness for several minutes, waiting, not knowing what for. Perhaps for Marcel or Jamal, who might be nearby, or could equally be far away by now. Perhaps for Dermann, who'd finally agreed to send some officers and said he'd come himself. Perhaps for another call from Schober. When Boni was sick of waiting she phoned Schober, who screamed that he'd been just about to call her – there *was* someone else, someone else was coming.

She leaped up. "How many? One?"

"Yes, yes, one!"

The helicopter was now directly above another person, who was coming down the stream. Moving slowly but steadily downstream, about two hundred metres away. Schober said they'd detected him or her near the restaurant at the summit, the Rappenecke Hütte. The person had run along the edge of the forest, anxious to avoid being seen, but not so anxious that they were going to let it cost time.

"Stay on them," she said. "Hans."

"A few minutes. But then we really have to get back."

They rang off.

"Illi, someone's coming from above."

Ilic was back on his feet now too. She saw him nod, but he just stood there without saying a word. It didn't seem to matter anymore.

*

They separated and took up positions behind trees on either side of the stream. But nobody came. She called Schober. Wait a second, he said, we'll take a look. She stared up the slope. Was it beginning to get a bit brighter above them, up at the top of the Rappeneck? Dark grey mingled with the black of the night. Why not, even this night must at some point come to an end.

Come on, come on, she thought.

But nobody came.

Her mobile vibrated. "Hans," Schober said.

"Yes?"

The figure had disappeared into the forest; at any rate they were no longer visible. Schober and the pilot would search for another couple of minutes, but then they had to get back. "Take care of yourself," he said.

She slipped the mobile into her trouser pocket, stepped across the stream and walked past Shahida who was lying in the rain because there was nothing to cover her with.

Ilic was sitting on the ground behind a small group of trees, his head leaning against a trunk. "Vanished," she said.

He nodded. He was pitifully pale. Louise was about to sit beside him, but he said "Don't". She realised that he'd vomited. She passed him the bottle, and he filled his mouth with water, swishing it around before spitting it out to the side. "Don't get up, Illi," she said. "I'll take a look around."

Searching the area around Shahida's body with her torch, she found footprints – too many different ones to have been made by just her and Ilic – as well as a bullet. She made a mental note of its location and left it where it was. There was nothing more to see, for the moment at least. But this didn't surprise her; Marcel and his team were professionals.

When she went back to Ilic he didn't ask any questions. She knelt before him and took his hand: cold and lifeless. Everything O.K., Illi? Yes, everything was O.K., he was feeling better, everything was better. Having a rest had done him good. His gaze and voice were both gentle and stand-offish. She was no longer getting through to him.

She sat on a root opposite Ilic and heard the helicopter approaching. Moments later Schober called. The second person was still missing – simply no sight of them. Schober sounded embarrassed, as if it were his fault that the camera couldn't penetrate the canopy of leaves. They would go back to Freiburg now; they *had* to go back. They were only on loan, after all. This time he didn't laugh. "Will you be alright, Louise?"

"Yes. Thanks for everything, Hans."

"My pleasure."

Looking upwards, she listened to the noise of the rotors fade into the distance. The blackness that swallowed the trees seemed to have become another degree greyer.

What now? she thought.

This time the decision was hers. Stay here and look after Ilic, or hunt for Marcel and look out for Jamal?

Her decision, her responsibility.

Come on, she thought, decide.

But she was far too exhausted.

Five minutes later she said, "I have to go up there."

Ilic cleared his throat. "Wait till we've got back-up."

She peered into the grey above them. All of a sudden she understood that for her this had nothing to do with Jamal; it was all about Marcel, Marcel who'd broken into her apartment, who'd tricked her. Who'd stood back and watched as people were killed, who might be a murderer himself. Marcel who was pulling the strings. Who, like Johannes Mahr, was employing in the short term the very same methods he was combating in the long term. She needed to see him, talk to him, now that they were at the end of this and they knew so much.

"No, Illi, I'm going right now."

"Well, I think I'll . . ." Ilic didn't finish his sentence.

"I know. Please don't worry, O.K.?"

"Please wait, Louise."

She shook her head, stroked his hair and walked away.

23

O nce again she avoided the stream and moved a little way into the forest for cover. The wet undergrowth made the ascent even trickier, and she kept slipping on the sodden forest floor and sliding back down. She was soaked to the bone and filthy. Her trainers were full of water and her hands hurt from pulling herself up, holding on, bracing herself. The wound in her left arm ached.

The wound that Marcel had bandaged.

Yes, she had to see him again. Had to track him down, intrude into a place where *he* felt secure.

At some point she crawled over a bank and found herself on a broad footpath that ran along the slope. She rested for a minute, squatting on her heels. No sign of Marcel or Jamal, no noise, nothing but the sounds of the rain and the forest. She was missing the helicopter most of all. The vibrant, friendly voice of Hans Schober. What she would give to be able to call him now in this dark silence. She wondered whether there was any particular reason for his friendliness. Whether her reputation had not only reached the Joint Centre in Kehl, but also the helicopter squad in Stuttgart.

Almenbroich was right. However much she'd changed, she was still what she had once been.

But that wasn't important. What mattered was the change.

She stood up straight, crossed the path and crept into the darkness of the forest on the other side.

Minutes later Bonì came to a clearing. A wispy mist rose from the knee-high grass. It had stopped raining. The sky was getting lighter, the cloud cover breaking up. But no ray of sun shone through. She had no idea where she was, how far from the summit, how far from the stream, from Ilic. Breathless, she stepped into the clearing and plodded over the soft ground. She thought of Shahida who had died before her eyes, and wondered whether Jamal was lying somewhere here too, a bullet in his head and one in his chest. She thought of the other dead in these terrible, sleepless summer days and nights: Lew Gubnik, Hannes Riedinger, Peter Mladic – victims of Aziza Mahr's innocent dream of democracy and freedom. Four people dead in the four days since Hannes Riedinger's shed had gone up in flames. And five people abducted, lives destroyed. Almenbroich on the verge of leaving. The dreadful result of a dreadful plan . . .

A sound made her stop in her tracks. A gentle rustling, as if the wind had wafted across the leaves.

But there wasn't a breath of wind.

She whipped around on the spot. Nothing to see, nothing more to hear. But Louise knew that she wasn't alone. That she was being watched.

Her heart began to race; Marcel was here.

She forced herself to walk on.

When she was halfway across the clearing the forest ahead of her came to life. A black, masked figure detached itself from the trees, diagonally to her right came a second, to the left a third. They wore uniform rucksacks and held pistols in their raised hands.

Lisbeth Walter's black hordes.

She had found them in the end.

The crunch of undergrowth behind, and Louise turned to see a fourth man approaching. Like the other three he was masked, but he wasn't holding a weapon. He knew that she wouldn't shoot him.

That she had no chance of sending him and his men to prison.

"O.K.," she said.

"O.K.," Marcel said. His voice betrayed no surprise. He must be used to unusual encounters in unusual places. A hillside in the forest above St Wilhelm. The apartment of a Freiburg chief inspector. A small clearing on the Rappeneck in the Grosse Tal at seven in the morning.

She stared at the eyeslit in the man's balaclava, waiting for her fury, her disappointment. But none came. Fury and disappointment required energy. All she felt was relief, because these terrible days, this terrible time would soon be at an end.

"You're under arrest," she said, then repeated it louder in English. Nobody reacted. She smiled. To go down with dignity was some consolation at least. She pulled the strap of the bag over her head and held it out to Marcel, then turned and let him remove her pistol from the holster.

"Let's go," he said, pointing in the direction from which she'd come.

"To get Shahida?"

He nodded. "You seem to know a lot."

"Not the answers to the key questions."

"Depends how you look at it."

"No, not the most important things." Such as where they would vanish to from here. Who they were. How they could be brought to justice. Who was in on it. Was F.I.S. involved, the F.C.P.O.? The Federal Ministry of the Interior? The C.I.A.? There was no way they could be operating without protection from on high, so who was involved?

She didn't yet have the answer to these or to so many other questions.

"You could tell me," Louise suggested.

"What then?"

"I'd try to make things difficult for you."

"You're too talented for that."

"It's my job, you know. Making things difficult for criminals."

Marcel didn't respond.

She glanced at the other men. Three unmoving, silent shadows, all but invisible against the dark forest. They'd dropped the hands that gripped their weapons, but seemed to be looking at the clearing rather than at her and Marcel. Undoubtedly professionals.

Professionals from which country? Working for whom? She'd never find out.

Other, fragmented questions drifted through her mind. Why did Shahida have to die? Who shot her? You, Marcel? Didn't you realise she was still alive? She postponed the questions until later. Now she had to focus on what was critical. If Marcel's black hordes were going to recover Shahida's body, then Thomas Ilic was critical. "My colleague is with her."

"The Croat?"

She nodded.

"Nobody else came?"

"No, but they're on their way."

"That might be a problem."

"Why? Shoot them."

Marcel said nothing.

"Shoot them," she repeated. Finally, a spark of anger. She came up close to him and said, "Take the balaclava off."

"Why?"

"Take the fucking mask off. I don't speak to people who hide their face from me."

He put a finger to his lips.

"The mask," she said quietly. "Off with it."

Taking a step backwards, he pulled the balaclava over his head. His longish, light-brown hair stuck to his head and brow. He appeared as shattered as she must look herself. His expression was alert, as it had been in her apartment, if a little impatient too. Time seemed short.

Marcel didn't look as if the four dead were on his conscience, nor any others for that matter.

Do something, a voice in her head urged. Don't just let him get away with it. This is your job. That's why you're here.

Her eyes filled with tears. No energy left for outrage, anger, the battle. She was running on empty.

Marcel touched her arm and pointed downhill. Side by side they headed towards the forest, two bleary-eyed wanderers in the morning, who had so much to tell each other and yet wouldn't speak about the most important things.

But even the unimportant questions demanded answers. "Why didn't you wear your mask in my apartment?"

"You know why."

She nodded hesitantly. He'd needed to gain her trust. Her trust had been essential to the plan. He had paid for it by showing his face. "And now? Now I can identify you. Are you going to vanish into thin air?"

"In a manner of speaking, yes."

"Oh, are we taking early retirement?"

"We're getting a desk."

"With a view of the forests of Virginia?"

He hesitated. At least it was still possible to catch Marcel off guard. "With a view of white walls."

"Walls inscribed with the names of dead people."

"One or two, yes."

"Lew Gubnik's name, for example?"

He didn't immediately reply, and then said, "The fireman from Kirchzarten?"

She nodded. There it was again, the telltale word. *Kirch*zarten. She played it cool. "The collateral damage."

He shrugged. "A regrettable accident."

"I see. Nobody meant for it to happen, nobody can do anything about it."

"Yes," Marcel said. "That's exactly right."

Marcel stopped at the edge of the forest. Again his hand touched her arm, to stop her this time. His other hand held a radio to his ear. He listened without speaking, then turned to the other men who'd followed them, spread out across the clearing, and whispered some-thing in English. The men moved to the edge of the forest on both sides and were soon no longer visible. "We're staying here," he said.

"No more time for Shahida?"

He didn't reply.

Louise looked at the clearing. Now she understood. The black hordes had a helicopter too.

In the end, she thought, luck played its part. If Schober could have stayed, if his instruments had registered the other chopper, if Stuttgart had requested interceptors from Berlin . . .

She rubbed her brow. Finally the chance to stop thinking, finally the chance to sleep.

She sensed that Marcel was looking at her. Was waiting for something. Another question, another argument. Waiting for the penny to drop.

Then the penny dropped.

Where the hell was Jamal?

"Jamal is a problem," Marcel admitted. They didn't know where he was. Shahida had tried to escape and in the tumult Jamal had fled too. That's why they shot Shahida – they'd had to go after Jamal. But they would have shot her anyway, Marcel said calmly. The four of them couldn't have coped with two terrorists. And Jamal was more important.

The more important one was allowed to live, she thought, the less important one had to die. This too sounded horrifically logical, like everything Marcel was involved in. As logical as Mahr's arguments, schemes and initiatives. If you decoupled logic from universal values, from human rights, and left it instead to the individual, everything could be regarded as logical.

If the moral code of the individual differed from that agreed by society.

And this was where she came in. It was her job to enforce society's agreed moral code. Could you say that? Yes you could, after four days and nights almost without sleep.

Bonì put her hands to her temples. Her words and thoughts had become treacly again. Tears of exhaustion ran down her cheeks. She felt the urge to laugh. There she was, standing helplessly in the forest at the Rappeneck, thinking about logic and moral codes.

She didn't laugh. Her legs were trembling, her arms were trembling. Fatigue sat painfully behind her eyes.

Marcel seemed to be waiting for her to respond, but she was too exhausted for discussions. He said that they'd lost Jamal on the other side of the Rappeneck. In the darkness and the rain he'd vanished without trace.

Jamal was armed. With a knife. *His* knife.

Louise nodded. They were professionals, and yet they were making one mistake after the other. "He'll come back," she muttered. "She was his wife. He'll want to avenge his wife."

"A romantic idea." But Marcel seemed to agree.

She smiled wanly. Romantic, why not? In some respects these had been days of romance too. Her time with Richard Landen, the political dreams of Aziza and Johannes Mahr, the grotesque German on his desert mount, Shahida's dark face, her dark death in the rain on a foreign continent.

Then she remembered Schober's second person, whoever had run across the Rappeneck plateau and had begun their descent along the stream before disappearing. Jamal? Marcel looked alarmed and turned away to talk into his radio. She could make out a soft voice somewhere nearby. A few English syllables, hissing static that ended abruptly, a fleeting movement in the corner of her eye, then silence. Her eyes scanned the clearing. Was Jamal hiding close by? Or was he going back for Shahida?

Would he meet Ilic there?

"Shit. I have to warn my colleague!"

Marcel shook his head. No way. Ilic mustn't know that she'd found them.

"If anything happens to him I'll kill you," she whispered.

"Jamal wants us, not him."

"I mean it, I'll kill you."

A serious, almost intimate look. "And change sides?"

And change sides, she thought, nodding.

Again it was wait, wait, wait. She crouched on the ground and leaned against a tree, trying to avoid looking at Marcel. The grey brightened and the cloud thinned, allowing a glimpse of the gleaming light beyond. The morning when everything would come to an end. Never in her life had Louise longed so much for the sun. With the arrival of the sun Lisbeth Walter's hordes would vanish. Creep back into their hideout, their non-existence, to devise more catastrophic plans and factor in other regrettable accidents.

When she heard her mobile vibrate in her bag she opened her eyes. Marcel shook his head.

The sound of a helicopter in the distance, a different sound from Schober's "Buzzard". Clipped, menacing, toneless. The sound of war.

She remembered what Wilhelm Brenner had said – someone's up for a war. Mahr, the Jinnah and their civil war. Marcel and his secret war.

She stood up.

An unintelligible voice droned from Marcel's radio. He listened, said a few words in Spanish, finishing with "*Bien*".

Bien, she thought. So that was it. The war lost, the important questions unanswered.

But she could have another try.

Bonì moved to be beside him and said, "Childhood in the Breisgau, adolescence in northern Germany, somewhere around Bremen. Years of elocution training to smooth away any remaining traces of dialect. Early forties, high social standing, an academic education. English and Spanish, both spoken and written. I'd wager that you spent some time with Kripo. You know how it works. You like it. You're ever so slightly disdainful, but you like it. In fact I sense a gushing of nostalgia in you when it comes to Kripo."

Marcel pulled the balaclava back over his head. She stared at his eyes, his narrow, uncovered lips. The lips gave a faint smile. Louise kept going – later a S.W.A.T. officer or Special Deployment Commando, or an immediate transfer to the secret service. Contacts in the U.S., later training by the Americans – surely he hadn't learned all of this in Germany? Marcel was still tight-lipped. "With a photofit, a personality profile and your voice, I'll find out who you are," she said. "I'll find out where you've spent the last twenty years, where you are now. I'll come into your office in Virginia and write the names of the dead on the wall."

"Then we can go for a picnic in the woods."

"I hate picnics."

His lips twisted into a grin.

"The Pakistanis you abducted in Emmendingen . . . Am I right in thinking your people are taking them to Ramstein or Spangdahlem? Putting them on a plane, flying them somewhere you can deal with them differently? Somewhere where these stupid democratic rules don't exist?"

Marcel took the mobile from her shoulder bag and passed it to her. "Ring the Croat."

She grabbed the phone. Echoing in her aching head were the slimy, sanctimonious words that Marcel and Mahr were so fond of using. "But not like *that*," she said. "Not with those methods, Marcel. What is democracy worth if it uses the methods of dictatorships in order to survive? What's going to become of us then? I mean, will we still be democrats? And who decides which methods can be used on whom, and when? What then makes us . . ."

"Call him, Louise."

"What then makes us different from people like Jamal? Certainly not our methods." She hit the speed dial for Ilic. "You're ruining *everything*."

"We're *saving lives*, Louise. We're saving democracy." Marcel was standing next to her. She felt his warm breath on her cheek. "We're bringing freedom and justice to the dark corners of this world."

"Rubbish," she said. "Such utter rubbish."

She heard the ringtone in her ear, then Ilic said, "Louise, thank God . . ."

Marcel moved away, but his eyes remained on her.

Jamal hadn't appeared, Ilic said, but Bermann, Pauling and other colleagues were there. Then she heard Bermann's voice: "I tried calling you, but if you won't answer your bloody phone."

"I was having a pee."

Marcel smiled; Bermann snorted impatiently. "The helicopter."

"Yes."

"Where . . . Christ, don't tell me you've found them! Are you with them now?"

"Yes."

"Shit! We're coming up."

"No, stay where you are. I'm coming down."

She ended the call and dropped her mobile into the bag. Boni stared at it for a moment, then looked at Marcel. She expected Bermann to call back, but he didn't. She knew what that meant.

He was coming up.

"Hurry up, will you?" she said.

Seconds later the helicopter appeared above the clearing – a slim, black, nervous insect. The noise was pure torture and the force from the rotors thrust back the crowns of the trees and sent leaves spinning. She screwed up her eyes and watched anxiously as the insect circled the clearing, then lowered itself slowly. Louise didn't know much about choppers, but she was sure that only military units flew helicopters such as these. Two rotors, a pointed nose, a sort of double cockpit with two honeycomb-like cells, one above and behind the other. "TIGER" was written in capital letters on the side. Perhaps it was better that Schober and his pilot had flown back to Freiburg after all.

A "Buzzard" from the Baden-Württemberg helicopter squad wouldn't have stood a chance against this tiger.

All of a sudden Marcel's men were back. One guided the helicopter down, the others secured the surrounding area. If Jamal hadn't known where they were before, he surely did now.

The same, she thought, was true of Rolf Bermann.

The helicopter hovered a metre above the ground. The pilots in the cockpits wore helmets, but not masks. Two men waited in the opened passenger cabin, one with a precision rifle to his shoulder, scoping the edge of the forest. In spite of the noise she could make out a voice – Marcel, talking to the pilot over the radio. She saw the pilot give the thumbs up.

Then nothing happened.

Seconds passed. The trees and leaves moved in the wind. The men stayed absolutely still.

Leaden seconds, until she understood.

They were waiting for Jamal.

He arrived half a minute later. She didn't see him at first because he was running towards the rear of the helicopter from the other side. Shots rang out, someone bellowed a warning in English, the black figures whisked around. Jamal reappeared on her side of the chopper, wielding a huge combat knife, his dark face rigid with concentration and resolve. Then he was amongst them, leaping and spinning in a bizarre, frenzied dance, grappling with one hand, stabbing with the other. Bonì heard screams, saw black bodies fall to the ground, Jamal's hands and arms were covered in blood, the knife red, blood everywhere. She was wrenched backwards, staggered past Marcel and, as she fell, saw blood again, a shower of blood, heard shots from an automatic pistol. She hit the ground, saw the clouds part in the sky above, the sun break through, then closed her eyes and thought, when is all this going to be over, when is all this going to be over at last?

*

When the shooting had stopped she sat up. In the harsh, burning morning light she watched Marcel and his men lift two dead bodies and a seriously injured person into the helicopter. One of the dead was Jamal.

Marcel came and knelt beside Louise. He said something, but in her exhaustion, and with the noise of the rotors, she couldn't understand a word. Blood was smeared across his cheek, his shoulder was covered in blood, blood was everywhere. She fancied that he might have said "Virginia", we'll see each other sometime in Virginia, and you'll write the names of the dead on my white wall. But she could not be sure; perhaps he'd simply asked whether she was alright. Bonì shrugged. His mouth moved and again she didn't understand. But she was almost certain he'd said "Virginia", perhaps because he was smiling. She nodded and said, I'll come in fifteen years, because that's how long you'll be banged up for, I'll make sure of it. Fifteen years on account of the moral codes. He smiled and spoke again. She was about to shake her head because she hadn't understood a word when she saw his expression and realised what he was trying to say.

Come with me.

She shook her head. The moral code, she said, is important to me. Who am I without my moral code? You can't seriously believe that the code doesn't count anymore, that the dead people, the murders don't count anymore just because it's all over?

An enigmatic smile darted across Marcel's lips and he gave her the shoulder bag. Not altogether aware of what she was doing, Louise now found her pistol in her hand. She cocked it, the good old, heavy Walther P5, a discontinued model, but if you were used to it . . . The Calambert weapon. It had done terrible things, but that wasn't the pistol's fault.

She put the barrel to Marcel's forehead.

His eyes narrowed. Yes, she was still capable of surprising Marcel. Slowly they stood up. Marcel said something, she shrugged her shoulders. She couldn't hear him anymore, didn't *want* to hear anymore. All she could hear was the infernal din of the rotors and a voice that had been unleashed in her head talking mantra-like about logic and moral codes. It tossed words around in her mind, words like bricks, each word a dull pain. She put her free arm around Marcel's neck, pulled his head towards her, stared into eyes that flashed a warning. This is how it has to be, my dear Marcel, now I'm going to empty a bullet into your head, now you're Shahida and I'm you. A shiver ran across her scalp, her arms and back. She knew this moment, hadn't it been similar with Calambert? Only she hadn't been quite so near to him, she hadn't wanted to touch Calambert, she had wanted only to kill him, and he'd had a weapon too. Unlike Marcel, who she was keen on touching and not so keen on killing, but now let's say you're Shahida and I'm you. From the corner of her eye Louise detected movement, in a blur she saw the man with the rifle coming closer, a small, dark something was aimed at her, behind it a wide-open mouth in a black balaclava. But she ignored the yelling man and the rifle, no bullet would penetrate the pain in her head, the pain protected her, the pain that was now in her belly, she closed her eyes and laid her head on Marcel's shoulder and asked him not to do it. She lowered her arm with the weapon, don't do it, how can you do that, I wouldn't really have done it, you know I would never have shot you, how can you do that? Louise dropped her pistol and wrapped her arms around him because her legs could no longer carry her weight. Marcel held her. The pain in her belly turned cold and biting, then the knife was gone and she felt Marcel's hand on the wound and she started laughing as she cried, the left, on the left, this was threatening to become a habit. And wasn't it funny, somehow, that Marcel had first plunged a knife into her belly and now was trying to staunch the bleeding? She felt him lay her carefully on the ground, push up her T-shirt, she saw again the masked face right before her eyes, the lips that once more were saying something that try as she might she couldn't understand, then it was over at last, all of it was finally over.

24

Incoherent, blurred days ensued. A weekend in hospital, more because of the exhaustion than the wound. The wound wasn't deep and certainly not life-threatening. Marcel seemed to have taken care not to injure her too badly. He'd wanted her to give in, no more. Then he'd patched up the wound.

Familiar and unfamiliar faces popped up around her and vanished again, and she tried to understand what had happened in those few minutes in the clearing. Was it possible that Marcel had saved her life? Had he thought that the man with the rifle would shoot?

More questions that would never find an answer.

Bermann, Ilic and Wallmer came, Almenbroich too, but she was barely aware of their presence. She nodded, mumbled something, nodded again in a doze, then closed her eyes and slept. At some point during this time someone told her what had happened in the clearing on the Rappeneck after the helicopter had taken off. Seconds later Bermann had arrived with a handful of S.W.A.T. officers. He'd carried Louise down to the footpath and waited with her for the paramedics. It was the second time he'd saved her in a matter of days, and the second time he had done it with no time to spare, she thought.

She began to feel comfortable in her small, white hospital room. Sleeping all day long, doing nothing – it wasn't bad. Thinking, allowing her thoughts to flow. At the Kanzan-an she had done little else for months on end; in the few weeks since she'd had scant opportunity.

Think, she thought and fell asleep.

*

When she awoke the first thing that came into her head was Marcel. Had he saved her life? Was he, even in those last few moments in the clearing, the one pulling the strings? Marcel, who did one thing and then the opposite, but saw no contradiction in the contradiction. Who broke the rules to protect the rules. How could he live with this contradiction? How could one live with people like him? But "rules" was perhaps the wrong word. These were fundamental principles, after all. You shouldn't take people out of the country against their will. You shouldn't put a gun to the head of a criminal and pull the trigger. Principles like that. It's not acceptable here, she thought, yawning. If it does happen, it changes the very fundament. Then we're no longer who we claim to be. It changes *everything*, she thought, and fell asleep.

Ilic came for the third or fourth time. He looked as if he hadn't slept a wink in days, nor had a bite to eat in weeks. He sat on her bed without saying anything. At some point she fell asleep. When she woke up he was still there. "It's really not your fault," she whispered. Ilic's face blurred in a torrent of tears. He passed her some tissues, wiped her nose, said nothing. "It's not your fault, for God's sake," she said, and Ilic nodded.

On one of those days Lisbeth Walter and Heinrich Täschle came too. They sat on either side of her bed, trying not to look at each other. Later Lisbeth cried. Louise thought she knew what was bothering her. Lisbeth's world had changed too. Nothing was as it had been before the day Henny came to see her with the policewoman from Freiburg. The protective veil around her world had been torn. It would be difficult to mend the rips. And: Täschle was back. He'd trudged up to the solitary house even though he didn't belong there. He was back in her thoughts. So Lisbeth Walter wept and Louise comforted her until she was overcome with tiredness.

*

Then, on Sunday afternoon, the stream of visitors dried up. Ilic came again, staying for half an hour and barely uttering a word, but nobody else. Louise had feared her father would appear, as he had in the winter, but she was spared this. To her surprise, however, she realised she would have liked to see the other brother at her bedside. Little brothers loved stories about helicopters and black hordes and knives that bored into bellies. Stories from her working life. She would have liked to see Richard Landen at her bedside, even though he didn't enjoy listening to stories from her working life. But Landen didn't come either.

Louise was discharged on Tuesday morning. Wallmer had offered to drive her home. Half blinded by the glaring light of the sun, she was led to the car, and by the time she got in she was bathed in sweat. The desert heat had returned.

During the short drive she slept.

Wallmer helped her up to her apartment. It was hot, musty and silent. Wallmer opened the windows and drew the curtains while Boni stood in the doorway. She saw the American in the hall, Marcel in the sitting room.

Her visitors had settled in.

She went to the telephone. Three messages on the answerphone, all from Friday, all from Landen. I can't get you on your mobile, I've got to go to Japan right away, our son will be born today or tomorrow, I'll call you from Japan . . . I hope you listen to your messages, I've got to go, call me, where are you . . . I'm at the airport now, I'll call you in a few days, where *are* you?

Wallmer looked at her; Louise shrugged.

They went to the door.

"If you need someone to change your bandages," Wallmer said, clapping her on the shoulder. She seemed to want to embrace her, but refrained.

Louise waited until the footsteps faded on the ground floor. Then she went to the front door of the neighbouring apartment.

Marcel Meier.

She rang the bell.

Nobody answered.

That evening Landen called. He had a son, he was happy, he missed her. He was, she thought, far, far away.

She congratulated him and asked him to pass on her regards to the mother.

As he talked about the birth and his son's crumpled face she saw in her mind the grassy glade on the Rappeneck. Jamal killing and being killed, all that blood, the warning in Marcel's eyes before he sunk the knife into her, the clearing at Heuweiler, the laughing, shouting Bo, Peter Mladic's fingers that had moved as if he were playing piano without a piano. How could these two lives ever mix? Dead bodies and murderers in the daytime, returning to one's cosy home for a meal together in the evening, tell me, what did you teach your students today, what wonderful things did you write, what's the little crumpled face up to, then watering the yucca, the cyclamens, the orchids and whatever the other one's called. With Mick her life hadn't mixed well either, and much had changed since then. Calambert, the alcohol, the self-destructive tendency. Hospitalised through injury twice within a few months – anyone might wonder where all this was going to lead.

Why she'd let it get this far.

"Louise? It might not be that obvious, but I'm really looking forward to seeing you."

She went to the kitchen window and looked down at the small square to the right of her block. Café tables, chairs, colourful sun umbrellas, palms in plastic tubs. Young waiters and waitresses hurrying back and forth, children playing by the stream. I'm really looking forward to seeing you. She thought of the wound, that terrible moment when she'd felt the knife enter her. "How could it work, Richard?" she said softly. "I mean . . ."

She heard him clear his throat.

"Six deaths in five days. That's what my life is like sometimes. Would you want me to tell you about it over dinner?"

More clearing of the throat.

"That's assuming I ever get back in time for dinner."

"Let's try. Let's find a way."

"The point is: I don't want to tell you about it."

"Because I wouldn't understand?"

"Yes, and because I don't want to have to justify myself. It is what it is. I do what I do."

"A Zen life." His laughter sounded sad.

She fell onto her back on the sofa. A cold pain shot through the left-hand side of her belly. She laid her hand on the bandage, held her breath until the pain was gone. "And *I* don't understand *your* life."

"Let's try anyway, Louise. Let's just carry on where we left off last week and see where it takes us."

She said nothing.

"It's important to me. I mean, *you're* important to me."

"Because I am what I am."

"And because *I* am what *I* am."

She nodded. "I'll bring chaos into your life and you'll bring a little peace into mine. That'll be fine to begin with, but at some point we'll stop liking each other for those very reasons."

"We're not living at some point in the future, we're living now."

"All very Zen, right?"

"Exactly. But I'm afraid it's not getting us anywhere. That seems to be the problem with Zen: it never helps in the short term."

She rolled onto her right side. The pain came and went again. She stared at the coffee table. The bottles had gone, and the demons too. Maybe not for ever, but they had been gone for a while now. That was the upside of days and nights like those in the past week. Injuries, hospital stays, extreme tiredness. All the euphoria and adrenalin.

No time for temptation. No desire for any substitute.

No loneliness.

"Let's try, Louise. Please."

"When are you back?"

"In a fortnight."

"O.K. You come over to mine, we'll sleep together, and then we'll see."

Muted laughter from both of them.

They said goodbye.

Bonì spent the rest of the week at home. Sleeping, listening to music, letting Wallmer change her bandages. Standing at the kitchen window, trying to understand whether the square and the café and the people beneath the umbrellas belonged to her life or not. Wondering why she didn't want them in her life any longer.

Ilic called, as did Hoffmann and Täschle. And Almenbroich. She begged him not to vanish without trace. He promised he wouldn't.

Bermann popped round, got her to approve protocols, flesh out statements and sign them. He sat impatiently on the sofa, urging her to be quick. Mahr and Marion Söllien had made detailed confessions, but Busche and Bo weren't talking. A deal with Busche seemed to be in the offing. They would get the routes of the arms transports, the names of the helpers, the helpers' helpers, and in return they would downgrade Busche's culpability in planning, organising and implementing it all. At this moment Marianne Andrele, Anselm Löbinger and Busche's lawyer were sitting around a table, thrashing out a deal. Bermann wanted to get back to seal it.

"What about Marion Söllien?"

"She cries all the time. Sits there with her face covered in snot and won't stop howling."

"Is she involved?"

"She slept with all the Yugoslavs – just imagine," Bermann said with a snort of disgust. "Bo and every other Yugoslavs who set foot in that house in the forest . . . I've got to get back, are you almost done?"

"Is Marion Söllien involved, Rolf?"

He nodded reluctantly. "She helped out when A.P.G.P.F. needed her. Dealt with the post, made telephone calls, that sort of stuff. Arranged meetings for members. And at some point she started opening her legs too." Putting on a high voice and fidgeting excessively, he said, "But you have to understand, I'm not one of *those* types, it's just that I was so lonely when Ernst Martin passed away, I was so lonely and so *desperate*." He got up. "Are you finished?"

She gathered the documents into a pile and handed them to Bermann. "What about the underground shelter? How did Söllien know about that?"

"His grandfather hid in it in 1944, when the British arrived." Bermann was already on his way to the door.

She followed him. "How about Rashid?"

"It's possible we made a mistake there."

"Meaning?"

"It's possible he didn't know anything."

"Well, that happens."

"An innocent Arab?"

"That we make mistakes."

She saw his shoulders twitch. At the door he turned and Bonì could see an intensity in his eyes. "By the way, back there in the forest . . . that blue bra – it really suits you."

"The red one's even better."

He faltered.

Yes, she could still catch Bermann off guard too.

Louise pushed him out and closed the door. There was one advantage to men like Bermann – they spent their whole lives at the same stage of civilisation, while the rest of humanity progressed. Which made them predictable.

Inferior.

Then she was alone again. As she lay on the sofa, with Pink Floyd on an endless loop, she thought of Marcel: had he saved her life or not?

How should she live with a question like that? How did you live with somebody like that? With all the other Marcels who might be here, there and everywhere? Who flew terrorist suspects in secret "tigers" and Gulfstreams to countries where they could deal with them using different methods to those that were regarded as "Western"? Who could make murderers, bombers and innocent people disappear in the no-man's-land of civilisation. Who breached agreements to protect these same agreements. She yawned and thought: democracies protected those who allowed themselves to be protected. Then she fell asleep.

Epilogue

On August 13, her birthday, Louise Bonì got up at half past four. By five o'clock she was sitting in her car. In the first greyish–black morning light she passed Kirchzarten, then the Himmelreich at the beginning of the Höllental. By the time she drove into the Upper Rhine Plain three quarters of an hour later, the sun was on the horizon. She took the motorway towards Singen and hit rush-hour traffic after Radolfzell. Dark rainclouds loomed to the north of Lake Constance. The city of Konstanz lay in gleaming sunlight.

She left her Renault in a car park on the edge of the old town. It was almost seven o'clock. She walked along shadowy lanes, passing colourful houses that were called names like "Zum Stern" or "Zum goldenen Löwen". In an Italian café Bonì drank an espresso. She felt at home in this colourful, lively, laid-back city where even the houses had names.

Then she sat on a bench in the sun and thought, this is madness, leave the old man in peace, he fled to Kaiserslauten, then to the Odenwald and finally to Konstanz – why can't you leave the old man in peace?

But she could not leave him in peace. After all this time she needed some assurance that he was alright.

Louise was keen to draw a line under the winter.

A few days ago she had been to Niksch's grave, then up to the Flaunser where Taro had died. Now it was Hollerer's turn.

She dialled his sister's number.

Hollerer's sister didn't know who she was. Oh, a former colleague? How nice that colleagues still showed an interest, after all this time.

But Johann Georg wasn't there; he was always out at this hour of the morning.

"So where is he?"

"Where is he? Every morning he goes for a walk by the pier. He's gradually getting used to all the water, it's taken ages, he doesn't like the water, he only likes his village and his fields and his hills, you see?" The sister laughed. "But now he sits by the water every morning, getting used to it."

"Do you know where, exactly?"

"Where? Beside the 'Imperia'. It's about the only thing he likes about Konstanz, he really isn't a fan of the water, but—"

"Is that a ship?" Louise interrupted.

The sister laughed, surprised. "A ship?" She laughed again.

The Imperia was a statue that stood beside the entrance to the harbour. A nine-metre-high female figure with large breasts, a half-open dress, one leg bent slightly forwards and two gnome-like male figures in her raised palms. She rotated slowly on her own axis. A buxom dream and nightmare of womankind immortalised in stone.

Louise crossed the railway tracks and headed for the lake. Small, gnarled trees stood in dense rows on either side of the footpath. Up ahead of her a heavy-set, stooped man walked with a stick. She saw this man lying in the snow, tears streaming from his eyes, blood streaming from his body. Then he was lying in a hospital bed, Louise holding his feeble hand. And then the man was gone.

She waited until he'd sat on a bench by the water before approaching.

"Hollerer . . ."

He turned his head. His face was paler and more wrinkled than in the winter, but he looked less scruffy, less unkempt. No crumbs on his chest, no stubble, and his shirt was tucked into his trousers. The sister, she thought. Doesn't just talk, she looks after him too.

"Well, well, well," he muttered. It didn't sound unfriendly.

"Hollerer." She put a hand on his shoulder and stroked it.

"Ouch!"

"Sorry." Now she remembered. A shattered shoulder, a shredded kidney.

"Look who's here," Hollerer said.

"Don't make me go."

"Make you go? Why would I?" He spoke more slowly than before and his movements were slower too. Life seemed to have become slower and more ordered with his sister in Konstanz.

Louise sat beside him. "How are you? Are you well? How are the ..."

"The holes?" He snorted. "They've closed up. My shoulder is knackered and they've removed the kidney, but luckily humans have two of each."

She grinned.

"You only get one life, on the other hand."

Just an observation, she thought, not a criticism.

Louise looked out at the lake. In this air all that could be seen of the far shore was a thin, dark line. The rainclouds hung close above.

What was true of the dead, she thought, was true of the living too.

She sensed Hollerer looking at her.

"How about you? What are you doing here? Taking a holiday beside this ghastly lake? Isn't this lake *ghastly*? Far too big, far too many people around. And this place, Konstanz." He snorted. "A *ghastly* place, far too neat and tidy. All spruced up like some cute little woman who thinks she's better than she is."

She smiled. She was familiar with the grumpiness, but the belligerence was new. Maybe it's the sister's doing, she thought. Sisters like shouting and howling and talking – maybe belligerence was a way of coping with that.

"Why don't you come for lunch?" Hollerer said.

"I'm afraid I can't."

"Shame. We're having fish, I bet you like fish. Nora cooks fish every day, as if there were no butchers here. But that's women's scheming for you. You keep eating fish until you like it so much that you sign up for an angling course."

They laughed.

"Can't you come, or don't you want to?"

"I've got to meet someone for coffee in Kehl."

"You poor thing. That's another ghastly place."

"I've got relatives there."

"Right."

"I've got a brother there."

"Right." Hollerer nodded. "Did you manage to crack it in the end, back in the winter?"

"Yes."

"Good. What about the other thing?" He raised a hand and made tilting movements.

She blushed. "That too."

"Good."

And somehow, Louise thought, for the time being everything had been said.

AUTHOR'S NOTE

Some of the events you have read about in this novel actually happened, but much is pure invention. I mixed the one with the other as I saw fit and sometimes tweaked what was real to make it correspond with the fiction. For example, "Rottweil 2002" took place in a different year, whereas "Rottweil 1992" did actually happen in 1992. There is no "Association for the Promotion of German–Pakistani Friendship" (A.P.G.P.F.), but Baden-Württemberg's "development cooperation" budget does exist. The dates and facts relating to the Yugoslav War and Pakistan come from the relevant journals, newspapers, magazines, monthly reports from political foundations and Amnesty International's annual reports. The Jinnah tribe does not exist, but I based it on the existing Bugti tribe in Quetta, Baluchistan. All the characters in this novel are fictitious. Any resemblance to persons, living or dead, is coincidental and unintended. This is also and especially true of the characters that belong to real organisations such as police authorities and the voluntary fire service, etc.

I should like to thank everybody who gave me assistance in writing this crime novel, especially Chief Inspector Karl-Heinz Schmid from Freiburg Kripo, who has since become a friend. Thanks also to Chief Inspector Roland Braunwarth from Freiburg forensics laboratory (dept. 6), Chief Inspector Rolf Bürer from Kirchzarten police station, Chief Inspector Sabine Heitz from the Joint Centre for Police and Customs Cooperation in Kehl, Chief Inspector Rolf Gröner from the Baden-Württemberg Helicopter Squad, as well as each of their offices, for the openness and friendliness with which my requests were treated. Thanks are likewise due to the many people who were kind enough to answer my questions about the former Yugoslavia, in particular Goran, Irena and Maja – as well as all those who cannot or did not want to be mentioned here.

OLIVER BOTTINI was born in 1965. Four of his novels, including *Zen and the Art of Murder* and *A Summer of Murder* of the Black Forest Investigations, have been awarded the Deutscher Krimipreis, Germany's most prestigious award for crime writing. In addition his novels have been awarded the Stuttgarter Krimipreis and the Berliner Krimipreis. *Zen and the Art of Murder* is now longlisted for the C.W.A. International Dagger. www.bottini.de.

JAMIE BULLOCH is the translator of Timur Vermes' *Look Who's Back*, Birgit Vanderbeke's *The Mussel Feast*, which won him the Schlegel-Tieck Prize, *Kingdom of Twilight* by Steven Uhly, and novels by F. C. Delius, Jörg Fauser, Martin Suter, Katharina Hagena and Daniel Glattauer.